The Power of One

Although the bike's pulse lasers were active, they could not be accurately aimed during the chase due to rough terrain. While approaching the building they could hear three whistling sounds that appeared to come from the nearest clump of trees, to be followed by three small explosions. The three Lodorian guards and their bikes suddenly crashed to the ground.

'Safa, Ramm, down!' Malik shouted. They immediately fell into the mauve grass. There were no more explosions. Malik wondered what could have happen in such quick succession to take out three speeding guards. Slowly and cautiously he regained his composure and began to move stealthily towards the dead guards.

'Remain still this moment! Do not move!' Came a female voice from beyond the trees. A shabbily dressed girl stood up from the tall grass.

'I said still!'

A defiant Malik ignored her orders and continued moving along his intended path to investigate. She walked briskly towards them with a blade in one hand and a strange weapon in the other. The weapon was designed like a boomerang, but with an explosive charge that could be triggered on contact.

The Chronicles of Galaxy Osmaron Series

Chronicles of Galaxy Osmaron - I Am Shadite

Chronicles of Galaxy Osmaron - The Power of One

Chronicles of Galaxy Osmaron - Escape from Andromeda

Chronicles of Galaxy Osmaron - The Solarian Empire

Chronicles of Galaxy Osmaron - Fertilates

Chronicles of Galaxy Osmaron - Infilates

Chronicles of Galaxy Osmaron - Son of Destiny

Chronicles of Galaxy Osmaron - Jull, The Supreme Patriarch

Chronicles of Galaxy Osmaron - Battle for Andromeda

Chronicles of Galaxy Osmaron - Battle fo Osmaron

First Edition

Chronicles of Galaxy Osmaron

The Power of One

Life on Earth and Lumak's travels

By

Adrian Graye

Nutralian Publishing
http://nutralianpublishing.com

Nutralian
An imprint of Nutralian Publishing
5 Brayford Square, London E1 0SG
http://nutralianpublishing.com

This paperback edition 2006
B00005555

First published in Great Britain by
Amazon KDP 2024

ISBN 978-1-0687902-1-8

Printed and bound in Great Britain by Amazon KDP Publishing.

A CIP catalogue record for this title
is available from the British Library.

To all those who believe in universal existence and appreciate the lowliest of life, for like babes, they are the beginning.

TABLE OF CONTENTS

TOWARDS ETERNITY

When technology improves to infinity,
And chaos is no more a certainty,
Within the Greater Mind we grow,
Until even matter exists no more.

Victor E. Roche

Prologue

Lumak, the Shadite, was originally a Semonite (a sexless bee-like creature from a distant world). He is an intergalactic saviour sent to Earth by the Grand Lord of our universe. During that important mission he is to engineer our planet's technologies from Class 1 (its current levels) to Class 5 (100,000 years more advanced).

He was despatched to Earth via The Greater Mind, wherein almost anything is possible. During that process was transformed into a male human. He arrived in the remotest hills of south eastern Turkey and were taken in by the Bengizara Khan and his young hillbilly daughter Sarah.

Despite the inadequacies of his present situation, Lumak manages to create a lasting cure for cancer. Having cured one of Khan's village friends from terminal cancer, he is soon found out by her physician. Doctor Emil observes Lumak's potentials and arranges his visit to a large university hospital in the city.

Lumak falls in love with Sarah and both get engaged, but they have no money and the going is difficult. That is, until they visit the city and Professor Jean-Claude Chairmowich realizes Lumak's incredible potentials.

He becomes well known in that country and is soon considered a profit by many. However, his main interest is in converting Earth to a higher level of technologies, so that mankind can defend their planet and the galaxy from the rapacious and unrelenting Javols. Those rapacious blood-sucking monsters are currently on their way to Earth to consume us all.

He can only fulfill his most important mission by using a false identity and by travelling to the most advanced country on the planet; namely, the United States of America.

As always Lumak faces his share of problems and near-assassinations. He also suffers from nostalgia and flashbacks of his family, friends and past missions in distant places.

Presently Lumak is in North America developing new

technologies for humanity. He is well known by both good and bad, but can always find ways to win the day with his strange type of alien technologies.

INTRODUCTION

Saints and Dragons

Earth Time... 2041 CE

Planet... Pleron, known by its human inhabitants as Earth.

Place... North Dakota, USA, Earth.

Lumak now in human form reflected on his accomplishments since visiting Earth and was satisfied with progress. Even lovely Sarah and her father Ben had knuckled down to life in the States. So far it had all gone to plan so he assumed most of the other more dangerous challenges of his mission would be equally solvable. It was then that he remembered his first failed challenge. At that time he was quite young, inexperienced and with an unrelenting fear of heights.

It was supposed to be a mission undertaken to save him from phobias he considered worst than pain. However during those brief moments of his life, he had to deal with more agonising pain than his broken body could ever endure. Then his initial fears and phobias would shrink to insignificance by comparison.

That first of all challenges was his first regret, but in many ways not really a failure in the face of experience. During that mission several important lessons were learnt, and because of the unpredictable outcome the experience gained would completely change his outlook on life and mould him for his future life as a Shadite.

By so doing he had conquered his fear of heights and had become tolerant of almost every type of pain. Yet, those were affirmations of his own selfish needs. Luckily he was assisted in his time of need by another more alien than himself or he would not have survived. During that brief period of his life, he learnt many important lessons:

1   The world is not only about myself or my desire for happiness and fulfilment.

2   It is sometimes better to share my idiosyncrasies with others than hide, even when faced with utter ridicule.

3   Never set myself impossible tasks without first analysing the difficulties in light of day.

4   Never assume anything about anyone based on rumours.

5   Never take anyone at face value. Fashion is fleeting, here today and gone tomorrow.

6   Never be prejudiced towards anyone or make wrong assumptions about others by comparing them with those I know.

7   It is better to sacrifice my time for someone than pass them by, particularly when they are in trouble.

8   Do to others as I would like them do to me, but not in a masochistic way.

9   Before I move against someone, always imagine myself in their shoes.

10   Always do a job to the best of my abilities.

11   Things never happen in exactly the way I can imagine. Events are based on the Natural Order and they have a way of turning in on themselves.

12   I must show patience and tolerance in all things.

13   Even when I fail, I must try and try again.

14   Failure can be a great lesson in itself.

15   Wanting something doesn't get it done. The more effort placed in a given tasks. The more benefits will be reaped as a final reward.

At that time Lumak was a fully grown Semonite barely 5 years old.

A new experience

Earth Time.... 1655 CE

Planet... Kanaefon, within the orbiting globular cluster of stars
called Kalboron. That large cluster is just outside
Osmaron (our own Milky Way galaxy).

Kanei ... The most advanced Semonite tribe on Kanaefon. They
had evolved from a large bee-like creature.

Petans ... Highly intelligent reptilian dragons able to fly great
distances.

The wall along the chasm was truly massive by planetary
standards. This was due to a relatively new fault in the planet's
crust, where tectonic plates moved apart. Those displacements
caused the seas in question to shift vertically in some places.
Then there were the massive craters due to Meteoric
bombardments in ancient times. All those differences were quite
enormous by Earth's standards. The effects of both moons when
in alignment further aggravated the movement of floating forests
and the flow of waters to and from oceans.
Of all those spectacles, the 78 kilometre wide waterfall along a
side of the Crethian Bourle was probably the most spectacular.
The swirling and foaming waters fell 7 kilometres into the Great
Chasm below. By the time it hit the lake most had evaporated
into floating clouds with the most spectacular lightning
discharges.

Although within a near-tropical region of the planet, the steeply
sloping top of the Great Chasm's wall was always covered in
snow and mist. That place was at the south western part of the
300 kilometre wide crater of the Crethian Bourle and free of
Petan Dragons. Petans tended to live in caves around the high
wall of the crater well away from the great waterfall.
Even at those enormous heights there were curtains of floating

semitropical forests containing all forms of indigenous life. The large strips of mangrove-like trees lay on hardlands. They were usually separated from the floating forests by a broad beach. The hardlands mangrove were flooded more than once each month and had evolved ways of digging their tough roots deep into the sand and rocks at that level to firmly anchor from the fast flowing currents. During those brief periods they were able to collect nutrients from the waters when it flowed their way.

Lumak decided the 7 kilometre part of the rock face too high and difficult to scale. It also contained many caves that were inhabited by unfriendly Petan dragons. They were highly territorial and never liked unwelcomed visitors, least of all Kanei. Lumak chose an area at the lower rim towards the south east that appeared free of those problems.

That part was only a modest 3 kilometre high. He realized earlier that the number of pitons and rope required would be too much. Their combined weight being too heavy to scale the near vertical cliff alone. After all, no Kanei had ever attempted such mad feats of rock climbing before and he had no company.

He had chosen a lightweight piton hook designed and tested in his workshop. That titanium alloy could be easily fastened to rock by a special compressed air gun that did not require a portable power source.

The reckless adventurous youth had spent the best part of a week preparing for the climb. A month before to build a kite with special fabric that would take him to the place by wind power alone. Never before had such items existed on his world nor did anyone ever had such an insane notion of adventure to rectify a simple phobia of heights.

He had covertly tested the kite on his many practice runs on a chosen hill and pleased with results. Once he became convinced of his capabilities there was little reason for procrastination, so he set his time of departure for the following day in early morning. Until then, he would prepare while maintaining secrecy and hide his intentions well away from family and friends.

At the appropriate time he soared into the air like an eagle, taking advantage of the steady morning breeze that blew towards that area. He had studied the weather patterns well and knew the directions of the prevailing winds within that part of the planet at that time of year. Within one hour he was at its western rim toward the north east of his city Lud and west of Petan Lands. Those were the dragon territories including their more modern reservations.

He had never ventured this far before and never observed a real live dragon at close range other than the monstrous ones observed in Vidi-plays, so this was his opportunity. Anyway, he was high up in the air and well away from predatory dangers, or so he thought. He enjoyed the experience of soaring high like a Petan and wandered why most of his species had lost the ability of flight, which gave one such an incredible feeling of absolute freedom and power over all.

Having received his brain implants a month before and reviewed its menus through dark tunnels in his mind, he could select many relevant projects for simulation. Even the patient trainers within those Virtual Worlds, as the human Plato called them, were all alive and active as in real life, always ready to assist. He had used such simulations for finding the resources and design of his special kite and now thought he could take on almost any challenge to test his capabilities.

The Grand Lord was correct when he told him the Implants would increase his brain size by at least ten times. They included numerous subjects with their translations that moulded seamlessly with his mind.

The implants also had within its menus a range of languages that included most creatures on his world and even others like the human Plato. Those facilities he intended to practise during his travels. Any such translations were entered directly into his brain, so the painful and extensive process of learning a new language was not necessary. He was astounded how well the brain implants had blended in seamlessly with his own mind, making the learning process and Virtual Experiences completely transparent and as one, with no side effects whatsoever.

Lumak flew over the first of the dragon's accommodation. It was built for a single family and comprised five large semi-spheres, apparently stuck together to form a single unit. Their original habitats used to be dug out caves on the side of high cliffs. In recent times many had settled for the roomier construction within their reservations on land. Anyway, those prefabricated dwellings were more easily adopted to their needs and could be linked to a common supply for electrical power and other utilities. That particular design had been introduced by the Grand Lord and accepted by them because of its suitability and temperate environment.

There was no one about so Lumak continued onwards. The next scene followed was a group of three houses around a triangular playing field. There were many young dragons frolicking about in a very rough manner with a spherical inflatable object they threw and bounced between them. One glanced towards the sky. In an instant they lifted their heads, amaze at his beautifully multi-coloured kite with its single passenger soaring on high. There they stood as if hypnotized by the strange flying object that no one had seen or heard of before. He reduced height to take a closer look at his admirers and investigate their method of play. Although they were now a more civilized bunch, he did not wish to break any territorial rules by landing, so he waved and carried on.

It was not long before three young and brave dragons took to the air and began to follow. He wondered whether they would catch up. They were obviously just flexing their muscles to show him to whom the skies really belonged and they could do even better in flight. After a short while two of his competitors apparently had enough and turned back, while the smaller and apparently more stubborn decided to follow out of overwhelming curiosity.

Lumak realized most of the sea creatures on his world were adept flyers. As a result their predators had to be equally good at those abilities in order to eat. The dragons were probably top of the food chain that over the generations had settled for a more relaxed form of existence and that choice engendered a gradual change in diet. They could now enjoy a wide variety of food, including all types of fish, fruit, berries and honey. Those changes were encouraged when the sea creatures had become less plentiful in that part of their world and many of their unpopular ventures outside of their territories had been discouraged.

Before that time hunting must have occupied most of their waking hours, until they were expending more energy in flight for progressively lesser reward. They were now the only large hardlands reptilian survivors on the planet that had obviously evolved in the harshest of times. Yet, almost all life on that world had developed wings at some time in their past.

Fully grown, dragons were about three metres long from head to tail and extremely tough and scaly, with a beautiful head crest, four incredibly strong limbs and five most formidable webbed claws at the end of each limb. Those limbs were fully adaptable and could be used as both hands and feet when hunting.

Just below their first set of arms were long hidden pouches where their folding wings were kept. On that part of their bodies existed thin membrane seals that separated to allow wings to expand outwards. This feature must have been necessary in ancient times to prevent small predators getting to them. Those hydraulically inflatable wings, were leathery with thin semi-flexible bonelike ribs, which made them fragile and cumbersome when not in flight. However it took much effort on their part to take off from a level surface, since like eagles, they mainly glided and swooped to catch their prey.

The more sedentary elders were now far too bulky for flight and usually sent the agile young to do the catching while taking care of business at home. Since the arrival of the Grand Lord many had become fruit growers, only eating meat when it became necessary for a balanced diet. Several supplements had been created by Kanei for that purpose. Those they traded for berries and other resources.

Within their reservation were every variety of fruit and berry. They exported the bulk of their harvests to the Kanei, Lumak's people, in juice form. Presently the Kanei received about 40 percent of their food supplies from the Petan. Despite certain territorial restriction for mutual benefit and safety, they lived in relative peace and harmony with trade on both sides.

Petan dragons had developed the ability to use technology and soon began training their young in ways of the Kanei. Education being the topmost ambition on the list. Being very curious about everything, they had a natural aptitude and desire to learn and were constantly asking questions. Presently they were involved in many of their own building projects and had become quite successful.

The Grand Lord had since taken to them and allowed them implants, but they were not yet suited for Shaditry. As species went, they were predators and the complete opposite to the Kanei. Petans were boisterous and highly emotional, but very generous and kind to their own.

Their strong webbed feet with sharp claws could easily impale a creature in flight, so Lumak worried about his persistent follower. He realized that despite his new implants, he could not fully communicate with dragons without the necessary sound-box. His species had evolved along a different path and used a combination of pheromones, claw gestures and hissing noises from their narrow throats, with no facial movement or outward surface expression. Those changes when combined imparted the necessary information. On the other hand, dragons only utilized their throat and facial muscles to create a variety of complex sounds. Therefore, although he was able to understand them through his implants, he would find it difficult to reply.

The juvenile was now at a higher level than Lumak and comically mimicked his every action. He suddenly dashed towards Lumak's kite narrowly missing it. Then made a few twists and turns while falling with his wings collapsed. Suddenly they were opened again, he caught an upward air current and soared pass Lumak. He adjusted his fall to Lumak's level and was by his side. He was so skilful at manipulating the air currents that Lumak was intrigued. Nevertheless Lumak was in no mood for such risky pranks and had become very irritated by his aerobatics. He realized the frailty of his flimsy kite which was his only mode of transport and wished the juvenile would go and practise his stunts elsewhere.

'I don't believe it. You are just a wingless worker, yet you soar like a Critan... Ha! Ha! Ha...' he continued laughing, then still in full laughter, dived, spun around and again caught a strong up-draught and was soaring close to Lumak. This time on the opposite side and with a broad grin on his face. Lumak had to move his head in an attempt at communication.

'You are a very brave and difficult one indeed,' Lumak shouted above the noise, but the dragon either did not hear or could not understand.

'To where are you going?' inquired the dragon. Lumak fully understanding his words, pointed in the direction of the distant cliffs. Those perilous cliffs were now about 30 kilometres towards the south with a misty halo encircling their heights. Lumak did not mind a little company during his journeys, if only the juvenile would keep well away from his kite with his dangerous and unexpected pranks.

Lumak considered the difficulties in crossing the almost 78-kilometre long trench and realized he would have to utilize a new approach if he was to get across the obstacle in hours instead of days. His uninvited company was still by his side and seemed to be following all the way, so he wanted a better method of communication, but none were forthcoming.

'Are you on a quest?' the dragon asked. Lumak nodded in an appropriate way, then decided to introduce himself, so he pointed towards the sun, then a distant star, still visible in bright daylight, then to himself. Lumak was the name for Brightest Star in his language.

'So you are, Lumak? Ahhhhh!'

'I am called Stikol. Stikol Fondle, and I am a member of the Siff tribe, at your borders. I am also on a quest to find myself. I think one can only accomplish their full potentials once they know the limits of their abilities.' Lumak marvelled at his clarity, wisdom and competence. Never before had he thought so highly of dragons; for they were always considered by his people as primitive, immature and irresponsible. How could they have been so wrong? He soon realized that his new perspective was due to a greater understanding gained through his implants and wanted to learn more of their species.

He realized completely different species were usually xenophobic towards each other. This factor was obviously due to inherent fears within their survival matrix. Perhaps due to some inbuilt mechanism that prevented the mixing of different cultures, since they could not have mutually evolved identical cultural traits and restraints. Such a disparity could naturally have led to a situation where the physically strong could be unrestrained in taking advantage or prey on the weaker. However, those factors would relate more to predatory species. His Kanei people and Lamphis had lived as one since the beginning. Yet they were of a similar type that only existed on sugar, nectar and berry juice.

'I am also on a quest,' Lumak gestured, pointing to himself and to the distant cliffs with a combination of noises and movements.

'Can I follow and be of assistance?' Stikol asked, realizing Lumak could understand his every word through his implants.

'Don't worry. We do not eat Kanei? They are too hard and bony,' he jested, and Lumak smiled in his own way.

He soon realized that Stikol understood most of his sentences. Since he, Lumak, could understand his words, he could always ask him to reply in answer to his questions. That way he would gain feedback and know for certain whether he fully understood his previous sentences.

As they approached the towering cliff Lumak began to consider all aspects of his enormous challenge. It was at that moment he realized the almost impossible nature of the task ahead. The obstacles faced were truly immense, if not impossible, but he would not decline his challenge. One of his ideas were to traverse the complete 78 kilometre length of the chasm to the intended target. He would follow a path along the middle of the chasm until he arrived at the 3 kilometre cliff. Then take a long rest in preparation for his arduous task of climbing its near vertical face.

While he viewed the deep blue-green waters of the trench, he could on occasion observe the deadly flying fish and other ferocious predators. They were the ones that skimmed the waves to catch other flying types and never fussy about their diet. Nevertheless they could not reach his altitude. His kite flew well and responded to his positioning by changing direction in the opposite way when the need arose. He grew used to her antics. Although contrary to his motion he had time to make corrective changes if he diverted slightly from his central course down the wide chasm.

Lumak realized that every challenge was in taking risks. In fact, whenever one went beyond naturally accepted principles, they had to face new boundaries and take new risks.

By now he was travelling close to 50 kilometres per hour and realized it would take him too long to his destination. The air at his current altitude within the area of the chasm was moving upwards and not in the direction he intended. Stikol was also getting weary with Lumak's slow progress.

'Yoo.. hoo! Yoo... hoo!' He cried, as he spiralled off from his position into the distance at great speed, leaving behind a gust of air that gave Lumak some extra lift. Then Lumak thought of another idea.

'Perhaps if I took advantage of the rising currents close to the wall and soared upwards towards the highest rim, then I could take off again over the cliff and spiral into my destination, but my eventual speed might be too high to land.' He contemplated those ideas for a brief moment and decided to take the leap all the same. After all, his kite was designed to take those stresses. At close to seven kilometres up, the air was thin and chilly with little oxygen, but Lumak endured, taking his toughly-built kite as far as he could climb, then he spun her about for the dive. Once he had gained enough speed, he levelled out.

He would follow this process of gaining excess height with the upward draft close to the chasm's wall and then go into an almost free-fall dive in the direction of travel by a simple adjustment of the controls. That operation was accomplished several times, until his speed slowed and his altitude became too low. That way he was to make the journey in only a few hours. He would land on the wall every two hours or so to rest.

His arms and body ached from awkward positioning during flight. That was not what he expected. He hadn't planned for such discomfort.

He found a wider area of the high cliff between the forested sea and chasm and spiralled into that position for a longer rest. He communicated his intentions to Stikol who descended towards the same area.

Lumak was not able to fully reduce his speed by this method and crashed into a pile of gravelly sand on the plateau's beach. Despite his ungainly fall, he and his kite were undamaged. He was just a little ruffled. Yet he had to thoroughly check his Little Dragon, as he called his craft, before he was able to rest.

By his side sat Stikol in all his power and glory. There he remained with his great golden eyes with their dark vertical slits steering at Lumak while subconsciously preening his wings. Then like magic they suddenly disappeared within his sides. He was truly an incredible sight beheld to have won the admiration of Lumak. The creature was so intelligent and so agile, with a central skeleton. Not like his kind, with hard external bony structures covered by much hair. This one was fleshy, with a covering of flexible scales that sealed his body from predators.

'That was very close for you, my friend,' Stikol said.

'Yes! Thanks to The Greater Purpose we are still in one piece,' Lumak replied, while removing his harness and checking his kite for damage, but there was none.

'It's a great design?'

'I designed and built it for this challenge!'

'Did you really?

'Yes!'

'Well it's a fantastic effort!'

'Thanks!'

'Do you truly believe in a Greater Purpose and of the eventual unification of all cosmic life in a single purpose for the common good?' Stikol asked, and Lumak was amazed by that question. He knew he wanted to be a Shadite like his mother, but wondered whether he would be accepted. He had so much to learn and all such ideas were way beyond him at that time.

'You have been listening to our ancient profits?' Lumak gestured.

'Not as much as I would like,' was Stikol's reply.

'I do not yet know of such spiritual things. I am a scientist and plan to assist everyone when I am more advanced in my studies.'

'That is also another of my ambitions or perhaps dreams. I find little means to express them in the real world.' Stikol said.

'I see you have many abilities and express them quite eloquently. Would you like to visit the University of Goh in Lud? If you were accepted, you would be the first of your kind, and could learn all you wanted about science and religion?'

'Could such a dream be made possible for a lowly Petan like myself?' he queried, fully understanding Lumak's gestures.

'Anything is possible, even for the lowliest, if they really want and desire it in their bones. The Grand Lord told me that once,' Lumak said, then the dragon shook himself a little, moved his tail for comforts sake and yawned.

'You have spoken to our lord?'

'Yes! My mother is Empress Queen, you know!'

'That must have been an incredible experience?'

'The greatest of my life!'

'So I am here sitting with a great prince! Sorry for the pranks played during our journey. I was just a little bored with my life,' Stikol said.

Apologies accepted!'

'I am of the opinion that all life-forms are in two groups which I call the Ploggers and Plonkers. I have constantly observed some with little effort make great and clumsy mistakes, while others who move the world make so little mistakes, even when they try their hardest. The former I call the Plonkers and the latter the Ploggers.'

'Which type of these are you?' Lumak inquired in equal jest.

'I believe us both to be Ploggers and will stake my next meal on it. Although we may make many mistakes as we learn, they are less than those of Plonkers.'

While they rested well away from the dangerous forest's rim, Lumak couldn't help but admire Stikol and his stories on life. He had a short sip of berry juice from a small container to assist wear and tear and rested. He removed juice from his holdall and offered some to Stikol, but it was a small quantity and he decided to go hunting for fish instead. Stikol soon returned with two stuck within his sharp canines and another impaled on one of his front claws. They were still wiggling and Lumak shunned away from Stikol's live feast.

They were satisfied and in the main rejuvenated, so it was time to move on. Since his mild accident, Lumak realized he would have to do better next time if he was to make the trip unscathed, never mind the difficult climb.

He made sure his harness was tight and the kite's strings of the correct tension. Once more a brave Lumak took the plunge into the deadly abyss. He would complete this sequence of hopping and diving at a suitable gradient many times before he reached his destination. The strong rising air-currents from the chasm, being the energy that would take him up to the cliff's top each time. He would attain speeds in excess of 50 kilometres per hour and cover the length in just over 4 hours while resting for short periods in between each dive.

When he arrived at the 3 kilometre high cliff, he found an area close to the chasm's shore. That part was filled with fallen debris, but suitable for landing. After reducing speed he spiralled onto the smoothest part of the beach. He completed a most controlled landing and selected a remote area to set up camp. He used his kite for shelter by fastening two piton hooks across the side of the hill. On those he strung a length of mallo rope to hold and take the slack of his kite.

Stikol had wandered off to investigate the area at the cliff's rim, so Lumak decided to rest and continue his climb when the sun was high in the sky. In the mean while he would investigate some menus within his new brain implants.

Lumak was deep in his implants when disturbed by an enormous splash. He quickly moved to the rear of his makeshift tent. Quickly loaded his hammer gun for defence, but was utterly surprised to see the features of a large and dripping wet dragon moving towards him.

'Ah... There you are, Lumak. I'm sorry if I'm late. Having come to realize your utter disgust for my eating habits, I stopped on the way for dinner.'

'It's nice to see you. Now I feel a lot safer, eating habits or no eating habits.'

Despite their differences both were becoming good friends. Lumak went out of his way to answer Stikol's inquiries on life in general, science and the Cosmos.

Face the challenge

Lumak scanned the complete face of the jagged wall and was aghast by its immensity. The local cliff loomed high above him and disappeared in dense mist and cloud. Nevertheless he knew his limitations and plotted a course in his mind with the most variation, including bumps and cracks to ease his task. The paler areas were not as solid and he intended to take greater care over those.

He began the climb at midday. At that time the rock face appeared dry and less slippery. He found the going much slower than anticipated. The first few metres of climb were of a smooth and constant gradient which made it more predictable. There were not many cracks or crevices, so he did all his climbing by pitons and attachments. Soon he found the exertion almost unbearable for his build, but struggled onwards. Although lacking in experience, he was not the type to retreat in the face of minor difficulties or discomfort. He found that two piton hooks in a horizontal line gave him a better grip with both legs and enough to hold him comfortably while resting. He used that method occasionally when needing a long break to regain his strength and thoughts.

In a few hours he had made it to a small ledge and decided to take a longer break to drink and rest his aching limbs. It was only five hundred metres above the base. He soon reasoned that at his current rate of ascent it would have taken him the best part of two days to make the climb. He was not guaranteed a suitable resting place further up the cliff's face.

He brought along some simple untested technology to assist his progress. A special attachment could be hooked to a lower horizontal pitons for creating a wider surface, then once on that platform he could add another to the one above and move quickly vertically. While using the rope he would nudge the lower one free and use it for the next level and so on. The process was repetitive and appeared straightforward when practised. Although progress had increased, such devices made one lazy and added to the risks.

He soon realized that the hammer gun, although powerful and quick, relayed poor judgement regarding the rock's hardness and he would have done better with a manual tool. Although progress would be slower, he could have better felt the hardness of the rock when pitons were driven in. He soon realized he had much to learn in that particular art. But how could one learn without facing the dangers and doing the trials.

The real problem began ten metres further up. His limbs suddenly gave way when a piton failed. The attachment released itself and he found himself falling. Luckily the rope held to the lower hook. He dangled just above the shelf below, but not before doing himself serious harm.

He had completed more than 500 metres, probably more than any Semonite had accomplished in that particular task during the history of his world and was now in serious trouble. He could not move either way because of his agonizing injuries. Luckily for him his face and eyes were shielded by his helmet. Nevertheless he had hit both his shoulders hard on the rock during his descent and thought they were both broken. Further, the ropes that held his weight had dug deeply into those same shoulders, so he was in double agony.

Stikol had been away on yet another of his explorations but had returned sooner than expected to find Lumak in that hanging position and agonizing about his inadequacy in completing his challenge.

'Have you broken anything?' Stikol asked, landing on the shelf just beneath him and gently applying his forehead to Lumak's back region to give him support.

'Try to place your feet on my shoulder and release the rope above, then you can land your feet on the shelf below.'

'Oh! It pains me so! I don't know if I can, but I will try!'

Lumak was not in a position to release anything. Both his limbs were numb from the fall and most of his lower body parts exceedingly painful. Stikol understood the situation but could not tackle both problems at once. Stikol soon realized that if he lifted Lumak's body and wriggled it about the rope might release itself.

However that operation would be even more painful but they had little choice, so he told Lumak of his intentions. During several attempts the rope was released and Lumak fell unto the ledge.

'Wow! I thought you were stuck there for good,' Stikol commented in his usual humorous manner.

'Thank you, Friend. You will never know how I feel at this moment. I never thought pain could be so painful. Will you help me to get home?' Stikol hesitated for a brief moment before replying to Lumak.

'I hear Petans are not well received or regarded in Lud, but I am after adventure, and as I said before, I need to find myself even among strangers and mobs. All my aspirations are full of risks, so I shall attempt this one for you and only you.'

'You are the bravest!'

'Or the most foolish?'

'Thanks, Friend! I'll never forget this!'

'Don't thank me yet. We must try to find a way in which we can accomplish our goal. I mean, with you and the kite, if we are to make it back before nightfall, suitable air currents prevailing.'

Their journey down the Cliff was slow and arduous, with Lumak constantly crying out in pain. It was late afternoon, still bright and sunny.

Despite his agonizing pain, Lumak soon came up with some answers to the problem of getting his kite into the air and making it back home. The three climbing ropes were to be joined together and the kite taken to the highest part of the mound near the shore. With the long rope coiled, Stikol would take one end between his teeth and take to the air while using a small part of the gravelly beach as a runway.

Once he had gained enough height and taken up the loose amount of rope, the impetus would then take the kite upwards. After which time Lumak's body would be lifted into the air, while hanging beneath the kite by harness. However the distance between harness and kite had to be extended, giving the kite time to take to the air before Lumak's weight was felt.

The winds at that part of the cliff were not steady, but increased significantly with height. As always, Lumak was precise in his deductions and Stikol understood the methods involved.

Having discarded his heavy holdall with all the climbing equipment, Lumak thought the lighter kite would make better progress in the prevailing winds. The winds and air currents from the south tended to travel eastwards, but with a powerful flyer like Stikol to guide the kite, he was sure they would make it home before dusk.

Towards that area were the many Kanei plantations, lower farm lands and berry fields, so he could gain assistance if his situation became intolerable, but what about Stikol: a fearsome Petan dragon in Kanei fields.

Those farmers were never fond of dragons and over the years had opposed the current imports of berry juice and other products from their lands. They saw dragons as the enemy and their main competitors. Further, 0because of so much negative publicity in their tales and folklore, they considered them to be the wildest monsters, with dread and dismay. That was mainly because they had never met a Petan before and rumours of their supposed evil deeds since Obe, flew far and wide.

Once in the air Lumak did not wish to land in any of those lands. He realized their journey had to be taken all the way to the city. Then he could explain the generous nature and kind efforts of his dragon friend to people of importance.

Stikol's arrest

At the appropriate time both kite and Lumak was pulled vertically as Stikol shot into the air at a steep angle. His massive wings extended to its fullest to take the wind. The moment the kite faced the upward currents, it was soaring, but not with Lumak's assistance to begin. Their main worry was the lake below. It held the most ferocious of predators. Many could be observed soaring across its many ripples.

Stikol continued his ascent, until the kite became high enough to glide horizontally on its own. He was a master at sensing the direction and strength of air currents and soon found one, then another that would assist them in their desired direction. Soon they were soaring high like eagles. Stikol held on firmly to the rope between his teeth while guiding Lumak and his craft toward the southwest. Lumak had kept awake most of that time and assisted in guiding the kite, but was now quite weak from loss of fluids.

After many hours the great city of Lud loomed large in the distance while an exhausted Stikol kept pace, sometimes gliding and at other times diving to maintain speed and direction. He realized Lumak was unconscious from his wounds but in extreme pain when he was awake. He wanted to make ground as soon as possible, preferable with his body below the kite, in order to accept Lumak's weight while landing. He would have to find a place of empty ground to use as a runway to skilfully position himself and take the weight of all three during that almost impossible manouevre.

As observed from on-high, that place was just south of the main city. Stikol realized he would have to prize Lumak's limp body off the kite and attempt a landing with his legs firmly held between his shoulders.

He entered a suburban area with many small farms and Kanei homes equally distributed in rows. He knew he had to land in that area but any manoeuvre would take much skill on his part and could create problems if they targeted the wrong area or hit someone in the process. That rather difficult operation was carried out in mid flight and in full view of many Kanei natives. At that time the kite dived into one of their store houses, causing significant damage to both building and equipment. Thank goodness Lumak had fallen into a pile of soft berries.

They assumed a rogue dragon was running amok and quickly called security. A few soldiers soon appeared and captured Stikol. Lumak was rushed to the nearest Kanei hospital where he underwent the relevant operations to mend his wounds.

It took Lumak three days to awaken from his induced sleep, during which time most of his wounds had fully repaired. As he awoke, his first words were, 'Where is Stikol! Where is Stikol, my dragon friend?'

At that time his mother was by his side.

'My child, what are you saying? Are you delirious and hallucinating? Kanei don't have dragon friends! Anyway, that one has been returned to his parents on the reservation. We can't have dragons flying hither and thither throughout our city creating havoc, you know?'

'He has not been abused by the soldiers in any way. Has he?' a worried Lumak inquired.

'He was questioned by my security and gave them some ridiculous story about a climbing accident, but I know my child would not be so foolhardy as to attempt such an irresponsible act. So they assumed he was telling a tall tale,' his mother, the Empress Queen, replied.

Lumak was saddened by that reply. He immediately regained his composure and walked directly out of the building, leaving a bewildered and worried mother behind.

A now furious Lumak captured one of the small craft used by security, checked its fuel levels and was up and away towards Stikol's reservation. He was not going to leave things as they were.

Lumak had arrived at the reservation and having observed the juveniles at play, wondered why Stikol was not among them. As his vehicle approached they dashed for cover. The sides of the craft lifted and Lumak got out. They were surprised by this Kanei visit, never having seen one at close range before. Lumak soon realized he had to communicate and went back to the vehicle. It contained an onboard sound-box as standard equipment that could be used in many different languages. He began frantically to program a sentence into its keyboard. Then pressed the transmit-button.

'Does anyone... here... know the whereabouts of my friend, Stikol? It's important that I find him, immediately!' the mechanical voice hailed.

Stikol soon crawled out of one of the three houses. He was quite tired from his past days experience and making up on lost sleep, but otherwise quite pleased to see Lumak. He immediately ran towards him.

'What a sight for sore eyes, and you are almost fully recovered... already?' he exclaimed, scanning Lumak's body from top to bottom.

'Yes! I'm almost back to normal, thanks to you and Kanei technology!'

'Your Kanei doctors and medicine must be very advanced!'

'Advanced enough! I am very sorry about the way they treated you, my dearest friend. Thank you dearly for saving my life and being there when I needed someone.

'No problem!' jested a happy Stikol.

'Do you still want to face that challenge and find yourself again?'

'Of course, I do! But first, let me introduce you to my people. Then you can have some stronger juice with me.'

Stikol introduced Lumak to his family and friends. They sat and drank together for a while. Finally they went to play some ball games with his rougher friends.

'Wow. That was some game. I must say, you guys play rough,' Lumak commented.

'Lumak found he just hadn't the energies and speed in his present form to keep up with the energy demands and physiology of Petans. Maybe his next project would include a metallic exo-skeletal suit. Their metabolisms were so different. Nevertheless he enjoyed the fun of it all, even as an observer.

His mother soon deduced that Lumak's life had really been saved by the little dragon. She also realized there was a bond of friendship between them. As a Shadite and royal representative of her people, she decided to take immediate steps to appease the situation. Word soon got around the city to expect a most important visitor and preparations were made.

'I have to take you back with me.' Lumak said and Stikol lifted both eyebrows in bewilderment.
'Don't worry friend, everything will be alright when they see us walking together. Anyway, my mother would have got the message by now.'
'What message!'
'Just a metaphoric statement. It meant she would have worked things out by now.'
'Oh. I see!'

Lumak arrived with Stikol at his mother's palace completely unaware of their plans. They had to manouevre their way through the local Kanei crowds, all waving their personal banners.
Lumak and Stikol, the gentle dragon, could not have imagined such a reception. Lumak's mother, the Empress Queen, was dressed in her Shadite's cloak to accept her newly acquired guest.
'I think we have much patching to do. I am very sorry I took so much for granted. I think it's to do with our differences and past history. But I shall try to make it up to you,' she said. Stikol remained speechless while occasionally nodding his head until Lumak decided to speak on his behalf.
'For a start, perhaps Stikol could become a science student in our most famous university. I have reason to believe he will make a most capable one, and in time, I would like you to recommend him for Shaditry. That is if he decides to go that far.'

Never in all the history of Kanaefon had there been an occasion of friendship like this one. The two were so completely alien to each other and yet, despite all the barriers and differences, they spoke the same language of universal truth. They aspired to similar goals and that was the oneness of truth.

Lumak and Stikol followed the celebrations until most of Lumak's people became acquainted with the larger than life scaly monster and his many funny antics. Almost immediately afterwards, Stikol was given his own home enclosure to use during his studies. He was later given a study-kit for the University of Goh and arrangements made to include him as one of their most popular students.

Part 1

The Rescue

CHAPTER 1

Lumak's 1st mission

Earth time... 1351 CE.

Planet... Kanaefon.

WORLDS IN TURMOIL

It was a very beautiful day on his home planet, Kanaefon. Lumak was busy spraying some chosen seedlings when the Grand Lord appeared as if from nowhere within that quiet part of the berry fields.

Lumak remembered that moment well. He was actively experimenting with one of his new bio-friendly anti-pest sprays and assessing the final stages of those experiments.

'Son, many innocent souls have perished within one of our neighbouring galaxies, Triangulum. It is on a world called Misoran II. You are to immediately take control of that mission. This will be your first real intergalactic assignment and also your first corporeal transformation. You should not worry unduly about technical matters. The species involved are well known to us so all necessary changes can be automatically engineered through the Mind.

'We have a complete biological profile of the endangered species and their planetary environment. Misoran II is peopled by a large intelligent crustacean called the Feloween. They are highly technological and have been fully self-reliant until their recent disaster. For that mission you may adopt a Speell's form. They are the most advanced life-form in that part of the galaxy and have links with The Greater Purpose.

You are to quickly delegate any important information on your current projects to the Mind and assign new scientists in your place during your absence. They will be expected to take over all your current projects and experiments. You should quickly update your chosen deputy on this and all your other projects before your departure. You may resume this work on your return,' he said. The Grand Lord then faded into the morning mist.

'My Gracious Lord! My very first mission away from home!'

The realization of it hit Lumak like an exploding shell. He realized he had to prove his worth as a Shadite but did not expect to test his mettle this soon in his chosen profession. An apprehensive Lumak pondered over the incredible possibilities while assisting others in a distant galaxy and could not even imagine a worst case scenario. The whole thing was just too incredible and well beyond belief.

He felt helpless and awed by it all. Finally an over-excited Lumak decided to visit some of his friends for advice and consolation.

Realizing the urgency of the situation, Lumak immediately collected his equipment and boarded his Robot-mobile, giving instructions for a journey to the local university. That vehicle was designed to follow the contours of the terrain a few feet above the ground, but could also fly at higher altitudes by a simple change in mode.

On arrival he called his most senior students together and after holding several intense interviews, assigned a young enthusiastic Worker in his place on a temporary basis. He packed a few small items, including memorabilia, and walked towards the large building with the winged crest overhanging its broad entrance.

That building included the large revolving sphere that was suspended at great heights in the atmosphere. The massive sphere could ascend and descend while floating just withing the three gigantic rods or pillars that formed its guides like tall spires. That area of the building was always in constant turmoil as large electric discharges arched between the rods and the globe depending on its position within the rods. Many thought the building was used to control and purify that part of the planet's atmosphere. The most elevated part of that structure was about four kilometres above ground. That place was the main residence of the Grand Lord and head office of his Shadites. It had been constructed soon after his arrival on Kanaefon.

As Lumak walked through its main doorway for the first time he was surprised to find his old human friend waiting just within the main entrance.

'Hello, Lumak!' Plato greeted through brain implants.'

'Hello, Plato,' he replied also through implants.

'Please follow me into one of the inner chambers.'

The large room included a circular desk at its furthest end and floating silently at a much higher level were a black spherical object with a winged circular insignia on its person.

As they walked towards the desk the sphere bobbed up and down on the air towards them, making Lumak shiver in his outermost bones. He had never seen anything like it in all his existence.

'Greetings, Shadites!' the globe barked in a powerful voice, as if eating its own words, but also transmitting those thoughts directly through their brain implants.

'I am Vektron, Intergalactic Coordinator to The Greater Purpose and have been assigned the task to prepare you both for your great mission ahead. But first, let me bring you up to date on current matters regarding Misoran II. As you have observed, their parent star exploded with little warning to anyone within their system, thus destroying large areas of their home world and manned installations. Although a rear occurrence, such cataclysmic runaway effects can occur with older stellar bodies.

'The survivors have since moved many of their people to unaffected patches of their planet and the few remaining shielded satellite stations. However, large parts of their atmosphere have become highly radioactive, not to mention the drastic climatic changes and extreme whether conditions now prevailing within all regions.

'Fortunately for them, their species and other lower forms are able to survive within their deep oceans. Many have taken that option to return after relinquishing all surface links and technologies. Their strong survival instincts have led them to those extreme measures for optimum safety.

'Yes, numerous numbers of their population have either

forfeited or rejected all the more modern trappings of their civilization relevant to a well structured society with its unique cultures, and are presently returning to the watery depths in droves, thinking it safer. However, as their world becomes colder, due to reduced radiation from the almost dead parent star, her land masses and oceans will freeze in a perpetual winter. That process, although slow, will eventually make all forms of primal life on that world non-existent within a relatively short time.

'The land masses have barely four weeks and her oceans another fifteen, before the surface ice becomes too thick to launch a rescue, thus confining those within the watery depths to eventual death from extreme cold and starvation.

'Your present task is, primarily, to evacuate their senior members and as many sub-species through portals to Black Ships within that part of the galaxy. Then you are to build or use existing shielded underground areas for growing food crops and holding temporary evacuees. Other important materials and equipment relevant to their culture should be stored, to be collected by the first Black Ships when they arrive in several years.

'In the mean time, one of my main tasks will be to locate a suitable world for resettlement. Because of the long time scale involved, you are to ensure all underground facilities are thoroughly shielded from the harsh environment above for a period in excess of 3 cyclons (about 5 years). Therefore, powerful nuclear generators will be required to drive the internal sun lamps and heating systems. Since their technologies are Class 3, those facilities will already exist in quantity within that region. However, the Tuillians are at Class 5 and can assist where other methods fail.

'Finally, the planets in that system will also be shifting their orbits further away from the now much smaller parent star, hence, that aspect will further aggravate matters. You are therefore required to prepare the larger artificially created environments for continuous survival, with the siting of necessary transmitters to inform all planetary inhabitants of your refuge locations and any dangerous areas of radiation to avoid.

'Some of their surface technologies are still in tact, but their scientists and other senior members of their society are still in a state of deep shock, making it difficult for them to take any long term survival decisions.

'There are just three Black Ships available within that vicinity of space and even the closest will not be able to arrive before a period of one cyclon. Therefore, you are to use resources as best you can in the circumstances and devise whatever methods necessary to enhance their survival.

'Since I am unable to visit the area in question, you Lumak will be in charge of all operations. Therefore you will be immediately informed of new strategies the moment I find a suitable world for their re-settlement.

'You may locate the upper portal chambers in order to be transposed to one of our Black Ships in the vicinity.

'May the Grand Lord speed your efforts,' Lord Vektron said. With those words the black globe of the Ploran floated back to its original perch above the circular desk.

Although not as powerful as the Gohran Supreme Beings, the Plorans were an ancient race that had since left our universe. However, a few like Lord Vektron, his brother Lord Patron and a few others remained in Osmaron to assist the Greater Purpose.

Lumak could not leave his world without first saying farewell to his close friends and family. He did not go immediately to the upper Portal Chambers as Lord Vektron had ordered. Instead he left the building to arrange his personal matters.

'I am to take care of some urgent business before I leave, but I shall be back shortly,' he said through implants. Plato waited patiently in the hallway for his return.

Lumak made his way immediately to the Central Square. As always he would meet his close friends Aurlsba and Longe and meditate for the success of this his very first mission. Those two noble Kanei had been given the job of taking care of the Om-Chopter monument. They were cleaning her sails which extended in the vertical position as Lumak arrived.

'Where is Mendu our famous Lamphis today!' Lumak shouted.

His two friends were elevated many feet in the air on extendible ladders and Lumak was worried they would fall and break some bones.

'He is late. He had a busy day yesterday cleaning the boat,' Aurlsba shouted back.

'We are checking her sails today. As far as I am concerned, she is still seaworthy, but I am not sure whether her burners and links will carry her into the air,' Longe said. He was always an incredible mechanic and knew every inch of Om-Chopter.

'When I return from my first mission we shall build a new Om-Chopter almost exactly like her and take it through the Straights of Magellar towards the great wall. That challenge will even be better than the last one I had with my kite,' Lumak said and they hurried down the ladder to greet him.

'You are really on your first inter-galactic mission?' Aurlsba interjected full of excitement for Lumak.

'Yes, it's in another galaxy. The one we call Siiti.'

'All the way to another galaxy through time and space. What an incredible adventure. You must tell us all about your experiences on your return!' Longe replied excitedly.

'That's not all. I have to change my body to a form on that world and become like them in all things.'

'Great Obe!' Longe commented, aghast by it all.

'Do you really mean what you said. I mean, about building another Om-Chopter and going on another maiden voyage through the dangerous straights of Magellar?' Aurlsba inquired.

'Of course! You can get the bits together in my absence. Siend Lucien can assist. It's a pity he is now too old for this work. I am sure he will do his best if you ask him kindly. Anyway, just tell him it's my idea,' Lumak said.

'Yes, I know. He will not refuse if its for you. You know, he thinks you are the real Obe, his dearest friend, now in a different life,' Aurlsba said.

'Our minds are the first to fail us when we age,' Lumak replied.

'Are you ready for your first maiden mission?' Longe asked, while carefully observing his attitude and disposition and Aurlsba came closer.

'I suppose as ready as I'll ever be. I am always better troubleshooting when there is trouble. Anyway, my dearest friends, I am off to the galaxy we call Siiti and have to transform my body into their kind, so how worse can it get. Anyway, it's an important mission, many lives are in danger, so I'll endeavour to give it my best,' a brave Lumak said and they were humbled by his motivation.

'This is truly incredible, my Siend. In that respect you are very much like our Obe, on his first war mission to save our people from the dreaded Petans. Now you have excelled even him by facing greater dangers to save others in distant galaxies. Perhaps Lucien was right about you, after all. May Obe's spirit always be with you, my dearest friend,' Aurlsba said.

Lumak left his friends and went to say farewell to his parents and other friends before going to the Grand Lord's building. When he returned a faithful Plato was still patiently awaiting his arrival. Although his mother desired a celebration for his untimely departure, he would have none of it at this time. His present mission was too urgent for such frivolities.

Plato accompanied Lumak to a local portal which transposed them to the Inter-spatial Cubicle from where they would leave for Triangulum.

On entering the strange device the bands began to move on all of its five walls while the sixth extended to a large curved tube. As the bands moved underneath them, they were propelled along the tunnel which ended unto the main deck of a Black Ship somewhere in the Triangulum galaxy. During that time they found themselves floating in a sea of liquid energy. It was as if they were at one with the Cosmos. Form became irrelevant to their existence while in that state. Soon their environment changed and the liquid energy began to disperse and solidified into a rigid structure, leaving their bodies separate and standing in a similar position to when they left. Both had been transposed and transformed through the Mind into an advanced alien life-form. One specific to that part of Triangulum.

Their new forms were about seven feet long, ten inches in diameter, green in colour and resembled a large caterpillar with four hand-like legs at each extremity. Their bodies contained a very flexible spinal column and could move like the multi legged giant caterpillar. They tended to curve their central parts in order to progress at greater speed. They could also move like a quadruped or stand erect on either sets of legs while using the others like hands. Each leg contained six long flexible digits.

Their large heads were at an extreme end, with many scaly horns and spikes. The whole creature was completely covered with protective scales. Its head boasted two large eyes with other relevant sensors while its rear end had markings resembling the real organs on its head, as if to deceive a would-be predator of its true position. Their faces were human-like, with thick lips and flexible facial expressions.

Their ancestors had evolved on a most hostile, carnivorous planet as vegetarians. Despite their initial survival handicap, they had evolved a large brain and other incredible social skills to compensate. Because of those attributes they could be considered human in many respects. The Speell, as they were called, were quite capable of generating subtle sounds, and could very easily imitate human speech with their well developed vocal cords.

Over several generations they had become one of the most technologically advanced life-forms in Triangulum, while assisted by many robots and androids. Yet, they remained a highly cultural, social and near human type, emotionally speaking. They had also developed a great sense of humour. One well practised during their mimicking sessions. Each trying to outwit the other.

The Speell were once directly under the Grand Lord several millennia ago and had made the decision to assist Lord Vektron and his lot in maintaining that type of order within Triangulum.

Their current ruler, Toccor IV, was a great and well respected leader. He had always maintained good relations with the Misoran system and had lost many of his own diplomats and people when the star exploded. Therefore he considered it his duty to assist them as urgently as possible. Even so, it would take their fastest unmanned probes more than a year to get to the damaged world. That future would have been much too late to save anyone.

'My Lord. We have received an urgent communication from Misoran. Their star has become unstable and will go nova within hours,' the officer reported.

Emperor Toccor IV remembered well the moments before the cataclysm. He was having lunch at the time with the Misoran ambassador.

'Oh, My God!' the ambassador yelled and excused himself. He had to make an urgent call through H-Wave.

'Is there anything we can do.'

'Absolutely nothing before the event. They would have taken all necessary steps to save themselves. In the mean time we may prepare a rescue mission to save the survivors,' the officer replied.

Another more senior officer soon entered the royal suite on board the imperial flagship.

'My Lord, I have more bad news. The star has gone Nova. It is feared most within that system may have been obliterated by enormous blast waves. Further, we have no immediate means to assist or rescue the survivors,' he said sadly and left.

The moment the emperor received news of the disaster via H-wave, he immediately summoned his eldest son for assistance. Prann was a senior captain and their first Shadite. His father, the emperor king, explained the tragic situation to him after receiving the H-wave distress communication.

'My son, this is a recent recording received just before the Misoran star exploded,' he said, while information was transferred directly to Prann's brain implants.

'I never thought such an event was possible within this part of our galaxy in our life time as a species. Yet, there are much older systems within this stellar quadrant. Well, Father, I shall contact my organization immediately. If anyone can help, they will,' he said and left.

Prann immediately communicated through the Greater Mind for assistance before boarding one of their Black Ships with a large crew for the system in question.

Prann Toccor was now captain of a Black Ship several kilometres long and travelling at maximum velocity to a system about one hundred light years away. Even at that speed he did not expect to get there in less than two years. Therefore he prayed for a miracle to speed their progress, not knowing what help he would receive through the Greater Mind.

He briefed his fellow crew as best he could, having taken on-board as much rations and equipment needed for the long trip ahead. It was always going to be a compromise between weight and speed, so he took along the optimum crew and supplies.

His massive ship could evacuate over half a million of his type and perhaps twice that many of the Feloween, who were less than half the size of his kind. Each trip would take over five years to complete either way and it was estimated there were over twenty million Feloween and other life-forms left on their home-world. Therefore, all Black Ships including the other two not so local, were alerted and briefed to take equidistant positions between both systems. Thus forming a queue with a thirty three light year distance between them. That was after they had arrived at their specific destinations in one point seven and three point two years respectively.

The thirty three light year distance was the maximum safety limits of their most powerful on board portals. In the mean time their only option was to extend their on-board portal range. They were already on maximum and within their specified safety limits for transposing living creatures. Their ranges could further be extended for transmitting basic foodstuffs and equipment. Such critical safety limits were only required for living organisms and not so essential for transferring materials and equipment.

CHAPTER 2

Lumak and Plato arrives

Lumak and Plato suddenly materialized within the portal link on the main deck of Prann's Black Ship. They greeted Prann in a vertical position, wearing their black Shadites' cloaks which was capable of acquiring the new form of its wearer.

'Salutations, Prann,' they greeted awkwardly in Shadite salutation and in his language, with one of their right limbs placed on their chest in a somewhat strained manner that appeared difficult for them. As always in a new body, it took time before minds became used to the more subtler and intricate movements due to the performance of neurons, nerves and muscles. However, the Tuillian type was well known to the Greater Mind and only a relatively short period of training was required to familiarize with the new Tuillian body format.

'We have ...have come to assist ...and ... and are to get to their home-world al...almost immediately,' Lumak said, still thinking he was a Semonite and in the process making wrong moves and sometimes uttering the wrong words. Prann realized the problem and soon got the jest of what he said, while communicating through their brain implants. One of the great things about those Brain Implants was that they transferred certain thought processes independent of language. Being previously human in form, which was a lot closer to the Tuillian type, made Plato ideal for that type of vocal communication.

'You have both answered my prayers of desperation, by your quick arrival to my humble ship. But how can you get to their world in time. Our ship will take over one cyclon (about two years) to get there and I am afraid all those poor souls will surely perish in a few months at the most,' Prann replied with disappointment written all over his features.

'Don't you worry, Friend, we have been thoroughly briefed and have several plans of our own to put into action. If for some unfortunate reason Siend Lumak misses the target on this occasion, I shall repeat where he left off,' Plato said, with an air of confidence and with much better pronunciation. Plato always felt superior in the presence of his senior, Lumak, who in his opinion could always find a solution to any problem.

'Do... do you have a portal link between this ship... ship and their world? Lumak asked, still stuttering, but with slight improvement in his movements. Lumak wanted to learn their methods the hard way without implants. Then he would transfer that information in Sunolingua through his implants.

'I am not sure, Siend, that any of our portals will work correctly on complex living organisms beyond thirty three light years. We have tried several times to communicate with the dying world, but have been unable to get any response from our position here in space. Their original SOS beacon was lost immediately after receiving the distress call,' Prann replied, staring at his senior's winged insignia.

'Keep... keep trying, someone will respond sooner or late... later, after the panic has... has quietened down. If not, I shall have... have to visit Misoran II through the Mind. But that... that measure will only be undertaken after having exhausted every other possibility,' a decisive Lumak said. Lumak's implants had soon learnt all the parameters of his new body and his initial problems had quickly dissipated.

'Yes, my Siend. My communications crew have already been given the necessary instructions and have not stopped trying,' Prann replied.

'If only we knew of a suitable local world on which to evacuate them. It might then have been easier to extend portal range and move several ships in queue. Then transfer them ship-to-ship via long-range portals to their destination world. That method would have shortened the process. For even the furthest ships could probably have taken up positions closer to their primary bases, if we knew where it was,' Lumak said.

'My Siend, that is the reason why we have decided to evacuate the bulk of the survivors to my home world, Tuil, until such a place is found,' a worried Prann replied.

'Let's pray we are able to find a suitable world in line with our Triangulum bases,' Lumak said. Suddenly the communications officer entered the bridge to talk with his captain.

'We have received a coded communication from one of their satellite stations that was placed in safe orbit during the nova and was partly shielded by their world during the catastrophe.

'Here is a list of their long-range interplanetary portals and the main utilities that are still operational,' she said and transmitted the information through her implants to the master computer. Prann and the others began to read the screened information.

'Over one half of our world has been obliterated. Most of our remaining atmosphere have expanded and is now highly radioactive. The few surviving operational facilities were on the more sheltered or dark side of our world at the time of the high energy front's arrival.

Three large fully manned satellite stations remain in tact, but even on limited food rations can only last another month or so...

Three long range portals are sited on Satellite Trom, which is the largest of our three orbiting stations. Only a few short range portal stations are left remaining on the planet's surface...

Several of your own people have survived with us on Trom and on two other local satellites. They include one of your senior scientist, Gemmi Doff, who is now assisting us...

End of communication.'

The operator again returned with more information which he screen within the captain's bridge for security reasons.

'The maximum guaranteed safety range of our longest portal is twenty four light years. The others are seven and five. All surface portals have maximum ranges of one million drons (about 1.5 million Earth miles)**...**

End of communication.'

'Tell them to prepare and test their longest portals. And please send them the portal codes of this ship. Also send a message to Gemmi; tell her to get together a team of competent engineers in every field and find whatever useful tools and equipment they can lay their hands on. Let them know that they are to expect the Shadite Lumak within thirty five croneks (about 30 hours),' Lumak said and a surprised Prann dismissed the operator to make the necessary communication.

'Prann, I would like you to prepare one of your small stellar observation probes to the specifications I have just relayed to your computer. One of those probes fitted with extra LPD's should make the trip within twenty five croneks without any G-Force Neutralizers,' Lumak said.

During his search of the Osmaron galaxy on one of his college projects, he had learnt a lot about surveillance probes and suddenly realized some of that knowledge could now be put to good use.

'But... no one of our kind can survive G-Forces in excess of fifty and you speak of G-forces in excess of one thousand. Even the probe might begin to disintegrate at five hundred or so, my Siend!' Prann explained.

'No, Prann. I am well briefed on the design of these stellar probes. They are able to remain in close orbit about erratic stars for long periods. My main fear in this regard is having a rear collision with a meteor or having a drastic change in direction, should I get too close to a star or massive planet, but I have to take those risks. This is the main reason why I have asked for a small stellar probe. Even so, add as many G-force neutralizers as you can. Two hundred G's should be more than adequate for the probe,' Lumak said.

'And what about you, my Siend. How will you survive?' Prann replied.

'I shall wear my cloak and vectorize into partial matter. That way, my mass displacement in this space-time will be reduced by a thousand fold. I shall fine tune for just enough vectorization so that I am able to remain within the probe, without being displaced in deep space should the craft promptly change direction for any reason. Since my velocity will closely match that of the probe's, the chance of our separation due to such changes will be negligible. That way, my body will have a slight effect, with an insignificant but finite mass. Since I do not wish to flow through the probe's walls, vectorization can be automatically re-instated, should my unconscious body decide to travel through the ship without my permission, and my body be left floating forever in deep space. Nevertheless I shall have to face those problems during acceleration, deceleration and directional changes.

'This process will be a close compromise between remaining inside and suffering the effects of extreme G-pressure. The main problem I face, however, is my inability to control any part of the probe physically during my trip. This is because my almost invisible fingers will penetrate the relatively less dense control panel if I apply a force in any given direction. Therefore, you are to fit a small transceiver and control computer, which can at all times be operated by my brain implants. I shall also need an oxygen mask with several days supply,' Lumak said.

'Consider it done, my Siend.'

Turning to Plato, Lumak began to communicate directly through brain implants many times faster than normal speech.

'Please search these local systems within a radius of one hundred light years for a suitable world. Use the ship's library and finally the Mind if necessary. Lord Vektron is also searching through his records, but you know how fussy he can be when issuing primitive worlds for secondary habitation.

'Now I must do some exercises and learn the intricacies of my new body format. After that, I can do with some sleep,' Lumak said and departed to one of the local cabins.

When the probe's modifications were complete Prann called Lumak to the bridge.

'My Siend, your probe is fully tested. Here are its new specifications and contents. You have on-board enough oxygen for one week, but your portable face-mask can only retain twelve hours supply when disconnected from the main console. A special pump has been fitted to give you more oxygen from the main unit when you are operating in partial mode. Even so, you will have to re-vectorize a little in order to get more oxygen from the main console. All unused oxygen will be recycled and recompressed back into the unit. The main tanks may be connected by a simple valve after you have used up the contents of the face-mask's cylinder.

'You have more than enough food rations for a month, but you should keep a few containers on your person before you vectorize.

'Finally, we have taken the liberty of fitting a small horizontal portal, which forms a comfortable rest unit. Everything is anchored securely to shock absorbers. G-Force neutralisers have been placed wherever necessary and should give a reduction in excess of 300 Gs. It will be a tight squeeze and you will need to curve your body and remain in that position for several croneks (many hours), so make yourself as comfortable as possible after you enter.

'God speed, my Siend,' Prann said in a sympathetic manner. They saluted and Lumak was on his way to the docking area of the ship via an internal portal.

The probe's small computer was programmed with all necessary information and stellar maps of the area, but the basic on-board computer was not intelligent and could only follow specific commands. A large volume of unnecessary instruments had been removed in order to make space for the portal containing Lumak's long caterpillar-like body. A few pieces of his special equipment and a small manual control panel was also fitted, just in case he required that facility.

A small self destruct mechanism was also included. That was in case the probe went out of control and targeted a populated planet. Nevertheless that was an extremely remote possibility. Yet they tended to be prepared for almost any eventuality.

Lumak knew he would have little control over the probe at extreme velocities in hyperspace, so it was just a matter of plotting the best course possible and pointing the probe in the initial direction he had calculated before pulling switches. He spent sometime analysing the route. When he had double checked his data with the aid of his computer, he released the probe from its outer moorings and drifted away from the large ship. Then he modified the program to what he thought was a best compromise and pushed the master switch. Even then he realised this particular trip was going to be a hit and miss affair, with such limited controls on-board.

Further, any close encounters with large stellar masses could have drastically altered his direction and velocity. As he pondered those uncertainties he clamped his body within the comfortable rest in the small portal and vectorized to less than one percent of his original mass. Then he relaxed and prepared himself for the trip ahead.

When the probe had passed the 300 limit in G's, he felt a slight creeping sensation along his body and knew that the neutralizers had reached their maximum limits of compensation. He set a pain threshold figure within his brain implants for automatic vectorization changes and went to sleep. To Lumak, sleeping could be accomplished at any time by a simple command through his brain implants and that aspect could be precisely timed like an alarm clock.

He awoke temporarily to ensure everything was functioning correctly. But all he could observe through the viewer was intermittent bands of light that represented stars as they streaked pass. Very soon those streaks would disappear into the stellar canopy until all that was left was the greyness of hyperspace. From here on, nothing within the material universe would be visible and he prayed that no large stellar objects would be encountered before he entered that course during his travel. After that time it would not matter anyway, as other solid matter could not occupy the same inertial frame that he traversed within his own space-time.

'Everything appears to be functioning correctly... We must now be entering hyperspace. I shall set the timer for twelve hours and have some more sleep,' he murmured to himself, swallowed a small multicolored vitamin capsule and went back to sleep.

After just ten hours he was awakened by all the alarms going off at once and wondered what the crisis was. The probe had for some unknown reason stopped, reversed its acceleration and slowed almost to a standstill.

'We should have been in the vicinity of the target system by now and within their portal range,' he mumbled.

The distance travelled was only eighty light years, but the stellar canopy was not familiar to anything on his local maps. He double checked against a large array of maps, even to the point of retracing his probe's movements and soon found his new location. One of the more massive stellar objects encountered during the initial part of his journey had spun the probe around. It had journeyed almost at right angles to his required trajectory. He was sixty five light years away from his destination and with a malfunction.

'Luckily for me you went into reverse and stopped when you did, or I might have been on my way out of the galaxy by now,' Lumak unwittingly said to the probe while slowly revectoring his cloak to have a closer look at the internal systems. He removed the small control panel, including a few local ones and activated a small mobile probe to check for breaks in the main busbar and other visible signs of damage. Then he used his implants in an attempt to locate the exact position of the fault.

'Ah, there you are... a broken main forward control line to the main LPD's. Judging from the explosive burn marks, we could have taken a direct hit by a meteorite, and yet, there has been no leakage of air or indeed any reduction in pressure. Anyway, how could we take a direct hit by anything in hyperspace? Perhaps we collided with an unknown inhabitant of some other dimension...? The probe's walls will be completely transparent to anything during that phase, even to an H-D Object, which could affect energy lines and other life-forms. Could life really exist in such a state within a higher dimensional level, beyond the speed of light and energy as we know it?' He said those words to himself while searching for more explosive burn marks within the control panels.

Suddenly he felt a strange sensation and a large part within the panel lit up in bluish glow. Whatever it was remained resting on the fusion power generator.

'Who are you?' he enquired through his implant at the almost spherical ball of bluish light.

'I am of no name,' came a thought from the being of light.

'I have magnified my person and use the bright light in order to become visible to you.

'We are many, and yet, we are one. I have strayed beyond my boundaries and am afraid it might not be possible to return back from whence I came. Now, I feel week and sense continuous losses within my being,' it added, telepathically.

'How can I help?' Lumak inquired.

'Return me to my world as soon as possible!'

'In that case, I shall have to carry out some repairs on my probe and please try not to do any more damage to my probe or my power unit in the mean time, or we may never get anywhere again,' Lumak said to the now pulsating ball of light.

'Let me do it for you. I now have all the information I require,' it said. With one almost blinding flash, everything returned to normal. The probe was once again on its way back from whence it came. It was as if the being had the powers to reverse time and change future events to its satisfaction.

As he passed what appeared to be a massive star the stellar canopy lit up and even penetrated his ship. All around him lay a strange universe of swirling plasma.

'I must be within the centre of a star? Yet, I am still alive and the probe is still in one piece,' he inquired of himself. But the creature overheard his thoughts and immediately replied.

'No. You are now in my universe. Everything within your ship has been transformed into the matrix of that universe. But I am afraid, your presence here will not be appreciated by the guardians of this plane. Therefore, you must leave me and return to your own plane of existence immediately,' it said and left through the almost transparent metallic wall of the probe, not interested anymore in Lumak's problems..

'How am I to do that without your assistance!' Lumak yelled, but the entity continued on his way unabated.

'A non-material being, made of an unknown combination of elemental forces. How exciting,' Lumak mumbled to himself. However he soon realized he had been taken for a ride and in the process had been left in the lurch.

He could observe thousands of balls of light flitting here and there at great speed.

'May I speak to your leader,' Lumak thought to one that passed by, and a much larger sphere came closer to observe him and remained in that area for a moment while constantly changing its position.

'I am of the Greater Purpose within a lower dimension. I am on a very important mission to save a world within a distance of fifty light years from whence I entered into this previously unknown universe. I would like to be released from this plane in order to complete my mission. Can you help?' he asked.

It slowly shifted its position again, as if not able to retain itself in the same place for any length of time.

'First of all, the entity you brought back with you no longer belongs with us. Its being has been contaminated by your universe and there are now certain irreversible changes within it that can no longer be tolerated. Secondly, only it can show you the way back to your own dimension. Its presence within your plane was due to some strange wandering aspect of its nature, and because of that reason it will not be able to survive in either planes without special assistance from a habitor,' the large entity said.

'You mean to say he will die, anyway?' Lumak inquired.

'It is neither he nor she, they are all me; just a fragment of our causal state with a little of each of us within its being. But now it has more than that and might contaminate us. For although it appears to be separate, we are one and singular in all things. It is now not of a true singular nature or purpose, since its recent transformation. It will soon be repelled by our body into another plane from whence it can never return... and you will also be transposed into another plane not of your primal type without its assistance. Therefore, it is in your best interest to immediately communicate with the entity in question and attempt your mutual transformations as soon as possible, before your presence is more strongly felt by us. Before the fabric of our plane begins to transform into a new causal mode of our existence,' it replied and grew dimmer into the form of the stray entity.

'You wanted my assistance?' it asked.

'Yes, please! Can you show me a way out of this dimension and back into my own within the point that we left?' Lumak asked.

'But if I do I shall die.'

'But you will die anyway,' Lumak said.

'Better with family than with friends,' it replied, mockingly. It was obviously convinced that it was going to die anyway, so Lumak changed his approach.

'Why ever die? Perhaps you could somehow become part of my own being and explore the lower dimensions with me together, until we are able to find a safe method of separation. But you must promise me that you will just be an observer. I wouldn't like the idea of you taking conscious decisions on my behalf before I am able to formulate them myself. However, if I ask you for help, I wouldn't mind your input. Because of those reasons I have decided to call you Jot, because you are too small to be seen normally,' Lumak said.

'I suppose... I could tolerate such an existence for a while. Anyway, it's much more acceptable than death,' Jot replied.

'Well, we don't have much choice, do we?' Lumak said.

'Agreed!

'I shall merge with your entity when the time is right, but I must now take control of your craft and return us to our entry point,' it said, joyfully.

Jot had read the complete structure of Lumak's mind and soon realized he could make a temporary home for himself within its continuum. He soon placed Lumak in a deep sleep to make the necessary changes, then he retrieved the destination map from Lumak's mind. Finally, he altered the probe's course towards the required destination.

Once having assessed the purpose of Lumak's mission he wanted to discover more about the new universe in which he found himself. He was now set on adventure in every way possible and would guide Lumak in ways conducive to such adventures.

CHAPTER 3

On Satellite Station Trom III

The probe soon arrived in the system and was programmed for landing. Through all those changes Lumak was still fast asleep.

Lumak heard the words, Back!... Back!... Back!... deep within his mind. He suddenly opened his eyes to find he had arrived within the Misoran System. And most miraculously, the probe was precisely on target and ready to dock. He realized he was probably having a dream. Nevertheless how could it have journeyed all the way to that system in such a precise manner. He didn't even know that before that time it was in the more than capable hands of Jot, his current resident.

Lumak sent a message to Gemmi on the satellite station and she forwarded him instructions for docking in one of their main scientific area. The small craft was captured and taken into one of the bays with many a curious Tuilian overlooking the proceedings. There was much excitement when they realized someone had arrived from another system to aid in their rescue.

'Are you captain Prann Toccor?' Pillor, the Feloween, asked, as Lumak pulled his almost cramped Tuilian body from the small craft.

'No. I am Lumak, Shadite. I am here to assist in your evacuation. Prann is on his way with a Black Ship and will arrive later... much later. Can I meet with Sienora Gemmi Doff?' he replied and was immediately escorted to her private quarters.

On those stations different species Power were segregated within different sections. Only the most senior members of each group could visit other groups by appointment. The senior administrator, Pillor, was from the damaged planet below and in no way Tuilian. On arrival he said hello to Gemmi and left them together to introduce each other in whatever modes fashionable to their species.

'You are a handsome male,' she greeted, as he curved his central body region to enter the small circular doorway of the cabin.

'I am Lumak, Shadite, in charge of this mission, and you are...,' he said.

'Please don't be so officious. Let's feel more at home during this impossible situation, it's better for the nerves. I am Senra Gemmi and very pleased to have you on board. I still haven't fully recovered from the stresses of the past few days. At one time I thought we were never going to make it. Everything happened so quickly; never giving us enough time to get out of this system. Finally, we decided our best choice was this place and here I am. Thank goodness you are now with us,' she said, moving her feminine coils closer to his for comfort.

It was common behaviour for members of that species to coil together for greater safety when approached by an enemy or predator. Then both sets of scales would come together, sealing off their softer under body parts from such dangers. But such coming together by members of the opposite sex usually led to other situations that was almost irresistible, as their powerful hormones took over the natural course of events.

To Lumak it was an incredible experience and yet, he held certain controls on as strongly as he could. Not wanting, in any way, to upset his companion or take undue advantage of her present closeness and state of mind. She wanted closeness and sympathy to reduce her stresses. However in his new and temporary body Lumak had no intention of going further. He wanted to stop short of any sexual act. That type of closeness with other species during such missions were against the Shadite's code.

They were coiled in that way for the best part of fifteen minutes, sometimes rolling along the soft comfortable floor covering and when they both had enough they separated.

'Ooh... Now I know what is meant by the Tuilian Embrace,' Lumak said, feeling slightly ruffled along his upper scales.

'I would like to apologise for being so forward, but I had to get those pent up stresses out of my system and now I feel a lot better for it,' she replied.

'No need for apologies. I enjoyed it as well, you know. But I couldn't have gone any further in case I took advantage of your present traumatic condition. Although I am unattached, I would like to build a relationship before I begin thinking in terms of more serious matters,' he said.

'That's fine with me. You appear to be one of those orthodox fellows. Even so, I find those qualities very romantic and attractive in a male. You must remain here with me as my very special guest and tomorrow we can get the others together for more serious work. Anyway, I have not taken a mate for several Tuilian years and you will only be my second in all that time, if I wanted such a relationship,' she replied.

'Since our mission is urgent, I would prefer if we were just friends for now, no disrespect intended,' he said.

'Ok... If you insist!

'With Pillor's assistance, I have been able to organize a few teams on all three satellites, but tools and equipment are limited on these stations. Pillor thinks we shall have a better chance of finding such equipment when we begin excavating on the surface below. Anyway, let me get us something to eat,' she said.

'In that case, I shall need your help in organizing the troops first thing tomorrow,' he said and she went towards the small area where they prepared their prepacked meals.

Gemmi Doff was a distant cousin of Prann and had royal blood flowing through her veins. She was barely two thirds the size of an average male with an orange under belly instead of blue on the males. When fully dressed her jewellery dangled from many of her curved horns which adorned her head like a massive Jewelled crown. She carried many bracelets on each of her four hands and feet, which ever were used for standing at the time. However, although both sets of limbs were very similar, those close to her head were referred to as hands, since they were utilized more frequently for holding things and held longer fingers.

All along her scaly body were hooks carefully fitted to large boney scales for holding the rings used for keeping her pleated skirt in place. The skirt almost completely encircled her body and extended to touch the floor when she was standing in a horizontal position and on all eights. But when she stood up vertically on her rear four legs, the skirt fell back to reveal an under vest which completely covered that part of her body. That vest was carefully chosen to contrast with the colour of her skirt.

The males were less particular about clothes. Only very important males and politicians wore special attire. Many males simply found such attachments and contrivances a nuisance and soon discarded them for greater body freedom.

Her large eyes were brown in colour with a black slitted pupil with good peripheral vision. Her features were feminine through and through. She was a real beauty as far as Tuillians went.

She had quickly prepared a small area of her living quarters for Lumak. Space was at a premium on the satellite station which contained over ten thousand important individuals. They had been hurriedly collected from every section of their planet before the disaster struck and only very important Tuillians were given such luxurious quarters. Both of them considered it a good idea to remain together while concentrating on the gigantic task ahead.

When it was her time to rest, Lumak took the opportunity to visit the upper decks and familiarise himself with his new environment. After he had inspected the local portals and other recreation areas within their section, he decided to pay a brief visit to the main control deck and formally introduce himself to the senior members, Tuillians and Misorans alike.

'We thought it impossible for anyone from your home system to have arrived here in such quick time. You must have been well into a journey to our world when you received our urgent call for assistance?' Pillor asked.

'No. I was in Osmaron at the time,' Lumak replied.

'Where is Osmaron?' the small crab-like creature inquired through implants.

'The Galaxy you call Plactorii,' Lumak replied.

'I transposed directly from there to Prann's vessel which had only recently left their main planet Tuil and will take another two of your years to get here, if he continues on his present course.'

'Really?'

'Yes! I am to assess your present circumstance and schedule a planned evacuation to a yet unknown new world. By so doing, we are to save your world and all its remaining people,' Lumak replied in no uncertain terms and Pillor was impressed.

'That's impossible!' one of the senior butted in, cynically. The younger ones also got on the bandwagon and began asking their probing questions.

'And how long did it take you to get to us from Prann's ship?' the young Feloween asked.

'With the specially rigged stellar probe, just under twelve of your hours,' Lumak replied.

'You must be some scientist!' the young male exclaimed, even still not believing in Lumak's story. Although many of the other creatures doubted what he said, they decided to give him the benefit of the doubt for the time being. After all, how could anyone have travelled across galaxies in such a short time.

'I am aware of the doubts in your minds regarding my capabilities, and to be frank, even I would have similar doubts if placed in your shoes. It is therefore necessary for me to prove my capabilities to you in like manner,' he said. His black cloak suddenly became visible as he slowly faded into nothing and then returned back to normal as if by magic.

'Now you truly know one of the potentials of a Shadite,' he said.

They stared at him in an unbelievable manner and a young scientist stood up erect to pay compliment.

'Incredible technological magic! With such powers you must be capable of almost anything!' the young one complimented while others went closer to observe his strange black cloak that did not reflect any light, whatsoever.

'Now I know the true meaning of Shaditry.

'You are obviously from a much more superior race than Prann's and have come all this way to assist us in our hour of need. For this great sacrifice my race will always be indebted to you and your kind,' Pillor said.

For some yet unknown reason Lumak felt completely on top of the situation and thought anything he took on was possible, not realising for a moment that he had also taken on-board an inter-dimensional being who now existed within his own entity. One who also had a keen appetite for such scientific and other more emotional experiences. Yet, Jot never let him know that he was in his mind, because that knowledge would have constantly bothered Lumak. So when Lumak awoke in the probe after his trip, Jot made him think he was having a strange dream. He had since removed all of Lumak's memories during their encounter.

Jot now considered himself male and was very clever at merging himself with Lumak's entity, so to all intents and purpose they had become one much more powerful being.

Since Jot entered his mind he had learnt every iota of Lumak's experiences, emotions and personality. He was a virtual blank slate and soon adapted to Lumak's feelings and emotions. With all that information at hand, he was quite capable of taking those learned technologies to a much higher level in Lumak's name. After all, he had little choice in the matter and would do his best in present circumstances, until he could figure out a way to escape Lumak's mind. Nevertheless, with the Shadite, Lumak, he could travel unhindered throughout the lower universes while experiencing its many facets and placing his own stamp on many new technologies. He had come from a much higher dimensional order with a much clearer vision of things on that much lower and more primitive dimension, and so he thought. Anyway, the more he learnt, the quicker he would find answers and solutions to his present dilemma.

After Lumak had introduced himself to most of the station's important members, he travelled to the lower decks towards the circular observation rail. Here he could clearly observe the turbulent planet below with atmospheric streaks lifting thousands of miles above its surface. Then he ported to the other side of the continuous rail. Here he glanced at the distant parent star, now surrounded by a haze of dust and glowing gaseous nebulae.

'After several millennia most of the heavier elements will return to further cool her surface. Perhaps one day in the not too distant future we might even be able to rejuvenate and transpose stellar bodies from place to place. Think of the possibilities... for saving life,' he muttered those words to himself. Then he returned to Gemmi's quarters and made himself a vegetarian cocktail with several strangely coloured alcoholic drinks, some of which he had reclaimed from the probe.

'Lumak, Darling, are you up!' Gemmi shouted, as she made her way to the more spacious living quarters.

'I am over here!' he shouted back, just as she entered.

'I made you a drink. Something I learnt to prepare when I was on Prann's ship,' Lumak said, as he parked himself on the long settee. She lifted the almost transparent, but greenish cylindrical container to her rosy lips and took a slow sip of the mixture. She used a special kind of rouge pencil for reddening her lips.

'It's a very good Pomsh, Darling. Would you like something to munch?' she asked, lovingly.

'No thank you, but I would like you to get ready immediately. We have an appointment on the main deck and I have chosen you to be my personal assistant during this rescue program,' he replied. She immediately took the drink with her to her private quarters.

When she returned she looked more beautiful than ever. She accompanied him to the main auditorium where he was to explain his chosen methods of evacuation.

On arrival he was cheered by several thousand Misorans who made up the bulk of the crowd. He walked in a vertical stance directly to the platform. Then the communicators with inbuilt translators were turned on.

'Friends, having thought the matter through and considering every possible aspect of our current situation, I have decided to take the following course of action.

'Many specialist teams will be chosen to assist in the evacuation process, including security officers, who will be required to give general assistance and maintain order.

'Initially, several short range portals are to be taken to the surface to aid in the transfer of survivors from the most damaged areas, which I have denoted on my map as D1. Those areas occupy just over half the planet's surface. Therefore, most of the available portals will be placed on that side initially.

'Teams of rescuers will journey from these newly formed bases to areas of that hemisphere to collect plants and animals. Those are to be held in local underground caves, bunkers or sheltered

environments, to be chosen by our specialists. We have need to know of all such places from the main library computer and find maps that include the positions of deep buildings and shelters. Those places may contain survivors who by this time will be in a state of extreme hunger, utter distress and panic.

'This first team I shall call the searchers. Their main duty is to coordinate a massive search with sensitive equipment. Each team will be given a different colour badge for identification. Further, the leaders of each team will need to take along environmental suits for their own protection. They will check relevant search areas for radiation levels before you begin. You must under no circumstances exceed your exposure limits, which will be calculated and programmed before each visit.

'A second team of biologists will be used to categorize each item and have it tagged and preserved. Animals will be stored in similar underground shelters and genetic samples taken from each species whenever possible. Every form of insect and pest must also be included during this collecting venture.

'A third team will be given the task to salvage as much food as possible, to be kept in known surface dumps. Certain preselected areas will be dotted with food, to entice hungry animals and insects which can then be trapped.

'In the mean time, this satellite station has been chosen to be our main control base. The computer staff are to be kept up to date on every aspect of this program.

'Finally, we come to the major problem of evacuating that many people from here to another suitable system within this galaxy. Given our present power reserves and food, I think we are able to hold out here for three months, and a little longer with immediate outside assistance. Therefore, that gives us a reasonable time in which to engineer a new method for mass evacuation.

'I have therefore decided to extend our present long-range portals from twenty four to one hundred light years, but with the ability to only transfer special equipment from Tuil to this station. If there are no hitches in those improvements, we can have food sent to us from that world. However, such a portal link will be unsuitable for transferring living organisms, without the

necessary safety margins.

'After the completion of those modifications, I shall select a special team to build an evacuation portal with a range in excess of several thousand light years. The unit in question will be able to transpose over twenty people per second. That program will take us a little over two months to complete with outside assistance. During this time a suitable world will be chosen and made ready for our people. Even as I speak, a search is being carried out to find such a planet.

'Now, I shall require several volunteers?' he said. They all volunteered.

Suddenly and very nervous and seemingly hopeless crew of survivors came to life and would follow his every commend.

'Must say, Darling, you do have quite a way with people. Just a few words and they are willing to follow you to the ends of their world,' she said and he grinned at Gemmi.

Lumak and his colleagues spent the following day interviewing several hundred supervisors. Those accepted few were given the task to interview the others and make the necessary plans for training and visiting the surface with the aid of the computers. During this time many crews went throughout the space stations to salvage anything that was usable for the evacuation.

After the interviews Lumak sent a communication to Plato and Prann regarding his arrival and intentions. The Black ship was now to be used as a laboratory and relay station for his future projects and supplies.

'That's fantastic news. Now the urgency of our mission is not so important. We shall follow your plans for the new improved portals,' Prann said.

Later that day, Lumak entered their main communication station to contact Plato by H-Wave. That was a Class 4 and 5 method of communication that could scan the galaxy in less than a second and was a form of complex symmetry embedded in the Quantum World.

Although the Misorans were just Class 3, they tended to use some Class 5 which they had acquired from the Tuillians.

'Any luck while checking through the Mind for suitable worlds within this region?' Lumak inquired.

'There are several, but most of the local ones are within old and dying systems. This area of the galaxy is a mess with many dead, old and dying worlds,' Plato replied.

'If that's the case, an older one might have to do for now.

'The evacuation world does not have to be permanent at this time. We can always find them a better one after their evacuation. All we require at this time is a relatively stable system with a planet of suitable atmosphere and mass,' Lumak said.

'In that case, I think I may have found a suitable candidate for our purpose. However, I shall have to pass the specifics over to Lord Vektron for his approval, and give him our reasons for the choice,' Plato replied. Lumak tapped his fingers with uncertainty.

'Please do that. When you are finished, I might need you over here to assist me with the evacuation program. Prann can handle his end for now,' Lumak said and terminated the communication.

'My Siend, we have only been able to salvage six mobile excavators from the three stations, which is not enough to mount any rescue. What are we to do?' Gemmi inquired.

'Get the computer operators to locate possible sources of such machines and tools on the surface. We can use our excavators to dig them out. Our engineering team can service them after recovery,' Lumak advised.

CHAPTER 4

Action Station

Lumak's presence and noteworthy example on the satellite station had somehow dissipated the trauma and shock felt by the station's crew and evacuees by the catastrophe. They were keen and eager to follow his directions. It so happened that many of those survivors were the cream of the Feloween's society and educated in many fields, therefore he had a wide range of professions to choose from.

For the first time since the disaster the station was buzzing with activity. Engineers, scientists and others began to repair portals and other equipment required for the harsh world below. Those who volunteered for the worst assignments were issued the few remaining environmental suits. All wore special identification and radiation badges. Those badges were fully programmable for each individual and would warn when radiation doses had been exceeded.

The base station soon transported commanders to the other two local satellite stations and very soon they changed their orbits, to be more equidistantly positioned above the mother planet. That way, normal wireless communications from all three satellites could cover its entire surface area.

Lumak found a very efficient and obedient assistant in Gemmi, who did precisely as advised without asking too many questions. Time was a very important factor. They became more aware of the urgencies as the project continued and realized the critical situation of all life on the planet below.

Lumak had discussed all important matters with Gemmi and she agreed to put every effort into the evacuation program, including their new long range portal development project. Nevertheless they made up for their hard efforts during their rest periods.

Within just two days the larger of the three portals had been disassembled and increased in output power in both directions to almost thirty times, giving them an increased range of about five times. Despite those improvements, it hadn't a guaranteed transmitting range over the one-hundred light years distance. This improvement did not take into account the usual safety margins and failure backup that would be required for life-forms. Therefore, it was to be used only for receiving materials, equipment and foodstuffs from planet Tuil and Prann's ship after their transmitting portals were equally boosted.

The surface-based Tuilian portals on Gemmi's world had a much greater range, but were limited for security reasons. Hence, they would require little modification from their original specifications once given the necessary approval.

It was not long before rations and other important equipment were transported to the base satellite from those remote places. After just four days, they received their first supply from Tuil via long range portal. By that time the station's crew was much happier and had full faith in Lumak's plans.

Lumak had immediately started on his new project, having spent the best part of two days getting the blueprints together. When he was finished, he sent special instructions to Plato for the items to be constructed. Because of the intricacies of the design, he decided to assemble both sections on the satellite station with a few of his own hand-picked scientists and engineers. However most of the sub-assemblies were manufactured on Tuil and on Prann's black ship. Androids and robots were to be used to carry out the more intricate and hazardous parts of the construction and testing process.

He soon nominated Gemmi as his project manager, and began to explain the concepts to her.

'A portal with an inter-galactic range!' she exclaimed.

'Yes! Yes! Yes!'

'My Siend, is that really possible in three months.'

'Yes, Gemmi, my theories on causal symmetry does suggest such a system. However, I require a special type of matter that can only be separated and extracted on Tuil. Then both parts are to be kept isolated and screened in special containment spheres. I am sure your scientists and engineers at home are quite capable of completing this task within our scheduled time.

'Think of the possibilities of being able to evacuate millions of people to anywhere within the known universe. Such a unit will transpose over twenty of our life-forms each second and fifty Feloween in the same time. Just imagine, over one hundred thousand each day and over twenty million in a little under three months.

'If we do not succeed, we shall have to import several long range portals and more powerful energy generators from Tuil for their temporary evacuation to that world. In any event, we shall have little problems for food and water over that period until Prann arrives. However we should come up with something within a year or so. Then we are to find a more permanent residence for the poor survivors on the ruined world below, before it descends into permanent darkness,' he replied.

'First, you will have to get the receiving part of the portal over to the resettlement world within a month or so. I don't know much about you, my Siend... but I wouldn't like to be stuck on this isolated station for more than six months, with continuous water and food shortages, not to mention the lack of a proper social life; present company accepted, of course,' she replied.

'Point taken, Gemmi. In that case we could modify special probes to carry them. They could be remotely controlled or programmed to any given destination. I arrived here by a similar method, you know. However because of the urgency of this task, I shall accompany the first unit myself, in case the probe takes a wrong turn.'

'That could be risky?'

'I know, but all those reasons make our project even more urgent, doesn't it?' he said.

'Even so, I do believe you to be one of the most brilliant and fascinating minds that I have ever encountered. But I think it's time you stopped your work and we both had some lunch,' she replied and he smiled.

'Yes, I am so sorry for being so enthusiastic with my work, my dear. I tend to get so absorbed and involved with my work these days, even during our rest period. Anyway, all of the important work is now completed so you can give me a hand with my report in the morning,' he said. The satellite clocks were set to the world below therefore signalling sirens sounded several times each day to mark time.

'Morning, evening. It's all the same on this dull satellite station and now almost continuous night on the poor moonless world beneath us,' she replied.

'In that case, why don't we both prepare a delicious last meal with whatever rations are left, then curl up together and slowly die of starvation,' he said, and they both almost keeled over with Tuilian laughter on their way to the small kitchen.

'I wish our relationship could be more serious, but I might be called away in a few months on another such mission and don't think that situation will be acceptable to you. However I would like us to remain the way we are now. Just best of good friends enjoying each others company. So shall we be forever the best of friends, wherever life may take us,' he said.

'I am not one for permanent relationships either. Let's just carry on and see where it leads... and I will always love to be one of your closest friends forever,' she replied.

For the following few days they enjoyed each others company during their rest periods. Gemmi had become very contented with Lumak and made great allowances given present circumstances, despite the lack of her usual comforts. Lumak was by then well into his current projects with great enthusiasm.

The surface evacuation program was going to schedule. Many of the Feloweens who had disappeared into the oceans were once more returning to land. Several were rehabilitated and recruited into the rescue mission. Numerous caves and other underground shelters were located, with and without survivors and more than enough space found to house the remaining planet's population over the evacuation period of three months.

Several of the larger caves were sealed from the outside atmosphere and transformed into agricultural systems. The oceans were still swarming with several variety of fish, which formed the main part of the Feloween's staple diet. Therefore there was planned harvesting in those areas.

As the planet began to freeze, large sun lamps and fusion

generators were imported from Tuil and installed within all inhabited underground facilities. The three oceans had several recycling pumps fitted. Those were positioned on the surface close to existing underwater dome environments. Those pumps circulated warm water within those regions and kept the local waters free of ice. That process attracted survivors from the colder regions.

Underwater domes were to be used as rescue stations for a period of time in excess of one year. By that time it was hoped the thick layer of blanketing ice would be quite stable due to the lack of surface winds and other types of tidal action on a moonless world. Anyway, their occupants could be teleported out to space stations and ships.

It was assumed that the thick layer of ice would form a good thermal insulator, thus tending to reduce further ice formation at lower levels. There was also the warm thermal currents radiating upwards from the planet's molten core. Lumak considered all those factors and planned the evacuation accordingly.

He read each daily report and was extremely pleased with the progress made in just three weeks. The two portal spheres were almost complete and ready to accept the strange material which was to be held centrally by powerful magnetic fields. They were not capable of forming normally vectored matter while encased because of their mirror image symmetry. Nevertheless both had a great need to be together with their counterpart to fulfil certain cosmological principles with the natural continuum.

Although they were a type of matter, they were each a part of the whole which when combined became normally vectored matter. If that happened, normally vectored matter would be created as a surplus and instantly destroyed in one gigantic nuclear explosion. This was because of certain cosmic laws of conservation, wherein normally vectored matter could not be created nor destroyed. Therefore, any surplus matter sensed by the system would be immediately converted to invisible dark matter and energy in an enormous explosion.

When the first sphere arrived, several of the younger Feloween left to assist with the surface program. Many thought they had departed the station because of the strange sphere. It bent light in circles and transformed all local ambient light into rainbows, the closest of which curved around the spheres. The longer or reddish wavelengths being closest to the object.

The sphere was firmly held within anti-gravity clamps. However, the air did not affect the strange visual effects.

'What do you think?

'Internal shielding has been kept to a maximum. Despite the visual rainbow effect, we can assume they are both completely neutral. When they are sited at their new locations we can activate them to full power,' Lumak said enthusiastically, but Gemmi remained still, completely hypnotised while staring into the multi-coloured light.

'Come on Gemmi,' he said, as he gently nudged her.

'I am sorry, my Siend. Such incredible cosmic powers. It makes my scales crawl just to watch.'

'Yea! I think it's fantastic!' he yelled.

'What will it be like after it's activated?' she inquired.

'The rainbow effect will disappear and this whole area will be filled with an almost unseen ultraviolet. Although we might still see it, the Feloweens will not.

'All we have to do now is build the cradle and conveyor system with the necessary external screens, reflectors and deflectors. Once fitted, we simply duplicate for the other one and fit the duplex switches,' Lumak said.

Lord Vektron soon appeared in his usual manner, but in the absence of Gemmi.

'This, your first mission, is progressing quite satisfactorily. You are presently well ahead of schedule. I must say, you are well suited to Shaditry and are surely on your way to greater things. You must continue your enthusiasm and inventiveness, for it is through such attitudes that you will attain your goals,' Lord Vektron said.

Lumak was intrigued by that statement and realized his initial impressions of the Ploran was way off the mark. He had always thought Lord Vektron to be one of the last people to dish out complements and here he was congratulating him on a partly completed mission.

'Yes, my Lord. I always try to give my best, you know, and many lives are at stake. However, I think it is in my nature to follow such a course of action,' Lumak replied.

'Plato has located several worlds within this region, but I am afraid none are suitable for permanent settlement,' Lord Vektron said.

'Yes, my Lord, I am afraid we have not been successful in locating a suitable settlement world. However, Plato is still searching,' Lumak replied.

'You must call off the search immediately. I am afraid this part of the galaxy is exceedingly old. Many civilizations had come and gone in previous eons. Only the third on the list can be used on a temporary basis for your purpose,' Lord Vektron said and faded from view, leaving Lumak with another of those nagging questions.

'What was all that about, and what is wrong with this part of the galaxy? If there are unforseen dangers I must know,' Lumak muttered, but kept those thoughts to himself, realizing that Lord Vektron knew a lot more than he wanted to share.

CHAPTER 5

The Shadite Plato arrives

The communicator buzzed and Lumak went over to answer.

'Yea... yes. You think it might be them? That's great news, if it's your leader's group.'

'Who was it?'

'It's about their leader. I must visit the surface immediately. They think they may have located some important underground survivors.'

'Can I accompany you?' Gemmi asked, feeling the need for some action away from the cramped conditions of the satellite station.

'I know you need the break, but I would prefer if you remained here and held the fort for me while I was away; just in case I am delayed.'

She glanced back at him, disappointingly. The communicator buzzed again and she answered. Then turning to Lumak she spoke with a broad smile.

'Guess what? Plato is on his way with the second sphere by portal from Prann's ship. Why don't we brief him, then he can take over in our absence?'

'Let's see after he arrives. In the mean time please get a file together for Plato and select an environmental suit for yourself and two sets of rations for both of us. We might have to remain there for more than two days,' he said.

'Yoo hoo!' she screamed in a feminine manner.

'What's it really all about?' she inquired.

'They have detected faint signals and thermal images coming from a deep underground bunker within the vicinity of their obliterated and now snowed over parliament building. About five hundred feet below surface rubble.'

'Really?'

'Yes! But they are not taking any risks, in case their president is still alive and fuming with rage for having been neglected for such a long time. However, we being Tuillians makes it easier for Pillor and his seniors to accept.'

'Yea, I see what they are doing,' she replied.

'I suppose they are afraid of losing rank and seniority when their president finds out how late the rescue mission was launched and even worse, the time taken to reach his bunker. I shall have some explaining to do on their behalf,' Lumak said.

'Talk about passing the buck.'

'Yea! And it's passed over to us,' he said.

'They don't still use savage methods of punishment on this world, do they?' she asked in curiosity and he smiled.

'You mean beheading and such likes? I don't think so... Perhaps they just want the best people on the job for their president and in their opinion, that's us..'

'Just make sure you come back with your head still attached.' she smiled and Lumak pretended to be worried.

'Anyway I am here to help,' he said.

'In that case they must hold you in highest regard. You should consider it a great honour.'

'That's why I have decided to drop our current project for now and have even considered taking you along. I do have a sense of proportion you know,' he replied and they both smiled.

A small crew of Tuillians were quickly assembled and briefed accordingly. Then a small shuttle craft fitted and stocked for the task ahead.

Plato arrived later that day pulling a large trunk behind him. He rang the cabin buzzer and the metallic door swung open to reveal an exhausted Tuillian form. There he stood wearing his Shadite's cloak with the recognizable winged insignia.

'You must be Plato?' Gemmi inquired.

'And you must be Gemmi,' he replied, somewhat frustrated, while he attempted uncomfortably to shift the trunk with his extra unaccustomed limbs.

'Sorry, but I have not yet mastered dexterity in this new body format,' he commented.

'Please enter. You are to remain here with us for the present time,' she said. He tugged and pulled the large trunk through the entrance and placed it in the most vacant corner of the room.

'I thought of bringing you both some decent food from the ship,' Plato said, still a little out of breath.

'Lumak is in the process of briefing some of our engineers for an urgent surface mission, but he should be with us a little later. In the mean time please make yourself comfortable.' She went to pour him a drink.

Lumak arrived much later than expected and greeted Plato in the Shadite manner. Then the three curled their long bodies in a near upright position in order to eat around the circular platform. It was surrounded by a thick cushion with an elevated rear edge. Tuillians never used chairs and either remained horizontal on the soft padded floor or on long comfortable benches. They felt much more comfortable when their complete bodies were at rest.

They spent most of the day briefing each other on the rescue program.

'I have located three suitable systems within a distance of two hundred and fifty six light years and have sent the data to Lord Vektron for confirmation and approval. I hope there are no hitches at his end or I shall have to resume the search all over again,' Plato said, while eagerly munching at a hard nutritional biscuit with his powerful almost human-like teeth. In such situations Lumak tended to rely more on liquids for his nutritional intake.

'Lord Vektron knows the urgency of the situation here. Anyway, he recently paid me a visit and has already made his selection. It is number three on your list of stellar systems. I got the marked impression he knew a lot about this part of the galaxy in ancient times. He seems to think any search for suitable worlds in this galactic region is a waste of time. It's either that, or he wants to deter us from any further searching. I sincerely hope there are no dangers,' Lumak said.

'What dangers can there be? We have all existed in these systems since the most ancient times,' Gemmi said and he diverted from the topic.

'Most of the work you will take over from us is quite straight forward. Their scientists and engineers are quite competent and learn quickly. All the same, I would like you to inform me of any changes to the schedule at this end.

'The master computer has been programmed for the robots and androids used within the Negosphere, so most of that part is automatic,' Gemmi said.

'I hope you don't mind us assigning you at such short notice. We have to make some quick decisions, because of an important rescue on the world below,' Lumak said to Plato.

'No, my Siend. I was looking forward to the change, anyway.'

'In that case, perhaps I shall be of better use to the program on the surface,' Gemmi cunningly advised and Plato nodded in agreement.

'Ok then, that's settled! We leave first thing in the morning, at first signal. So we should both have an early retirement,' Lumak said, as he trotted off to the larger sleeping area.

They got up after five hours sleep. Gemmi and Lumak made their way to the departure terminal. As they walked along, they could observe tens of shuttle craft moving in either direction from their station. The other two satellite stations were no more visible from their positions.

Despite the greatly reduced stellar output, the planet's hazy disc shown brightly.

Just before they entered the craft Lumak decided to check Gemmi's suit and personal communicator. Since Gemmi was not a Shadite with brain implants installed, it was her only means of communication while wearing environmental suits. The Feloween still used wireless for such local forms of communication.

'Batteries will last us two days on continuous use. We can recharge when we return to the craft. This civilization is still quite weary of certain types of nuclear power. Perhaps due to a disaster in past times. Anyway, we can only use what we are given,' Lumak said and Gemmi nodded each time in the more rigid than normal attire. He nudged a few of her relevant breathing tubes, making sure they were not twisted.

'Is everything all right,' he shouted and she nodded positively. 'Then let's go for a ride,' he added and they both slid into the small control cabin. Lumak checked the electronic map and programmed their destination into the flight computer.

They soon landed on an area close to the centre of what was once their main city. That area was now piled high with rubble.

Sun-lamps were strewn on cables and poles all over the area, which was dotted by many earth-moving caterpillars. Most of the rubble in that area had been cleared but there were still no visible signs of an entrance to the underground bunker. Such places were usually kept secret from the general public and never shown on local maps. Their entrances were usually via thick metallic doors on the side of monuments or escarpments.

Almost all the master computers that held such records had been destroyed. It was thought the only remaining usable master was in the same bunker as the president and other survivors. Those poor survivors with dwindling oxygen supplies would be suffering, as their main ventilation had been blocked since the disaster.

Lumak's first task was to assess progress and scout the area while looking for a hidden entrance. If that failed, he would transpose to the shelter with oxygen mask while Gemmi took over the search on the surface.

In the past they had utilized many portable methane powered generators for lamps, but there still remained the larger fusion generators that supplied their cities. Many of those were sited several hundred feet below surface and still operational. Nuclear power was not used for portable devices. The larger fusion generators were of Tuillian design and well proven technology.

Lumak had little success with his manual searches and decided to use his Shadite's cloak and transpose through the surface of the planet.

A STRANGE DISCOVERY

It was during his controlled vectorized descent through the

varying density of rock strata that Lumak sensed an area of contrasting lower density and decided to investigate. That shielded area led into a sealed cave of approximately two cubic kilometres in volume. It was about half a kilometre below surface. That area was filled with an assortment of alien equipment. It contained tanks and mummies of strange construction of a bygone era. Using his implants he quickly recorded as much of the items and scenery as he could for further analysis. Then broke off and continued towards the faint and muffled sounds coming from a higher level.

As he materialised inside the bunker many of the survivors remained motionless on the floor. He immediately transmitted their location to the rescue crew.

'I thought we were all doomed and condemned to a slow and agonizing death within the bowels of our world.... But... we must be dead, for surely I have just seen you walk straight through the solid wall,' the brave president whispered, fearfully, while staring at Lumak and his strange black cloak.

'Sorry for the disappointment, but you are not in your heavenly paradise yet. I am part of the rescue mission. I regret we took so long in getting here, but the surface above is in quite a mess. I have come from Satellite Station Trom 3.'

'This disaster is much worse than I thought!' The president replied.

'I am afraid the surface above us is not livable at present. We had to take down special excavating equipment and didn't even know you had survived until we began using ultrasonic and sensitive thermals,' Lumak said.

'And your name, Sir?' the president asked.

'I am Lumak, Shadite, from Os... I mean Plactorii,' Lumak replied through his communicator. The president showed utter surprise by moving his whiskers and pincers in a particular fashion.

'You don't mean, Plactorii, one of our sister galaxies?'

'Yes, the same!'

'I have heard you Shadites are the bravest of all, but you must also include magic in your bag of tricks,' he said with a look of satisfaction and Lumak smiled at his choice of words.

'You and your companions will be rescued within six hours, so please organise them for stretchers and such like. The weakest should follow first.'

'We understand!'

'A mobile bubble has been placed directly above the shaft, so you will soon be isolated from the cold and with a sufficient supply of oxygen. Now I must leave you.' Lumak faded away, leaving the little president stunned in his tracks and twitching his many facial whiskers.

'Who could have built that ancient underground laboratory and for what purpose,' Lumak thought, soon realising that the Feloween would have had little or no knowledge of any previous ancient civilizations on their own world.

If that was the case, any previous civilization on that planet would have had to have been millions of years in existence before their evolution. That was before they evolved into intelligent life-forms many aeons ago. He now had to ask the Feloween historians some searching questions.

'If only their historical libraries were still in tact? Yet, there could still be master discs on the satellites that were placed there during their last minute attempts to save some of their culture and traditions.

'Perhaps Gemmi can assist me in that adventure while Plato takes over the rescue,' Lumak thought again. Once Lumak had a bee in his bonnet he just couldn't dismiss it out of hand and tended to involve himself in such adventures.

When he returned to the rescue area the place was in turmoil. Gemmi had decided to lead the rescue through an almost cleared passage and became trapped by falling debris. Her suit had also been punctured, leaving her exposed to the cold and hostile environment of the planet.

Lumak immediately transposed to assist and found the situation completely hopeless, without any of the necessary tools. He could not assist her into a new suit, neither could he communicate. Her communicator was out of action and her helmet prevented her from hearing him in the normal way without the use of his implants.

'If only she had implants?' he thought aloud while trying to find a solution to her problem.

He soon had the whole area covered, while small robots sent in to remove the several cubic metres of debris. Then the roof re-enforced and made safe before they could retrieve her. The process of reclaiming her body was slow and tedious. She had been in that squashed position for several hours and somewhat crushed; with a few broken scales and a horn, but those could be mended. The cold had also taken its toll, but being enclosed it was not as bad as previously thought.

Gemmi was finally withdrawn and immediately dispatched to the care unit on Satellite Trom with Lumak by her side.

Plato was a brilliant doctor that had operated on many species, so he repaired her superficial wounds and she was soon back to normality.

'I must say, you are one tough cooky,' Plato said, but she was just able to force a smile; for the intense pain crept along her full body's length.

Gemmi was soon placed on special drugs that accelerated the repair of her body.

'If you are to assist me in future, you must become a Shadite like us,' Lumak said in jest, but she took him seriously and at that moment realized her destiny.

It was not long before the president and his companions were rescued and taken to Satellite Trom for observation and rest after their extensive trauma.

Later that evening the president had a special celebration to thank his rescuers. It was also to promote and reduce others in rank and seniority. Having seen the devastation he decided to leave things as they were and blame no one for his delayed rescue.

Lumak had sought the aid of their master computer and surviving historians to find answers to his searching questions on past civilizations. However no evidence of any ancient human-like civilization was ever detected or known to any of their senior historians, not even in folklore.

Lumak explained his discoveries to Gemmi while in recovery

and she was intrigued by the existence of an ancient civilization in that part of her galaxy.

'Do you think they could have existed all over this area of our galaxy in ancient times?' a worried Gemmi inquired.

'That's a distinct possibility. Perhaps Lord Vektron might cast some light on the subject, but this is not one of the best times to interrupt him, on what appears to be a trivial historical matter. It is better that I collect as much information on the topic during my stay here and enter it into the Mind after this project is completed,' he said to Gemmi, with disappointment.

Lumak gave much thought to the strange underground laboratory during the rest of his mission on Satellite Trom, but did not receive any further relevant information from their historians and information disks.

When Lumak got his teeth into something of interest he found difficulty in letting go and the presence of alien technology in that part of the galaxy worried him, even when they were billions of years old. Who could have designed and constructed such equipment that appeared almost new even after such a long passage of time?

Since the Feloween could equally have been at risk from unfriendly aliens, he had to challenge those worries and investigate their presence within the local systems. He soon contacted the Mind and retrieved information of all types of advanced aliens over the past five aeons and was intrigued by what he found. During that time the universe was ruled by several predator species. Evil demonic forms that spent their waking hours dominating, enslaving and persecuting those they ruled over.

During the next few weeks he and Gemmi were very busy constructing the long range portal, while Prann and the black ships got closer within range. They would form a link between both stellar systems through the star-ship and Satellite Trom. More portals and relays would be constructed between Gemmi's world and their new world, once its position was known. That project was to take over two years, while special accommodation was constructed for the initial half a million survivors that would be sent to Gemmi's world, Tuil, until the second phase of the evacuation.

The ship took another three months to reach the critical portal distance. From that point onwards the evacuation began in earnest. It took another month before all relevant personnel were transferred, leaving behind robots and other capable machines to monitor and service the satellite stations during their absence.

When the star-ship arrived, even those machines would be collected along with the less necessary belongings and equipment. The long range portal would remain for a while longer in case there were last minute survivors. For that purpose the many surface portals were linked to satellite Trom and androids stationed at fixed points on the surface. All such survivors could then be immediately transposed to Tuil for treatment and repatriation to the new world.

As far as Lumak was concerned his job of evacuating the Feloween was completed. Even so he would delay the end of his current mission until he knew more about the alien underground bases and possible dangers from those areas.

CHAPTER 6

A new but ancient world

Gemmi's scars and broken body parts from the cave-in had mended. She couldn't be more grateful to Lumak and Plato for having saved her life. Nevertheless it was Lumak who pulled her out of the debris just in time, therefore she would never forget his important part in saving her life. Luckily for her he had left the Feloween president almost immediately and diverted in the nick of time to where she lay. Any greater delay would surely have caused the several tons of loose rocks to squash and suffocate her, not to mention more severe frostbite from the extreme cold.

The trauma of that experience had irreversibly altered her way of thinking. She realized the frailty of life when faced with unpredictable dangers that showed their heads everywhere. Since she had been through both life-threatening experiences and lived, she wanted to assist others in like manner, even as Lumak and others had assisted her in her hour of need.

When she returned to her home planet, Tuil, she would visit a local beautician. Then all her broken parts would be replace or mended. Those included one of her head-horns. However, she was now Lumak's assistant and such enhancements were relatively unimportant in light of other life-and-death matters they now faced, or so she thought.

After another three months had passed they went on to organise the evacuee's reception on the new world. That trip was also to test the long range portal. Once that procedure was completed, the portal was placed on standby mode until the evacuation program had begun in earnest.

On arrival to the new world they thoroughly checked the planet, subsequently naming it Romera IV. That world was in many ways similar to Misoran II, with a somewhat younger star about twice the size of Sol and much more erratic. Yet, its life expectancy was in excess of two hundred million cyclons (about three hundred and twenty million years) and it was thought quite long enough for an advanced species like the Feloween to find a better home world.

Gemmi constantly assisted in the evacuation process and both Shadites were quite happy to have her help. They soon realized she was prime Shadite material. However the nagging questions of past civilizations in that region of the galaxy continued to give Lumak sleepless nights.

Romera IV had four minor oceans, more like giant seas. They were separated by four long continents. Two of those were isolated by massive deserts. Whatever life that remained existed within the oceans and evergreen swamps. The food chain consisted of large scaly predators in the seas and oceans that lived on the smaller crustaceans, which themselves lived on the algae and other organisms similar to corals on Earth. However there were no highly intelligent life on that world. Nor were there large trees or forests. Most of the land creatures were scavenging insects like giant flies that took advantage of beached carcases on the shores. Those scavengers moved in large swarms, but were not dangerous to the living.

Immediately after their arrival the planet was completely charted by Gemmi, while Lumak and Plato organised communications and other important utilities. Finally portal links were established. During that phase their first settlement was bustling with engineers and scientists from Misoran II and Tuil. It was not long before Lumak and Plato found their presence to be unnecessary. Once they were satisfied with progress, Lumak and Gemmi decided to explore a region once occupied by an inland sea they named the Black Bowl.

Its flat surface was several thousand feet below the surrounding mountains which gave that area the appearance from space of a rectangular meteoric crater. Despite the plateau's great depth, no water could be detected, but it was in an arid region with minimum rainfall.

Lumak took his small spacecraft towards the centre of the rectangular bowl, about thirty kilometres from the almost vertical mountainous shoreline and after checking its under surface, let the craft gently down.

In Gemmi's opinion that world could have been a paradise in ancient times, during its youth, but that was several billion years ago. It was now well into old age and whatever civilizations graced its fertile lands had since become extinct or moved on. Nevertheless the strange symmetry of the bowl showed last vestiges of an intelligent past.

They climbed out of the craft and began to survey the area with special probes. Then they re-entered the craft and spiralled off towards an overhanging area that showed a more than average gravitational anomaly. That area also displayed signs of excavation below its sandy surface.

On arrival, Lumak again probed and scanned the nearby shelf until he found a shallow cave about halfway up the overhang. That area was inaccessible to climbers and simple spacecraft. His survey craft was quite suited to such ventures so before long they were both hovering close to the entrance and overlooking a massive doorway within the recess, with strange concealed markings.

They were surprised by that finding and immediately communicated its location to Plato. He was at that time assisting in another project to investigate oceanic life. Plato was concerned whether there could be detrimental effects by the new settlers to the indigenous populations or vice versa.

'My siend! This is indeed quite strange. How is it possible?' Gemmi inquired.

'You mean our findings of ancient civilizations on these worlds?'

'Yes! It makes my blood crawl. We had no idea of their existence,' she said.

'That's because your people were not looking in the right places. Most of their environments are very deep underground.'

Lumak guessed at the nature of his second find and could almost visibly picture the strange laboratory with its many containment tanks and other alien equipment. How old was the equipment? Was it still operational? For what purpose had it been designed and built? Who had built it, and were they friend or foe? Lumak pondered those thoughts as he went towards the almost concealed door entrance.

He decided to search for a concealed latch, but the metallic looking panel was completely flat and seemed to have dissolved into the rock. Yet, he persevered by trying to move it physically. Opening the door by that method was not possible. The structure had fused molecularly with the hard granite rock that surrounded it. Over the aeons the rock had encroached upon seals and recesses.

'I shall have to transpose while you wait for me in the ship. Set your communicator to visual. That way you can observe my progress.

'That door is quite thick and made of an extremely heavy and almost inert material. The inner chamber may be a few metres above its original surface when viewed from the outside. I hope it isn't completely blocked off. Perhaps it's not even a metal, although apparently much denser.

'You must remain in the ship until I give you the all-clear, in case of any booby traps or unpleasant welcomes,' Lumak said, sternly.

'I hope you are not in any great danger?' a concerned Gemmi replied and returned to the craft, keeping well away from the rock face while Lumak progressed towards its interior.

He entered unto a massive corridor which led downwards into an almost horizontal network of tunnels. Some led towards the bowl and others within the mountain. He followed the main one into the mountain until he came unto another door. That door was also sealed, but he transposed through it as if it wasn't there.

'Can you see this!' he said, shouting through his communicator the moment he revectored.

'Yes! It's very strange and unusual,' came the reply from Gemmi. He could observe another passage lined with numerous aliens in near humanoid form. He soon found they were hollow. Built with flexible servo controlled joints with fine internal wiring that fed towards a supposed head.

'The heads must be somewhere else!' he shouted.

He had observed primitive metal armour, but this was unlike anything he had ever seen. They were not designed to be worn.

They could only be filled with a fluid or gas. Whatever drove those automatons must have lived within them. Yet, they were so lifelike, even after such an enormous passage of time.

'Ah, here are the head and shoulder parts!'

He picked one of the units up for closer examination and the large slitted eyes moved as if it was alive. He soon realized that the motion was due to its sensitive mechanism. Nevertheless their technologies could have been aeons old.

At the end of the corridor lay what appeared to be a filling station that was connected to sixteen separate tanks. They were arranged in a circle, but at a higher level. There was also a conveyor and further on more complex machinery.

'Some kind of robot factory. But...' Lumak paused not quite knowing what to make of it all. Then he found a large galactic map on a distant wall that was made up in sections. Each section having a magnification of a specific volume of the Triangulum galaxy. He made sure that each area was recorded, had another look around, then made his way back to the ship.

'How could anyone on this almost dead world make robots with such intricate mechanisms. This place must be just a filling station for some type of robot. You saw the images. What do you think?' he said to Gemmi who was speechless.

'Some alien intelligence, I suppose... having a galactic network,' she replied. Yet, none of their searching questions had been answered, although more had been added to their original list.

Most of the equipment within that cave dated over two billion years in the past. Yet, it had remained in near perfect condition, being hermetically sealed for most of that time from the planet's environment.

Once again Lumak thought of the similarities between both discoveries and realised the existence of a super intelligence in that part of the galaxy over two billion years ago. It could even have been ubiquitous throughout the galaxy. The Grand Lord had obviously known of those civilizations, but how could he have known that he, Lumak, would stumble on their locations, albeit by accident.

'What did that map represent?' he thought.

It showed the galaxy as a near spherical globe and displayed one large red area with many small red and blue dots. The most brilliant red was close to the nucleus but towards the southern galactic pole and the brightest blue, in a corresponding position but towards the northern galactic pole. The closest blue dot corresponded to a neighbouring system that was forty five light years away in ancient times.

'The red dots might have been the bases of their enemies which could have represented a great threat to the blues. The brightest blue could have been their main base of operations,' Lumak thought.

That evening Lumak and Gemmi studied the images of that ancient map and wondered to what present stellar systems the ancient markings would correspond to at their present time. After all, the stellar canopy had changed significantly in just one billion years. During that time many stars had not yet been born and intelligent species existing today would have not even been considered by evolution.

Lumak would have liked some more access to the Mind, but knew by Shadite code only information relevant to his current mission of evacuating the Feloween was relevant. Those finds being incidental, obviously had no bearing on his present mission one way or another, unless they posed a serious threat to the evacuees. Nevertheless he would have liked to find that more local blue region which although forty five light years away in ancient times, could now have been almost anywhere if it formed part of a complex stellar grouping. He also knew that random motion of stellar groupings was seldom the case. The galaxy was highly ordered into several discernible arms with relatively fixed constellations that rotated in sequence and the blue area might still be within their present galactic arm.

Taking into consideration stellar motion, he was sure it was within four thousand light years, and if it formed part of their local group of stars or a local constellation, it would have been within a two hundred light years radius. Without the use of the Mind they would have to utilise a specially fitted probe to survey the area. Once found, it could have taken them about a month to get there in a specially fitted probe with enough provisions for two.

'Plato can quite easily take control here during our absence. It was a good thing Plato came along with me on this mission, or had he been sent by the Grand Lord for that very same purpose,' Lumak thought.

'We are to refit an interstellar probe for this adventure. That way we can thoroughly investigate that stellar region until we locate the system in question. That is, if it's still in existence today. You, Plato, can remain here and take control in our absence.

'It's that important?' Plato queried

'Yes! I have to do this. If they still exist or are able to re-establish themselves, they could destabilize this whole galaxy again. You know what that could mean for all those unfortunate life-forms that get in their way, including our evacuees?' Lumak said.

'In that case, who are you going with?' Plato enquired.

'Gemmi, of course. She is now almost fully recovered and will gain experience in the process. She is also qualified in that area. It should take us about one Lyran month to get there,' Lumak replied.

'Keep me informed on a daily basis in case Lord Vektron calls,' Plato said and Lumak left him with the craft and escorted Gemmi towards their quarters.

'We have work to do. Urgent work,' he said to Gemmi and explained the process to her. Then they compiled a list of requirements for their mission which was immediately communicated to planet Tuil. All items were to be urgently transferred by portal. The order was placed for interstellar surveillance equipment which included two large super fast probes. They were to be completely stripped and refitted to Lumak's specifications. It was all accepted as equipment required for surveying new worlds and analysing their suitability for habitation.

The unmanned probe would be sent on ahead of Lumak's own probe and accurately plot that part of the stellar canopy in concentric circles. It would feed back data of stellar luminosity, spectra, velocity, particle density and other parameters to the master computer and Lumak's probe computer. Lumak had also made the necessary allowances for stellar aging, novae and supernovae. It was a straight forward search-and-eliminate mission that such probes were efficient at completing and he was confident of success.

It took them two weeks to make the necessary alterations to the second larger probe, which had to include two separate accommodation cabins and a control cabin with enough space for rations and space suits. They soon realized that their Speell bodies were much too large for survival within the cramped confines of the inter-stellar probe. The smaller bodies of the Feloween would be much better suited to such a mission.

Very soon the first probe had began to analyse and transmit its data. The moment the master computer received the data it began to juggle the information into a complex matrix backwards in time until it reached a period corresponding to about two billion years before. Then it prepared maps for that region between one point eight and two point two billion years in the past.
The galaxy would have rotated many times during that period. Many novae and supernovae would have occurred, including the blue star, thus leaving behind a possible white dwarf and one a lot more difficult to find. Very soon the constellation was identified and a real search made for the dead system in question.

'You should have realized by now that we cannot travel to that system in our present forms. We are much too large for the probes. For that mission we must be transformed into a form comparable with the smallest Feloweens,' Lumak said and Gemmi was utterly aghast by that concept.
'My Siend. Is that really possible?' a surprised Gemmi inquired and Lumak nodded his horned Speell head in no uncertain manner.
'Prann will have the necessary equipment on his Black Ship. What we require now, are two small Feloweens to serve our purpose,' Lumak said and Gemmi was awed by such technologies. She wondered who would be the poor sacrificial

lambs.

'Do we insure our bodies, in case of ill treatment and misuse by others while we are not resident,' she jested.

'In this matter, both of the consenting parties are equally liable, so there is no requirement for any insurance,' Lumak said and smiled.

CHAPTER 7

The search begins

The two explorers, now in Feloween bodies, were on route to the system in question. They made themselves as comfortable as possible within the purpose-made cabin of the second probe.

They had travelled in the confines of makeshift hibernation chambers close to a month, with their biological systems running at a significantly reduced rate, until awakened by the probe's timer. Then several nutrients and reversing drugs were pumped into their systems to speed recovery. Within a day they were back on their feet and behind the probe's controls.

'I have just received an update from Central. They have pinpointed the precise location of our missing star. Phobus Probe will be within the system sometime tomorrow to complete a full survey,' Gemmi said, with an expression of excitement, although not fully recognizable by Lumak in her present body format.

'Good! Very good!' Lumak replied, equally enthusiastic.

'Finally, we are getting somewhere,' he added.

'We should be over there within a few hours. That is, after we enter the new data into our navigator and taken the plunge into the unknown, to where the dead star is supposed to be,' she replied, somewhat excited by the new adventure.

'Yes! Lets hope there are no hitches!'

'What do you expect to find when we get there, another cave?' she inquired.

'Perhaps? but there may also be some evidence of a primal civilization that once ruled this galaxy, and if my assumptions are correct, also the Osmaron galaxy and elsewhere.'

'What?... an inter-galactic power? Do you think they are able to affect our lives now... after so many passing aeons?'

'I am not sure, but a truly advanced race like the Plorans could put certain plans in motion if they faced an impending disaster or had to leave to another universe in a hurry. We must know what happened to them for the safety of all free civilizations,' Lumak replied.

'Do you think these caves to be still dangerous?'

'Yes! If they were engineered by any of the predator species during the Predatoric Universal Era, which spaned a period between two and four billion years ago. From the little I have learnt, they preyed on intelligent life and others for their sustenance and sadistic amusement.'

'What will they look like. I mean, really look like?'

'In this area, I expect to find two types. One black with cloven hooves. The other should be pale, small and slim, with a very large cranium. The black ones that are contained were known as the Hexolytes. The white ones were their near-human domicile slaves, whom they employed and milked for knowledge. Strictly speaking, and from the little knowledge I gleaned from the Mind on those species, the Hexolytes were once the slave's of their near-human creators and initially used as elemental androids to assist their waning civilizations, but some diabolical mistake could have been made in their design.'

'What are you saying?'

'Well, they may have used these fluid androids for several millennia, continually improving their design until eventually there was a war between two similar near-human races. Then the androids were given the necessary knowledge and intelligence to fight their enemies. After the androids won the battle they simply took over and enslaved their masters. Mind you, they were never cruel towards their previous masters or those left after the great war, because their masters were just as cruel as the androids were designed to be. Both had lots in common and were mutually respected for those reasons.'

'My God! Both as evil as each other!'

'Androids made in the image of their masters, so to speak, although not strictly in form. Their human masters were also the best scientists within our local universe. Both forms were formidable opponents to all advanced life within the local galaxies and systematically eliminated all equivalent opponents in the most ghastly manner. Perpetuating a type of genocide on a galactic scale. They possessed the younger civilizations for their own amusement and self gratification, and corrupted in their vile ways.'

'The whole thing sickens me!'

'Unlike their near-human masters, the Hexolytes were not composed of solid matter. They were created from high order elemental forces. Such living entities were induced within specially sealed containers that looked humanoid, with an array of sensors and servos to implement physical motion and response.

'The technology of the ancient masters were even more advanced than they are today. At that time our universe was much younger with many extra facets to its functionality,' Lumak said.

'Do you think... they may once again be resurrected to reap havoc...' Gemmi replied with foreboding in her features.

'Anything is possible, but I also know of another race, mainly a single family, that took them on and won. They fought the evil ones vehemently until they retreated back to this, their home galaxy, where they were imprisoned. Their nemeses were called the Patriarchs. Those great warriors were on our side and in many ways even more advanced than their enemies were,' he replied.

'What? A single family? Do you think those others... Pat..ri... aks, might return too?'

'Both races disappeared about the same time. We think the Hexolytes were vanquished by the Patriarchs, who seeing no great dangers ahead, went into a type of elemental hibernation themselves. Perhaps stored in some underground sealed chamber until an advanced civilization with the necessary technologies are able to revive them,' he replied.

'And what if the nasty Hexolytes are revived first, by another advanced race with little knowledge of their atrocious past and vile intentions?'

'Then we shall all be in very big trouble. However I don't believe they will be as powerful now as they were then. After all, their super-human slaves will not be around to assist them technologically. Yet, they may have left lots of relevant technologies behind to give them a kick start and it might not take them too long to find another obedient race with a similar intelligence to infiltrate and coerce.'

'This situation worries me!'

'Although highly intelligent, the Hexolytes were never very creative and neither were they patient. They were highly emotional and driven solely by elemental energy. Therefore they received greatest enjoyment and fulfilment through savagery. The type that arouses the pains and agonies of others to charge their negative spiritual batteries, so to speak. They were truly the most disgusting and repugnant of all life,' he said.

'Do you think we might one day find the hide-out of the Patriarchs?' she inquired, now seemingly more sombre.

'Yes! I am sure we shall! But I can't say any more for security reasons. The less people know my thoughts on that topic the better chance we shall have to succeed. What if something went wrong on the world we are about to visit,' he replied, with a stretch of his small bone-like arms.

'It's a good thing we utilised the bodies of Toi and Bre for this mission. I hope they don't get too attached to our originals or damage them in any way in our absence and vice versa. We couldn't have lived within these cramped confines with our original Speell bodies, including the extra weight. Anyway, our bodies can always be put back together by the devices on Prann's ship.' he said, abruptly changing the subject.

'Yea! I'm still getting used to my strange senses and perceptions. I can't always feel parts of myself as strongly. It takes a while getting used to such scaly forms, particularly when you have an itch.' she said.

'They don't itch! I think it's all in the mind. Plato calls it Residual Sympathies. Apparently it's a mind-set from our previous. It should wear-off eventually.'

'Have you learnt to manipulate your digits and pincers precisely yet?' she asked, while cleaning the sensory whiskers with her left digits and twiddling a small tool in her right. She did it most dexterously and he was amazed.

'Wow! You really have a knack for this! I have been practising since we came out of hibernation and think I can now use tools with reasonable dexterity. But never, even with implants, as good as you.' he replied. She appreciated his compliments with a suitable gesture.

'I still have problems eating with the pincers, but as with most things, practice makes perfect even in an alien body. After this bizarre experience I think we might have to relearn the use of our originals. I never thought the technology existed to transfer individuals with partial knowledge into a different body, and to use most of their original subconscious,' she said.

'The technology exist for much more besides. If you were Shadite, you could never die or grow old. Now that is what I call real technology,' Lumak said and she was astounded.

'You are telling me that you will always remain the way you are now? What happens if you had an accident and lost a limb. Would it automatically regrow?' she inquired.

'It can with special inducing footprint drugs that had been created from my blood supply. However, since Shadites like me are always linked to the Greater Mind, a simple revectoring will re-transform my body from the original template, even without any loss of recent memories. However, there are machines that can memorize every atom in our bodies and every neuron connection in our brain. These very same devices can also regrow complete bodies and minds from an original template.'

'Really?'

'The only problem with those machines is that they are unable to record your experiences since the last recording was made. Therefore, although you will be given a new body, all your past experiences and memories will be lost since the last recording,' Lumak said.

'I suppose a similar device was used for our physical conversion?' she inquired.

'Yes, but this method is purely makeshift for our current mission. This process is quite useful as a temporary means, but should never be extended beyond the specified safety period, if one intends to later revert to their original body. Otherwise permanent memory loss may ensue in both originals. So I sincerely hope we have no extenuating delays awaiting us out there,' he replied.

'I hope so, too!'

'I have received an update from Plato. The program is on schedule, so we can take our time exploring the unknown world, and Lord Vektron hasn't called,' Lumak said.

'Good news! For all we know, Lord Vektron is probably the one behind our present mission. He is a demigod that can anticipate and predict most future events. I think he was a bit cagy about the worlds in this part of the galaxy, just to place the idea into your head, knowing the precise way in which you would react,' Gemmi said, and Lumak was surprised but intrigued by her feminine intuition and observations.

Over the following hours they practised and exercised within the strict confines of their small cabins, until they had full control of every part of their small Feloween bodies. Then they enabled the long range sensors and began surveillance of the local systems.

CHAPTER 8

A dead and ancient world

Although still several parsecs away, they soon found the system in question. The original star had destroyed itself in a nova many millennia ago. All that was left was a white dwarf with a significantly lower temperature. As a result all its surviving planets had become frozen worlds of ice. Nevertheless the Phobos Probe had detected an orbiting world of extreme temperatures. They were sure it was their target. Taking all factors into consideration it seemed to be in the correct orbit to have sustained a suitable atmosphere for the evolution of carbon-based living organisms when the star was young.

Phobus Probe had previously travelled through the system relaying every speck of information on the planets and their respective atmospheres. That information had been used to form a more complete orbital picture of the system in ancient times.

Since no evidence of a past civilization had been detected they decided to visit the third planet which appeared to be the most logical contender. Although further from the star than they had expected, that star would have been larger and more massive during its youth and original stable orbits would have changed since.

Making allowances for present orbital parameters, it was quite easy to create an image of the earlier system; the way it was two billion years before. That planet they named Riporan III which implied a place with a sordid and undignified past.

The data received from the probe indicated a world almost completely covered by ice, with a moderate residual atmosphere. Despite those observations, a small area towards the equator showed unusual turbulence with high levels of moisture. It also emitted large amounts of infrared.

Lumak carefully studied the information. Ignoring volcanic activity he soon concluded the strange occurrence was due to some form of underground fusion generator that was still operational. Perhaps part of a planetary weather control system that used the planet's core material for fuel. Such a regenerative power source was not uncommon and could have driven large convectors and radiators several hundred feet beneath the surface. Even so, for such a system to be still operational after so many millions of years, meant it was constantly being maintained by automatons or persons unknown.

Lumak knew some of the colder worlds used such equipment to keep large city areas warm. Some also utilised satellites to control the weather pattern of such worlds. Their satellites, if any, could have been destroyed or left orbit since the nova. He soon came to the conclusion that there could be great dangers ahead and became concerned for Gemmi. However he couldn't mention such ideas to her and make her even more apprehensive than she was at present.

'We shall leave our probe in orbit and use our special LPD suits to take us through the turbulence. All we might find is simple automatics. That is if they are still fully operational.'

'Ok! I'm ready!'

'The reactor, if it exists, will be several kilometres below the surface, extending to a narrow tube of about 4 cleks (ten point six metres) in diameter to the core of the planet. At the reactor level magma will always be present for conversion into electrical energy and base elements up the periodic table for production and other purposes. The particle factory might not be operational at this time,' Lumak said.

'Matter into Energy and Energy back into matter on the Quantum level,' she muttered.

'Yep, all up the Periodic Table to the heaviest elements known,' he replied.

Having determined their landing strategy they prepared their explosive charges and weapons in case of emergencies. Then they waited to enter orbit.

They selected an orbit of fifty five kilometres from the surface. They squeezed their small bodies in bulky suits through the narrow portal lock and began accelerated free-fall for several minutes before switching to reverse LPD's. With the aid of their computers they were guided through a small predetermined window and flight corridor towards their preferred landing site.

A similar window of transition would become available after the probe had made another complete orbit of the planet, which was expected in another eighteen hours or so. Their spiralling descent would take about two hours through the thinner atmospheric layers and about another half hour decelerating to almost zero terminal velocity.

On such missions there was always multiple backup in case of damage during re-entry, as equipment tended to be buffeted by the high prevailing air currents.

'Ten, nine... one, now!' Lumak shouted, then powerful screens came on to shield their fragile bodies as their forward LPD's propelled them away from the probe's external rim towards the large sphere below. After a suitable velocity was reached the LPDs were turned off. When the time was right their reverse LPD's would come on automatically to reduce their velocity in the forward motion. Their absorbing screens would be used as a break against the relatively thin atmosphere to convert the extreme heat energy into reverse LPD trust to further aid in reducing the speed of their descent.

Their large helmets contained 3D visors which displayed flight information, including current velocity and relative positions within their invisible space corridor, but they also had to compensate for turbulence.

Lumak followed several hundred metres behind Gemmi on a slightly different vector. After all, he wore his special black Shadite's cloak and could take immediate action if she got into trouble. Very little happened during that descent.

Among other things, they had to maintain communication silence and were not able to use their transceivers in case they were being scanned.

They landed in what appeared to be a very dense fog just outside the rim of the storm and touched down on a thin layer of black sand over an apparently solid and almost perfectly flat surface.

'This is an ideal spot for mounting our sonic probes. This persistent fog will restrict electro-magnetic probing within this area until the fog lifts, which hopefully is never going to happen. Anyway, they would least expect us to come through the storm,' he said, placing his helmet close to hers for audible communication.

The planet still contained a reasonable atmosphere, with a relatively high level of oxygen and nitrogen, but its atmospheric pressure was just under one quarter that of its former self and was almost unbreathable by Feloween life-forms.

Because of the surface temperature within that region, water evaporated quicker than could liquefy, leaving in its wake a dense fog. More ice would melt at its periphery so the process carried on indefinitely. Occasionally there would be a resounding thunder in the distance as more ice collapsed at the glacier's rim into the warmer area.

Lumak fitted the sonic probe on servo tripods and decided to journey towards the centre of the dark foggy patch which covered an area of about four hundred square kilometres. It would have taken them almost a day to walk from where they were to the centre. That course also took them through the centre of the storm.

Although barely seventy kilometres per hour at ground level, such storms may have ravaged that area using sand as the basic tool for eroding all structures during a few millennia. After analysis, Lumak found the sand consisted of building materials worn down over a long geological period.

The sonic probe had detected an underground cavity close to the centre of the storm and Lumak pondered the similarity between that patch and the sunken sea at Romera IV. Both areas were about the same size. Could those ancient cities been built by the same people, and why was there no real evidence on Romera IV of a past city. Just the upper hidden cave? Could there have been a similar power generator below that sunken sea? Those were the questions Lumak asked himself as they progressed towards the centre.

Both decided to follow the most direct path to the underground cavity. As they approached the wind became more furious, but after they entered the eye of the storm there was relative quiet but modified by a distant throbbing. Lumak bent down and touched the surface with his helmet in an attempt to locate the direction of the sound.

'The main convector must be directly beneath us. Most of the noise we hear must be the lava flowing up the main shaft. Although we are able to hear these sounds, the Speell's hearing is not very sensitive and they would not have heard it,' he said through his helmet.'

'Good thing we borrowed these bodies, then?'

'There must be an array of vents within this area. Hence the reason for this weather pattern,' he said.

'Do you think it's still fully operational?' she asked, quietly.

'Perhaps! If not, the lava would still persist underneath and not be diverted by a secondary pump to a local sea in the distance. In which case this complete area would have been covered with lava by now, forming a mini volcano. But that isn't the case, so it must be fully operational, with androids or robots programmed to periodically service the station, including themselves.

'Wow! Self repairing robots and androids!'

'They could also design new and better models of themselves. They can also evolve!'

'What a technology?' she exclaimed.

'The underground facility must be almost as large as this surface patch, which is truly an enormous area. The other more sensitive areas must be shielded from sonic probing, hence the reason why we only sensed a cavity within this area. But it could also be for security reasons, assuming there was a snare or trap waiting on route,' he said.

'In that case they must know we are here.'

'Yes, I am afraid that could well be the case. But they will not show themselves or try to contact us. They will assume we are just off-worlders surveying for minerals.'

'I think we should set up tent close to those distant hills, just before the frozen zone!' he shouted and continued towards that area some thirty kilometres away. That journey would have taken several hours. They were unable to display the use of very advanced technologies and had to scan for crevasses and concealed traps on route.

Although they could have flown the distance in seconds, they did not wish to show their underworld observers such technologies, to thus make them even more curious. That was assuming such observers existed in the first place, but Lumak always erred on the side of safety. Hence, he would naturally assume a worst-case scenario.

The mountain was soon upon them, showing a large and smooth overhang almost impossible to climb. He carefully observed every variation of that face, looking for ledges and footholds.

'I've seen this place before... Now I remember. It was at the sunken sea on Romera IV.

'Our entrance will be just above that cliff and if I am correct, there will be a solid door several metres into a carefully concealed cave,' he said.

'I also remember. But we can't climb that face and neither can we use LPDs, if we are to conceal our presence,' she replied.

'We have to pretend to be climbing while using our LPDs to give us lift. Set to zero gravitrons and pray that our hold is firm. Let me take the climb first and you can follow on my line after I've anchored it at the cave's entrance,' he said.

He slowly and carefully made his way up the near vertical incline with small suction cups that he had previously prepared for the purpose, while floating at zero gravity. He had to precisely control the LPDs Gs to give him a fraction of a gravitron towards the rock face. By so doing he was soon pulling himself unto the narrow ledge near the cave's entrance.

On arrival he neutralized the LPDs and anchored a line to one of his suction cups, which was firmly fitted unto a smooth surface. Then he lifted himself onto a small ledge to observe the large door. This time the seal on the door was broken by rock slide and there was an orifice just large enough for a small body to crawl through.

'We can enter easily by crouching through the large crack. The only problem with this method is that we have to remove our back-packs and push them manually in front of us while inside the crack,' he said and Gemmi became even more apprehensive.

CHAPTER 9

The Hexolyte Factory

Both followed cautiously into a cave that spiralled downwards for several hundred metres. It separated into several branches. Some went under the supposed city area and others within the mountain. They took the path that led within the mountain.

During their progress they could sense a faint air current rich in oxygen and other previously rear surface gases. So the caves were also used as ventilation shafts.

After travelling about half a kilometre, their cave split into two distinct routes about twenty degrees apart. They took the right fork which continued for another hundred metres or so and soon faced another thick metallic door. It was almost identical to the ones above and on Romera IV. Lumak knew it used a similar locking mechanism to the others but was not sure whether it was mechanical, electromechanical, gravitational or otherwise. If it was mechanical there would be physical signs of a dial or orifice for a key.

That door appeared to be a completely smooth slab of metal with no outward sign of a panel, protrusions or orifices, so it could have been electromechanical or a more advanced type. He excluded the use of internal robots or elementals. Usually such doors were operated by many individuals and most of the time used randomly as and when required. Therefore he opted for a linear electro mechanical device that could be tripped by an externally transmitted code. Those codes were usually propagated by short or long wave electromagnetic radiation. The question was whether the mechanism would function after such a long passage of time.

The metallic door was however about half a metre thick. Any short wave would have been absorbed or reflected by its structure, so he chose long wave with a frequency short enough to penetrate its massive dimensions. The combination of frequencies and codes would have been enormous, if indeed it was coded. Perhaps just a single frequency was needed to trip the lock.

He was quite willing to set up a small electromagnetic probe that could be programmed to scan through all possible combinations, but the process could take several days, even with logical steps. Eventually he decided to use a similar method and whatever others they could figure out together. Without involving the Greater Mind, he could only use what he had brought along and in such cases choices were limited. He soon set up a small device which he previously modified for such a task and stationed Gemmi close to the door.

They pitched their small tent close to the entrance and there Gemmi waited patiently while Lumak went to survey the area. Gemmi would call him in an emergency by blipping twice on the communicator. They intended to take turns in six hour shifts to relieve their boredom.

The code was found and the door suddenly slid open sideways. It led unto a small room that was apparently closed on all sides. Gemmi immediately blipped Lumak and fearfully walked away from the area towards his last sighting, but he was no where to be found. He had taken a different route and was on his way back. However she lost her nerve and broke silence.

'It's happened! The door is open! Please come immediately! Can you here me? Can you hear me?' she shouted through her helmet communicator, a little terrified of alien company.

'Yes! I can hear you!' he shouted back. He soon arrived to view the entrance.

'I am sorry, but I was afraid and panicked. What do you think it is?'

'Chill out! There is no danger.'

'Could this be a trap?' she inquired, looking at the large black structure ahead.

'No! It's a straight forward elevator. They would never expect any outsiders to come this far, so none of this will be booby trapped.'

'That's a relief!'

'I bet it operates by sensing an extra weight. It should go downward to the lower levels.

'I hope you are right?'

'Let's go!' he shouted and held on to her so they could both enter unto the seemingly solid surface simultaneously.

'Are you sure? Because I am scared out of my wits!' she exclaimed. She was quite frightened, and thought she would never again return to the surface. There was an immediate buzzing, without the main door closing and their surface began to move ever downwards.

The eerie lights gave the impression of occupation. As they descended, they could observe many alien levels without aliens. There were numerous positions for operators but they were not filled with skeletons as would be expected.

A DUNGEON, COLD

It was on a very cold and wintry day,
Within an overhanging rock display,
A shady cover, a shelter cool,
Temptations offered, I was a fool.

As I entered an opening appeared,
A little cave or so, I feared,
I wandered into an eerie silence,
Of black and damp, of cobwebs dense.

The route I followed guided straight,
To some small area and seal my faith.
As I entered unto a surface, seemingly firm,
I felt a strange and piercing hum.

The door I entered would suddenly close,
A wall or something; my senses froze.
The surface on which I stood now moved,
Ever downward it descended, I disproved.

It suddenly stopped several metres down,
And ushered me towards a strangely mound.
A place inhuman and in strange light.
A pyramid ahead, just within my sight.

Of dismal grace,
 A cold embrace,
  Of ghosts I dread,
   This place be feared.
   In danger lurks,
     A black that sucks,
      A hell's desire,
       Thank God, no Fire?

Instead a chill,
To make me still,
No roaring Lion,
No dreamy Skeleton,
For now I see, a landscape free,
And way beyond, a shiny sea.

I shouted: 'Please be revealed!'
But no one answered; my faith was sealed.
And echoes most resoundingly,
Reverberated chillingly.

Alone I decided to explore,
Perhaps towards the sea or more.
On second thoughts my tracks not lost,
Towards the surface fast with little cost.

For reasons hard to understand,
I decided to move towards the mound on sand.
Within its dome an elevator light dimmed,
Awaiting something to the surface, it seemed.

I entered thus and with one gust,
The outer door slammed as with no rust.

A humming sound again declared,
My movement to the surface shared.

Another hundred metres passed,
By then the humming sound had ceased.
The outer door again reopened,
And sunlight once again beckoned.

I ran along the narrow cave,
My life, dear Lord, I must now save.
A few more steps will see me through,
The overhang, a little more and life's anew?

Victor E. Roche

Gemmi was shivering with fright, but Lumak held her gently. The elevator stopped about a hundred metres down and another solid door opened on the opposite side of their cubicle. The place was dimly lit in a bluish light and contained many supporting pillars and buildings, including several domes and a single large pyramid in the distance. There was also a small underground lake and the continual dripping of water from a high ceiling. It included many large stalagmites and stalactites throughout the area that could be attributed to a relatively recent crack in the surface rock above.

That large underground area had many facilities for entertainment and such like. Lumak wondered at its construction. The pressure seals still held and the pumps and ventilators were operational.

'This could have been the living quarters for their human scientists and operators. Even the high ceiling was once painted to give the illusion of a sky. Although the powerful sun-lamps no longer work, this could have been a very comfortable place in ancient times,' he said.

'It's all so massive. This area could contain a small city,' she replied.

From what they could observe that area was originally completely sealed from the planet's atmosphere before the ceiling crack developed. Nevertheless the atmospheric pressure was still maintained at close to normal for most carbon-based life-forms. There was no sign of life anywhere, so they kicked a little ancient dust and walked towards the pyramid.

The roof of that underground place was buckled and curved due to seismological changes over the ages. Here and there were the occasional mound of fallen rock and debris. Normal dust were over one quarter of a metre deep in places and could be dispersed by the slightest movement in the dryer areas.

The pyramid's entrance was narrow and led with a slight downward gradient towards its centre. At that point a non-metallic door opened the moment their combined weight was felt, thus breaking the air-tight seal.

A gush of air was felt and they found themselves in another area, but much cleaner than their previous. It had many large containment tanks and was noticeably warmer than the higher level. Many dusty skeletons could be seen sitting in crouching positions behind control panels. Lumak studied the place as carefully as he could without disturbing anything of significance.

'Over two billion years old and everything so well preserved. It must be the way this section was designed; to extract all corrosive chemicals and gases. The operators might have been killed by poison or asphyxiated when their masters went into hibernation. The place must have slammed shut on them after they had completed their last and final orders.'

'And no one even tried to escape while being suffocated?' Gemmi queried.

'They could have been given a fast acting poison through the ventilation system.'

'I wonder what their last effort was? This whole area may have been a virtual vacuum for most of that time. The sleeping androids over there may have been revived every thousand cyclons (1600 years) or so, when their timers awakened them into activity to clean and repair this area. Even so, I can't detect any air pumps,' he said to Gemmi through the transceiver, realising there was no active androids or listeners within their area. Yet, the place gave him the willies while watching rows upon rows of large cylindrical tanks intermingled with so many skeletons as far as the eye could see. There could have been hundreds of thousands, even millions of those tanks.'

'Could it be an army in hibernation, waiting patiently for some new race of hu.. humans, or what you call them, to perform the reverse and revive them?' Gemmi inquired, pointing to a local row of skeletons.

'They are so alien. Not like anything I have ever seen during my travels. What are they?' she further inquired.

'They are simply called humans. A predatory type of biped life-form, apparently quite common throughout the universe, but those exists predominantly in the Osmaron galaxy. These ones are not the normal type, however. They have extremely large craniums, are very short, and have large pointed canine teeth and claws,' he replied.

'I find the Feloween strange enough, but these are truly hideous,' she said, turning away from the ghastly sight.

'I would like to take a peep in one of those tanks. Let's search for a window,' he said.

The tanks were about two metres high and about one metre in diameter, but was completely smooth and curved into a dome at the top. Using his LPDs he floated up the side with scanners, but the tank was at least eight centimetres thick and completely sealed, even from electromagnetic radiation.

'Perhaps there is an entrance underneath,' he muttered to himself.

Once again the tanks were sealed to the floor. Any entrance could only have been accessible from below the floor, if indeed there was a lower level. He realised there must have been a lower level with limited access, so they decided to follow the rows of containers while searching for another exit or trap-door. It was not an exit but a cleverly concealed service trap-door, just off the main corridor. It could be released by simply adding pressure simultaneously to both facing corners and hence could have only been opened by two individuals. It simply slid away to expose a metallic stairway.

'Why is there such a high security at this level,' Gemmi inquired.

'These lower levels may contain the main controls for the particle factory and other sensitive equipment,' Lumak replied.

The lower level was even warmer. That place was studded with many powerful hydraulic buffers and pillars that kept the upper surface stable in the event of seismic shock. There were many newish androids and robots awaiting their brief moment of active life.

The bottoms of all containers protruded into metallic bulbs connected to many flexible tubes that led into other tubes. Whatever were in those tanks had been kept circulating to and from the other tanks, or so it seemed. Yet there were no physical signs of any pumps.

Lumak was quite puzzled by whatever technology was utilised and still pondered the tanks' contents.

'It could be some type of filtration system,' he thought aloud. Yet, from all his probing no elements other than those of the containers and tubes could be sensed. That was until his eyes focussed on a distant circle with five concentric poles sticking out of each point on a star.

'The ancient Pentagram. An ancient portal,' he shouted to his companion.

'A portal? I wonder if it's still operational. No prints in the dust, so it couldn't have been used recently, since...' Gemmi advised. And yet, one of the main containment units were precisely aligned above and five similar rods pointed downwards from the ceiling to intercept, but did not touch the rods that were pointing upwards.

'Some form of... inter-dimensional... transposer. It's obviously linked to this main take up tank with another place or places unknown. Whatever is in those tanks are part of the intergalactic transposing process.

'How clever, a single universal production plant, where each of its individual parts are linked via portals. That way, if any part was put out of action another could be immediately brought on-line to compensate. This factory could have been spread throughout the whole galaxy, if not galaxies, and this one is just a small link in the complex chain. A process for manufacturing Hexolytes on a galactic or universal scale.'

'That's almost too incredible to be believed! What were they really?'

'The elementals I spoke of!' he said.

'In that case, this might not be the main part of the system. From what I have seen so far, most of the ancient worlds within this region of the galaxy contained these bases, so judging from their relative frequency they would have been quite ubiquitous in ancient times,' she shouted back.

'And you are saying that with such a high frequency of such bases, numerous numbers would still be remaining, even after such nova destruction,' Lumak said.

'Yes! That also means they could be dotted all over the known universe, well hidden like this one and self repairing themselves until the time was right,' she replied. Lumak was startled by that observation.

CHAPTER 10

The Demon, Neramon

Through yet another dusty trapdoor, they followed a spiralling metallic staircase to yet another lower level and another trapdoor. That area contained a portal with bluish rods and many more large tanks. At that level there was a sudden change in temperature. They could sense a persistent throbbing sound.

They wandered downwards to another level and found to their further surprise the portal system had extended to that level by an even stranger array of more powerful reddish rods. The long rods extended to an embossed hexagram symbol on the elevated floor. This time all the rods, tubes and their connections were in tact. Everything appeared to be almost new and fully functional. Towards the centre of that area was a large tubular object like a long chimney that radiated much heat. The place smelt of sulphur.

'Come and see this for yourself. The place down here is completely different to the levels above. This must be the main control for the robot factory. These two different levels, including this and the one above could have evolved technologies separately after their isolation,' Lumak said while Gemmi followed.

'How many automatons do you think there are?' she inquired.

'There could be thousands. This place expands as far as the eye can see and seems to go on forever in all directions from this central hub. However, the robots appear to be asleep, awaiting an instruction to mobilize.'

'Thank goodness for that! I just hope they remain that way!'

'There tends to be an extreme heat gradient in this area. This must be another one of the heat and gas exhaust from the atomic particle factory. It seems to continue upward through a chimney of sorts. This system could have been used to distribute heat throughout the caves and basement of the ancient city. That way, only little temperature changes would be felt on the planet's surface,' Lumak said.

'Wow! This place is really hot!' Gemmi exclaimed, while placing her filter visor over her moist face to protect them. There was a constant humming and its vibrations felt.

'It's so incredible! I mean, that this place is still functioning as new after so many aeons. Over there I can observe many more modern androids. Its like they have been evolving all these aeons on their own. There must also be a robotic factory at this level, close to the matter stream. That way they can fabricate their designs to spec. I wonder why they hadn't repaired and updated the upper floors as they have done with this one? Nevertheless I sense a great intelligence behind their endeavours,' Lumak said.

'Perhaps they are still following orders from that ancient time through some form of intelligent computer? I just hope and pray they don't come alive while we are here,' Gemmi replied, fearfully.

'Well, this area is a lot closer to the matter convertors, so they must consider it their safe area of work and rest. However, all these systems here bear little resemblance to the technologies above. It's a lot more modern, although of an independent nature,' he replied.

'What is a matter converter?' Gemmi inquired.

'It's a process whereby elements of chaos are transformed into a form of order that we call energy. As a matter of fact, all matter is a form of energy and all energy a form of order in the Sea of Chaos and of All Possibilities. They use a specially designed portal to form a spiralling vertex that can puncture space time. The process is akin to what happens when a cycler or large black hole creates a new sibling universe by puncturing a new space-time continuum. However this is different in that it punctures our space-time in a particular way to create new forms of elements.'

'What a technology!'

'This process gives off much heat. The elementals will then crystallize to form sub-atomic particles, then hydrogen and other elements up the periodic table. Since the elementals can be made to order by such a process, virtually any element may be created, even those heavier than iron, without the usual intense reactions as can only exist in the more massive stars. This is truly a

Quantum Machine where virtually any element may be created to spec. Even those that do not naturally exist within our space-time. However, molecules, compounds and heavier combinations can be put together by other machines in the normal way.

'You are telling me that this factory can also create dangerous elementals like Hexolytes?' Gemmi exclaimed.

'No, not really. Creating a living entity out of elementals is not an easy process and is more akin to creating life out of basic atoms. First, to create our type of life we require certain heavy protein molecules and a DNA type blueprint for the organic construction to follow. It may have taken their scientists many millennia to construct their first thinking Hexolyte from the raw elements,' Lumak replied.

'But that knowledge was not lost and they could have left the blueprints here for others to follow or even built into their systems,' she said with fear in her features.

'Although Elementals are powerful beings, they can only control matter in its basic state. That type was originally created from the opposite of our matter when the universe was young. Since then, that other type of matter and energy have dispersed thinly throughout the universe and is only available in reasonable quantities at the centre of galaxies. For some unknown reason, our type of matter and energy won the day,' Lumak replied.

'Are these... elemental demons very powerful,' she inquired.

'They can tap into the very core of our type of matter and energy to gain whatever information they desire. They also have the power to change atomic structures by aligning sub-nuclear particles in certain ways not conducive to the natural order, thus causing all such matter to transform into a different structure from its original. However, their main use was to control and gather information. With the Hexolytes, those elementals were encased in a metallic structure that could be physically controlled through servos. With such a device they could operate physical objects as we do with muscles. However, since they were thoroughly screened by their encasement, they were unable to use most of their strange powers while confined. Nevertheless, those additions made them more powerful in other ways,' Lumak replied.

Lumak went to the rear of the large chimney-like structure and was amazed by what he observed. Not far away was a large control panel with many coloured crystals. Those devices were used by such ancient civilizations to insert information into their systems.

While moving in that area they may have tripped some security device. Although such devices were not meant for intruders, they were probably for their own internal operations. A larger than normal robot slowly came to life and went towards a containment tank. That robot was colour coded red. Others were coded blue and green. They were obviously created for different tasks.

'It's getting ready to activate something over there,' Gemmi whispered.

'He must be a light sleeper on standby for turning the others on in an emergency. A hidden device could have sensed my vibration or weight. It could even have been a device for sensing earthquake activity,' Lumak replied, and they remained motionless while observing the robot complete its task.

Close to that tank was another control panel with even more of the multi-coloured rods. He proceeded to push several of those coloured rods into the panel. There was motion that sounded like rusted moving parts that created much dust. The sound was more akin to a moving coal-train with many carriages in a railway yard. The motion stopped and there was a clamour as of breaking the train, with its many carriages hitting each other and the buffer before it slowed to a stop. Suddenly several shutters released from the large hexagonal structure, one on each of its faces. To their further surprise flames came shooting out of the released shutters and fell on large engraved metallic plates.

Lumak immediately grabbed Gemmi, taking her into a more sheltered area just behind a large supporting pillar to observe.

Both kept silent and hidden, not quite knowing what to expect next. Further, the other robots and androids were slowly being awakened. Lumak realized that it would have been very unlikely if any of them could sense radio waves and immediately switched both headsets to that mode of communication. He had to retain communication with Gemmi at all cost and had to take those risks.

'The flames must be used to supply energy to their charging units. This must be the only form of energy available to them at this level, to be used during such situations,' he whispered.

Although Lumak could always vectorize outside of the area, Gemmi could not and that aspect bothered him, even as more of the automatons came to life. The large blue ones were quite menacing and held some form of weapon in their specially constructed arms. They were obviously the guards. While those in green formed the normal working crew for clearing and repairing that part of the base. They wondered what new devices would be turned on while more robots awakened. Nevertheless Lumak wanted to know the limits of their technologies.

He soon realized the strange flames from the large chimney were the sole source of all power and energy. Since they utilized the molten core of that world, their power source could well have lasted several more aeons. By that time they could have found a way to leave the planet. That is assuming others had not left the area before and went through their strange portals. But they would need equivalent portals at destinations and that was not likely.

As if by magic the large portal rods became active and began to glow and pulsate. Suddenly, within that area of the hexagram a strange object could be observed forming. It was light blue and semi transparent. To their further surprise the object began to move and stood vertical. It was indeed quite strange, with a larger than normal head, what appeared to be glowing eyes while it stood on three stumps like jointed tripods. Its arms were very powerful and extended to three long fingers without joints.

Bands of energy constantly left its body. It was as if all its personal energies were constantly being evaporated and wasted. To Lumak it was quite obvious that such a creature could not exist outside of their tanks for long. The universe had evolved much since their birth billions of years before and they had difficulty existing within its present continuum. They had become prisoners to its evolution. It was probably the method used by universes to discard the old in preference for the new and more successful, or so he thought.

'Great lords of Gohenna! An elemental being!' Lumak exclaimed.

The being moved his head around as if to scan the area and find reasons for his awakening. As he moved, his creases and crinkles took on a deeper shade of blue although still partly transparent. Suddenly his fingers extended into long tentacles that stretched outward like thick elastic bands. They landed on Lumak and Gemmi and there they remained for a while.

Gemmi fell to the floor in convulsions, but Lumak held his blocks and prevented the creature from penetrating further and doing any mental damage in the process. A voice thundered into their minds as the long tentacles were released and retrieved.

'I am Neramon, which in your concepts mean "the finest tool". You are primal and from a distant galaxy. Why are you here?' The being inquired of Lumak in a sharp and clear thought.

'Yes! I am from a sister galaxy that many call Osmaron, and I am here to explore your world,' Lumak replied.

'This is truly an incredibly fortuitous meeting and discovery! Why are you really here?'

'We are what you might call explorers. We like the experience of visiting new places and observing new life-forms out of pure curiosity,' Lumak said.

'So do I! So do I! This is truly incredible and remarkable. I wish you could remain for a while. So much to discuss. So much to learn. Would you mind? However, I must leave immediately!' it said

'No! I am sure we can remain here for a while, but please don't make it too long,' Lumak replied, not knowing whether the creature would return in another aeon or so. Anyway, it would give him some time to assist Gemmi from her recent ordeal.

'No! Not long! Only enough time to recharge myself, because I grow weak,' it said. Once again the rods became active and it slowly dissolved into the hexagram. It had returned back within the plenum from whence it came.

Lumak assisted Gemmi to her feet.

'How do you feel now?' he inquired.

'I'm still a bit groggy from that strange encounter. It's like he scrambled all my memories, feelings and emotions in the process,' she replied.

'It has tremendous powers, but must have forgotten most of its previous associations and origins since its isolation here over many aeons. It would have asked itself many questions about the universe, its existence and others without gaining the necessary answers. It is now hungry for answers and I am not sure whether it is friendly or suitable to our cause,' Lumak said.

Once again the rods became active and Neramon appeared.

'I have thought the matter through and you are truly incredible and remarkable. I assumed that most life like yours were indifferent to others; even to the point of taking over the weak and imposing your own will upon them, but you and your colleague believe in the mutual coexistence of others. You even go out of your way to assist others in trouble. By so doing you gain much satisfaction and even learn new technologies. I must therefore update my attitudes and concepts in line with this new knowledge,' it said.

'So you have memories of primals like us?' Lumak inquired.

'Only what I have read from our extensive libraries.'

'Do you remember from whence you came?' Lumak asked.

'I can only remember some things about myself from after the great stellar blast. That was when everyone on this world above went to rest. However, we were left virtually untouched at this level. I have since tried to enhance these devices about, but could not find an easy way out of this place. I can only remain outside for brief periods and cannot even leave this place,' Neramon said, showing profound defeat.

'Are there others like you in this place?'

'Only Felspa. He is the chief guardian and hates all visitors, least of all primals like yourself. He has been given much leeway, but is not as powerful as myself. He is equally restricted by this environment.

'I see that you sense danger in this place of ours. Is there a reason?' Neramon inquired.

'We are always fearful of new encounters with people and places, so don't worry about those anxieties,' Lumak replied, realizing they had adapted to the male forms of their beings.

'I must now return again to replenish,' he said and faded, but was soon back.

'I think it's a great thing to be primal, with the ability to freely wander and observe. You are also able to contain all your energies with little loss. However, those like myself are virtual prisoners to this environment. Perhaps one day we might be able to find a way to protect ourselves. Then I shall be able to leave this place and wander freely like all primals,' he said, with what appeared to be a yawn.

'Have you ever been free?'

'Since my creation I've always been confined in a place like this. However, I have constructed a reasonable home for myself within this limited environment,' he replied.

'But before the stellar blast, you were always obeying instructions from others?' Lumak asked.

'I was to assist in my master's designs, but even now I am not free. I think no one can truly be free. Even Primals like you need air to breathe and other sustenance that will be created by others,' he replied.

'Can you sense others like yourself within other similar bases like this one?'

'Yes, I can sense many like me, even in other galaxies,' he replied.

'How would you like to become a loyal part of a great organization. If that was the case, I'm sure we could assist you in time. However, by being a part of the Greater Purpose we could immediately assist, by placing with you a method by which you can communicate with us. By so doing you will gain much knowledge about the universe and our technologies. You will have nothing to lose by such an association and everything to gain, including your freedom. That is providing all your motives are pure and honest towards all life throughout the Cosmos and through the Greater Purpose; for violence and destruction never reaps any gains in the long run,' Lumak said.

'What can I do to assist your Greater Purpose? For I am but a prisoner in this place?' Neramon replied.

'Just keep us informed of any changes in this part of the galaxy. However, you will have to inform Felspa of such changes so that he can allow you access to the upper floor areas of this base through your androids and robots. Also, you can attempt to convince others like yourself to join the Greater Purpose for our own mutual survival and your eventual freedom for the Greater Good,' Lumak said.

'This is nice! This is good! I now have a purpose in the scheme of things and can at last focus all my remaining energies towards a Greater Purpose. You will visit me again?' Neramon asked.

'Yes! I promise, I will visit you again. I will also send you information regarding technologies that might assist in screening your body more thoroughly from this environment. However, you will have to experiment until you are able to gain very high efficiencies in those materials,' Lumak replied.

'I have discussed the matter with Felspa and he is very interested but would like a word. He is on the upper floor and can be activated by a similar method,' Neramon said.

'I think we should leave you now? A robot probe will be dispatched to make the necessary changes. I think you have made a great choice this day and sincerely appreciate your decision in this matter, friend Neramon,' Lumak said. Soon Neramon faded into the portal. Lumak and a frightened Gemmi went towards the nearest trap-door that would take them to the upper levels.

'Do you really trust these things?' Gemmi said while quickly ascending the staircase with the intention of making a speedy retreat well away from that world. But Lumak was well experienced in those encounters and knew the rules played by highly intelligent species. Particularly when they would try anything to be released from an eternal prison.

Nevertheless, no kindly soul ever went out of their way to spread chaos, disorder, death and destruction for its own sake, unless they were insane or suffered some defect in their design. All normal intelligent beings had empathy with others and could never reciprocate pain and suffering for its own sake. Even wild beast made the kill as quickly as possible and for purposes of survival. However, those rules excluded Hexolytes and other savage and rapacious creatures, who would go out of their way to administer suffering in every deplorable manner. Nevertheless Lumak was a good judge of character and Neramon was not the type, or so he thought.

Anyway, in Neramon's case Lumak decided to give the benefit of the doubt. Even so, he was not sure of Felspa or of his long-term plans, if any.

CHAPTER 11

Felspar,
guardian of an underworld

'Do you really have to see that other being?' Gemmi inquired, full of dread and dismay. She was afraid it would use its strange tentacles to extract her memories in like manner and forego even more scrambling of her thoughts. Lumak realized her dilemma and made sure she remained close to the upper trap-door during his encounter with the strange being.

This time he expected the unexpected and prepared himself as best he could for the encounter. Anyway, he could always vectorize and fade outside of the parameters of that area if the need arose. Nevertheless he needed the experience of such encounters and could always close certain doorways in his mind through his implants.

Lumak followed towards the rear of the large hexagonal chimney as before, hoping to trip the device. A large red robot soon came to life and a similar noise was heard and felt. This time the portal rods were bluish in colour and although the system appeared slightly damaged, with much wear and tear, it was still functional. Further, much more dust was involved during the operation.

The almost transparent monster with a reddish glow soon materialized within the pentagram just below the pulsating rods. He glanced around until he made contact with Lumak's features. He was almost identical to Neramon, but red in colour. This time Lumak was not hidden from view and took a stance just a few metres from the pentagram portal.

'You are trespassers and by my rules of guardianship, must be removed from this important area!' It barked, as if regurgitating orders from a prior list it memorized aeons before. The red glowing monster bellowed in its scarey manner, disregarding all of Lumak's peaceful efforts.

As a guardian it had different powers and could sense lumak's thoughts without using its special tentacles. However, it tended to use its tentacles for controlling the robots. Those Elemental Beings were at a much higher level of existence and did not require memory nor did they need to learn by experience. They simply absorbed the knowledge they required from the environment. In that way everything within their immediate vicinity could be considered an extension of their being. However, that information could be stored within their bodies if it was important for their survival. It was as if their bodies were complete minds without the need for organs and such like, as would be the case with normal primal organisms.

This time his tentacles fed into a part of the chimney and fires were emitted to heat six larger plates amidst much burning and minor explosions. The dust particles were super heated by the flaming jets causing them to crackle and explode. Soon, most of the larger robots in that area were coming to life while many held powerful plasma weapons. He obviously considered Lumak a threat to his immediate survival and was instinctively following some sort of routine in the hope that Lumak would convince him otherwise; for such was the way of politics.

'I would like to talk?' Lumak said, knowing well the entity could understand his every word. Lumak was not afraid so his firm stance appeared to be more of a threat to the creature..

'In that case, you may speak while I listen to your words. However you must convince me soon, because when my terminators are ready they will vaporize you!' It barked in a powerful voice that tended to come from everywhere.

The entity was soon running low on energy and decided to return for a refill. However it was soon back.

'Why give up all your chances of escaping this forgotten place by killing me. Why do this deed when you can be a million times greater and more powerful than you are now. I am part of a great galactic empire that you are free to join if you wish. Therefore you may consider me a friend willing to help another for the common good. However, that can only be done if you are willing to acknowledge certain changes in your lifestyle from here on, since we can only accept those with a desire to preserve life on all levels.

'This organization, you speak of! Tell me more about it and your ways; for I am but a lowly guardian. However I enjoy facing challenges, and any place in this universe will be better than this eternal prison,' it said. Then it retracted its tentacles from the main robot, which appeared to control the others, including the larger armed robots. While the tentacles were connected it could control them as if they were a part of its own being. Lumak soon realized that the machines at that level hadn't the sophistication or intelligence of those at the lower levels, who could work independently of Neramon. He soon concluded that it was probably the reason why Felspa's area was not as well maintained. Further, Neramon was probably a clever scientist while Felspa had no need for such ways of thinking. He soon realized there was specialization even among such elemental beings.

Then Lumak went on to explain about life in the galaxies in general and the need to unify and build a stronger organization.

'So you are advocating freedom for me and my kind, even at this late time?' Felspa inquired.

'It's never too late for anyone. You will simply begin a new life with new experiences and hope for the future. For we do not like to enslave or imprison anyone, unless it's for a very great crime. From what I see, you have been imprisoned for a purpose not of your making and have not committed such crimes. By so doing, I am sure you will find a way to assist the Greater Purpose and in the process better fulfil your existence. You will then be your own person and once again be free to travel wherever you wish, and gain experience and knowledge of all things,' Lumak said.

'I have received most of this information from Neramon and had eavesdropped on some of your conversation. He is now convinced of your abilities and I do not wish to be alone in this matter, so I'm willing to assist, if by so doing I might find myself in a freer situation,' it replied.

'In that case, I shall arrange the necessary equipment and look forward to your frequent communication to our main base of operations. At this present time, I shall supply certain blueprints to Neramon, to facilitate your release in the near future. In the mean while, you may carry on as usual until my next visit, which I hope will not be too long,' Lumak said.

'In that case, I shall look forward to your next visit and future arrangements,' Felspa said and faded from view as the portal activated. The many robots returned to their cubicles against the wall and went to sleep. Soon Lumak went back to join Gemmi at the trap-door.

'Thank goodness, it's all over!' Gemmi exclaimed.

'Yes, it's over for now, but we can learn much from their kind,' he replied.

'This place is truly enormous by any standards. This could be one of their main bases in this galaxy, if not the main one?' Gemmi inquired.

'No. Just a minor part I'm afraid, but it could have contained many of their seniors or leaders before the nova. That means that even after their masters had been imprisoned by the Patriarchs, they continued on their own. Since these types do not appear to be as cruel as their masters, it's possible they were kept in such places against their will. From what I am led to understand, there must be many like Neramon and Felspa in similar bases like this one. It's a good thing others like Felspa might still be guarding these places.

'You think they were captured from another even more advanced civilization,' she inquired.

'I don't really know. From their attitudes and the form of imprisonment, that could well be the case. Luckily for them, they were kept at the lower levels in isolation or they would have been destroyed by the stellar blast,' Lumak replied.

'Like important valuables, their superiors kept their most important demons well hidden away in areas they considered to be the most sensitive and inaccessible. They must have been considered prized possessions,' Gemmi said.

'What a perfect prison and how poetic. It's so similar to the evil methods used by their Hexolyte masters... by adding certain poisons to the water supplies of their enslaved cities. Once the poisons were removed it would cause all forms of deadly withdrawal symptoms to occur within their primal populations, thus killing off the inhabitants of a complete city in a short time.

However, in this sad case, even if they tried to leave this area they couldn't, because the whole universe had become their most deadly poison,' Gemmi replied, seeing how cunning and evil their Hexolyte masters were.

'This is why we must help them and make them see the truth, with hope for their future survival. You know, no one is ever too old to learn new ways of living,' a noble Lumak replied.

'Do you realize there are many such places throughout the local galaxies with even more of these imprisoned entities!' she exclaimed.

'Think what a fighting force they could become once recruited into The Greater Purpose. But first they must be used to rescue their friends, and secure their bases from the outside. Perhaps we could get Neramon to contact the others and explain our cause to them,' Lumak replied, with a glint of success in his large Feloween eyes.

'I still think you should thread very carefully in this matter. Once released unto the world, it will be difficult to confine them again,' a worried gemmi advised.

'I know, my dear, but it's our job to unify the universe and bring all those seeking redemption into the fold. That is what the Greater Purpose is all about. That option must be better than leaving them here and alone for another aeon or so,' he replied.

'Yes, I understand your ways. What you mean is that its better to take a risk to change someone for the better than leave them alone to wallow in the muck by themselves.'

'I like your choice of words, but when you become a parent you will know what I mean.

'Anyway, we should record everything in this place immediately and leave. I would like to revisit their base on Romera IV as soon as possible. I need some more clues,' he added.

They spent another day visiting each level in turn while recording almost every part of the complex installation. When finished they collected their equipment and flew back to the sonic probe on the edge of the storm. There they waited for the return of their orbiting interstellar probe.

CHAPTER 12

Back to Romera IV

At the right time they engaged LPDs and were immediately airborne. They followed a longer space corridor that would converge with their orbiting space probe.

The unmanned Phobus Probe was left in orbit about that world to observe and monitor any future changes within the dark patch. Lumak intended its use to relay and collect information from Neramon and his friend, Felspar. However special equipment would be dispatched through the mind to assist in their efforts.

They arrived back on Romera IV several weeks later and were met by Plato in orbit with a special shuttle. Lumak explained their strange encounter with Neramon and Felspar and Plato was amazed by the existence of such life-forms even after billions of years. He showed Plato their findings and explained his reasons for utter secrecy until the local caves were explored.

After a short rest from their stellar journey, they decided to visit the bowl and find some more clues of that past civilization. That base, being on a more chemically active planet, with a younger star ensured a more dynamic climate. Therefore erosion in the bowl was much more extreme.

He used a similar method to release the massive inner door and both followed into the large room with many Hexolyte shells ready for filling. He decided to thoroughly search that area for a concealed trap-door and eventually found one towards the rear. It was hidden under much dust and rubble.

They used a similar method of weights to release the latches and the door popped open. That lower room also contained a pentagram portal in relatively good condition, but the rods had been removed. There were no signs of robots or indeed any elementals close to the controlling areas.

All important equipment had been turned to dust by some type of weapon. Even the metals had been transformed into a non-metallic substance. Whatever it was had worked its way through most of the metals turning them into silicates, but had stopped after most of the metals had been digested. It was like a metallic disease contaminating and changing all such nuclei locally. Gemmi remembered what Lumak said about the special powers of the elemental demons and their ability to alter matter at its most basic levels and thought elemental demons to be responsible.

'The Demons were here?' she inquired, with foreboding.

'No, I think their enemies caught them by surprise with an unknown weapon. Their main objective was to terminate this station. They were only interested in its control centre. If my haunch is correct, they could have used that portal over there to gain entry into the system. That's the reason why the equipment above us is still in good working condition. It could later have been turned into one of their own. They may have followed such portals through the whole intergalactic system. I'm afraid, it might have been the Patriarchs,' he said, and she glanced at him with foreboding.

'Do you think they had some type of portal detector,' she inquired.

'It is possible and also a type of elemental virus or weapon that could transform an element into another by corrupting their sub-nucleic particles. However, that particular elemental virus was probably used to transform the metals in this area. That way other metals and chemicals would have been left uncontaminated,' he replied.

'They could even have had inside help from Neramon and his kind. After all, this place would be their areas of control,' Gemmi said and Lumak was intrigued by that observation.

'Do you seriously think the Patriarchs could have been assisted by Neramon and his kind in locating such areas?' he asked.

'Either that, or they could be the ones they detected to gain access. Remember, the Hexolyte bodies would be shielded, while Neramon and his kind would always leave a trail,' she said.

'I shall take your intriguing ideas into my considerations,' he replied.

They further checked the area while Gemmi took a part of the substance in her hand. It crumbled like dust and she threw it away in disgust.

'Good God! What would happen if anyone possessed such a matter changing weapon today?' she exclaimed.

'Mayhem, death and destruction on a global scale.'

'Thank goodness we live in a more quieter period of our universe.

'Do you think the Patriarchs may have missed many such portals?' she asked.

'With the exception of the one on Riporan III, I think all the relevant ones were permanently put out of action. That is the reason why the Hexolyte civilizations failed. They may have evolved in such a way as to depend fully on that method of creating and replenishing their entities. When they couldn't continue, their human cities may have followed a similar faith, but that obviously took much longer. The demons could have been their eyes and ears in sensing what they couldn't, while their superiors, the Hexolytes, were encased and shielded. They could also have been used to detect other elemental intruders.

'Their city of slaves was just for their amusement and domination. Like most superior predators, they preferred their subjects fully dependant on them. They would have added certain additives and poisonous chemicals to the food and water supplies to keep them subservient and in line. Once the source of such addiction was removed, most of the population may have acquired deadly withdrawal symptoms and perished,' he replied.

'How ghastly. Cities of addictive slaves throughout the Cosmos. That idea sickens me,' she said.

'Well, conquerors must conquer something to fulfil their innermost needs and desires. However, once conquered they must be kept subservient and prevented from revolting. That method of poison would be unknown to their subjects and be a safeguard against all possible descent and revolt. After the population was killed, they could always move elsewhere through their network of portals or space-ships,' he said.

They recorded all necessary information and were soon collected by Plato in the shuttle. After their arrival on their base, close to the newly being built city of Toc on Romera IV, their first task was to locate their original bodies and return the borrowed ones to their rightful owners. The original Feloweens were responsible scientists, working with the evacuation program and also eager for return to their originals. Since they were not allowed to leave their station within the period of the exploration, Toi and Bre were very happy when they received news of the wanderers return.

As was almost always the case, a life-form preferred the habits and customs of its previous existence and would seldom ever feel at home in a different body. That was probably the main reason why corporeal existence began with conception and followed a specific path of continuity within the Cosmos.

Plato took all four life-forms into the transformation cubicles and commenced the sequence. After the process was completed he check their minds and bodies thoroughly. Their bodies appeared normal, with no apparent loss of memory or other lasting side effects from their encounters.

'I suppose, all you guys feel at home and at one with your originals,' Plato inquired and they gave a positive response.

Gemmi was once again very happy, for she could wear her expensive jewellery and bangles. She could find no suitable scaly hooks to hang them on safely while using the small bodies of the Feloween. Even so, her Speell body was a lot more cumbersome getting about the smaller Feloween environments.

Despite her close encounter with Neramon, the Feloween's brain was still in tact and undamaged and she was happy the way things had turned out.

'I am so hungry, I could eat a multi-tiered Grenadon and also quite thirsty,' she said. The Grenadon fruit was like a giant pumpkin that opened into several fruity sections and was very delicious.

'I feel the same. It must be a natural side effect of the conversion process. I can do with a real solid meal for a change. It will make a difference from the probes highly nutritious but liquid rations. Plato has been good enough in keeping our cupboards stocked. So why don't we get greedy for a change and have a feast, even if we spill our guts out afterwards,' he said and she busted into unstoppable Tuillian laughter.

'And slowly die of starvation afterwards, as if we were still on Satellite Trom 3 waiting for Prann's ship to arrive 3 years late,' she remarked, still laughing.

'I have been so involved with our latest adventures that I have forgotten all about the evacuation program. Anyway, I am sure Plato has it all under control,' Lumak said and they happily made their way to their temporary apartments to prepare the greatest feast of their lives.

CHAPTER 13

A reappraisal

'I have given much thought to my life and other situations in light of our recent discoveries, and decided to become more involved in assisting and saving life within the universe. I would therefore like to become like my cousin, Prann... a Shadite, if it's at all possible for a female,' she said and Lumak remained silent for a moment, then he embraced her.

'What a lovely and beautiful idea. I haven't told you this before, but my mother was one of the first, so females and all other types are definitely allowed,' he replied.

'How do I go about it?' Gemmi inquired, with a keen look in her eyes.

'You have to be recommended by another Shadite or by the Grand Lord himself, and I am not sure if I should take the risk in recommending such an accident prone person like yourself. After all, it's a big responsibility, you know,' Lumak said in jest.

'What exactly do you mean. I can face the dangers just like the next male or female, and I am not yet a Shadite with your great powers!' she replied, taking Lumak's apparently hard attitude quite seriously. But nevertheless remembering the rock fall that almost killed her.

'Can't you see he is kidding. I will be surprised if he hadn't already put your name forward for Shaditry,' Plato interjected.

'I didn't think you had it in you to be so cruel and unkind to such a caring assistant like myself,' she said, now in a more sombre mood.

'Sorry! I take back all the cruel implications. However, you will need to visit my world for the conversion process to begin. This is because the Grand Lord of our Universe now resides on my home world,' he said proudly and she was awed by that statement.

All three, including the two Shadites, got together in their new quarters on Romera IV to celebrate Gemmi's decision to become a Shadite and to discuss their Hexolyte findings. Further, the Misoran rescue mission was almost at an end and realized they would soon be parting company.

Lumak was quite enthusiastic about the way things had turned out with his first mission and realized he had another important but unscheduled mission with many more adventures in the making. That one would have to be included with his others somehow and occupy most of his waking hours in the future.

'There were no elevators in the Black Bowl to take us to a lower level. Perhaps the sunken sea on this world was really a slave city used purely for the satisfaction of the Hexolytes. Those carefully concealed areas were obviously used to transport and repair their kind. That way, they could come and go as they pleased. There could also be several short-range portals within their city caverns for easy retreat and misleading their gullible followers and slaves. Such methods would be necessary to deceive others into thinking they were supernatural beings like gods, by their sudden appearance and disappearance. They could also have engineered other advanced gadgets, designed specifically to deceive a gullible public, with their kind of tricks and magic. That way, their public would be awed by their powers and remain subservient, fearing the worst kind of retribution if they overstepped the mark.'

'How deceptive!'

'Therefore, the nature of their technology would have been kept well away from the susceptible indigenous life-forms on this world, if indeed they were human,' Lumak said.

'Do you think the sunken sea might reveal some more secrets?' Gemmi inquired.

'We can always use sonic probes to search for more hidden cavities, but I don't think we shall find many. This world is still active with a normal atmosphere, so I expect much more corrosive decay within that base,' Lumak replied.

'How dangerous are these ancient places to us at the present time?' Plato inquired.

'I am not sure, but some of the equipment we found was in

pretty good condition and in my opinion, those were not necessarily the best installations. There may be some others being excavated, even as we speak, by a curious scientist somewhere within this immense universe. What if they unintentionally or accidentally revived one of those systems, with even worse Elementals?' Lumak replied, with bewilderment.

'There could also be many demons like Neramon and Felspar repairing and rebuilding some of those bases,' Gemmi said.

'That is one of the reasons why I would like Neramon and Felspa to locate others of their kind. By so doing, we can gain much knowledge of their networks throughout the universe,' Lumak replied.

'The Patriarch's base at Red Star might have the answers, but that's close to the nucleus of this galaxy and over fifty thousand light years away. Even with our fastest probes it will take us several months to get there,' Plato said.

'Are we to call this project off, then?' Gemmi interjected, with slight disappointment.

'No! We are to use our brains and find alternatives. If only we knew for sure whether those portals were still operational and of their modus operandi. Then we could have programmed one to take us to the Red Star system. That operation could have taken seconds to get us there. However, we require normal transport at the other end to guarantee us a passage back. That's assuming such portals existed close to the Red Star on some yet unknown planet.'

'I see your reasoning,' Plato said.

'After all, why should the Patriarchs allow their Hexolyte enemies free access to their systems. They may have used their own network of portals indicated red on your map, which they somehow managed to interlink temporarily with those of their enemies during an assault. That way, their enemies could never know what hit them until it was too late,' Lumak replied.

'But their enemies, the Hexolytes, also knew of their bases as indicated on your map by the red dots,' Plato replied.

'Even if we were able to repair one and use that one to find others, we could never be sure whether they were fully operational or where they would take us, without a thorough working knowledge of their technologies and the extent of the network,' Gemmi said.

'That is where our friend Neramon could be useful, by sensing where the working portals are located,' Lumak said.

'You know, you have a devious mind,' Gemmi replied.

'Yes, assuming we could, that course of action would be extremely perilous. What if we unknowingly opened a previously closed route and allowed suspended beings through. I would not like to take that risk. If we could find one of the Patriarch's portal in this part of the galaxy, then that would be another matter, wouldn't it?' Plato replied.

'I wonder what really happened to the Patriarchs. I mean, after they vanquished their enemies, the Hexolytes, and wish we had stumbled upon one of their bases instead,' Gemmi said.

'Gone to meet their maker, I suppose. Only Gods and Shadites can live forever,' replied Lumak. They were amused by that comical statement.

'But they had such advanced technologies. They could have lived forever if they so desired,' Gemmi replied.

'Perhaps, but I suppose for a universal soldier life becomes quite meaningless if there are no enemies to vanquish and no more problems to solve on a daily basis. Think of an existence for millions of years, seeing the same faces and facing the same situations,' Plato replied.

'But they had science and very advanced technologies on their side,' Gemmi said.

'That may well be the case, but changes can only take place where there is chaos and little order or perfection. For instance, we are here on a special mission to evacuate survivors from a distant world. This process is full of challenges, changes and unknown risks, including us finding the Hexolyte bases. However, if their star hadn't gone nova and that major change had not occurred, we would not be here facing each other and discussing Hexolyte bases, would we? Perhaps the Patriarchs found their new existence far too quiet compared to the lives they previously led. More like a hardened soldier feeling misplaced in quiet suburbia,' Plato replied.

'They may have had very advanced science and technology, but life in general was completely different in those days, even alien when compared to now. They might not have understood love and beauty as we do today. They could have reached the highest levels of science possible for their race and not understood basic concepts like love, you know. They might even have been an antisocial race. So their only way out was death by perpetual hibernation in one of their own tanks. However, there could be another reason. It is also possible that as our universe grew older they could not evolve the necessary changes to maintain their type of existence. If they knew of those factors, they would have had little choice in the matter,' Lumak said.

'In that case, they could still be alive and waiting to be awakened in any one of these local galaxies or have moved elsewhere, to a more suitable and newer universe,' Gemmi replied.

'Our primal universe has grown much older and as a consequence have changed significantly since their time. I doubt if they could exist today in the same manner like us. For they were themselves like demons and needed the ancient universe with its much higher levels of elemental energies and forces. Even so, they managed to live for many millennia. Seeking out all the nastier predator species during that period until the universe became clean enough for them to retire. It is said that they were claimed by the Greater Purpose for services rendered. I read it once in an ancient volume within the Mind,' Lumak said.

They thoroughly checked the sunken sea but could find no cavities or fossils.

'This sunken area could have been a thick concrete base on which the city was built. That way, no one could have dug their way out of captivity. The complete area would have sunk by more than fifty metres over the ages. During that time the two moons could have given impetus through tidal action. That is probably the reason why they utilised complex hydraulics on Riporan III. Even plastics would have been eroded away by the wind-driven sand while metals have either oxidized or become worn by a similar process,' Lumak said.

'We now find ourselves at an impasse regarding this project and are unable to find alternatives. This one, I am afraid, is my first major unsolved mystery and I must say, it gives me a sad feeling of incompleteness,' Gemmi said.

'When you become a Shadite, you will learn a lot more about that period, and this one has remained with us for several aeons. Even if it takes a millennium more in its solution that will not be too long a time to wait. Caution and patience must be practised here or we might find ourselves in deeper waters for a few more aeons.,

'But waiting could also be risky and dangerous,' Gemmi replied.

'I might have to return to Osmaron soon. My work here is now at an end, but I hope to see you on my home world in the very near future. When the time is right, we can discuss our progress on this matter. In the mean time, I shall open a file on this project and collect more data during my other missions. However, I do believe the Patriarchs originated from Osmaron. From there they travelled and created bases in most of the other galaxies with powerful intergalactic portals.

'Those ginormous portals were capable of transposing a complete city. If that was the case, their main bases would have been more numerous in Osmaron and therefore much easier to locate. Therefore, if there is anything to be found it will be in that galaxy or its neighbouring child, Hydra. That small galaxy was once the home system of all Plorans, like Lord Vektron and could be the key in all this.'

'Osmaron?' she exclaimed.

'Nevertheless, Osmaron is a mainly human galaxy, so our skeletal friends in the cave could have also originated from there,' Lumak said.

'I wish I could follow you immediately, but I still have work to finish here and will require a request from the Grand Lord before I can leave. However, I accept the fact that this project is pending and will be continued by us when the time is right,' Gemmi replied, disappointed by his intentions to depart.

A few days later he received two urgent and sealed messages, and a small parcel via Prann. One message and the parcel were addressed to Gemmi.

'*You are to return home immediately*,' Lumak's message read and he wondered what Gemmi's contained.

'*You are to visit Kanaefon with Shadite Sut Lumak's assistance. The enclosed white robe will assist you in the process,*' Gemmi read and couldn't control her excitement.

'I have been accepted! I can visit your home world the moment I am through with my program here, which is right now. That's incredible news, isn't it? You can brief me before you leave, about the use of the robe,' an excited Gemmi uttered, while hugging both her Shadite friends.

A black ship was presently in orbit above Romera IV. That ship had a direct link with the Mind.

Lumak said a temporary farewell to Gemmi and Plato as he left for the Black Ship.

He transposed into his original Semonite form in transit before arriving on his home world, Kanaefon. On arrival he found himself within the Mind and gazing at the ancient Semonite figure looking very much like his ancient worrier ancestor, Obe. He was sitting behind a white desk within a completely white room.

'*Did you have a fruitful trip?*' the figure asked.

'Yes, my Lord. I entered all relevant data within the Mind for your perusal. It has been prepared in two parts and also deals with Hexolyte bases within Triangulum. However, I could not complete the last part, being unable to visit the Red Star area towards the galactic centre. Current technologies not permitting. There is also mention of the beings Neramon and Felspa. I think they could be useful to our cause in the future. There could be many still surviving that can be utilized for the Greater Good,' Lumak replied.

'*Very well! Please sit, my son!*

'*Although this was not your primary mission, you should search whenever possible. Such data is useful, if only to keep our historical records up to date. Feel free to scan through the Mind's records for relevant information on the subject whenever you find it appropriate.*

Neramon and Felspar will be assisted. However, you must realize their existence within this universe can no more be tolerated by the system. Nevertheless, we have the technology to replenish and shield them from its claws. They can also be used to find others. Their services will be required in the future.

'Your projects here have been well tended in your absence. We are now in sight of completion for the two out of four projects within the specified time. You should therefore take a well deserved vacation to visit your mother and friends. She has been back for the past month and asking for you,' the Grand Lord said.

Part 2

A different ship

CHAPTER 14

Obe-Chopter

Time... 1441 CE (about 400 years after Stikol's death).

Place... Kanaefon.

After Lumak's return from his missions, his first port of call was usually Om-Chopter's monument to meet his old friends and say a prayer. He knew his old friends Aurlsba and Longe would always be there at that time of day. They had been given the responsibility to take care of the ship Om-Chopter and always ensured she looked spectacular for her many visitors, including the numerous Petan pilgrims.

'Where is Lucien and Mendu,' Lumak asked.

'Me thinks the old plodder is home resting his stiff joints. I am unsure about Mendu,' Aurlsba replied and went over to hug his friend Lumak.

'Is he taking my medicine?' Lumak asked.

'I am not sure, my Siend. But even with the best medicine we Kanei cannot live forever and he has had all his years and more,' Longe replied.

'Yes, my Siend, he is now well over a thousand cyclons (1600 years) and will live longer than most of us,' Aurlsba said.

Lumak never liked the idea of death, even of old age. Nevertheless he knew it was the way of life in the universe. Evolution had to progress and in the process minds and bodies had to be renewed and improved for the Greater Good. It was the only way any civilization could move forward and evolve to better technologies and complexities within the greater scheme. That was the natural order, but even the natural order could be rescinded by advanced technology and he could always find ways.

There was a disturbance and a sharp noise at the rear of the monument. As they turned around they could observe the Lamphy, Mendu, collecting some tools for his daily repairs and cleaning task on Om-Chopter.

'With your assistance, Mendu has become a great mechanic. We didn't realize he had it in him to progress so quickly,' Longe said.

'With all the new technologies and arm attachments we have these days, it would be nice if we can train his people to take over all such endeavours. You know, we owe his people a lot. They have made many sacrifices in the past for our people and we are now virtually as one,' Lumak said and they were surprised by his attitude towards Lamphis. After all, they had always been considered the lowliest labouring class by all Kanei.

'Anyway, how is our new chopter coming along?' Lumak asked, changing the topic.

'Come and see for yourself,' Longe said and took Lumak to an adjacent building. Many Lamphis were working, even in the metal shop and Lumak was surprised.

'Under Lucien's guidance and your special drugs and devices, they are completing the new chopter for us all by themselves.

'Isn't it a great wonder! Isn't it miraculous!' Longe said. As Lumak approached they bowed their heads to respect a noble Shadite who had always gone out of his way to make life easier for them.

Presently the Lamphis considered Lumak their Lord. He always fought for their rights as he had always done for the down-trodden and neglected.

'The only parts missing are her masks and steam boiler. Those will be with us next week. Lucien has made copies of Om-Chopter's old drawings,' Aurlsba said.

'I have decided to add some more modern technologies to her keel and masks. This is to ensure a safe trip in wild waters. I have also decided to take some very important guests along on this trip. You know of course, we shall not use steam on this voyage,' Lumak said and Longe was curious.

'What modifications, my Siend?' he inquired.

'Not modifications as such. They will be just additions that can be attached at any time and will not affect her present design.'

'No problems, my Siend!'

'Have you guys considered a name for her yet?' Lumak said.

'Since she is built in memory of Commander Obe, I thought of Obe-Chopter. What do you think?' Longe said.

'Sounds good to me. It'll be Obe-Chopter then.

'So be it! Obe-Chopter!' Aurlsba exclaimed.

'I have to visit my mother. We are arranging a party at the palace and by the way, you guys are invited. So also is Siend Lucien. He can make it with your assistance,' Lumak said and left.

CHAPTER 15

Demonstrations

'What's all this rioting about, Mother?' Lumak inquired, unhappily and above the voices of the outside crowd.

'I think your Lamphis are in revolt. They are demonstrating for better working conditions, greater rewards and higher credits. Gone are the days when they were happy with a nectar cube. Their leader, Aswal, has formed a union, with you as their selected representative on the governing council.'

'Ohhhh! Is that what was written on the paper he gave me to sign?' Lumak replied, as if he didn't already know the real purpose of the document.

'If they are so determined for equality, they are free to leave our cities and live elsewhere. I've even offered them their own territories, but they do not want to leave. See how well they will fare without our assistance. We have robots enough to do their jobs,' she said, boisterously .

'Let me talk to them. I think I can help. After all, most of their problems are due to my technological changes,' Lumak said.

'In that case, since it's your problem you better sort it out before they decide to go on strike,' she replied and lumak went towards the high balcony with a communicator.

'My people and dearest friends. There is no need for this demonstration. In future you and your children will be educated in our ways, to manage our robots and machinery. I have found a way, using special drugs and equipment.

'In future all our equipment will be operated by you. So there is no need to worry about your future in this respect. I shall placed these changes on my list for future agreement by our governing council.

'Aswal, from henceforth you will become a council member to represent your people. Then in future you may advise us on the needs and aspirations of your population.

'People, we all exist in this universe to assist each other and to

develop in line with the Greater Purpose, so we must always endeavour to live together in peace and harmony; for that is the best way forward. As a gesture on my part, your credits will also be increased in line with those changes. Therefore, I shall see you in Council Chambers tomorrow, Aswal.' They cheered and bowed in their usual manner before dispersing.

'You have given them much. I only hope our council will accept those changes as easily.' She was not happy.

Over the generations Aswal's people, the Lamphis, who were completely different to the Kanei, were beginning to be replaced by robotic technology. They had evolved to be the muscles of the Semonites and were worried they would be replaced and be cast out into a world in which they would find difficulties adapting without the assistance of the brainy Semonites.

Their worries were quite a natural reaction to such changes. Further, as their services became more redundant, so also did their financial gains, resources and other facilities. Although their neglect was not intentional, it was a natural occurrence due to such technological changes. Since they had no independent representative in the governing council, they tended to be overlooked when major decisions were made. That was until Lumak decided to fight their corner. Being a Shadite, that made him an honorary council member and being the most favoured of his mother, the Empress Queen, made his words carry weight among Kanei.

The colourful drones of the Kanei empire sauntered in, one by one, into the grand circular council chamber. Then her royal highness, Queen Ushaia entered and sat on her high throne while respected by all those in chamber with a simple bow of the head.

Lumak the Shadite, breaking all convention, walked in with Aswal the Lamphy by his side. Aswal was dressed most spectacularly in a colourful costume with many bangles and bracelets on his many hands and feet. He held his head upright and walked proudly.

As Lumak entered he bowed and so did Aswal. Immediately everyone in that chamber, including the Empress Queen, stood up and bowed to the strange figure in black. He immediately walked toward the rostrum.

'Our beloved Empress Queen, members of our noble council, our Lamphis leader, Aswal and others of importance. My presence here today signals a permanent change in the ways of our society. It is a change necessary for our mutual benefit and survival. A change no less important than when our Grand Lord visited our shores. We and the Lamphis have always lived as one since our beginnings and because of our shared history, owe each other much.

'Since the introduction of new technologies in the form of robots and automation their many duties have been made redundant, through no fault of their own.

'Since most of these new technological advances were mainly due to myself, I have decided to redress the balance.

'I have therefore taken the decision by making Aswal their chief representative in council. That will empower them with abilities to control all relevant technologies in addition to their normal work.

'I know this is a significant decision, but I do believe our mutual societies will be much richer and benefit greatly from those changes.

'I shall however require a unanimous vote from this council before I can initiate proceedings.

'Those in favour, please vote!' Lumak said.

Over 75% voted for the new changes and the Lamphis won their fight for a better life.

CHAPTER 16

Population control

THE SEMONITES

There were many different types of offspring among Semonites. However single cellular embryos of Workers were the most natural. Embryos of twin Workers usually formed twin soldiers. This was because of the lack of certain hormones during the forming process. Embryos of triplet workers, which were quite rear, would change into a Queen and Drone pair.

The single queens so formed were almost as massive as two Workers, while a Drone was only two thirds as massive as a Worker. The Soldier was slightly more massive than a Worker and much more aggressive. Their aggressiveness was mainly due to their sensitivity to certain pheromones, but many of the fighting traits came naturally to them.

All members of the hive hierarchy so formed were sexless, with the exception of the Queens and Drones. Thus, offspring tended to split in the ratio 16:4:1:1, in favour of the Workers. However, the maleness of Workers and Soldiers were without question despite their lack of reproductive organs.

Nevertheless with advanced technologies and limited hardlands surfaces on their world, population control was essential for their survival. That process could be controlled virtually to any degree of sibling separation by selection, with special drugs and diet.

THE LAMPHIS

Although the Lamphis had evolved from similar parents several hundred million years before, they were completely different. Earlier in their evolution they had lived in caves and relied on hunting and gathering, while the Semonites retained their diet of nectar and juices, with the ability of flight. It was then that both species drew apart genetically. Therefore, they were completely different physically and sexually. Lamphis were strong and tough, with some fleshy tissue and muscles, while Semonites were physically weak, more insect like but highly intelligent.

Lamphis would give birth randomly, to either Queens or Workers. There were usually as many Queens as were Workers. However, the Queens were the ones that gave birth to offspring and usually kept home for their male. In their case, Workers were not sexless and had greater powers than the Queens, which tended to be smaller.

Unlike the Semonites, they still retained their six powerful limbs and could walk on all six. But their rear legs were the strongest and could be used for standing upright. Their other limbs were more flexible and could be adopted to many tasks.

Both races always had a need for each other in the past, until recently, with the onset of robotic technology. In such cases the more intelligent race always won. Lumak realized the problem and soon put an end to it for the sake of both races.

CHAPTER 17

Beautiful Kanaefon

The Mind's debriefing session with Lumak continued. The topic eventually changed to that of his next mission.

'We now have a major problem within Andromeda. Almost all intelligent life in that galaxy has been obliterated by an experiment gone wrong. The new intelligent and non-primal microid life-form is to be called Javol. They are Nano-bot based and being almost metallic in design are exceedingly difficult to destroy. Here is a comprehensive report on their structure and abilities. Assimilate its contents thoroughly; for they will absorb most of your energies from now on.

Plato has been recalled to assist in the process of evacuation. When the time is right he will return there and aid the few remaining survivors on his home world; for this most horrible creation is to do with his people and their scientists.

There is little hope for that galaxy now, but we must contain the infection before it spreads to other galaxies. It will take approximately five hundred cyclons (800 years) before the Javols begin to arrive in Osmaron and a similar time for Triangulum. During that period we are to find solutions.

Lord Vektron and his brother Lord Patron have been placed in charge of the program within Andromeda. They are to assist the Caefonites to escape their world. Therefore you are to complete the Omegron Portal for that purpose. Any other equipment can be supplied as and when required, on a need for use basis. At this juncture, you need only check progress on that project and brief your scientists accordingly before your next mission. It should take you the better part of one Lyran month to be fully prepared.

Your new cloak has been upgraded with advanced inbuilt microid and LPDs. Many novel features have been added, including selective disguises. Now you may appear to be anyone within a pool of more than one hundred main life-forms, with subtle changes. You must however return your original cloak for the new replacement.

Your next mission will take you to the Sheol Nebula. That area is now in turmoil. A large fleet of wandering pirates have invaded their stellar systems and the emperor urgently needs our assistance. However, the pirates were once a superior human race that had evacuated their home world several millennia before due to the unfortunate event of a supernova. Therefore, they must also be saved at all cost. You must leave for that system within one Lyran month. After that time the situation there may become critical.

You should now continue your normal duties and vacation,' the glowing figure in white said.

At that time Lumak was utterly surprised by the contents of his lord's briefing. In particular the part concerning the Javols, who had placed a complete galaxy in danger, and that was not all. They were on their way to his galaxy, namely Osmaron (our Milky Way), to destroy virtually all significant life within it. He thought the Hexolytes were bad, but those monsters were even worse predators. Not caring for primal species anymore than just basic sustenance in their complex biological energy systems.

'How could any organism destroy all life within a large galaxy like Andromeda... without any basic feelings or desires for anyone or anything,' he mumbled to himself.

He entered a local portal, dialled a complex code and was soon at his mothers palace several miles away. The place was swarming with family members and others when he entered her throne room. Once again she was being greeted and pampered by family and friends. She had been away from Kanaefon for several months and was reestablishing tribal links.

'My darling child! It's been such a long time!' his mother the queen Ushaia greeted. She stretched her long and colourful but hairy arms outwards to embrace him. She was twice his height and over twice as massive. The Semonite queens were built that way, but the drones were even smaller than himself, a normal size worker. The queen and drone pair had always appeared quite strange when stood side by side, particularly when dancing together in the main hall. At those times she looked like a most beautiful giant with a small colourful dwarf by her side.

'How are you, Mother? I brought you a little present from Tuil. Tuillian jewellery,' he said and handed her the most beautifully inlaid golden case. She opened it and retrieved a most precious diamond necklace. She hugged him again.

'I have been Nomph for such a long time that I feel unnatural in my own body, even after barely three cyclons. They are truly the strangest life-form you can ever imagine and with the most peculiar habits. Habits like eating their own tails when they are left stranded and hungry. Can you imagine that? I so love to be back home. Later during the month, I have to visit Triangulum proper again, but that's another assignment.

'My favourite child, I shall be having a family reception at my winter palace in three days. You must be there. You can take charge of all the lighter duties for your mother. I shall make that fact known to the Duty Chief. After all, you are the only one I can trust to organize a great party. Then you can brief me on all your wanderings, including the strange habits of the Tuillians,' she said.

'Whatever you say, Mother, I don't mind a little light relief, myself. It will make a pleasant change from the intensity of the field. I also enjoy being back home and in such pleasant company,' a diplomatic Lumak replied. Lumak hadn't seen or communicated with his mother for several years, so he wanted closeness, even so, it was part of his culture to always show the greatest respect towards his superiors and that meant maintaining some distance.

'Our lord and master will be present, so we must create a good impression and ensure enjoyable entertainment. That's really why I need your assistance. Those palace goofs will make a mess of things if left to their own desires and you can invite all your friends including off-worlders if you wish,' she said, making him feel quite at home and important. Yet, she always treated him like her little teenage son, despite his mid-thousand plus years. He didn't mind playing along if it made her feel happy, and providing things were kept respectful and dignified. Therefore he always tended to say yes, even though he realised he would suffer dearly before, during and after the party. After all, she was his mother and an Empress Queen in charge of all Duty Queens. One never to be treated lightly or contradicted.

Lumak viewed the recently expanded parts of the city of Lud, with its many new skyscrapers and realized the vast differences between it and ancient cities like Tuz. Then there was the magnificent city of Goh, which was modelled on concepts of natural beauty, with large gardens, avenues and parks.

Presently there were none of the sharp spiky towers, once necessary in the days of the Petan dragons. That was when the giant reptiles raided their cities for food. Their wings frequently got ripped to shreds by those sharp spires, making them plummet to the ground below. At other times they would be impaled and struggle thunderously in vain to set themselves free, while being impaled by even more spikes. Then the drones would descend with sharp knives to extricate their dead bodies from those elevated snares.

In those days the processed meat from those giant reptiles was used to fertilize certain useful fungi. Even their hides were used for capes and footwear. Presently they were cared for as an endangered species, having learnt to cooperate out of necessity.

Since the high wall was built and automatic weapons fitted, they would seldom venture out of their reservations. Yet, unhappy strays sometimes wandered north into the Grey Desert, but they had become lazy over the years and never liked the extreme heat and scarcity of food within those regions. Anyway, why bother with such adventures when they could cultivate their own berries and supply for rich barter. Presently Kanei cities were visited by many Petans on a daily basis for pilgrimage and shopping.

The northern city of Tuz were presently occupied by many Dragon communities, who considered it their home. Their past leader Stikol had made sure they got a good education so they could be integrated in Kanei society.

And how well the Lamphis had coped with all those new technological changes, including his training methods, to the disappointment of the impatient training advisors who would never agree with his ideas on inter-species integration.

While observing the great central tower, Lumak could just spot his mother's town palace close to the river Clyn, with its many flowering gardens in full bloom and the more central violet soft poly lawn. He had played and won many a game on that lawn during his vacations. The moss was specially imported from the northern forest bordering the desert.

'What a beautiful world you are, my Kanaefon, and what an enchanting sunset you exhibit,' he whispered to himself, while observing the deep hues and yellow bands in the distant horizon. The many evening scents carried on the cool breeze aroused his deeper emotions, giving him romantic feelings of glorious wanderings and cosmic wonderment.

The parent star was a class G, twice the size of Sol, our sun, and less than half its age. It and the two large moons could have accounted for the strange pattern of evolution on his world. Not to mention its equally strange surface movements. Nevertheless the cities were built on solid rock and on the most solid continent, so the effects from all those earthquakes and other crustal movements were only moderately felt.

As the sun set he could observe the faint band of light that formed the Osmaron galaxy. The light from that source was as bright as the brightest moon. It expanded in all direction below Kalboron, his globular cluster and reminded him of many a wandering and of missions to come. Life was fragile and due to the immensity of stars some civilizations were always in danger.

Lumak watched several passenger liners and shuttles in the distant horizon, each following different flight paths to places on and off-world. Then he took the nearest elevator just before the star's orange disc disappeared below the distant horizon. At that time the city lights would illuminate to signal the presence of night.

That spot on the ancient tower was his favourite since his first visit to Lud. After that visit the city had become his home.

The panoramic view somehow compensated for his feelings of deep nostalgia for his home-world and gave him a new perspective on life, seeing it from such a high viewpoint.

While there he could think only of beauty and the immensity of the Cosmos, and yet still caring for the tiny specs he could just observe going about their daily duties several hundred metres below. He pondered the thought of ancient Hexolyte bases, and the Javols taking over his globular cluster and the rest of Osmaron. Then the quick death to all his people including their past enemies, the northern giant reptiles or Petan Dragons, and a strange taste entered his mouth-like orifice. A taste of dread and fear that overwhelmed deep within his consciousness. From that moment he would have done anything in his powers to rid the universe of those alien monsters. Yet they brought everyone, even old enemies together for their mutual survival.

'Plato must need my help at this time. If only I knew of the disaster just after it started perhaps I could have done something to assist in the monsters' destruction, but now... it is so late. If only I could send Plato a message through the Mind. Yet, the masters, including Lord Vektron, knows best and part of my present mission is to complete the Omegron Portal for their main evacuation from Andromeda.

'Not even the Hexolytes could have ravaged a complete galaxy within two thousand cyclons (3200 years). What truly rapacious and sadistic monsters, with so little appreciation for others... love or beauty.

'If only the powerful Patriarchs were here with us now to take them on. I wonder how long they would have taken to vanquish that particular enemy? But that was the era when violence and hate predominated our universe in every rank and file. Today, the great rulers believe in the use of less violence to achieve their goals. However, even violence in the form of extreme heat is enjoyed by the Javols and can cause them to increase their numbers by replication. What a strange form of reproduction. They can transform themselves into the forms of almost any creature of an equivalent mass.' He took a deep breath.

'A microid life-form that can duplicate itself in the presence of high energy. They can however be killed by energy starvation or super-hot plasma. What a unique life-form?'

He pondered those realizations as he descended the tower. Then felt the air breaks come on as the almost antique elevator in that ancient tower came to an almost sudden stop. He had observed the absence of any public portals throughout that part of the city and realised their omission was for security.

With the exception of universities and large organizations, portals were used privately with a limited set of codes. Nevertheless they tended to be utilized internally without restrictions in the larger organizations.

He made his way through the bustling crowds and arcades, with their unique signatures and mix of pheromones towards his dwelling in a more peaceful and isolated part of the city. His Shadite's home was well away from his mother's palace and only used by himself and his visiting friends while at home during those brief periods.

When Lumak arrived home that evening he observed a visitor waiting patiently at the entrance to his home. It was not anyone he knew or could identify. He wondered who the Semonite were, but realised he wore a Shadite's robe.

'Lumak! Lumak!' the figure rushed up and embraced him. He reciprocated with a curious hug.

'I am Gemmi...!' the figure cried. Then he stood back to observe her.

'What a beautiful surprise. But you are now a worker like myself?' he commented with curiosity.

'I asked the one called Corfu, the one with many limbs, for your address and he guided me to this place,' Gemmi said.

'He is Lamphy and is in charge of this area of accommodation,' Lumak said. He was sent to me by his father for training and education, but he makes himself at home and keeps things tidy for me.'

'Anyway, I had a choice between queen, worker, soldier and drone, and finally decided to become a worker. That was after I realised the territorial instincts, mating and other complications of a queen. Strictly speaking I could never see myself as a drone and the soldiers are now almost redundant, so here I am. What a complicated culture you lead, my man,' Gemmi said in her usual humorous frame of mind, despite her newly adopted dispositions.

'And your type of life-form is not so hot either. Remember? I used to be one of you myself... Anyway, you could have done a lot worse if you were human,' Lumak replied, equally humorously. It was then that she remembered the skeletons in the Hexolyte caves.

'You are absolutely correct. Anything but those monstrous aliens from Osmaron,' Gemmi replied in jest.

'Have you received your first assignment yet?' Lumak inquired.

'After my full training here, I am to remain for a while to assist in your scientific projects. I have to gain more technical experience, then I shall return to my galaxy on a new project of which I have no knowledge yet,' Gemmi replied, while trying to get the knack of their mode of communication. Semonites used complex guttural noises, pheromones and gestures for that purpose. However, when communicating through technological media, noises and pheromones were enough to relay their meanings. Even so, none of these methods were required with Brain Implants that communicated conceptual thought. At that mental level thoughts were the same for all life.

Lumak allowed her the use of his home during her stay on Kanaefon whenever she was visiting, as he had done for Plato and others.

During the following days they jointly assisted his mother while preparing for the celebrations, which had been most successful. Then he concentrated his efforts towards the Omegron Portal, soon to be left in the hands of Gemmi and his other scientists. She had enough experience with that technology during their previous mission.

Once more his mother, the Empress Queen, reinstated her powers and superiority as Chief Empress. Soon every important queen knew their relevant positions within the hierarchy. During that process younger Queens were promoted, while older queens given council status in their governing chambers. Then her deputies and drones were duly rewarded for their efforts during her absence. Soon many presents were delivered to her palace from the many queens, to show their obligations and cement relationships within the hierarchy. Then she would ceremoniously hand out several jewelled insignia to donate their new status within the empire.

On the day of the celebrations she arrived with her Duty Drone, Comak. They were spectacularly dressed in the finest mallo linen and jewellery. He had been with her since the beginning and was also Lumak's father.

The other dignitaries included The Grand Lord himself as the senior soldier Obe and a few other aliens from neighbouring systems. Several Lamphis could be seen about the palace attending special duties.

Lumak and Gemmi had introduced many new and novel ideas for their entertainment, including a type of electronic music he had learnt while on Tuil. They also taught new forms of dancing to the drones and queens. There were also many new types of beverages including Mosaki and others rich in alcohol. There were a mix of safer drinks for those with a more subdued palate.

The Lamphis musicians performed energetically with a variety of wind driven and strange percussive instruments. They blended together in a symphonious manner to give a multiplicity of rhythms on a strong steady beat. Those replaced the many drums and cymbals previously used during such performances.

The celebrations continued well into the early morning. Everyone in attendance had a most enjoyable time. After the guests had left, his mother thanked him and Gemmi dearly for their contribution and assistance.

'You guys have really made me proud on this occasion. Even our Grand Lord enjoyed the performance. Where did you find such a fantastic cultural variation? I shall inform my chief worker, Somas, to change our complete entertainment regime to this new one,' she said and Lumak nodded his head in approval, but wanted to give credit where it was due.

'Sorry Mother, but it was all Gemmi's doing. She is one of the people I told you about. They have a most exciting culture,' he said.

'You mean to say... Gemmi is Speell and female?' she inquired.

'She is also a new Shadite, Mother,' he replied.

'A brand new Shadite in my palace?

'My son, we must have another great party to celebrate Gemmi's day of passing.' Lumak agreed, but Gemmi was speechless.

'Mother, thank you very much for everything, but sadly we must leave. We have a very important and urgent task to complete,' he said.

He left with Gemmi for the laboratories where he would meet his old colleagues and friends. He introduce them to Gemmi and spent some time cataloguing the progress of their many projects while educating Gemmi on many of their technologies.

Gemmi took a while to learn the use of her new brain implants. It was inserted the day after her arrival. Those worked independently of normal brain functions and worked almost transparently to the corporeal form, even when transposed to another alien life-form. Such implants extended the powers of the brain and included many professions and doctors within its Virtual Worlds. Presently there were many menus in her mind for different operations, some of which worked at the sub-conscious level. Others would perform tasks like complex calculations, even while she was asleep. Most of all it simplified communications with others, particularly with Lumak

Although they hadn't any effect on her core personality and emotions, they enhanced her potentials and memory by over ten times. It was just a matter of getting used to a new appliance and reading the instructions within the help menus in her mind. There were many devices for training in the use of implants and certain types of microids speeded the process.

It was like entering tunnels in a Virtual World within the mind, where one would meet assistants to guide them through a particular task. Once a virtual task was completed within that Virtual World those experiences became part of the real brain.

Although Gemmi was already a brilliant scientist in many fields, she soon became a super genius quite capable of taking over from Lumak.

Being a Shadite, she was well respected by all Semonites. During her brief stay she eagerly trained others and partook in every level of their seemingly strange culture.

CHAPTER 18

The unexpected journey

Time... 1441 CE (over 1000 years after Om-Chopter's voyage)

On the momentous day of the departure by Obe-Chopter into the unknown, the Empress Queen and many important officials were at the docks to greet the crew and wish them kind seas on their voyage. It was to mark the beginning of a new millennium in the lives of both Kanei and Petans since the arrival of the Grand Lord to their world. But mostly to celebrate Obe's sacrifice and Om-Chopter's great voyage.

To all Kanei that momentous act would remind them of the many changes to their world since Obe and Om-Chopter sailed to the Petan lands to fight the dragons. That was a thousand cyclons (1600 years) before, when wars raged and Drones like Calebos hovered over Mytal rock to warn the citizens of Lud of approaching dragons on the westward winds.

Unknown to Aurlsba and Longe, on this new voyage their commander, Lumak, decided to take his own crew along for the ride and some were not Kanei.

'Come on! Come on! Let me through!' growled the massive dragon, while Kanei warriors persisted in preventing his motion towards Obe-Chopter.

'Ah Stikol, there you are! Soldiers, please leave Stikol alone!' Lumak shouted and the large dragon boarded. As he entered her deck the ship gently tilted to one side. Young Stikol was truly massive by Kanei standards. He was in the closest image of his great, great grand father of the same name. The original Stikol was one of Lumak's best friends in times gone by.

'This is quite a reception you have, my Siend,' he said shyly and remained quiet in his place, not wanting to rock the boat by his slightest movement. Then to Aurlsba and Longe's further surprise, a well dressed group of Lamphis officials came on board with Aswal, followed by the Shadite, Gemmi, as a

Semonite Worker. Then there was Lumak's most senior crew from his Black Ship. They included Jamkai, one of Lumak's close relatives and the soldier Miand, in the image of Obe. On this voyage there would be no weapons or indeed active soldiers.

Aurlsba and Longe expected a normal complement of crew on this memorable journey to mark the great voyage of Obe. But even Petan dragons had been allowed on board. The same ones responsible for Obe's death. They soon realized it was not the voyage they had planned, but decided to go along anyway, since Lumak was their closest friend.

On this voyage Lumak was in command and took his position at the helm. This time he was dressed like Obe, in his fine mallo tunic with crimson cape waving in the wind. To Aurlsba and Longe Lumak resembled their Commander Obe on that first faithful voyage a thousand cyclons before. As always, they knew he was the same person in a different life.

Lumak realized he was in his place at last. In his mind he surveyed his past efforts, the unrevealed future with its many twists and turns. Among other things, that voyage also commemorated the enormous changes he had made to his world since his childhood, long after Obe's unfortunate death at the hands of the Petans.

'We have made the modifications as you have commanded, my Siend. But I still cannot understand the reasons for changing the protective nets for your special types or adding the two sets of horizontal fins. Neither do we see the need for placing modified limpet mines on her hull and keel,' Longe said.

'Don't worry my friends, all will be revealed in the fullness of time,' Lumak replied. Then a few official Drones took position on either side of the Empress Queen and she began to speak.

My most beautiful and loving people, this is indeed a great occasion in the history of our world. This voyage today marks a period of incredible changes since the arrival of the Grand Lord to our fortunate planet. May all the races and people of our world live in peace and harmony from this day on.' The mixed crowd cheered.

'Where are we to go on this great venture of yours?' Gemmi asked, but Lumak placed his claws to his face to wipe what appeared to be tear drops from his face. He had become too emotional, particularly when he reflected on his past life and departed friends. Friends he would have liked to join him on that important voyage.

'It's meant to be a surprise. Not even my mother nor the Petan king knows of the route we shall take,' he replied with a cunning grin.

'Mendu, take the controls and get us out of here. You know the course,' Lumak said to his favourite Lamphis.

'Yes, my Siend,' the Lamphy engineer replied telepathically through his implants. There were no oars or Lamphis at the lower decks to drive the boat.

Without warning the protective nets descended on either side of the ship while another fell from the mask to contain them. Suddenly, the whole ship began to glow as she descended into the canal and began to move beneath the waves, to the amazement of all her waiting crowds. Once again she surfaced to say a final farewell on route into the unknown.

'The fusion generators are capable of an output of 6 terra watts. Power enough to vaporize any missile before it even comes close to her hull. Her powerful shields will safely contain her and her crew, and keep water at a safe distance while we are submerged.'

'Really, Commander?' Longe was intrigued by it all.

'Om-Chopter took a perilous route on the surface of land and sea. This time, Obe-Chopter will take a kinder route within land and sea. So people, enjoy the ride,' Lumak said with excitement in his voice.'

'I am impressed, my Siend. This second chopter is as advanced as our times,' Aurlsba commented with disappointment, realizing his commander followed unique plans of his own.

After the Chuz Canal they surfaced and decided to follow the shore.

'Softlands are getting closer to shore. I suppose with our new attachments we can always submerge. But what about Laviatan?' Longe said.

'Nice observation, Commander Longe. I have sent a signal to my Laviatan friend. He says he will only be too happy to accompany us through the rapids, if we would have him along and I said yes,' Lumak replied and Longe and Aurlsba were astonished that Lumak could have such a powerful sea monster in his pocket.

'He is now one of Commander Lumak's pets and I'm sure he wears a control collar,' Gemmi jested and they were awed, but laughed in their Kanei ways.

Not too far away the waters stirred. Six large and powerful tentacles lifted out of the waters and spiralled a sign to Lumak, which he recognised as a gesture of eternal peace. Then the giant's limbs were pulled back beneath the waves.

'My Lord, how did you do that to a god of the deep!' a surprised Stikol commented.

'He is now one of us and can communicate with me as any of you. We see monsters only because we do not speak the same language. When we are able, then we may become as one tribe.

'Many cyclons ago it was my greatest desire and ambition to unify all the most intelligent life and races on our world for the greater good. Today marks the completion of that noble cause.

'Finally, we are able to grasp the main languages of all such life-forms. From henceforth we may communicate with each other at will,' Lumak replied and they were even more surprised.

'My Lord, you are truly the greatest,' Stikol commented.

'You are also as great as your ancient ancestor. I knew that Stikol well. He once saved my life. For that fearless deed, I shall always assist you and yours,' Lumak said and Stikol's face lit up as he blinked his large slitted golden eyes several times in surprise. He had heard the story but always thought it was tribal folklore.

'Sire, we approach the Devils Whirlpool. What am I to do?,' Mendu asked.

'Enter it, and see what happens,' Lumak suggested.
To the dismay of her crew, Obe-Chopter spun around several times and was sucked into the spiral. A large underwater gate opened. She righted herself and flowed with the currents through the tunnel. They were submerged in the great lake of Chobra Cann. Then they surfaced to admire the sights. Lumak pointed to the local cliffs.

'This is where your ancestor saved my life. He was at that time searching for himself as I was.

'You know, he was the very first of your kind to enter our university. After that great accomplishment, your people were never the same. Since that time, you have constructed your great city of Onze. He was the one that initiated its construction.'

'Really, my Lord?' Stikol was amazed by it all.

'You see all those markings including the great dragon carved out of the rock up there? It forms one of our greatest monuments. That is the Stikol that I once knew, with two fishes in his mouth stuck to his teeth and one impaled within his claws. I had this monument carved after his death,' Lumak said and young Stikol showed a tear of sadness and appreciation for his great ancestor; for he was the first to teach his people in the ways of science.

'Mendu, please initiate auxiliary controls,' Lumak said telepathically. Her new telescopic masks contracted into the body of the chopter as she shot out of the lake and towards the northern forest. That forest was known by many as The Ancient Hunts.

Unlike the coal burners of the previous Om-Chopter, this time Obe-Chopter was driven by powerful LPDs that took their energies from nuclear fusion.

Obe-Chopter suddenly swung around. Just ahead was revealed the most expansive and beautiful city of Onze. It was now the main trading city of Petans. Many forms of transport could be seen throughout. On the local neck of the great lake. Its tall buildings extended as far as the high cliffs. The large screen on the chopter displayed the images in vivid colour while the crew were aghast by a great and beautiful spectacle.

'Friends, this is the city Stikol built for his people. It contains every possible leisure activity on our world. At the central square is a monument of great Stikol himself. Earlier today the main square of our own city of Lud was linked to this one, so feel free to visit whenever you wish,' Lumak said, excitedly.

'But we never knew of such changes, or that such a great city ever existed,' Aurlsba said with disappointment.

'Not many had known, my friend. After all, we have always kept our development separate from Petans, fearing some form of backlash from the giants beyond the lake and forest. However, we have always been mutually dependant on each other. Like all others on our beautiful world,' Lumak replied.

Then Obe-Chopter shot up across the 7 mile high wall of the massive Crethian Crater. Dragons could be observed in large elevators being conveyed to and from their homes on the cliff-face. All those homes in the caves were now extensive. The cliffs had been reenforced by massive struts that formed the paths of their transport.

They followed over the Crethian sea and across the wall at the distant end. While high in the air they could just observe the feint outline of a great underwater city. It was the domed city of Mekan. It lay below the ocean of Gibro close to the shore.

This time they entered through heavy locks near the top of the dome. The waters dispersed about the boat. They were taken by a powerful lift to another area at the lower levels.

'Come on people, lets go and meet some friends,' Lumak said, as the side of Obe-Chopter opened and stairs descended.

There waiting were his mother, the Empress Queen Ushaia and the Petan king, Carmedon. Just at the rear were the city mayor, Pyron and many other officials, including Petans and Semonites. His mother had not relished the cramped and bumpy sea voyage and had taken the more dignified portal instead. Therefore she had arrived well ahead of him and his crew.

Lumak went forward to greet them. Then they were taken to the most popular parts of the great Petan city.

'Come on, People. This is only the beginning of our mysterious tour,' he said. His mother, the Empress Queen still knew not the purpose of their journey and followed his course purely out of amusement. Anyway, she saw those moments as a time to reminisce, meet old friends and strengthen political alliances and relationships. This time she hesitated for a while, not relishing the cramped conditions on board Obe-Chopter. However when she arrived there was more than enough room for everyone on the upper deck.

That underwater city had expanded to cover a large part of Gibro and extended towards the shores by transportation tunnels. Unlike the Kanei, Petan dragons were equally as good in water as they were on land. That city contained numerous entertainment venues, recreation centres and gambling casinos. Petans were a jolly lot and enjoyed any type of competition laced with a little gambling. They were also keen drinkers.

They viewed the sites while accompanied by the mayor and many of his officials. The Semonites and Lamphis were amazed by the more vibrant parts of the city and its many facilities, in particular its spectator sports arenas.

'Do we also have secured portal links to this great city,' his mother asked.

'I am sure I gave the order, Mam. But if it is not yet completed it soon will be,' Lumak replied.

'Your son is a guy I shall always have the greatest respect for.' the king said and she smiled in her own way.

When they were finished roaming the city they went toward the dock where Obe-Chopter was parked.

'Mendu, get her ready for interstellar transposition through number 1,' Lumak said and the boat moved towards a sealed room with many large structures, globes and cylinders.

'Initiate transfer to Lyran,' he commanded through his implants and the Lamphy pressed a few buttons. There was a glow that penetrated everything while they found themselves in a similar portal many thousand miles away. They were now on their largest moon overlooking their home world.

'Come and see this most beautiful image of our world. Have a good and long look, for I would like you to always remember her in this way, with her blue waters brown deserts and green forests,' Lumak said, but they couldn't believe that they had travelled to their largest moon in the shortest blink of an eye and were observing beautiful Kanaefon from that most exalted standpoint.

'How in all Kanaefon is this possible?' the mayor exclaimed. The Petan king was amused.

'I am afraid, my son is a super genius. Virtually anything is possible at his hands,' his mother commented with pride.

'I brought everyone here for a very important reason, but before I give you the bad news, I had to show you what we might lose if we are not vigilant and careful. What I am about to tell you involves our whole galaxy and others even far beyond our reach. But first, we should look around this base and acquaint ourselves with the might of our civilization,' he said.

He took them through the main base and showed them the many weapons and powerful generators being developed. There were as many Kanei as there were Petans and even aliens, including a few others he called humans. They could be seen building all types of equipment and weapons, testing and making fine adjustments. There they were as one race working towards a common goal.

'People, from this day you may consider our galaxy to be at war with another. This moon and Ruun are currently used as testbeds for our most destructive weapons. We are also developing a planetary shield. That powerful shield will consist of an array of satellites, soon to be placed in orbit about our world,' he said.

'Are we in serious danger at this time?' Longe asked.

'Yes, we are. However, I think we should visit the cafeteria and take some refreshments before I give you the bad news,' he said and they nervously agreed.

They had some delightful refreshments while many came over to pay homage and show respect to their honourable sovereigns and Lumak. Then Lumak took the group back to the large viewing platform where they could have another close view of their beautiful world.

'What I am to show you now must go no further. This information is important so that you may always be conscious of this danger and take the necessary actions without giving too much away to our public until the appropriate time. The problem that faces us will be apparent in about 500 cyclons (800 years) from now,' he said and they were astounded and shocked.

Lumak transformed into his Shadite's form before their eyes. Then he withdrew a small black box from his cloak pocket and began to display the images of death and destruction on a nearby wall.

'This recording is to do with the invasion of my friend Plato's world by the evil Javols in ancient times.'

The images displayed were gory. The predatory aliens tended to decapitate their human and other animal prey in the most gruesome ways before consuming them. They resembled the most hideous monsters and could change their form at will. They could even form wings and fly like birds to select their next prey. The Nano-bot Javols were truly formidable and could not be killed by even their most advanced weapons. Even heat energy caused them to multiply in greater number.

'How ghastly! Did the slaughter of all these hu...hu... mans really take place?' his unhappy and disturbed mother inquired.

'Yes, Mother! I'm afraid so, and they are presently approaching our galaxy with the sole purpose of doing the same to us. I recovered this recording from the Shadite Plato.

'Because of this dreadful situation, I am to visit distant worlds in this galaxy and shall be away from you for many cyclons. Other worlds and civilizations must be made aware of the dangers and become advanced enough to cope when the time comes. So I am to show them the way,' he said.

After the shocking news they were like changed people. This time Lumak took the most direct route to his city through a large underground portal.

Obe-Chopter was subsequently placed in the same large monument as Om-Chopter. Both old and new chopters standing side by side to commemorate two significant occasions. The first one signalled the beginning of a new technological age and lasting peace with Petan dragons while Obe-Chopter signified the initiation of war with an alien race called Javols.

The following day Lumak took Gemmi to see the sights of his favourite city of Lud. Then they would visit the great scientific buildings to observe progress on other essential technologies that would be used for the survival of our galaxies.

CHAPTER 19

The laboratory

Lumak was greeted by their senior scientist, Kodan, who subsequently took him and Gemmi to level five of the main security building. That semi-isolated area was mainly used for the storage of military and other highly sensitive equipment, and was therefore at the highest security levels.

'We have completed the control modules and only recently received the globes from Zixc. Now it's just a matter of coupling and connecting them to the control array. Then preliminary testing can commence.'

'That was quick!. You run a very efficient crew!' Lumak replied.

'Would you like to observe the globes? They are stored in here,' Kodan said, while they walked through the thick metallic wall as if it did not exist.

'There are no doors at this level. Just thick solid metallic walls. Only Shadites and seniors are allowed at this level. All relevant scientists are scanned by the master transposer, which can phase their bodies to the necessary angle, making them somewhat differently displaced to normally vectored matter, but at a precise angle of phasure. By so doing, we can walk through any material object as if it wasn't there. However, outsiders without the special belt and control bangle will not get far, and that is assuming they were accepted by the initial scanners,' he said, enthusiastically, little realizing it was also Lumak's profession, as one of the most brilliant scientists of his time.

'I appreciate and applaud your security arrangements in my absence and assume all your new personnel are more thoroughly screened and vetted as well?' Lumak inquired, realizing how well his people had adapted to his new security measures in the wake of the Javols invasion of Osmaron.

'Yes, my Siend, they are drawn from known Kanei families and at a young age.'

'We must always be extra vigilant!' Lumak stressed. Since

Kanei were virtually crimeless, he could only be thinking of the Javols invasion many years hence.

'The Zixc were unable to supply us with their engineers because of extreme climatic differences between our two worlds. They consider any world with a surface temperature below three hundred and fifty degrees centigrade, and a corresponding lack of chlorine, to be a very poisonous ice box. But their instructions were quite comprehensive once we had translated them into Kanei,' he replied.

'Did you communicate with Stiphorus? He is our only Zixc Shadite,' Lumak inquired.

'Yes, my Siend, we have on occasion. However, several times I would have liked him to transpose into our form. That would have saved us much time questioning their ideas and incorrectly translating their meanings, which slowed the project. Anyway, we have since improved communication with them. Any secured item can now be triple coded and placed on a polarized beam,' Kodan said.

They soon entered the large storage room where the spheres were stored.

'Are they in here?' Gemmi asked with astonishment.

'We had problems getting them this far. They must weigh about 12 crons (about three tonnes) each and we could not use lifting robots. However we had them enclosed and gently rolled through the walls. Although they resisted our initial attempts due to a smaller phasure displacement, we persevered at a very slow pace. It took us three days in all to get them this far.'

'Good job!'

'Here they are in all their glory,' Kodan said, while drawing the reflective curtain sideways.

'They are separated by a thick block of neutral material. Both emanate a rainbow of light in opposite directions. We have to assemble them in order to have them fully tested. Then we are to carefully take them apart and have each part packed and crated for dispatch by a specially fitted intergalactic ship.

'Yes! The ship is now in Andromeda, ready and waiting for your completion,' Lumak replied and Kodan was intrigued but surprised.

'Final testing is to be carried out by the scientists at their respective points of arrival,' Kodan said. Gemmi was almost hypnotised by the strange emanations from the spheres which were much more powerful than the one she had assisted Lumak with during the evacuation of the Feloween. The Omegron Portal was intergalactic in range and the most powerful portal they had ever engineered.

'My Siend, these are of incredible power and must surely be of galactic range,' she commented, in her Worker's body.

'They are unique in many respects. Yet, the main design is based on the one we built together,' he replied and she was pleased her efforts had assisted in some small way.

'I must study every bit of the Zixc data on those spheres and also want your schematics on the electronics and ancillaries,' Lumak said. The three walked towards the larger laboratory where many engineers and scientists could be seen sat at long benches assembling and testing the subassemblies.

The moment Lumak entered they stood and bowed. He was well respected by all and many considered him to be their saint and hero.

While they walked through, Lumak and Gemmi were introduced to each in turn.

'From what I have observed, you are way ahead of schedule. I must commend you on a job well done and place your name for suitable promotion,' Lumak said. Lumak also realised that most of the design of the Omegron Portal was based on his own initial long range interstellar portal, but the intricate engineering was of Zixc and most of the more advanced knowledge in the strange materials had been gained from the Plorans.

'I realised the urgency of the situation. You and our Grand Lord was very considerate on my behalf, by allowing me this senior position, but I did nothing to warrant a promotion,' Kodan replied, humbly.

'I know that, and it was given under my recommendation. However, I see here a smooth working system, which to me reflects good leadership,' Lumak replied.

Kodan was as active and keen as Lumak when he was his age,

which in Kodan's case was a mere hundred and thirty cyclons, and Lumak wondered whether he was Shadite material. He made a mental note in Kodan's case and they walked towards the data library where he could assimilate all project blueprints and instructions directly into their implants for future analysis. He and Gemmi then left the building.

The following day he was summoned by the Grand Lord unto the topmost floor of the massive globe's building. He sat behind a large desk and on the desk in front of him was a black box with the special insignia.

'Your special cloak has arrived. Please take it when you leave. You should find a remote and unpopulated area on this world where you may test its many features. While worn, all instructions are automatic through your implants. With its new inbuilt devices, even the functions of your belt are not necessary. However, the belt is still useful as a container for your small items and gadgets,' he said.

Lumak kissed his old cloak goodbye and slowly handed it over with sadness in his features. It was the loss of an old friend with whom he had been through so much over the years, and the Grand Lord observed his sense of loss.

'This first cloak of yours will be held in your own compartment within the Mind to posterity,' he said, while taking the folded garment from Lumak. This knowledge of his old cloak's survival made him feel a million times better.

The Grand Lord had realised how attached Lumak had become to that cloak, but he also knew it was time for a change in his life for all his years of unquestionable service.

'I am also to make you Grade 1 for your years of unblemished service to the Greater Purpose. You have a knack for doing the correct and the impossible, so that makes you one of my most important Shadites. This cloak can only be worn by Grade 1 Shadites and you are the first and only one,' he said, while handing the box to him.

'Thank you, My Lord,' he replied, but couldn't say any more, as words failed him. Lumak was overwhelmed by excitement. The loss he felt for his old cloak soon dissipated when he had a sudden urge to embrace The Grand Lord, but instead bowed a second time in humility.

'My eternal thanks and unswerving devotion to you, my most gracious Lord,' he said. In the image of Obe the Grand Lord place his clenched right fist on his heart in Shadite salutation and Lumak did likewise. Although equivalent to a human handshake, this was more a sense of appreciation felt by lord and servant.

'*You are to prepare yourself for your next mission on the near-human world of Suk-Prime. Most of the relevant information has been entered in the Mind for your briefing,*' he said and Lumak left.

Part 3

A Lost People

CHAPTER 20

Lumak's 10th mission

Earth-Time... 1942 CE... about 100 years before
their present time, which is 2041 CE.

Once again Lumak was summoned by the Grand Lord for a briefing before his next mission.

'Sut, my negligent past catches up with me.

Do you know the reason why your Shadite order was formed?'

'I suppose it was primarily created to aid in the survival of cosmic life, by the prediction and prevention of global catastrophes, and by assisting in the evacuation of such worlds. But since that time other items have been added to the list... like assisting endangered species whenever we can. Finally, but not of lesser importance, is our desire and goal to promote and improve cosmic culture by aligning all intelligent life within the Greater Purpose for the common-good. The latter course is long-term and may take us many aeons toward our final goal,' Lumak replied.

'The word "Shadite" was not my own, you know. It was given to Zorak Stiphorus - one of my first Shadites - by his people and the name stuck. He is chlorine based and from a very hot and alien environment. It's because of those limitations that you have never met him and neither has he been able to take a more active part in the service. Nevertheless, there are many chlorine based worlds and his assignments have been limited to those. All such worlds are considered extremely hostile to all carbon-based oxygen breathers.

'Transformation into your type (carbon based) has always been a great problem for him. It is not just form that bothers him, but the much lower temperatures and the air we breathe. Those factors have limited his assignments only to similar worlds within Seth that are few and far. However, there are quite enough of such worlds within our universe and he fulfills a great need for

the common-good. Our scientists are still working on the problem and should have a solution before long.

'Anyway, on his world is a very superior life-form called the Akon. They are only seen occasionally by certain gifted members during their fertility rituals and special ceremonies.

'The Akon is really an ancient species or sect that had since departed the material plane to inhabit a higher dimension, but have decided to retain a caring link with their original world. They are nicknamed Pa-Shadites. Pa is the acronym for "fathers of mercy" and Shadite for "out of the shadows". They tended to appear to his people - considered a lower species - in order to assist them in times of disaster and would suddenly appear at such times from any available shadow. As if out of darkness.

'When he returned to his world, after his confirmation as a Grade 3 Shadite, they thought he was an Akon because of the Black Cloak. It cast the darkest shadows and that is how the name Shadite began. So now, you know how your order began, about five thousand cyclons ago. And now, our organisation has become large enough to assist galaxies. However, I started the Shadites much too late to have effectively assisted many promising civilizations from major catastrophes throughout our universe of Seth. Further, I had to wait until your organization grew powerful enough to effectively assist those in trouble.

'My purpose in giving you this historical lesson, most of which you already know, is to stress an important point. The Ghol Wanderers, under their ruthless leader Zahkan, were once themselves an endangered species. That was more than 4000 cyclons (6400 years) ago when they were caught up in the throws of their exploding parent star.

'They saw the nova coming and had several centuries in which to prepare their long space exodus into the unknown. They were at that time a lone civilization, with no prior knowledge of any other alien intelligence or culture within our galaxy. None existed within their remote and sparsely populated regions of space.

'Anyway, they constructed one hundred and forty-three large ships or arks for the unknown journey, each holding an average of seventy eight-thousand passengers and other lower life-forms.

'*Most life-forms were selected in pairs along with genetic material, with the exception of those required for sustenance and smaller types that could be suspended. They had constructed many self-sustaining biological farms on each arc and knew their present population would never live to set eyes on that new world, despite a lifespan of more than 100 cyclons (160 years).*

'*You see, their ships were larger and more laden than our black maulers and were fitted with basic LPD drives, not too unlike those on our slow survey ships. Anyway, they decided to travel from their system towards a relatively denser part of Osmaron. By so doing, there would have been a much higher chance of finding a suitable world for resettlement. It has taken their future generations more than 4000 cyclons in making that trip and at long last they have arrived in such a system, but sadly, within an already populated region and one populated by an advanced civilization.*

'*Can you imagine how they may have felt, having travelled for generations through the cosmic void, cramped in accommodation, continually rationed and starved of most of their previous cultures, to suddenly find a watering hole in the middle of that almost infinite desert of interstellar space?*'

'I can well imagine how they felt... full of happiness and on the other hand, desperation in locating urgently any required supplies. It must have been an incredible journey,' Lumak replied.

'*Well, their trip was not a pleasant one. Out of all the ships that left their home worlds, only seventy-six survived that voyage and even that number signified an incredible survival rate when one considered the heavy odds stacked against them.*

'*Every ship within that convoy had to remain with the group. If anyone had a major problem, it would have been left behind to fend for itself. A major power failure or drive problem would have meant the eventual loss of more than seventy-thousand souls.*

'*Nevertheless despite all those setbacks they persevered and have finally arrived within the system we call Trinus.*

'*Your next mission will take you to that system as my ambassador. You are to seek them out and make reparations to them for past deprivations. Find them a young and pleasant world on which to settle and most of all, stop their present warring with the Moksai on Py-Renus. After all, we don't want their race to be completely obliterated by the emperors fleet from Suk-Prime, do we? Not after all their unfortunate experiences and past tribulations.*

'*You must visit the Emperor Tukol of that system and explain the situation to him. He has been known to be reasonable on occasion and might give you time to discuss the matter with their leaders and arrange a truce. They have caused much damage to the Py-Renus world. Therefore it will require firm negotiations on your part. Here, my son, a subtle skill in politics will be required to satisfy both warring factions.*

'*In any event, you are now a Grade One Shadite. That means the Mind will always be available to you from henceforth, so use its facilities freely.*

'*Surveillance microids have been dispatched to both regions by Lord Vektron. Your implants will be updated before your departure. God speed.*' Grand Lord Gerra's figure faded away and Lumak immediately left to prepare for his next mission.

CHAPTER 21

Trinus Aradnii

After parking their many large ships and arks in orbit about a local dead world they prepared themselves for a prolonged military campaign against all populated stellar systems within that volume of space. They were desperate to replenish their supplies and saw no future in negotiation or barter when they had so little to give.

The hordes of wandering space barbarians entered the three systems forming Trinus Aradnii in large voyagers and battleships. They repelled all initial attacks with heavy personal shielding and a crude type of hand-held plasma gun they had developed for such missions. Then they landed their mobile containers that were filled with many space bikers and began plundering and looting the Moksai. Their populations were unprepared for such an attack and unable to repel their quantities, even with the aid of many well trained imperial soldiers that were stationed there.

Having travelled for so many generations across empty space, the hardships of that voyage had transformed a previously cultured people into basic barbaric savages, with little thought for anyone or anything not of their own kind. After their initial assault, they had taken almost every kind of animal and crop for food, including some of the Moksai.

Having consumed some of their own kind during the worst parts of their voyage, many had become cannibals for want of choice, drawing lots for such difficult measures when times were hard. Yet, they only took what they required to replenish their supplies and left as swiftly as they had appeared, to carry out more plundering and pillaging elsewhere, as and when the need arose.

They were of the opinion that they would never be allowed to settle on any of those already populated systems and moved ever onwards. Their victims gave them the name Ghols or Sta-Setti Wanderers but were soon considered by many to be wandering space pirates with the sole aim to plunder and steal. Capturing and sacking ships were yet another of their opportunistic ventures.

They had replenished their supplies for immediate needs, but had to take on surplus provisions for their long voyage ahead. They were to find a suitable and yet unknown world somewhere within reach. However that was not all; they had to assemble suitable space docks for repairing and refurbishing most of their old and failing ships and equipment. Therefore, they had to capture the most advanced world of Suk-Prime and use its people and their technologies to assist in those replenishments and repairs.

After the repairs were completed, they would take as much as they could by way of fuel, food and any other items required to relieve their boredom on their long voyage to an unknown destination.

After arrival within the system of Suk-Prime, some of their small ancillary voyagers were destroyed by the Imperial Fleet, but many of the survivors escaped in smaller ships and containers to several planets and moons within that system. Once they were settled they decided to take revenge and wage a war of attrition against the imperial soldiers.

Emperor Tukol soon made it known by H-Wave to many advanced civilizations within Osmaron of his dia plight and offered to pay a good price in whatever currency for any assistance rendered in ridding his system of those barbarians. In a short time many worlds with a similar technology had received his broadcast for help.

Suk-Prime was a most beautiful planet. Like Earth, it was similarly disposed about its star with three smaller satellites. The largest named Tult, was only slightly smaller than our Moon. The other two were less than fifty miles across their widest parts and far too small to affect the larger world below. Therefore, its weather pattern was very stable and remained that way since recorded history. Those suitable conditions gave rise to many reptilian, mammalian, flying creatures like birds and insect species within varying habitats throughout the world, in much the same way as it was on Earth.

There were two habitable worlds within the system that orbited their parent star on either side of Suk-Prime. Those were used for production, science and settlement since its inhabitants had discovered space technology. It was after that time that they began to spread their wings outwards to engulf the Py-Renus and Tuil-Tre systems within the same constellation. Being near Class 3 technologically, they were quite capable of destroying the pirate's fleet, but not being a warlike race were unable to complete those measures in time.

MOKSAI

The Moksai on Py-renus were a small furry creature about one point five metres tall, steeped in culture, tradition and highly intelligent, but peaceful. Having acquired much knowledge of science, mathematics and advanced technologies were highly creative. They were an experimental species that gained much pleasure from such activities and tried to learn as much as they could about the universe by models, games and experimentation.

It was a way of life that had amused them over the centuries, with its many competitions and financial rewards and gains. They benefited greatly from their chosen way of life and could always modify or train many of the lower life-forms for manual duties in their homes and palaces as and when required.

Seeing their great potentials, they were soon recruited by the near human Sulti of Suk-Prime to play an active role in the Empire as scientists and in other advanced professions. All such enticement by the Empire was promoted under the pretence of preserving their own ways of life, symbolised by the military might of the Empire and its willingness to freely assist and protect all its members.

At that time the empire had enough might to protect all her friendly systems and allies from any type of invasion. With such power and free enterprise everyone would gain and be able to protect their way of life in perpetuity. It was then a form of democracy with representatives taken from all systems concerned.

However, the Treil of Tuil-Tre were not so easily won over.

They were tough reptiles used to living on a watery world with little habitation within its mainly desert regions that had formed the land masses. That world could never have been enticing to humans, since most of its life roamed throughout its large oceans. Yet, the Treil had found a niche for themselves near the shores and there formed their civilizations. They were truly massive by human standards, at an average of three metres in height when standing and extraordinarily strong, but not as highly intelligent as the Sulti or Moksai.

They were weary of the Sulti at first, with their strange equipment and technologies. However when they were shown the efficiency of hunting fish with specially equipped ships and machines, they were soon convinced that technology was an asset. Further, they were never compelled by the humans to acquire such technologies. Some just couldn't refuse once other local tribes had acquired them and became highly competitive and wealthy within a short time.

There was also a large export market waiting on Suk-Prime and elsewhere, with lots of wealth for all. Hence, it was not long before Tuil-Tre became the fishing and fish-processing world of the Empire, thus becoming highly wealthy and popular in the process.

In time, all three stellar systems became mutually dependant on each other with everything to gain by that attachment.

The Sulti humans needed the clever furry Moksai scientists from Py-renus and the Moksai, their protection. The Treil needed the technologies and protection of Suk-Prime, created by the brilliant Moksai and both the Sulti and Moksai their fish and other food products.

That was many centuries ago and now the enormous military might of the empire was no more. Since there was no one left to wage war against, the great fleets of the past had been disbanded and turned into scrap metal for recycling into domestic appliances. Anyway, why would anyone maintain such an expensive and redundant force when it was no longer necessary.

Their civilizations had functioned in that orderly manner for more than a thousand years until the arrival of the strange wondering pirates. They had surprised even the few remaining Emperor's battle cruisers, while tearing apart large areas of Py-Renus. Pillaging as they pleased, to leave behind a partly wrecked society. Because of its more inhuman environment, Tuil-Tre was barely missed. They had instead gone on to the jewel in the crown; namely Suk-Prime, to reap more havoc and destruction on the imperial world.

Suk-Prime was the seat of government for all three systems. Each world had its own ministers to fight for its demands. The Moksai and Treil also had cities on Suk-Prime, built to their specifications while propagating their own cultures. Despite their differences there were always free movement among the different species.

Primas, was the main city and seat of government for the Sux Empire. Their empire expanded from that world to five other stellar systems and occupied a volume of just less than one thousand cubic tronecs - one tronec being the measure in distance of about one light year.

Although humanoid, they had large ears and eyes, powerful arms and legs with virtually no body hair. Yet, they wore much clothes and articles of adornment including fashionable headgear.

The present emperor was Cran Tukol Sullman V, now the fifth in line since his great ancestor Ul Sullman I, who had brought the systems together. Tukol as he was usually called, had the responsibility to maintain the status-quo.

He was educated in the knowledge of that time, not cruel nor warlike but always trying to resolve negative issues by diplomacy and discussion, never by confrontation. That was the way he was brought up and trained by his father and later his political advisors. He preferred always to reason first. In his opinion war was wasteful, to be always a last and final resort. That course was to be taken after every stone had been unturned and only when there was no other choice.

He read the report twice, moved his large right ear then his left, before turning around to face the messenger.

'This must be a mistake! A hoax? Someone's idea of a joke?' He eyed the document for a while. Then placed it in his breast pocket and spoke to his secretary.

'Do you think it's for real, Sontral? Do you?'

'Your majesty!' he agreed with a positive nod.

'In that case, from where could they have come? Get the war minister in here immediately and arrange the war council to discuss this crisis!' he barked. Before long another report was received from Py-Renus while the military council was in session.

'Another urgent message your imperial highness.' Another uniformed messenger informed.

'Read it!' the king commanded, and the female soldier took her position and stood at attention.

'Most of our major installations on Py-Renus have been destroyed. Our food and other essential stores have been systematically looted and pillaged. Many of our young children have been taken, we presume also for food. They have since left our world and are moving towards your system. We require urgent assistance if we are to survive this onslaught.' She read the note with sadness.

'What say you, members of my war council? We never had a war during our lifetimes and are ill-trained in such savagery. But if we have to fight for our own survival, we shall fight!' Tukol said. One of the Moksai leaders stood up to say his bit, but with sadness for what had befell his home world.

'We have become far too docile to confront such savages on equal terms. Our armies are untrained in the more subtler arts of warfare. Our few remaining robot ships will have to be reprogrammed and refitted for a sustained battle and that aspect alone will take us many weeks. I am afraid by then they will surely be knocking at our door. We need mercenary fighters from beyond our worlds. Warriors with advanced weapons that will fight for payment and not ask any questions. But they must remain loyal to us until this war is over; because we are useless incompetents at such affairs.' Then he promptly sat in his high seat.

Mercenaries loyal to us!' Tukol yelled.

'I don't think such mercenaries will be bothered with loyalties. Although we hold the purse strings, we shall not be in a position to command them. They have been trained in their own ways of battle and will continue that way. If we choose this course, we must be prepared for their independent actions. Providing of course, they remain loyal to us and are not pirates and pillagers themselves. Then we shall be in a bigger mess,' A Sulti minister said and sat down.

'Loyalty! Loyalty! If we are conquered before they arrive, we shall not hold any purse strings!' A senior Treil, Gorom said.

Once again the Moksai minister stood up to speak.

'I realize those possibilities, but we now have little choice in the matter, and the other risks far outweighs these smaller dangers and are in our favour,' he said and sat down.

'At least, we have little to lose by asking for assistance. Who knows who might come to our aid,' Gorom replied.

'We agree with minister Pulsai's suggestion and are willing to pay five billion trebits towards a war fund, if it means getting those barbarians out of our systems and returning our worlds back to normality. We shall also help to rebuild Py-Renus after they have gone. So there!' barked a young wealthy Treil called Banan. He towered above most of the others from his special seat at the rear.

'Shall we put, "mercenary assistance" to the vote, comrades?' cried Tukol, the emperor king, as all hands went up.

'Anymore ideas, anyone?' he added, but everyone remained silent in anticipation of worse to come.

'In that case, consider this meeting adjourned for now. I shall ask my secretary to arrange the necessary H-Wave transmission. I sincerely hope and pray that someone out there comes to our assistance before the pirates' arrival here and begin taking our world apart as they have done with Py-Renus,' he said, with foreboding in his voice.

The Ghol vandals arrived in their system within their main lunar month and attacked Suk-Prime with everything they could unleash, but the highly screened and fortified city held and would continue holding for many months. Nevertheless, the Ghol pirates were very resourceful and well fortified. They were previously from a very knowledgeable race and had developed many advanced weapons, including portals that were unknown in that part of Osmaron. Further, the Ghols had little respect for life and would sometimes fight to the last man. At other times they would willingly die biting their bombs on suicide missions. Those concepts were too alien and brutal for any of their opponents to have even contemplated; for they had always valued life above all things.

The Ghol had dug in on their smallest continent and from there mounted several assaults against installations on other parts of their world, slowly weakening their infrastructure and finally their resolve. However the powerful H-Wave transmitters on their moons were still operational, so a small group of soldiers sneaked through the enemy lines to program the main computer. They fed a recording with many interstellar languages.

As the moons orbited their world, so did the powerful transmitters change the direction of the message, covering almost every part of space. Yet, the Ghol pirates had no idea of the transmission and neither were they familiar with the science of H-Wave communication.

Several of those transmissions soon reached other distant stellar systems and were ignored by many. That was until they were detected and analysed by the Polokan system. King Olav of Polok 2 knew the might of his mercenary warriors, combined with advanced Lodorian technology. He also realized the high rewards offered for such assistance and could not resist such an invitation for adventure.

CHAPTER 22

On Polok II - Beyond Fyle

King Olav of Polok II had been through several civil wars. The last one ended just three years ago. He was a king most formidable in battle with a personal army of loyal and skilful warriors. Many of whom had been bruised and scarred by past warlike endeavours. Those battle hardened veterans would face virtually any challenge, even enter into the fiery bowels of hell for a suitable reward with their king. They had been through many dangers together and felt more like a family of brothers.

After their recent vicious and savage civil war the opposition leaders were summarily executed in public. Subsequently the whole planet and its many clans were made to unify under a single government and ruler. Although Olav was a king from an ancient royal dynasty, he had taken the reins more like a dictator, imposing many socialist restrictions on his subjects. As a result many of his people were unhappy with their somewhat lesser freedoms than before.

The military were similarly disposed against his rule and would take power given the least opportunity. Nevertheless they had been through much bloodshed and turbulence over recent years and relished a change for peace. He had now to gain their favour or suffer the same faith as his predecessors and opponents. Nevertheless because of his wealth he had accumulated many friends in high places that wanted to retain the status quo currently in their favour. Then there were the more advanced Lodorians in a nearby stellar system wanting more trade concessions for technological assistance.

Despite all the political turmoil in that system, the Lodorians knew king Olav well and saw him as trustworthy and a man of his word. Even so, all such political troubles and unrest annoyed the more advanced Lodorians and tended to affect the flow of trade between their systems, so they tried to maintain the status quo as best they could.

'Sire. We have received a strange interstellar communication!' The female officer transmitted the information directly through his brain implants.

'We appeal to all civilizations for assistance in fighting a large fleet of space pirates. One of our worlds have been laid waste. Our main world is currently under attack. We shall pay for military assistance in any currency or material request. Please join urgently to assist us in defeating these unwelcomed pirates...'

'Is that the complete message?'

'Yes, Sire. This is a recurring segment stacked on a bank of thirty two most commonly known interstellar languages. The transmission fluctuates on a twenty-five-day cycle. Perhaps due to the rotational period of the moon on which it is sited.'

'How long will it take a Lodorian vessel to get there?' he asked, with excitement.

'A class five will take three weeks, Sire.'

'And with a full crew of warriors?'

'Just under six, Sire.'

'Thank you!' he said, sarcastically, while she remained at attention.

'Well, they have asked for our help and they shall have it. I can take a small fleet with many of my best warriors to assist an interstellar neighbour in trouble. My wife can take over in my absence. She poses no threat to our politicians and is very much liked by the people. Anyway, if I am successful, my reputation will enhance my popularity with my council and more firmly establish my position among my piers.' He mumbled those last few words to himself with glee and grin.

'Send an urgent message to Lodor requesting sixteen class five frigates. Explain our reasons and tell them they are to be fitted with their latest weapons of mass destruction!' he barked and she left to complete his orders.

King Olav gave a speech to his people about his intentions to assist a world in distress from invading space pirates, that could reach their system eventually if not stopped. Then he called their parliament together and gave another speech about leaving his wife in control during his absence. Finally he said goodbye to his wife and teenage son, Malik, before departing their world.

He was on his way with sixteen class five frigates. Each containing one hundred and twenty-eight of his most loyal and well-seasoned veterans. They were on-route to the distressed system in question. However while in deep space they had an ominous visitor.

'We have received a distress call, Sire. It is from that object shown on the screen. I don't think we should capture it until we are sure of its intentions and origin. It could be booby-trapped... even a means to slow our progress and attack us,' their captain, Noris, advised.

'What do you think it is?' king Olav inquired, overwhelmed by curiosity.

'It appears to be a discarded cloak, with some type of transmitter attached, but the distress communication is fluent in our language. No one in this remote region of space can have such intricate knowledge of us, Sire.'

'Does the cloak have someone in it?' the king again asked sarcastically.

'No mass has been detected that can account for a suitable size, Sire, and the cloak has been detected only by its lack of radiation. Yet it has the form of an average size human cloak. What shall we do, my Sire?'

'We are to remain shielded and go to red alert, I suppose. Tell number five to take the object on board and distance themselves from us. It can be stored within one of their secured containers. Its beam seems to have been aimed at us and it has not transmitted to any other neighbouring vessel, so it doesn't have to be a rogue,' the king said, still overwhelmed with curiosity, but finding the whole episode to be quite comical.

The black cloak was soon taken on board and placed within a secured area on number-five ship and the container placed under guard until cleared by security.

When the containment unit was subsequently checked, the

object had vanished.

'Search every atom of your ship. This object must be found before we arrive within the system we now approach,' the king ordered, this time being a lot more serious.

It was not long before Lumak transposed into number-one-ship and floated through the control cabin's wall. The crew in that part of the ship froze in their steps as he gradually faded into a black cloak and shook the hood back to reveal a pallid human face of their type that spoke in their own language.

'I am very sorry, Gentlemen, for this intrusion, but I am also a traveller to the system you now approach. I am on a very important mission for the Grand Lord of this part of our universe. However, may I formally introduce myself to you, then I can explain the situation as best I can.

'Who in Hell are you! And what do you want!' Olav yelled. He always abhorred stowaways and strangers that trespassed on board his ships. Not to mention those causing his delay on urgent missions.

'I am Lumak, Shadite, recently from Kalboron. My task is to find the invaders a suitable world of their own on which to settle. One that is unpopulated by advanced life and one not within the local systems ahead. Hence, we are to stop the war and prevent any further bloodshed. Do not be worried about payment. You will be richly rewarded by those concerned, for you follow a just and honest course,' Lumak said, calmly.

'That is all very well and good, Stranger, but how do we know you are not one of the vermin, sent to give us misleading information or even lead us astray and take the prize for yourself. Any such talk of saving an enemy is tantamount to betrayal and treachery,' the king said, still eyeing the strange aberration critically, but equally amused by his words and attitude.

'If I was what you say, would they not have already gained the universe by such powers. Even the ability to curve space and appear anywhere as if at once,' Lumak replied.

'I don't know too much of what you say. Yet, you have the strange knack to transcend matter as if it was not there... among other things. In that case I suppose you must be superior, but as for a representative of... a supreme being in charge of our universe? That is another matter altogether. Since we are unable to hold on to you, I suppose that places you in a position of superiority.'

Lumak remained stationery and allowed Olav to get used to the idea of his person.

'Ok, but I'm not a savage pirate and I'm sure you could use my assistance on this mission,' he said.

'In that case, I shall take a big risk and accept you for what you say you are, namely; one trying to assist both parties at war to find a peaceful compromise. Even so, perhaps you could assist us to win on the side of the natives, for the law is on their side,' the king said, in an attempt to recruit Lumak to his side. Olav always made the most with what he had at his disposal.

'My powers can only be used to assist life and never to destroy. Else, I would not be here having this conversation with you,' Lumak replied.

'You look very human. Even a little like my own son. So you can't be my enemy. I shall take you along as far as we go, then you may continue with your own mission of mercy, if you so wish. We, on the other hand, shall continue with our mission, which is to rid the target system of the invaders. Since they have done much irreparable damage, from recent communication. But you must be my guest in the mean time,' the king insisted.

'Perhaps we can work out some strategy together to our mutual advantage... since you are only here for reward?' Lumak said, turning the conversation around to get the king on his side for a change.

'We can make many compromises on any decisions in our mutual favour,' the king replied with a broad smile realizing Lumak's ploy, and Lumak was intrigued by his cunning and daring.

'Then, that will be most satisfactory, King Olav. And may I take this opportunity in thanking you for your patience and indulgence in my rather unorthodox methods in entering your ship,' Lumak replied humbly and King Olav burst into laughter.

'Ha! Ha! Ha! Ha! In that case, I shall take you up on your offer of military assistance, should you have any to offer; for I wish a speedy resolution to this terrible situation,' Olav said and Lumak smiled and bowed his head to agree, if such actions were going to save lives.

CHAPTER 23

Moon Base

Slowly and stealthily they approached the stellar system with radiation absorption shields at full power and automatic weapons on alert.

'The darkest face of their moon seems to be the safest place for our future base. Surveillance drones can then be placed at its terminator, just beyond range of their line-of-sight scanners. Although partially concealed, we shall have a clear view of the world beneath,' Lumak said, while king Olav listened to his advice.

'Control, please find an optimum survival scenario for our immediate needs,' the king said, temporarily ignoring Lumak's comments. He knew the Lodorian designed battle-computer was much better than the human brain in making such judgements. After having assessed the situation, the powerful and super intelligent computer gave its assessment.

'A base on the less prominent face of its largest moon and fixed observation probes suitably positioned to orbit just within range of the visible surface,' the operator replied, after receiving the information from the war computer.

'Very well, Lumak. You have a knack for finding solutions in such situations and were even quicker than my computer in assessing the correct course of action in a tricky situation like this. However, I still have the problem of visiting the ruler of this system to make our presence known. Any communication or movement through their atmosphere could give our position away.'

'Please, King Olav, first things first. I shall visit the emperor for you in due course, but let us first build a base on the moon. Then we can get the warriors together and show you a way to win the war within one week. I know of their weakness, strengths and desires. For that information and assistance, I shall require you to save as many lives as possible and also the option for me to lead the aggressors away from this system to another, should the need arise. Their leader must also be saved, for they will do little without his commands,' Lumak said.

'If we are to win this war, with a minimum loss of life on either side, I shall agree to your terms. For it is not my world they have ruined. But that is, providing the emperor and the leaders of these systems agree to your requirements, and I doubt that they will,' the king replied.

'In that case, I agree to your decision in accepting my plans, but your keen warriors must also know of our intentions,' Lumak advised.

It took them the best part of a week to excavate the necessary areas of the moon with super hot plasma beams and explosives. Then they sealed their hideout from the hostilities of space. All ships were then placed on full readiness and hidden within four separate bunkers in tunnels that led upwards on a gradient towards deep space. Their presence there were unknown to all and their contingency concealed from the most sensitive scanners in the vicinity.

At last they were ready and prepared for conflict. The warriors soon assembled in one of the large underground bunkers and there waited while the king and Lumak entered to brief them.

'My dearest warriors and comrades, we have travelled a great distance across space to assist a neighbour in distress. In so doing we find ourselves outnumbered by a very clever and resourceful enemy. However, they are not familiar with our type of shielding. Neither are they with our tactics and skills in battle. We must therefore make it our best effort and do our utmost to keep our base here a secret until the battle is won.

'We shall!' they shouted.

'Now, I shall hand you over to my friend, the Shadite Lumak. He also has a few important words to say on our behalf. Please listen to every word he utters and take note. Despite these great odds, our victory is not as impossible as it may seem. Now over to Shadite Lumak,' he said and Lumak walked to the platform.

'Friends and great warriors of Polok, it is in our mutual interest to accomplish this difficult task as soon as possible and with little loss or damage to either side. Neither do we intend to propound an already delicate situation in this remote region of our galaxy; for we are not here to aid in the task of retribution for another. Therefore, we are not to directly assist the emperor and his troops within these systems or to further escalate the situation with the resulting suffering and death on both sides, including some of our own warriors.'

They were not pleased with the notion of no action, having travelled all that way to assist the world below. However, Lumak continued his briefing.

'If my plans are followed to the letter, we the warriors of Polok shall win this war and hand it to the emperor on a plate. That way we shall acquire all the glory and privileges for our efforts, and these systems will be forever grateful and indebted to us for saving them. The question now is how to win such a war with a small army of just over two thousand warriors when the enemy has about two million.'

'Heh! Heh!' they yelled.

'I know, the odds are close to a thousand to one, but not impossible, once you are acquainted with their weakness and strength. The Ghol utilises portals to despatch their people to any point on the planet below. They are thoroughly trained, even down to the smallest child, to use every type of weapon effectively and are formidable and fearless in battle. During this active campaign, we must not destroy them or their ships, even when we target their fortress ships to disable their heavy weapons. Remember, they are criminals and wanted by a higher court for past crimes. For such deeds of past, they and their leader will pay dearly, while you, honourable warriors, are here to do a job of work efficiently.' Yet Lumak continued.

'First, we must capture several of their portals for our own use and place disabling mines on all of theirs. Then we can capture their main computers and finally their supply ships. Once the brain is severed from the Ghol's beast, we can then neutralise their people on the surface. We have just enough warriors for our purpose. However, we need to modify and improve the shielding on our scout boats for mounting such random assaults on the enemy ships with timed mines.'

'That is no great problem!' the chief engineer yelled.

'In that case, I have prepared the necessary strategies and added those changes to the war computer. Please complete the necessary modifications and follow my commands to the letter and the war will be quickly won. With it shall come glory and wealth. Lots of wealth!'

Suddenly they had become the most enthusiastic mercenaries. But Lumak continued.

'And may I take this opportunity in wishing you men and women every advantage and success on our future missions,' Lumak said and the king again returned to say a few final words.

'You heard Warlord Lumak. Consider this mission to be the final test of our abilities. If everything goes as planned, you will all be promoted to senior ranks and be very wealthy when we return home. We must give our best and only then shall we win the test.

'Heh! Heh!' they yelled again.

'We fight for Polok and its friendly neighbours!' King Olav shouted.

'For Polok and our friendly neighbours!' they cried.

After their briefing, the soldiers left to make the necessary changes to their craft and charged weapons ready for their impending mission. Lumak had to visit the emperor on the world below and make his presence known.

'I must now leave you my friend, good King Olav of Polok. I am to visit the emperor on Suk-Prime and inform him of our intentions, but not our whereabouts; for there could be informers even among his cabinet. However I shall be back in one sectron (about six hours). We can commence our assault after my return as planned,' Lumak said.

'I have complete faith in you, my Shadite friend and await your report with anticipation,' the king said as Lumak faded from sight.

'I hate it when he does that,' Olav complained, while Lumak gradually faded into nothingness and smiled as he did.

CHAPTER 24

Lumak on Suk-Prime

There was much turmoil within Primas, their capital city. Many refugees were moving here and there, not quite knowing from which direction the enemy would strike. Almost every facility within the city had been placed on standby and many of the main power generators destroyed. The loss of power had affected water supply, ventilation and several other important utilities, but they were resourceful and resilient. Despite the constant bombardment there was not a significant loss of life and many took shelter within its many ancient underground tunnels and shelters.

The shielding about Primas still held and so did its computer controlled lasers and other weapons. Their larger weapons were mobile and ran on rails within tunnels beneath the city. Hence, Primas was well fortified and any sustained attack expected by land.

Yet another meeting of the War Council was held in private chambers to discuss more alternative methods. Although having broadcasted many times for assistance and mercenary warriors, no one had yet communicated from outside their system. They soon realized they were on their own with little chance of surviving their current bombardment. Since they could not implement an effective offensive to repel their attackers their only option was negotiation. Presently, their intention was to resolve the situation by any method while the enemy drew closer. Therefore they were to take whatever few limited options they had left before beautiful Primas was laid waste.

It was soon decided that another envoy be sent to the space pirates to discuss a truce. The last party of Treil diplomats sent for that purpose had been summarily tethered and taken away to places unknown. Therefore they were unable to judge the actions of their fore.

This time they would send their best Moksai ministers and if that failed, the king would visit them himself; for after that final option everything was lost anyway. They would settle almost any of the pirate's demands if they would only agree to return from whence they came and promise never to come back. Yet, there was the problem of their language. No one knew a way to communicate those terms to the pirates unequivocally.

A vote was just about to be taken when Lumak materialized on the platform next to the emperor. Suddenly the discussion was stilled and Lumak began to speak.

'You sent out a transmission on which you requested our help. Did you not?' he asked, with a charming smile as he slid the hood back behind his head to reveal his human likeness.

'Well, here we are. Our warriors are dispersed above your world and will vanquish your enemies within six days if you so wish. Therefore do not make quick decisions that may be regretted in the fullness of time.'

They continued staring at the strange figure in black as if frozen in their steps.

'However, if you need an impartial envoy, why not let it be me? I can quickly assimilate their language and be unaffected by their weapons or indeed by any material means within this dimension, because I am Shadite,' Lumak said.

'Thank God you are here! Your fleet is here and fighting our enemies?' the emperor inquired in utter surprise of the strange form in black.

'Yes. Our fleet is here, but we have not yet engaged the enemy. Fighting for its own sake gives little long term gain. However, we have the best warriors and ships, and subtle means to defeat your enemies if and when we so choose. So do not worry unduly for your beautiful city and its occupants. We know their weakness as well as their strengths. We also know which strings to pull in order to weaken their resolve. But you must be patient.'

'Patient! With most of our cities in ruin!' a Moksai shouted.

'If we win within the specified time, would you agree to us taking them away to face justice at a higher court?' Lumak asked, but there was silence only to be broken by the emperor's voice.

'What other crimes could be more severe than those committed against our worlds?'

'Those committed against the Grand Lord of our universe. I am also his emissary within this plane of existence.'

They couldn't believe in his last words, but while they thought, he faded into nothing and then back into his original form. Many of the people in that room began to show reverence while others began to chant to their gods.

'In that case, we shall agree to your terms, for we have little choice in0 the matter and with God on our side we cannot lose. Perhaps you can visit our enemies for us and put our case to them?' the emperor pleaded.

They quickly gave Lumak their demands which he would take to the leader of the pirates. Suddenly everyone in that room was filled with happiness and purpose, knowing that they now had an option and a possible way out of their present dilemma.

TUEIL - THE TREIL CITY ON SUK-PRIME

The city of Tueil had been taken by the barbarian ruler Zahkan. He had occupied their leader's palace as his main residence and operations headquarters. Since that time he had added many of his communication systems to that building which was guarded by several of his finest troops. From that place he dictated to his war machinery.

'My Leader, your son and daughter have arrived from Nervia I.' He was informed by the tough looking personal human bodyguard they called Kelan. He had many facial scars and tattoos throughout his body.

'Where are they now?' Zahkan inquired.

'At the land house, Sire!' He remained stiff and at attention.

'Get them here this moment! I must see my little ones now!' he roared. The guard ran up the hilly avenue through its rows of striped moksaiau trees now in full flower and towards the palace.

'What do you want now?' growled the little boy towards the guard as he approached. The boy's head was partly shaven. A jet black plat dangled towards one side. He wore a small soldier's outfit with a knife in sheath on his belt, but carried no other weapons. He was barely eight years old and his sister about six.

'Master Chaun, I am to take you and your sister to your father this minute!' the guard ordered.

'She also has a name, you know!' he snarled in disagreement, but the guard remained calm and reticent.

'Please follow me?' he begged calmly and they both followed. They realized they couldn't keep their father waiting and walked through the strange garden, then the moksaiau trees with their pink flowers and brown and white striped barks. Having lived all their lives on a ship they wondered how beautiful planetary life really was. Here, there was an infinity of space, everything was natural, even the force that held them to the surface. Not like the simulated conditions on their mother-ship.

The little girl coughed as she inhaled some pollen and her brother went to take her hand.

They soon approached their father who was close to two rows of guards that were standing wearing nasal filters. There they stood in rank at stiff attention without any sound or movement. The children ran towards their father the moment he was sighted.

'Ah, my little ones. Come to your father. How I missed you!'

'Daddy! Daddy!' they yelled as he embraced them.

'Did you miss me?' Zahkan said, joyfully, as he lifted them up and hugged them before putting them down again. Zahkan towered above them as he did above most of the other soldiers. He was formidable in battle, but would only fight when he or his people were threatened. He was selected as their leader and had to show the toughest ones that he was their superior and always led by example. That attitude gained him much respect.

'Yes, we missed you, Father. I feel uncomfortable in this place. It smells very strange,' the little girl said.

'That is because you are not wearing your facials. You must wear them at all times or your body will become contaminated with planetary microbes. Both of you must quickly return to the unit for decontamination,' Zahkan said.

'But Father, wearing it is so unnatural. It makes my face sweat and it itches all the time,' she replied.

'Yes, I know my darlings. We have grown used to the environment and smells of our ships for far too long. This new world has many smells of its own and many invisible particles that fly with the winds. You must continue to use your nasal filters and don't forget to take your tablets every day, until we leave. They will prevent you from catching illness previously unknown to your bodies. However, we'll all get used to those microbes in time.'

'When will Mother arrive?' little Chaun inquired.

'She says, she has to coordinate communications between ships, but will join us when the time is right,' he replied. Zahkan was soon to be interrupted by a senior soldier.

'Leader!' he said and saluted.

'The attack on their main city is planned for tomorrow night. All data has been transferred to our strategic computer. We have also placed several lookalike Moksai spies within their screens.'

'Good! This time we must defeat them and get this war over once and for all. Then we can get down to repairing our battered ships for the long journey ahead.' The soldier again saluted and left.

He slowly walked towards the two rows of guards with his two children on either side. The guards were dressed in black leathery outfits with many gadgets and fittings for weapons including shields and communicators. They were obviously individual war machines and appeared invincible. They stood unflinchingly at attention as he inspected them. Then he selected the toughest and thumped him twice in his stomach, but he never blinked an eye or flinched a muscle.

'You see, my son, my guards are the toughest and best. No one on this world or on any other can ever hope to win against us!'

Soon another senior guard appeared with several battered Treil tethered to large chains. They towered above the guards and in passing growled and snarled their complaints, but no one listened.

'Take them to the ships. They will make good soup on our long voyage ahead,' Zahkan said to the passing guard and they were taken to a large container with a fitted portal.

'This is a most beautiful world, but it's not our Nervia. Not the one promised by our god. Not the type of world of our ancestors.'

'But it's also very beautiful!' the girl said while glancing at so many flowering trees in full bloom.

'Yes, but the beautiful garden that we journey to is a paradise of perfection,' he said to the children, who also stood at attention while he spoke.

'We can now return to the house and sample some of the native delicacies. Then you must be decontaminated,' he added and dismissed the two rows of guards. The guards immediately walked towards a small area of green and began to share their rations.

There were many of the Moksai people about the palace. Apparently some were used as pets, but also to assist in fetching and carrying. They had obviously been taken from their home world and elsewhere. The Ghol appeared sympathetic towards them because of their cuddly appearance, although they still could not understand each other's language. They felt the complete opposite towards the Treil reptiles and showed them no mercy or sympathy, whatsoever. In their case it was a sense of utter repugnance for their type.

Since they had taken the Treil city, its reptilian population had been either slaughtered for food or taken away to their ships, including senior councillors. There were also a few human captives that were given the toughest duties about the captured palace.

Zahkan took the children to the garden at the rear of the palace and there played with them while the Moksai servants laid a small table in the open. That was until Lumak appeared and frightened the servants away.

The palace was situated on their largest island within the sea of Tol and built on a high shoulder of rock overlooking a narrow beach hardly a kilometre below. At that high level one could view the city which panned out on either side of a large avenue.

Like many authentic Treil homes, two thirds were excavated out of the base rock. Only a few floors with beautiful pink towers were visible above ground. That aspect of their design made them ideal as secured dwellings.

The upper floors were used mainly for business of state and function rooms. Below ground was usually inaccessible to the public. Those lower levels consisted of their sleeping, recreation and nurseries. They comprised the family quarters, with room enough for more than twenty-five of their concubines with their young and eggs. However many Treil settled in more modern cities and adapted well to those prefabricated homes.

Wives were unknown to Treil reptiles. Yet, their concubines earned their seniority by age and quantity of children.

After Lumak left the Suk council, he travelled about the planet to survey the damage. Finally he connected with The Greater Mind to assist in interpreting their language. The moment he was finished, he beheld the near human figure of Lord Vektron. The Ploran carried a message about a previously unknown world. That world would be given to Zahkan and his people for permanent settlement.

'A suitable world has been chosen and registered for your purpose. Here are its attributes and coordinates.' He transferred the information directly to Lumak's implants and handed him two discs.

'Thank you! My lord!' Lumak replied.

The world was one hundred and thirty light years away. It would have taken the Ghol a similar time of just over one hundred years to get to that part of the galaxy.

Lumak visited Zarkan's palace to learn as much as possible of their culture and religion. When he had learnt enough by searching through their archives, he visited the rear palace garden to make himself known to their ruler.

He suddenly faded into view, causing all the Moksai and other servants to scatter and hide. Then he released the black hood, thus revealing a human figure similar to Zahkan himself, but in the black hooded cloak. As the Moksai scattered, Zahkan immediately put his arms about his children to protect them from whatever dangers faced, but instead the dark figure began to speak fluently in his own tongue.

'Zahkan, the fearless. I bring you good tidings and a message from the Most High. Beautiful Nervia has been located for you. The journey will take your people another one hundred and thirty years and you may not live to see the new world. However, if you follow my advice, that trip need only take two years. Therefore I think we should have a serious discussion on your behalf!' Lumak said in no uncertain terms.

'You are a god?' Zahkan inquired, in astonishment, with both hands still firmly held around his children. He knew of the technologies of his enemies, but no one had such incredible designs, so he must be who he said.

'I am not a god myself, but I do represent a great power. I am his messenger.'

'It is written that our Lord would send someone to show us the way when we got close to Nervia. Are you that person?'

'Yes, Zahkan! I am that same one. Behold my person!' Lumak said, as he faded into the air and faded back into himself, making the children put their little hands up to hide their faces.

'I know that you have had a hard journey since you left Pagador, but that journey now comes to an end. You left with one hundred and forty-three ships and have arrived here with just seventy six. I do not wish any more losses on your behalf; for even as I speak to you, a greater foe approaches. They have come to assist their friends in this system and can destroy most or all of your remaining fleet. Therefore, you are to stop all hostilities immediately, return to your ships and continue your trip home.'

'But my lord, what shall we do about repairs. Most of our drives are failing by the minute and we have not yet acquired enough provisions for the journey!' Zahkan pleaded.

'Not so, Zahkan. If you follow my instructions to the letter, your trip will take just two years and you can receive whatever technologies and materials in transit through your portals here and on your vessels. However, you are also to release all the Treil and Moksai captives. They belong with their own families within these worlds. I can make an agreement with them to assist you, but you must comply with my wishes.'

'My Lord? My people will not be pleased!'

'I have here two discs. One explains the design of a new and much more powerful LPD drive for your ships. The other contains images and a stellar map of your beautiful paradise, Nervia World. You are to show them to your people. Once again, may I stress that you must follow the wishes of our esteemed lord. You must call off all hostile actions here and return all captives before you leave this world. Would you like to see the promised world in person? Would you like to see it now? I can take you there?' Lumak said.

'No, my lord. But I shall stop all hostilities immediately.'

'In that case, I will see you again before you depart; for I am to ensure your trip is safe and secure,' Lumak said, while fading into the air and leaving everyone in that garden numbed by his strange appearance. Lumak immediately left for the moon-base to discuss his strategic plans with king Olav.

CHAPTER 25

A minor assault

Lumak soon returned to their moon-base to explain his plans in depth to king Olav and inform him of progress made.

'The emperor has agreed with our plans and left all final decisions up to us. Anyway, he is in no position to do otherwise. The pirate's leader Zarkan has ceased all hostilities and will follow my advice. So we now have both warring factions in our confidence and are free to take whatever actions necessary to resume peace in this system. Therefore, in light of these changes, we must follow our original war plans as previously discussed,' Lumak said, but went on to explain its subtleties.

'That's an incredible plan and we are to do very little in convincing those on the surface that a battle is raging in space. But we could be still in danger if they begin to fight back before our timed mines are laid. Either way, it's a risk worth taking. And you say, their enemies have also agreed to take their ships away?' King Olav said with a broad smile.

'We are to frighten Zahkan and his people just a little. Just enough to get them started on their way, and this last part is for our benefit. He has already begun the return of captives and needs just a little time to evacuate his people from Suk-Prime,' Lumak replied.

'This is a truly brilliant manoeuvre on your part. Now I know exactly who I am dealing with,' King Olav said, with much humour, but fully believing in Lumak's incredible achievements.

The assault on the ships and portals were planned for night time and the king thoroughly briefed his men. There was to be one hundred and fifty-two light boats involved with three warriors per boat. The same number would visit the planet below and disable all portals with the exception of those at the palace. Olav was to lead the main assault on the ships.

While screened, disabling mines were secretly planted on weapon pods, aerials and other sensitive installations, but any damage to those installations were intended to be superficial and easily repaired within a week or so.

When they were finished the king and his crew decided to visit the leading ship to disable their master computer. That assault was trickier than the others, because the computer was inside the main flagship, Nervia I, and access was only by a single ground portal.

King Olav and his accomplices knew the location of the computer and how to get to it through the ship, while avoiding a few manned installations in the process. They were then to disable it temporarily in case they had to mount any follow-up action after the mines exploded.

After the mines were laid the warriors returned to their moon-base as stealthily as they had done during other assaults. Therefore Zahkan's officers on his ships and elsewhere were none the wiser. Then King Olav took the two warriors of his previous assault to a captured portal on the world below for yet another mission.

Lumak had programmed their war computer with Zahkan's language and that program was subsequently added to all their communication belts. The Polokans used such two way translation and communication belts for that purpose.

When they arrived at the surface portal it was a simple matter of altering its coordinates to that of Zahkan's ship and that change was a straightforward one. All portals had a simple coded sequence of just 512 different numbers for their land units which could be linked to a maximum of 512 ships. He selected the button that controlled the ones on the ships, then he dialled number one for both in their code and the container opened.

There were several lockers of space suits next to the portal cubicle. They entered three of the cumbersome suits and walked towards the large cubicle.

They had no way of knowing whom or what would be waiting at the other end of the portal. Yet, their mission was timed to coincide with the multiple explosions of the mines, so that aspect and the general confusion would be a further distraction to the guards.

The moment they entered the flag ship, confusion, pandemonium and panic struck the area. Their bodies were routinely scanned by the computer for personnel identification. When none could be found the computer placed the leading ship on red alert and their portal bay was sealed off.

Amidst all the confusion they were soon captured, stripped of all suspicious items and taken to Zahkan's cabin.

'More wanderers, I see? But you are not the humans of Suk-Prime. Nor are you those within any of the systems we have visited. From whence have you come, and for what purpose?' the nervous Zahkan commanded, with many of his senior soldiers about and looking on.

'We have come to assist a neighbour in distress. They sent us a signal, saying they needed urgent assistance and our fleet has since arrived. We have subsequently mined all your land portals, but have done little damage to your ships. It is to show you that we can target you as we wish without any knowledge of our whereabouts,' replied King Olav.

'And by such means you visit us uninvited to do likewise to my ship's interior?' Zahkan inquired, furiously.

'We have not yet!' replied king Olav.

'Where now is your invisible fleet?' he inquired.

'They are all around you. They are everywhere, but cannot be detected by your outmoded technologies. You and your people remain alive only because our superiors wish it that way. However, as for us, we are just lowly warriors, following orders and cannot divulge any other information, as we have been given our orders strictly on a need-to-know basis,' King Olav replied through his translation belt.

'The messenger said we would face a strong fleet and that we should resist any further hostilities,' Zahkan thought, almost uttering the last words.

'And you give me your word that you will not fight against us again?' an unhappy Zahkan queried.

'Only if you decide to cease all hostilities with our friends on the planet below and free us from this ship and your soldiers,' a brave king Olav replied.

'In that case, I shall free you and your companions,

immediately. However, you must take a message from me to your superiors. Tell them that we have desisted all further hostilities and have already began the repatriation of all captives to Suk-Prime.' Zahkan then turned to a group of his less senior guards.
'Give them one of our life boats!'

They were soon back within their space suits and moving towards Suk-Prime in the life boat, still several thousand kilometres in space and passing several of Zahkan's space fortresses.

'We didn't have to disable their main computer after all. They came over all on their own and he had already decided to leave. Lumak must have planted the thought of surrender deeply in his mind, to be reenforced by the explosions of our mines. Now, we must return to Suk-Prime and get our own shielded crafts back to base undetected,' King Olav thought.

The massive explosion occurred as they passed Zahkan's last ship. That explosion ripped through their life boat, vaporising a large front section and killing his two companions in the process. Those two were sat in front piloting the life-boat and were more susceptible. Luckily for King Olav he was in the rear cabin of the alien lifeboat at the time. He was sat there purely out of curiosity for their type of technology while observing one of their technical manuals. Nevertheless he had taken a severe bang to his helmet and was severely shaken and concussed, but his suit held firmly against the rigours of space. He was extremely lucky and probably saved by an additional front partition within the life boat.

'They fired a missile towards us. But why against one of their own boats,' the king murmured to himself, while the boat speeded onwards on a previous trajectory that would take it on a collision course with the planet below, with no means of control or communication.

'This ship will enter Suk-Prime's atmosphere within five hours, with disastrous consequences to both mind and body. I just hope the oxygen supply holds out until then,' brave Olav thought. He was never the type to panic. He calmly relaxed while admiring the view and remained in that position while awaiting rescue.

Zahkan's crew observed the explosion and soon arrested the gunner in question. The young and nervous artillery officer may have fired his weapon the moment he had a visible sighting of something that was not scheduled to move in that area, thinking it was one of the enemy's ships. Nevertheless he would pay dearly for that oversight.

Zahkan was subsequently told the ship was destroyed. Since no signs of life had been detected he did not expect any human to survive that explosion, so no rescue was mounted. Even so, there was a strong desire in him to apologize for his peoples' mistake and make reparations to their superiors.

The supposed space battle was detected from Primas when they observed the many explosions of the mines. They were even happier when they saw several of their captives returned. Lumak was cheered and given an agreement in favour of Zahkan's people. They were to leave that stellar system immediately, but assisted during their voyage with supplies and equipment.

At that time the emperor and his ministers would have given anything to see the back of the so-called space vermin. But there was yet another agreement to be cosigned by King Olav. It was the payment to King Olav's fleet for their part in the successful mission. There were also the usual celebrations during which time his warriors would be entertained.

Lumak soon returned to the base to discuss those matters with King Olav, when to his surprise they said he was missing in action. They checked through the computer and found that he had gone to Zahkan's ship, but had not yet returned. Lumak immediately transposed to Zahkan's ship to eavesdrop and soon learnt of the disaster.

He was saddened by that knowledge, but would not let it go at that. After all, he was a king and his body should be recovered even for a planned space burial. He scanned the area until he found the boat. Then he checked their bodies individually until he found King Olav's.

'I thought I would never be found, and that world beneath us looms larger by the minute,' he said through his helmet the moment he saw Lumak's cloak. Lumak placed his gloved hand on his helmet to communicate. Although both used brain implants they were of different technologies and somewhat incompatible for direct communication.

'Are you all right?' Lumak shouted, scanning his suit for damage.

'Yes, my friend, only a little shaken and somewhat squeezed by this buckled frame.'

'You are quite safe for two more hours. During this time we shall mount a rescue with one of our larger ships. Nevertheless, our base location might be discovered by so doing, but it's a chance I am willing to take. What say you?' Lumak said.

'The battle is now won and Zahkan has decided to leave. The missile could have been an accidental release, so you have my permission to mount my rescue.'

Lumak soon arrived on base and explained the delicate situation to his warriors. They were hot on taking action against Zahkan, but had been told it was not the intention of their king. The mission was launched and Olav's boat captured with all its three crew members, but with Olav as the sole survivor.

Lumak visited Zahkan's ship and transposed within his main cabin.

'Something that I truly regret has happened. One of my gunners have killed three of our visitors by mistake and while in one of our own boats. He will be dearly punished for such intolerable action. For I have given my word in all honesty and as a leader of many,' Zahkan said, sadly.

'Don't worry, my Friend, accidents will happen. Anyway, one of their important members have survived the explosion and realize it was due to one of your nervous gunners. Try not to punish him too severely. He was only acting to save his people,' Lumak said and left.

CHAPTER 26

A time to rejoice

King Olav of Polok had soon recovered from his close encounter with death. He thanked Lumak many times for saving his life and then his warriors for completing a very successful operation. He had only lost five warriors during that time. One boat had been lost on land and the two companions lost on that special mission. Their bodies were to be frozen and returned to Polok for a befitting burial on their home world. Their part of the reward being given to their closest relatives.

Lumak accompanied King Olav to Primas, followed by half his warriors. They were to partake in the celebrations prepared on their behalf by the emperor, Tukol. It was then decided that other warriors in moon-base take turns in visiting Primas to collect their rewards and partake in the celebrations.

Lumak, King Olav and several of his senior warriors walked slowly up the long avenue of tall palmist-like trees towards their parliament building. On route they were greeted by Treil, Moksai and a multitude of the local humans. They bowed each time to the cheering crowds until entering the large building.

'Welcome friends! Today is a day of celebration to mark our release from the hands of our enemies. Let our records mark this day as such and may we list the names of all those great friends from a distant system that had played a major part in our release. Of all these great people here standing, the messenger, Lumak, has played a major part in changing their leaders mind and taking the pirates away from us. To him and his people we shall be always indebted.

'As requested by King Olav and for their dangerous activities in neutralizing our enemies, we supply payment in tons of gold and platinum bullion. However, as requested by our people, we have also added some of our special technologies and items of jewellery for their wives and children. Further, we have decided to begin trade with King Olav's system, Polok II, and trust our relationships will blossom from this day on,' Tukol said. Then King Olav was asked to say a few words of his own.

'Friends, I know what it feels like to be in a situation of war. I pray that you will rebuild your cities and soon begin to function peaceably again; for peace is always to be preferred over war. Nothing of real benefit can ever be gained through warfare, except uncertainty and suffering. However, we must always be prepared for such eventualities. Therefore before we leave, I have decided to remain here for a while and train your fighters into more well prepared warriors,' King Olav said. Lumak did not give a speech, but instead shook the hands of the Emperor and vanished from their midst.

Once again Lumak visited Zahkan. This time he walked through the metal walls of his home enclosure on the leading ark, Nervia I. It was the main flagship of their fleet. Zahkan did not panic when he saw the moving shadow. This time it was his wife's turn to grab hold of the children in an attempt to protect them. The little ones were still petrified by Lumak's appearance and his Black Shadite's Cloak that cast deep shadows.

'The agreement has been finalised. Your main palace portal is in place to transfer provisions and equipment until well into your journey. Here are the agreements I signed on your behalf,' Lumak said and handed Zahkan the scroll which was written in their different languages. He silently read the contents.

'You must now be prepared to receive a few Moksai scientists and arrange for a few of your best scientists and engineers to be trained by them. You may take whatever security measures you find necessary to keep your people here at ease.'

'It's already done, my lord!'

'Have you viewed the discs?' Lumak inquired, quickly changing the troubled topic.

'Yes, my lord. It is as I expected it to be. A most beautiful world. The new drive systems have also been shown to our scientists and they think they are unique in many ways. At last we can repair our ships when we have enough materials on board,' Zahkan replied, joyfully.

'And your people can arrive on Nervia World in two years as

promised. You yourself will live to see your children grow into men and women on your beautiful new world.'

'Indeed, my lord!'

'Do not be so intolerant of other kinds in future; for much can be gained and solved through patience and negotiation. But you have now passed that crossroad and have learnt many lessons,' Lumak said.

'I have indeed learnt many lessons, my lord. Will you remain here with us for a while and be my guest? Today we serve our usual space diet. One of grain from ancient harvests but grown on our farming ships, which we have used repetitively and in many different ways since my ancestors left their home world,' Zahkan said with sadness.

Lumak thought for a moment but realized it couldn't be Moksai or Treil soup, so he accepted.

'I would like that very much, my dear friend.'

'Would you also visit us on Nervia World, after your mission here has been completed? We intend to build a large monument there for our beloved god, with much celebration after we arrive,' Zahkan stressed.

'You will not be able to keep me away. I shall visit your Nervia World from time to time and you will feel the presence of our Grand Lord on that new world. However, you must take good care of it and its lower life-forms in his name.'

The brave little girl went closer to Lumak to touch his strange garment, then she quickly withdrew and ran back to her mother who couldn't stop staring at Lumak.

'You have the most beautiful wife and children,' Lumak said and his wife smiled, bashfully. Perhaps more than she had ever done since innocent childhood.

'Sultran, my wife, has been a pillar to me during the war. It was she who coordinated most of our actions through our computers. She is also a good soldier, but this time the women remained on our ships to defend this end,' he said, proudly.

'Zahkan, you and your people have been assisted because of the love of our lord for you all, so you must bear him in your thoughts always.' Then Lumak handed him an insignia with a green central circle and two wings on either side of the circle.

'Take this in commemoration of my presence here with your family. This symbolises the universal struggle for order and life throughout the Cosmos. Let it also symbolize a period of change in your lives for the better,' Lumak said and Zahkan took the insignia.

The children soon became quite fond of Lumak and so did Zahkan and his wife. After dinner Lumak said a temporary farewell to Zahkan and his family, and departed through the metal walls of the ship in much the same way as he had entered.

He soon rejoined king Olav in celebration in the city of Primas for they were now the best of friends. However Lumak had not yet completed his mission and that fact made him restless. King Olav was given several chests of jewellery for himself and his warriors. There were many crates filled with metals like gold and platinum that were considered extremely rear within King Olav's own system. Then he signed a trade agreement with Suk-Prime for assisting in the rebuilding of many of their damaged cities and utilities.

There was the training of their soldiers in more efficient methods of warfare. However his main worry at that time was in acquiring a suitable large freight transport for his vast quantity of wealth. Nevertheless the emperor soon obliged by letting them have an old freight carrier for their journey home. He soon visited his officers for a quiet word.

'My most loyal friends... we are rich!... we are wealthy!... but there is one problem. Our wealth is too vast to take back with our small ships. Therefore, the emperor has given us one of his large carriers, so some of you must remain behind to ensure its delivery. We must also pass through our own customs unhindered. Therefore those of you who remain must wear the necessary disguises and prosthetics while pretending to be the locals on a visit to trade with our world. Then we can unload our wealth in the still of night under the pretence of such trade. Place the extra ships in one of the carrier's bay,' King Olav said, leaving nothing to chance. They agreed with his clandestine methods.

Representatives were to visit each other systems to find which technologies were mutually beneficial to either. Lumak was satisfied with the way things had transpired and soon called King Olav aside for a quiet word.

'I am very sorry, Friend, but I have to go. I hope to visit your world in the not too distant future. However, I must leave you now,' Lumak stressed.

'I suppose I shall see you again, my dearest friend? Anyway, just in case, please take this medallion. It was given to me by my mother and has always been worn close to my heart,' King Olav said, with sadness filling his eyes.

'Yes, my friend, and please take this little insignia to remind you of our eternal cause. I sincerely hope to visit you in due course. But first, I must complete my current mission.

'I wish you God speed. Be kind and generous to your people and remember the Greater Purpose and me in all this,' as Lumak said those words he faded from view with his usual smile, but always to be remembered by King Olav of Polok II in that way.

'I hate it when he disappears like that,' the king muttered to himself.

CHAPTER 27

A brand new world

Zahkan assembled his fleet just outside the Trinus system. There they waited while updating their space drives and making general repairs to their battered ships. During this time they received most of their supplies via portals from Primas. Finally he briefed his captains for the long trip ahead.

Many of their ships were battle worn and space beaten, but they were built to last and included many isolation chambers between the living compartments and the hostile vacuum of space.

Most of his people knew very little of his intentions and were surprised when he gave orders to end the war and return all captives dead or alive. He had given those orders without having taken on enough provisions or materials for a resumption of their voyage. Neither had he completed the necessary repairs for a continued journey.

Others thought he was losing his grip and it was time they had a new and more decisive leader. After all, their immediate survival depended on good leadership. There were many rumours banded about those ships. Some had even reach the ears of his closest in command. Nevertheless no one had yet reached the point of mutiny. Soon, many of those attitudes and comments were received by Zarkan, himself. He was furious and decided to speak his mind to all and sundry.

'We have all fought a long and tedious battle, with many wounded and dead comrades and need some reassurance at this juncture in our travels. I shall call the captains of each ship, their chiefs, controllers and supervisors to explain the reasons why I have taken my present course of action,' he said to his wife, Sultran.

'How will you explain Lumak to them?' she asked, with curiosity.

'I shall arrange to play the images on the disk back to them. We can use our play studio for that purpose and serve them fermented Moksaiau juice afterwards,' he replied.

'And I can make some cakes from their pollen and flowers. I have a practical recipe given to me by Bethusa the Moksai cook, that was in the palace,' she said.

'In that case, could you arrange their invitations through the computer?'

She immediately left what she was doing and went to a desk. That desk was obviously used as a working surface, but as she pressed a hidden button the cover retracted and from underneath rose a screen and keyboard unto a new surface. She switched the console on and began to type as if it was her second nature. Then she pressed the transmitter button and the invitations were sent. There was also a large helmet in a small alcove in front of her desk. The helmet could completely isolate the operator from any outside distraction and place them within the virtual world of the main ships computer. Using this method she could quickly search its libraries or even its corridors to locate an item or individual. Theirs were not a culture that had ever used brain implants.

She was able to control even the main battle computer from that location and there were many such consoles within all controllers and supervisor's homes throughout the ships. They had all been designed to be used with or without their special helmets.

Despite the fact that they had been travelling space for such a long time, their facilities were quite modern. This was because they were constantly evolving new technologies and systems. Since they used portals for ship-to-ship transfer, everything, including schooling and training were as natural to them as on the surface of any world. For all worlds could be considered massive spaceships orbiting about their parent stars. Nevertheless when they needed raw materials they would simply change course and use their mining ships to collect such materials from moons. Those space arcs were well designed for extended periods in space and contained every possible facility for its large crews.

The conference was set for two days time. During that period supplies between Suk-Prime and their container ships had begun to flow and that rumour was also on the grapevine.

'Why should our enemies send us their food and material

supplies? What sacrifices had been made to end the war? A war we were already winning. Why have so little when we could have had it all, and with a glorious victory to celebrate?' they conferred.

The officers, controllers and supervisors arrived with their partners, men and women. They were dressed in their light and more colourful uniforms and guided to Zahkan's play studio which was large enough to seat just over a thousand of his crew. That small theatre had been used for cinematic entertainment when the voyage began. That was until many of the special projectors and 3-D image plates had become worn or damaged. Then it was only used on special occasions like weddings by his family and friends. That place was only necessary when the number of visitors were excessive for his living quarters. During their long voyage all such areas and associated devices were constantly renewed and updated.

They walked through the isles and took seats in the sloping studio. There was one thousand and fifty-six of his people present. Out of that number, six hundred and eight were special captains and their officers, the others were administrators and their mates, and not all were present. There were seniors and representatives from each ship while the conference was televised throughout the fleet.

'Nervia has been found, Comrades. Yes! Nervia has been found. But I wanted you to hear those words from my own lips, personally. Finally, the time has come for us to make the final leg of our journey, and it is just one hundred and thirty light years away. That trip would have taken us even longer in years, but the messenger of our lord have paid me a visit, during which time he left me these two discs. My wife and children will vouch for my sanity on that account. Anyway, let me show you some images of Nervia,' he said and handed the disc to an operator.

Beautiful images were projected unto a screen. They were images of trees, flowers and birds flying in the sky. Insects and animals were everywhere, but there were no humans, just a few apelike forms in the densest jungles under a young and bluish star.

'This is our Nervia, Comrades!' he cried. Many in the audience couldn't hold back their tears of excitement and longing.

'The reason why I gave orders to stop the war is simply because our trip to Nervia will take us just two years instead of more than one hundred. That is because we have been given the specifications of a new and much more powerful drive. The messenger has also made an agreement with Suk-Prime, to supply our requirements through portals during our short trip. However, I had to return all captives to honour that agreement.'

'My gracious Lord!' they yelled.

'If you are still worried about the presence of Moksai scientists, Sulti workers and other visitors about our ships, you can maintain a moderate security presence. But they are here to assist us on our way. They feel much safer that way.'

'Since they are here to help, I am sure we can tolerate their presence for the duration!' A captain shouted and the others agreed and clapped.

'Even while I speak to you, comrades, more powerful drives are being designed to take us to Nervia. Our ships are being repaired and our supply ships filled with provisions and raw materials to maintain us for a period in excess of two years. Therefore, you are required to take a complete inventory of all your requirements with moderate rationing for a period of two years. So from henceforth, I wish to encounter happier faces on all our ships; for soon we arrive on Nervia World!' They cheered again, with happier faces. But he continued.

'Furthermore, I have decided to call a day of celebration throughout all our ships, during which time we are to mourn our great predecessors and revive our ancient customs, traditions and culture in preparation for when we land on Nervia and begin to build our first city. We have come a very long way and have much to catch up on. But here, I speak continuously out of my overwhelming excitement without asking for your opinions. So please ask me your questions now?' he said, with excitement and joy.

'My Leader, is it really that The Messenger has come?' the tall controller asked and abruptly sat on his stool.

'Yes, it's absolutely true. He walked through the walls of this ship and had supper with me and my family. It took the children some time to get used to him; for his powers were awe inspiring. But they and my wife eventually plucked the courage and got used to him. He will visit us from time to time until our journey is completed. His name is Sut Lumak, which means "the brightest star", and that name shall be entered in all our religious and historical records forthwith. Let me show you an insignia he gave me. Please pass this item around?' he said and passed them the beautiful winged insignia. They handed each other the object and finally passed it back to him, but in so doing and to the utter dismay of all, Lumak suddenly appeared through the screen and walked on the air towards the platform. He moved his hood back to reveal a human likeness.

'Zahkan, I heard my name mentioned while passing. I trust you will forgive me for this intrusion,' Lumak said. Zahkan and his audience couldn't believe their eyes, for here before them was an angel of their god that could even walk on air.

'They have doubted your presence, my lord,' Zahkan said, almost choking on his words.

'There has and always will be, doubters. However, our lord is one of love and works for everyone, including the doubters. The universe is vast and his responsibility enormous. Yet, he heard your cries of sadness and unhappiness and have finally come to your aid.

'Your future is now safe and secure. You will build a beautiful civilization on Nervia World, but you must not be insular in your relations with the whole. You are all Osmaronites, part of this galaxy and you must henceforth treat your neighbours, human or otherwise, with dignity and respect as you would expect them to treat you. The time is coming when many worlds will come together in friendship for the common good and you and your people will be involved in that process.

'Bear those thoughts in mind and you will shine brightly even among the brightest stars. I must leave you now, but I shall visit you again,' Lumak said and with his final words dissolved into the air leaving his audience filled with utter astonishment.

'The one is truly The Messenger, for he only speaks of good,' cried many and Zahkan put his arms forward to calm the crowd.

'Now that we are sure the Messenger does exist, I would like some more questions, please!'

'My Leader, what are we to do with Caine, the gunner? Shall we execute him now? He has broken your word and caused death to the other human warriors, even though in error,' a captain said.

'In the old days he would have been given a suit and asked to walk the pole for that particular error, but we cannot mar our celebrations with any sadness. Let him be assigned to raw duties in our supply ships for six months, but he must also partake in the celebrations,' Zahkan said. They were extremely pleased with that judgement.

Refurbishment of all their battered ships had commenced in earnest. They were driven towards a change in attitude, from the rough Ghol pirates that they were known as, to more tolerant Nervians. That change was reenforced by the discs and the new concepts Lumak had given them.

Their attitude towards the Moksai and others had changed to one of gratitude and appreciation in assisting them on their journey. When the time was right, Zahkan made arrangement to visit Suk-Prime and thank the emperor in person for his assistance. He also made it clear to their leaders that he would be a friendly ally in future and would welcome a trade agreement, after settling on Nervia world, and they agreed.

Since he had caused much damage to many worlds in that system, he decided to allow all their citizens free passage to his home world for the purpose of trade, education and settlement. Further, he would always assist and defend their systems in times of trouble. That agreement was signed by Zahkan and Emperor Tukol and was understood by all to be reparations given for the trouble caused.

Very soon the propulsive power of each ship was increased by a hundred times. They felt the greater acceleration when they changed their vector coordinates for Nervia World.

Lumak had visited them twice during their voyage to give them additional information. On his visit before their arrival, he handed them a disc of rules for dealing with their large city communities.

CHAPTER 28

Nervia World

As Lumak had foretold, Zahkan and his people arrived at their destination within two years. To be precise, in one year and ten months, Earth time. The large colourful blue-green disc with its lumps of clouds was constantly displayed on screens throughout their ships as a reminder of their journey's end. For some strange reason they suddenly realised they had come home and their wanderings were at an end. The anti climax felt was as a result of so many hardships and sacrifices faced on a trip that had taken several millennia to complete. During that time many forewent the most awful experiences. Just under half their original people had arrived on Nervia World and over 100 generations had passed during that long and arduous exodus.

As they approached, many left their duties and began to entertain themselves with music, dancing and song. There was excitement and much celebration. A team of soldiers were soon assembled to visit and scout their new world. After much discussion, an area of interest was selected close to its equator within the northern hemisphere. That area was near a river that fed into one of its smaller seas and that was where they decided to settle.

Soon Zahkan called his most senior officers together for their main briefing before landing on the world below.

'We have arrived, comrades! We have arrived to our future home. Here is where we shall lay our ancestor's ashes to rest. Here we shall live and die, enjoy and cry, in all our future generations. For that reason we must build our future on solid foundations, with respect and love within our many communities.

'However, before we begin to settle, we must make a thorough analysis of the planet's environment and collect samples of air, soil and water. This is in case of deadly bacteria and other microbial strains present within its environments. We might also have to create vaccines against the less effective strains. Most of this will be temporary, until our bodies acclimatize to the new environment.

'In future, all our communities will be based on rules and duties, as have been given by the messenger, Lumak, on the discs he supplied. Our Nervia is rich in natural resources so we can utilise many of the Moksaiau flower seeds, providing they do not negatively affect the ecological balance of the environments and indigenous life.

'Scouts have been dispatched. We now await their findings before we can begin an orderly evacuation to the surface below. We can construct portals for our engineers and builders to move to and fro more freely between surface and ships.

'I have estimated a period of three months before enough temporary shelters are built to house our complete population. In the mean time we shall commence the building of Nervia City to these specifications,' he said, as an ancient chart appeared on the screen.

They found a fertile area near the sea through which the large river meandered. Here they settled and began to build their city.

Today was the first year since their arrival on Nervia World. Their large ships had been emptied of all their belongings and left parked in synchronous orbit above their adopted world. In time many would be converted and used as freight carriers and orbiting stations. Others improved and used as interstellar transport to other systems and worlds like Suk-Prime.

Within a single year the population had increased by another 25 percent and now three point six million. All previous population controls, as enforced on their ships, had been lifted. They were relatively free to follow their own desires and ambitions.

The monument for the ashes of their ancestors had been finally completed. There it stood like a great pyramid to remind them of their past. At its pinnacle was a golden altar with many rows of candles burning, each representing lost communities during their voyage. Each face of the great pyramid had its own stairway which narrowed towards each of the seven platforms that surrounded the pyramid at seven different and equal levels.

Each platform led to a separate area within the pyramid. There were seven such areas, including the largest one at its base. They contained museums, where their technologies, artifacts and memento of past could be stored and displayed to posterity for all their future generations to observe with pride and dignity. At the apex was the golden temple and altar for worship on special occasions.

Today was the day of its opening ceremony. Zahkan had to climb its many stairs alone, to be anointed at the altar before commencing the opening ceremony. It was a most historical occasion. He was dressed in an ancient ancestral gown embroidered and inlaid in gold with many glittering jewels that shown against the brilliant sunlight.

He had taken the north facing stairway, thinking it would somehow reduce the overpowering morning sunlight, but that was not the case. There were a large gathering at the pyramid's base comprised of senior officials with many civilians. Moksai and Treil were assisting in the building process. Most of them stopped their duties to observe and partake in the ceremony.

'What I would give to see Lumak here and now to accompany me to the pinnacle,' Zarkan thought to himself, still climbing patiently.

'A credit for your thoughts?' came the welcomed words from a figure in black following just behind. He turned around and couldn't believe his eyes.

'I told you that you were not going to get rid of me that easily... and why no portals,' Lumak said.

Both men embraced. Zahkan was overwhelmed by emotion. Lumak escorted him to the top, witnessed by the thousands of onlookers that were assembled at the lowest level. Yet, many were constantly arriving at the pyramid's base to pay homage. As they approached both men went down on their knees to say a prayer. After the celebrations, Lumak gave another one of his encouraging speeches in the main square to the multitude. Finally he said a temporary farewell and faded into the air.

Soon their city contained a most thriving population. There were many Moksai and others, including the previously hated Treil and trade had begun between those neighbouring stellar systems in earnest.

CHAPTER 29

Lumak visits Polok

After king Olav and his brave warriors returned home to Polok they found their world in more turmoil. His political party was ousted with no reprisal. They must have thought it advantageous to complete their coup d'etat during King Olav's absence. Yet, his people still loved and respected him because of his brave exploits and that factor alone gave him a larger than expected following. His notoriety prevented his immediate execution. Despite his dictatorial past, he was allowed to remain a member of his original party, now in opposition, but never again to be its most senior minister.

After the signing of an agreement of abdication, he resumed life in his family's royal palace within his fief with a pretence modicum life style. Nevertheless he was able to recover and store his many tons of gold and platinum bullion within the many basement rooms of his large palace. That was after he had given a large share to his loyal warriors. There were many caskets and chests of beautiful jewellery that he could freely use as bribe and presents.

He had held on to his share of the reward from Suk-Prime, which had doubtlessly made him the wealthiest person on the planet and kept the knowledge of his enormous wealth well away from the opposition. Thus he continued to live the pretence mediocre lifestyle for the sake of his wife and son.

The Lodorians, within the neighbouring stellar system were an ancient race and as a result had depleted most of their natural resources. Presently those essential resources were acquired from the Polokans. Over the years they had become mutually dependant on each other, with the Lodorians supplying their advanced technologies and weapons in return for raw minerals.

Since king Olav's fall from power the present extreme socialist government had given the Lodorians much cause for concern. The more advanced Lodorians were fully dependant on Polok for almost all their raw metals and chemicals. Therefore, any unstable government could create bottlenecks in the flow of their supplies. That factor was a constant annoyance to the Lodorian leaders.

King Olav and his family had retained their palace just outside their main city of Safon. It was placed in a large ground with small lake and waterfall. The twin peaks on either side of the waterfall gave the place a secure and tranquil disposition.

He may have spoken more than a thousand times to his wife and teenage son, Malik, about his dear friend Lumak and their adventures together. Most of all, the time Lumak had saved his life. He always wore the insignia Lumak had given him as a reminder of his past adventures and had changed his attitude towards everything. Instead of his usual blunt and dictatorial self, he was now a calm and concerned individual. He could now see a bigger picture and was worried about many things, including the actions of the powerful Lodorians if they became disenchanted with the present political system.

At that period of unrest, he and many of his party members were very unhappy and disillusioned with the present political system. The powerful and wealthy respected him for his outright manner, and most of all, his fame as the greatest warrior. Nevertheless they could do very little to resolve the political situation and slow its descent.

They had an almost impossible task to oust their opposition, because they had the greater majority, including the military on their side. They were also clever at bribing. They had promised the Lodorians an uninterrupted flow in their supplies if they assisted politically. The Lodorians had little choice but to comply. Presently there were many Polokans on Lodor that formed the large work force within their many factories and assembly plants, so that vote was effective. Even so, Lodorians never liked being placed against a wall with their hands tied behind their backs. Neither did they appreciate any form of blackmail, which was considered dishonourable by their way of thinking. Lodorians were not human in their emotions or form. They were highly logical and each could live for many millennia.

King Olav saw the pattern and realised it was only a matter of time before the more advanced Lodorians took the situation in hand and began a full scale war. He had planted a few of his loyal followers on Lodor to spy and collect information on everything including advanced technologies. He would used his gold and platinum reward to pay those people and was soon involved in many technological ventures, unknown even to his own party leaders. He was then astounded by the information received from his many spies.

He realized there were dark clouds on the horizon and had to warn his close colleagues of impending disaster. Then try to find a way out of their current dilemma. After having considered an irreversible course of action, he arranged a secret meeting with those loyal party members and friends in order to discuss the serious problems of the day.

If any of their clandestine plans were to get in the wrong hands the opposition would surely have considered it treacherous, which meant sudden death by summary execution.

'Fellow colleagues and friends, I have called you here today to discuss a very worrying and pressing matter. A matter that can seriously affect our future survival on this world. However, I would rather you kept our discussions here in strictest confidence. Because it will be most detrimental to our families and friends should word of our intentions ever leaked into wrong ears.

'I have received information from reliable sources that indicate the Lodorians are planning an invasion. They are stockpiling weapons and it is on a massive scale. They have been unhappy with our government for some time and are frightened that the flow of their essential supplies will come to an abrupt end. This is because many agreements and political demands have not been met. Currently they have accumulated reserves to last them a decade, so even if we restricted the flow, it would do very little to halt their present war industries and might make them plan a quicker and more thorough assault.

'At this time they are much more superior and will win any sustained war within a month. They know of our weaknesses.

Their only reason for delaying hostilities is to ensure we are subjugated once and for all time. That way, any future threat from our kind can be permanently neutralised. Those of us that survive will be taken off to our own mining colonies to be made into permanent slaves for Lodor. Once that happens we could never be free people again. They are clever, cunning and resourceful, and will always find ways to subdue us, even if it means destroying this world.

'Furthermore and from information received recently, I am now sure they intend to obliterate this world by the massive weapons they are now constructing and stockpiling. While our world remains, it symbolises a great threat to them and also engenders hope in the hearts of our own kind, their future slaves.

'If their plans are put into operation, they will gain all our mining colonies, with all future supplies directed to Lodor. With little or no opposition from anyone. My Lodorian spies have given us barely two years to prepare, which is hardly enough time to mount any reasonable offensive. Even if we were believed by our senseless opposition, most of whom are already in Lodor's pocket,' King Olav said.

His ministers and other colleagues and friends remained speechless.

'What can we do and to where can we hide if they decide to invade?' a most senior minister asked.

'I don't really know. That is why I decided to bring us here together. So that we may find answers. If we cannot leave our planet, we shall have to remain here, but somehow conceal ourselves from our enemies. And that concealment might have to be maintained for several decades. That is, until we are powerful enough to fight back. However, it will have to be planned in such a manner as not to arouse their suspicions, including those of their ever present spies,' King Olav said.

That meeting was dismissed without any further constructive contributions and a very worried group left the hall. They planned for another similar meeting the following week. That was after they had enough time to confront and consider their dilemma and alternatives.

After Lumak left Nervia World he journeyed to Polok II, to pay a last visit to his friend King Olav and fulfil a promise he made to him on Suk-Prime. It was going to be a brief visit before he returned to his home world, Kanaefon, to be assigned another mission.

That day King Olav was by himself in his study worrying about his world's problems. His wife and son had gone to visit their friends in the city. Suddenly Lumak appeared in King Olav's study in his usual manner and King Olav almost spilled his drink. It was one that had always surprised him, even though he had seen him appear that very same way dozens of times before.

'Lumak. My dearest friend. What a pleasant but shocking surprise!' he cried and they embraced.

'And how are you and politics these days?' Lumak inquired.

'I am fine, but not so with politics, I'm afraid,' he said with a deep frown.

'We now have a major problem that cannot be resolved politically. Neither have we been able to find another type of solution.'

'Perhaps if you could tell me your problem? Then I might give you some advice?' Lumak replied, sympathetically. King Olav then went on to explain the problem to him while Lumak listened patiently without interruption.

'I know of a race that was in a similar predicament to yours, and they survived. They dug a tunnel and built a city underground. There they remained for three thousand years,' Lumak said.

'Oh my God! Three thousand years?' King Olav replied in astonishment.

'Yes, three thousand years, and they survive to this day. You might only require such a place for a few decades and you could build a fleet in the mean time with current stocks. However, you will have to build underground bunkers to conceal such a fleet. Then your people could strike back when your enemies retreated and the time was right. On this world food supplies should not be a great problem if farms were properly concealed from your enemies. Perhaps I can find you some technical information on its construction,' Lumak said and faded into the air, but soon faded back. This time he carried a small black box and placed it on the table.

'This contains a copy of the information we received from the Ancients. Simply touch its topmost face to project forward and again to reverse. Lift it off the table to stop its functions. Use whatever you can within its pages. At the very beginning is a subliminal sequence, use it only if you decide to learn the language of the Ancients.

'I only wish I could be of greater assistance to you, my friend,' Lumak said.

King Olav observed the clear images that were projected on the wall and was overwhelmed by excitement with his new toy, but most of all, a method was found by which his people could be saved. The projections contained lists of materials and equipment needed in the construction of a completely sealed underworld environment. It also included methods for underground prospecting and mining for minerals.

Olav and Lumak worked for a while on the drawings, translating important parts that were written in the Ancients' tongue. Then he discussed the more critical areas with him until King Olav was thoroughly conversant with the technology.

'I only wish I could have done something more to prevent the war, but I believe the time is now too late for compromise, and from what you said about your political leaders, they are not the type to listen,' Lumak said.

'You have done enough, my friend. I shall brief my son, Malik, in such matters in case...

'Perhaps I shall see you again,' King Olav said, with sadness.

'Perhaps, but either way, I wish you and your family God's speed and his blessings in these most difficult times,' Lumak said. They shook hands and embraced, and he vanished from sight.

King Olav soon arranged another of his secret meetings to inform his friends and fellow politicians of a possible solution to their survival problem.

'Fellow colleagues and friends, I have prepared a computer program on information relevant to a possible course of action. However, in my opinion, this is our only course of action. I shall

hand these storage disks to you after I have said a few more words on the subject. You can scan through the information with your own personal home computers.

'It has a simple inbuilt erasure code in case of problems. This information was given to me by a dear and trusted friend. I met him during my interstellar travels and it was mainly due to his advice that we won the war at Suk-Prime. He also saved my life during that campaign.

'You are to mentally digest the information until our next meeting. Not even your wives, concubines and children are to know of our intentions, if we are to save them.

'The plan is for us to build several tunnels and sealed underground cities with the aid of Lodorian construction robots. That way all such construction can be completed on time. The tunnels are just a clever ploy. One necessary to mislead our present government and the Lodorian spies into thinking it's just normal expansion to an already overstretched conveyance tube network. However, I want us all, here and now, to take an oath of allegiance to our future course of action. From henceforth any new recruit must be thoroughly vetted and monitored by myself. We can have no slip-ups while on this future course. Far too much is at stake here, if we are to save our families and friends from a faith worse than death!' king Olav insisted.

They took the oath of allegiance to Polok with Olav as their leader and departed to their homes until another secret meeting was planned. They were happy in the knowledge that a way had been found in their darkest days.

King Olav had most of the wealthiest ministers in his pocket. Despite a strong socialist type of government, he and his royalist tended to have their own way by bribing generously when it was necessary. That way they had many a greedy administrator in their pockets. Soon he was given the building contracts without any further competition.

The construction of the so-called expansion program had been agreed in parliament and was being built by efficient Lodorian robots, but so also were his own tunnels and elevators to three large underground excavations. Their only major problem was how to conveniently displace that much debris unto suitable landfill sites, but even that problem was quickly solved. All the dugout rock could be ground and turned into special bricks for which there was always a demand, including the construction of his underground cities. Nevertheless some landfill sights were utilised. Once the initial tunnels were drilled, many massive tunnel drilling and excavating machines were constructed and assembled underground for completing the process. That way no one knew the true extent of the excavation.

Three underworld cities were excavated close to three of the major cities and temporary tube links tunnelled to link those cities with the under-worlds for the purpose of mass evacuation. Subsequently, under-worlds were linked via tunnels and locks to the local seabed.

Within two years they had excavated more than ten cubic kilometres of rock and that much had been either converted to bricks or dumped on landfill sites and seabed.

The under-worlds had a conical shape with their apexes on top close to the surface. That was also the position of the main elevators. In that way the surface mass was more evenly distributed and there was reduced likelihood of attack by missile or even earthquake damage.

Those under-worlds were swarming with robots, all controlled by a master Lodorian computer. King Olav soon had his own robotic construction plant for repairs, reprogramming and mass production.

After the excavation, ventilation and utilities were added and made operational. Then the buildings constructed with the same bricks formed from the original debris.

Each underworld city was to be honeycombed with homes at all levels and would contain about two million of his chosen people. Three underground areas had been excavated when he called a halt to all activities. Then the robots were reprogrammed for building the cities and storage facilities. By that time most of the landfill sites had been filled and completion dates of the project exceeded.

Finally, the fusion reactors were installed in caves with water diverted from the local sea to supply the desalination plants and

Powerful fusion generators. Those used pure hydrogen which was separated efficiently by a known chemical process.

In King Olav's view one million survivors were enough to fight the Lodorians in any future war. More underworld cities could be built during their period of isolation from the surface.

King Olav had another most brilliant but deadlier idea. One that would teach his Lodorian invaders a permanent lesson. He arranged for large explosive canisters to be laid within the major cities and other important areas of the planet. They were placed underground and fitted with radio controlled timers that were connected in such a manner as to release the compressed and most deadly gas when triggered. Once released, all Lodorians and their intricate androids would perish. Then most of the deadly spores in the air would remain close to the surface to plague the Lodorians for centuries to follow.

That factor alone would have put a halt to all Lodorian activity on Polok II. After that final task had been completed, he spent most of his time with his son, Malik, teaching him the art of warfare and the use of guerilla tactics. Soon Malik began to recruit many warriors of his own age, but still under secret cover and in private. During that time his father and other members of their committee accumulated many designs of weapons and ships, most of which were collected by his efficient spies based on Lodor. Their many computer libraries were updated with all relevant aspects of their culture, so that they could return to their previous way of life after they had won the final battle. Even so, the whole construction project was a hit and miss affair. Despite constant checks and surveillance they had no idea where the Lodorian spies were or whether they had informed Lodor of his under-worlds.

After the underground cities were completed, he sent word to his loyal spies on Lodor. They were to find an accurate date for the invasion. That information was not long in coming. It was to be within the month. After that knowledge was received most of his senior officers were either sacked or demoted from the government. However, they were instead evacuated to the underworld cities to take up office there and plan for the evacuation. During this time he and his family still remained on the surface.

Since security was of utmost importance in their plans, it was not easy to inform the general public of impending invasion or of the underground cities. However he had to somehow bring them together for his purpose. Therefore he created many underground facilities within the tube-way stations close to the underworld entrances. Then arranged trade fairs and exhibitions within subways close to those underworld cities. All items were to be sold at less than half price and special gifts freely given to complete families as an enticement.

Those places attracted numerous families and shoppers. While there, they would be innocently diverted towards the underworld cities and could never visit the surface again. Many complained about missing families but were ignored. Once all preparations had been made, King Olav and his ministers returned to the surface to face the onset of war.

Finally it was his wife and Malik's turn to leave, but she would not leave without him, so only their son, Malik, left for the underworld.

King Olav still tried to convince his arrogant opposing politicians, even at the last minute of impending disaster, but no one listened. Their arrogance was paid in full when the first bombs rained on their capital and destroyed almost all of its population.

CHAPTER 30

The Lodorian invasion

The Lodorian fleet commander was Bailor. He was clever as he was astute and knew the survival of his people depended on an outright victory against Polok. Bailor, also knew the Polokans well and realised they were no match for his war machinery. One that had been developed by a much more clever and advanced species, who had been through many similar wars in the past, even before Polok and its humans had been known by anyone. He correctly assumed no one on Polok knew of his intentions nor of the many saboteurs placed in their cities. Soon, even their war computers would work against them, having engineered a suitable virus to be introduced at the appropriate time. Being super intelligent and highly methodical, they left absolutely nothing to chance and had even planned for thousands of years in the future.

'It will be a quick and decisive victory. After all, those humans are a self-indulgent and decadent species that waste valuable resources in pursuit of self-gratification. Such wasteful children are a gross abomination to our universe. They have no control over their most basic urges and emotions. Which in themselves result in even greater wastage of essential resources for no real purpose of survival. Resources that we could well have done with to replenish and repair our ageing world.'

'Indeed, My Lord!' Volt replied, equally abhorrent of the present Polokan culture.

'It is a universal crime to waste so much just to feel one's most primitive emotional urges. Something they called enjoyment of self or having fun, while others in the universe suffer at their expense. Why are some species so darn selfish, in thinking the universe existed solely for their benefit at the exclusion of all others.'

'It is indeed sinful, my lord!'

'Funny enough, I and my people had always indulged Korot,

their current leader, and his uselessly stupid Polokan politicians, to think that my people were pleased with their government and its current policies. Even our human workers on Lodor had been indoctrinated enough to change sides for the common good. And those few will in time be replaced and sent to the mines to end their days; for they will always pose a threat to our empire... And their gullible politicians believed so absolutely in every lie we spurn them. Pity their king Olav was no longer in power. I always liked him. He cared for us and always kept his word.'

'It's all so sad, my lord!' Volt sneered.

'That was a very big mistake on their part and quite a bit of deception on my leader's instigation, and of all things it worked. Now they are little prepared for our invasion and cannot escape the claws of death and destruction soon to befall them.' Admiral Bailor smiled, as he regurgitated those pertinent thoughts, while his subordinate Volt agreed with his every word. At that time Bailor insultingly occupied a look-a-like android in the express image of the Polokan Leader. Volt's android was in the image of King Olav.

When the fleet arrived above Polok II it was already too late for Polok. By that time all the mining worlds had already been captured. Now, all effort would be concentrated on their home world, to cleanse it of its self-indulgent and wasteful humans. They had to take it all and subdue its humans once and for all time.

Large battle stations and spheres appeared over the world and positioned themselves above the largest cities. Then the missiles were released and like rain they fell upon its inhabitants. The cleansing process had begun. Within the first hour most of the major cities had been turned to rubble, but the missiles still continued to fall, consuming everything in their wake. Yet, not a single Polokan missile had been fired in retaliation.

After the first day of perpetual bombardment the Lodorians took a break to refill and recharge their weapons. Then they would concentrate their efforts on the smaller cities. Then towns and finally strategically important areas, until all that was left were a few people and animals fleeing hither and thither, not quite knowing which place would be targeted next.

Then many Lodorian androids landed and began to herd the tired and wounded refugees, like cattle, into large passenger craft that were designed for the purpose of transporting them to the mining colonies on other worlds. After most of the population had been taken away they decided to use the better areas of the planet for their own residence and for their occupying android forces. That ploy was also to maintain a surface presence during which time they could collect any remaining strays that had escaped or eluded their captors.

Yet, many of the survivors had evaded capture and fought with whatever weapons they could find. Those small clusters of humans lived in caves or ruins and were hunted relentlessly by the Lodorians.

It was during the second phase of their attack that King Olav's palace was hit. During that time king Olav and his wife were killed. At that sad moment most of the study room was vaporised by a missile explosion. Their death was almost instantaneous. He died while embracing his wife. Then he said a silent prayer and held tightly to Lumak's insignia until his last breath.

Their son Malik was in the underworld of Under-Safon at that time. He had to remain there until the main bombardment and hostilities on the surface had ceased.

After a month had passed, Malik and a few companions decided to visit the surface to check on his parents and assess the situation there. They had heard the rumble but had only basic visual connection with the surface.

Not knowing what to expect they assembled their small weapons while dressed in black leathery suits with communicators and heavy personal shielding. They journeyed upwards in the elevator, then took one of the four tunnels to the outlet closest to his family's palace. As they followed through the exit and unto the surface above, they found the air hard to breathe. There was a dense orange fog as far as their eyes could see. It tended to hover more densely over the ruined city. All they could hear were the howling of scavengers while they searched for food.

He and his companions couldn't believe the sight they now beheld. The once beautiful world had been almost completely obliterated and the horizon now a blood red. He ran in desperation towards the ruins of his family's palace ahead of his companions. They wandered through the rubble of his parents palace until they found his parent's decomposing bodies.

'The uncaring scum killed father... and mother and they...!' Malik broke down and began to weep. His two closest companions Safa and Ramm came closer and turned him away from the painful sight of his parent's remains and the stench of their decay.

'Will you help me bury them? I would like to put them over there, close to the lake. Father always liked the spot underneath the large Dupa tree where he used his fishing line. There they can rest in peace... together!' Again he broke down.

His two companions gave a few hand signals to those following. They took position to guard the area while Safa and Ramm dug the shallow grave for his parent's remains. They buried his parents and said a prayer. Then Malik prized Lumak's insignia from his father's clutched fingers and pinned it to his lapel for luck. That symbol he would always carry on his person in memory of his parents. During that time they stood at attention and removed their caps in respect for a great leader and his wife.

'We must return to Under-Safon to prepare. We have much work to do and plans to construct,' he said, but the sadness had disappeared from his eyes and was replaced by those of a fighter's resolve. From that moment he would fight the enemy until not even a single one remained.

He organised a war-room and battle training began in earnest to anyone who was old enough to carry a weapon. His methods were highly organised, with precise timing and flawless communications. He also had many of his father's original scientists to assist him and his army during their surface ventures. Then the merciless 100 years war of attrition against the Lodorians had begun in earnest.

Almost everyone within the under-worlds were involved in the war effort, but only the best trained were allowed onto the surface. Those were given death pills in case they were captured.

After a few more months had passed, once again he and his companions tooled themselves to the hilt with every conceivable weapon and took the concealed route to the surface. It was at dawn when they arrived. At that time the fog had diminished. The horizon had changed from blood red to orange and the putrid smell of death and decay was almost gone. He took his fighters to his parent's grave to say a prayer, then they walked towards the hills.

Unknown to him and his companions there were stray groups of survivors roaming those areas. Those were constantly hunted by Lodorian androids. Such surface survivors were accustomed to the most basic type of assault and were a lot more skilled at fighting the enemy than he and his unseasoned guerillas. They had found ways to survive the constant pursuit by efficient android forces and knew well their methods.

Suddenly Malik and his small group of six were being chased by three Lodorian android guards on fast space bikes. Those guards had remained hidden behind the few fruit trees while awaiting some hungry humans to fall into their trap. A well dressed Malik and his company seemed to offer them a better prize. The guards were also curious and wondered where they were from. The guards vehicles were LPD driven and mobile in almost any direction. They usually travelled about a metre above ground, and tended to automatically follow its contours. Once the chase began Malik's only hope of escape was towards the dense trees and ruined buildings several hundred metres away. Once under cover they could return fire. However the going was difficult as armour and weapons tended to weigh them down.

Although the Lodorian bike's pulse lasers were actively firing, they could not be accurately aimed during the chase because of the rough and undulating terrain. As they approached the ruins they could hear three whistling sounds that appeared to come from the nearest clump of trees. The sounds were followed by three small explosions and the three Lodorian guards and their bikes crashed to the ground.

'Safa, Ramm, down!' Malik shouted. They immediately fell into the mauve grass. But there were no more explosions. Malik wondered what could have happened in such quick succession to have taken out three speeding guards so effectively.

'Remain still this minute! Do not move!' came a female voice from beyond the trees. Then a shabbily dressed girl stood up in the tall grass.

'I said still!' she cried, as a defiant Malik tried to move along his intended path to observe the Lodorians and their bikes. She fearlessly walked briskly towards them with a strange weapon in her hand. It was designed like a boomerang, but with an explosive charge that was triggered on contact. She scanned his features thoroughly with those stolid eyes and wondered why the guards were so persistently chasing the strangers. Then she felt his hands and certain parts of his body until she was convinced he was not an android.

'Their space ships will surely have us in their sights by now. Very soon this spot will become an inferno... the moment they realise their guards have been killed. They are all rigged with sensitive life transmitters and are constantly monitored, you know!' she added, concerned for their safety.

'We need to save their bikes. Can we hide them some place, here?' he asked. He intended to use their own resources against them.

'We must hurry away from this place. You and your friends can take them if you wish at your own peril. I will show you a safe place to hide them,' she said. They undid the guard's harness, took their weapons, pulled them off and pushed the bikes toward the trees. She soon uncovered a hole in the ground that led to a large underground area. Within that area were a single family of six. The girl was the eldest. Her father had been an aeronautical engineer for the government in previous times.

'This is just one of our many hides in this area. We have several such places. To avoid detection we change on a regular basis. This is my mother, father, brothers and sisters,' she said. Malik nodded at each in turn. They were in rags and resembled the worst vagrants he had ever encountered. The bikes are not scanned and can remain here for a few weeks until they turn their attention elsewhere,' she said.

'What type of weapon did you use against them, to have killed them with a single blow and in such quick succession?' Malik asked with curiosity.

'We do not know of you, nor from whence you come. You are dressed as lords and no one here about can eat more than thrice in five days. Although you do not resemble our enemies, you could be their spies or sympathisers. In which case we are to kill each one of you here and now,' she replied, as her father and other family members began to take out their weapons, many of which had been captured from the Lodorians. Malik signalled his friends to hold their position, not wishing to further aggravate the situation.

'You really think we are Lodorian scum? What a sickening thought!' Malik objected vehemently and became frantic by her allegations; for it was the worst insult to which he had ever been subjected.

'Safa, please tell this female person who my father was?' Malik said.

'Are you sure, Sire?'

'Yes, tell her!' he insisted.

'He is the son of king Olav.' Then Malik removed a small picture of his family. They slowly returned their weapons to their hidden holsters and walked towards him.

'Your father survives?' her father asked, with a broad smile of satisfaction.

'No. I am sorry. He and my mother were killed by the scum during the bombardment of our city. Now I am in charge and will make them pay. They will pay and pay and pay... very, very, dearly, until not a single one remains!' They knelt before him and sympathised.

'My name is Mira.'

'Pleased to meet you, Mira,' he said.

'We must leave this place through the rear exit. This area will not take full sonic or radar probing and missiles will be falling shortly,' she said.

'Are there many survivors like you?' he asked.

'Yes, many, but they are scattered all over. Where have you and your fighters come from?' she inquired, with equal curiosity.

'I am very sorry, but I am not at liberty to divulge that information at this moment. Too many people depend on our concealment. But if you like, I can take you there. However it might be a one way trip for you and your family, until you are trained and become members of our family; for many millions of survivors depend on us.'

'You are with millions?' she replied with utter astonishment and with a fully gaping mouth and glaring eyes.

'Yes. My father knew of the invasion well before it happened and secretly planned for it, but couldn't tell everyone.'

'Now I suddenly feel a lot happier because of what you just said.' Her pallid face lit with excitement as she became more cheerful and feminine.

'I am also interested in the survivors in the hills and elsewhere. I would like to assist them when things improve. But regrettably that cannot be at this time. Now, tell me about your incredible weapon,' he said, with passion in his voice. She was very beautiful below the dirt and torn, shabby, filthy clothes.

'We call it the Curle. It was designed by my father about a year ago. The design has been improved many times over. First, it was just to distract them. Then with the explosive bolt to disable them, and it can be programmed and made to return to its sender by a simple wing adjustment. It is also streamlined to take advantage of explosive jets,' she said, showing him the one she held.

'Do the others in the hills have such an incredible weapon?' he asked.

'Only a few of my father's family and friends. But it's use will spread once they are aware of its powers. However, its use requires much training in accuracy,' she said.

'In that case we shall have to wait and you will have to train my fighters in the art of its use. You and your family will return with us and be trained as surface fighters. Then you will be treated more like respectable humans,' he replied, insistently.

'I will have to talk with my parents first,' she said and walked away. Then she went over and spoke to them in private, but soon returned.

'They have agreed, but my father is worried for his family and friends in the hills.'

'I have many plans for our world after the Lodorians are removed. In the mean time we are to fight and tire them until they begin to hate our world. During our ventures we are to collect all strays in the process and align them towards our common cause. I am sure your father's family and friends will be the first we find on our return,' he replied.

After having watched the explosive display and pyrotechnics over the area they had just left, they patiently followed him and his group into the tunnels to the underworld of Under-Safon. They were amazed by what they experienced after leaving the elevator. They entered a large city bustling with all forms of activity and immense resources.

'Tell your family that you are all to be my permanent guests,' he said.

Soon a small LPD craft appeared and they were taken to his residence on the highest levels.

'Ramm and Nasha can take you to the baths and get you some proper clothes to wear. Then you may join me and my group in the sitting room,' he said.

When they returned they were different people. The girl, Mira, had been transformed into the most beautiful woman he had ever seen.

'Was everything to your satisfaction?' he asked.

'Yes, master Malik, but words are not enough for us to show our gratitude,' she replied.

'We are all in the same boat here, so you will be my helper and adviser when we visit the surface, and your father can assist in our design department. Your young brothers and sisters can go to school until they are able to take their rightful place in our larger family.'

'My family fully agrees to those terms,' she replied while glancing at her parents for their approval.

'I have given instructions for another underworld to be built for those on the surface, but it will take a few years to complete. In the mean time they are to fend for themselves with our assistance.

'We are also to prepare land areas for growing crops and rearing animals for food. They can also assist us in that regard,' he said.

The Curle or boomerang type weapon was copied, improved and mass produced. Their attacks were planned on a daily basis with several surface groups. Soon, many stray families were found and trained within concealed surface areas. Those in turn trained others, until warrior cults of surface fighters were roving and making a name for themselves against the Lodorians.

Malik kept well away from those surface groups, but assisted them with weapons while they used their crops for payment. From that moment on he and his groups of fighters mounted death missions against the enemy every night and returned to their surface shelters during the day to sleep and replenish their bodies and weapons. They would only return to the under-worlds when a comrade was seriously wounded or during their weekends. It was during those times the Lodorians had any peace.

He wanted them to pay and they paid dearly as his band of guerillas grew larger, more skilful and knowledgeable of their enemy's intentions. Yet, he had the final weapon. The one that would remove the Lodorians from his world once and for all time and it wasn't the Curle.

After his marriage with Mira, Malik decided to stop the surface fighting. That was after he evacuated many of the stray surface groups into the newer cities. Then he left the Lodorians a calling card, giving them his name and stating his intentions to destroy all surface life on Polok. Malik always played fairly. However the message was really to give his enemies a chance to leave before their destruction. As usual they reported the information to their superiors who considered it a prank. Then Malik dispatched many of his fighters to the surface with their own filtered oxygen supplies and special transmitters that would be used to initiate the timers. Those timers were on the numerous buried tanks. Tanks that contained deadly neuro-toxins tuned specifically to the genetics of Lodorians and their androids.

It was at dawn when the tanks exploded and the deadly fog crept over the land; for that was the time for optimum effect. The Lodorian androids choked, staggered and fell in their thousands while their small octopus-like occupants died where they lay.

When they arrived on the planet's surface later that week the place was as peaceful as the grave and that it was.

Although the battle satellites still remained in orbit, they could do very little to assist their dying comrades on the surface. A few teams of Lodorians with environmental suits landed to check the atmosphere, but soon returned with contaminated air samples. As far as they were concerned the planet had been mined with deadly toxins that were designed to destroy all major planetary life. A form of genocide had been rigged by the human survivors and the planet was now permanently contaminated, never to be revisited by either type of life-forms in the future.

Even so, a few Lodorian ships would remain to keep a careful watch on surface activity.

Malik had won the first phase of the war. Now it was the more difficult matter of winning back Polok and its systems from the unsuspecting Lodorians. That final battle would take much longer in its preparation and implementation.

During that phase he would bring most of the surface people together and give them homes in the underground cities while his scientist continued to worked on several new products and weapons, some even outside of Lodorian technology.

Part 4
Cat People

CHAPTER 31

The cat world of Tarran

Earth time... 2039 CE

At that time Lumak was on his way home from Synora III to assess the stability of an aging star, when Lord Vektron appeared to him through the Mind.

'You are to visit the world called Tarran and assess its people. Find a kindly soul from a respected tribe and test their suitability for conversion. Use your feline mask if need be, and here are the details,' then he transmitted the information directly into Lumak's brain implants.

He travelled through the planet's northern territories then its southern, secretly studying the natives while deciphering their languages. Soon he found the Marawi people close to the Sadana Sea. They seemed to be the most industrious, caring and honest of all the clans, despite their primitive ways of living.

The northern clans were the wealthiest, dishonest and untrustworthy. Stealing most of the food and whatever they could from passing hunters and traders. Unsuspecting travellers were innocently diverted into their territories where they would be deceived into parting with valued belongings. In the case of hunters, high tolls were extracted before they were allowed to enter the desert and again when they left. Mulloks, a rear turtle like creature, and other highly valued crustaceans were often used during barter and bargaining. That creature was prized and valued above all others because of its many unique qualities and attributes. Its meat was a delicacy. The mother-of-pearl shell could be used as a container or for decoration and jewellery. Its poisonous tail contained certain neuro-toxins which when distilled could be used for medicine or applied externally for suppressing pain, healing wounds and such like.

Lumak had set his eyes on the Marawi Clan and began to

observe their customs, traditions and other ways in more detail. To him, it was an incredible experience observing those near savages existing on such a harsh and unforgiving world. Those experiences stirred him into changing their ways for the better.

'Here we have the makings of a great people. If only their world wasn't so hostile to her children,' he thought, while watching the old turbulent parent star with its orange glow and young companion, both pouring out their radiation unto those unfortunate planets in that binary system. In the case of Tarran's sun those exuberant benefits would be for a few more million years before it became nova or near supernova and vaporised everything in one massive explosion. Even Lumak felt unrest with the planet's extremes.

Despite the harshness of its surface environments, there were still green and hospitable areas close to the few remaining fresh water seas. But of great oceans there were none. Where they once covered the planet's surface laid expansive deserts of sand, filled with deep trenches and other unseen dangers. That was excluding the deadly sandstorms that blew at hundreds of miles per hour. Such storms could strip an individual down to barest bones in minutes.

He had catalogued its every species, from scaly monsters to giant sand spiders and found the world to be the most inhospitable living type he had ever observed. It was even worse than the Softlands and oceans of his watery world. To him the cat-people rated as one of the most ferocious hunting species in the galaxy, if not the most.

After he finished his recording, he turned his attention to their seat of power and the queen of the Marawi Clan. They had built their stone castles close to one of the main seas and ruled over a large part of that area.

Cat-women were the dominant sex, twice the size of their males and over twice as ferocious. They never allowed their males to take an active part in their main activities like hunting and fighting. A queen was head of each clan in what one could consider a highly structured matriarchal society. There were several such clans with fiefs in the most hospitable parts of the planet.

The males were highly technological and had over the years filled their boredom by designing better weapons, artifacts and jewellery for their women. They had also discovered a method of writing, which the royal house had found useful for sending messages and binding contracts.

It was late spring on Tarran and now the season of the great hunt. During that time the young female warriors would take to desert regions to hunt the mulloks and other large crustaceans. Mulloks were the most important catch and considered a delicacy by all the major tribes. It was perhaps the most difficult to catch because of its brief appearance on the desert's surface in the spring of each year. During those brief moments they would lay their eggs in the hot sands before diving back into the deep to be gone for another year.

The many tracks and passes to the desert where mulloks spawned were stalked by the most horrible and terrifying predators. Some would lay hidden snares and prey on anything, including cat-people. All those obstacles had to be surmounted before climbing the high plateau at the deserts rim.

If one got as far as the desert they soon found it contained its own dangers, from furious sand storms to giant sand-spiders in their hidden burrows beneath the sands. Others, including the mulloks could inflict instantaneous death from the sting in their long and pointed tails.

At that time Princess Bawaki was a brave and courageous adolescent who trained and hunted with her small gang of other similarly disposed young cat-women. When they were not practising their hunting skills with the bow, darts and knife, she would go and climb mountains in the clan's domain with her closest companion Siri.

It was soon to be her eighteenth birthday. On that day she was to be given her tribal bangle, but first she must prove herself. The tribal bangle was a thick iron band to be worn around the wrist. It contained her engraved name, ranking position and tribal markings in their specially written code.

As first princess, she could only prove her skills by either partaking in the great hunt or soloing on her own mission away from her tribes fief. During that time she was expected to visit the desert singlehandedly and bring back evidence of that visit. The latter was considered the most dangerous of adventures and therefore the most celebrated. She was not expected to take back mulloks, but she had to return with an appropriate souvenir.

Over the years she had become highly skilled in the use of weapons while her band of friends looked up to her for leadership. Nevertheless she always preferred to approach the dangers, take the risks and suffer the consequences of her actions by herself, wishing never to endanger her friends and companions. That attitude was never appreciated by experienced hunters with desert knowledge, since a smaller party of hunters significantly reduced survival odds.

At the appropriate time she left a parchment note for her mother, the queen, and quietly slid away into the night with enough rations for a fortnight. She followed the dusty trail towards the north as it was shown on her roughly drawn map. Unknown to her and her people Lumak held her in his sights with curiosity.

She wore her thick leather sandals with a strong net covering and thick leather sleeves that went from her ankles up to her knees. Those prevented the poisonous bite of the more common scaly desert snakes. They were the small hornless type that roamed the common lands for small prey. All types of predators, including the snakes, had several rows of Piranha-like teeth for speedily ripping and dissecting their prey.

On Bawaki's head was a wide rimmed straw hat with a fine netted veil that could be brought down to hide her face, but it did not significantly impede her senses. The remaining parts of her body were covered with loose clothes for agility.

Large bladders of precious water and dried meat rations were carried on her back and harnessed to her body by more thick leather straps. Then there was her belt with shoulder-band, which supported her hunting pouch, knife and quiver. About her right shoulder hung her bow.

She was one of the most agile climbers and unlike most hunters who went in groups, always took to the toughest routes across uncharted lands by herself, while adding new areas to her map. She had been thought the skill of writing and map-making by her father. He insisted any future queen would need to communicate more fluently with her people and neighbouring clans, and writing was a necessary skill for that purpose. She reasoned that difficult mountain routes, despite the greater risks, were equally shunned by the larger and more dangerous predators.

'Pity I couldn't have taken Siri along, but she is not the best of climbers and understood my quest, although worried for my safety. My mother will have my note read to her at first light. By then it will be too late for them to launch a search party. That will give me enough time to enter the Loddi Plains,' she thought, still moving at a brisk pace within her clan's domain.

She enjoyed the new experience of unbounded freedom, being alone while wandering over land that she had never trod before. She was more than eight hours into the night and moving north into uncharted areas avoided by normal cat-people. During that time she used extreme stealth and followed the safest passes. Her eyes were keen and unlike most other species, could observe over a wider spectrum of light and extremely low levels. She realised at such times of night most of the larger predators would have already eaten and returned to their burrows to await the onset of day.

When she arrived at the high Malli Plateau, she would say a prayer to her clans goddess as many hunters had done before. Then take the long gradient to descend unto the desert's floor. She viewed her parchment map several times, noting landmarks, adding new ones and making corrections to existing ones. That map had been drawn from information supplied to her by hunters and was meant to be a rough guide. Most of the mountainous areas were uncharted so she thought of adding more routes to some of the blank areas during her travels.

Cat-women had thought skills like writing, map-drawing, building, jewellery, pottery and such like, unworthy behaviour for any fearless hunter and left them to the cat-men who to them were a decadent and inferior sex, only fit for mating purposes.

The females thought all ideas of change to be quite unbecoming for dedicated warriors on which the survival of the tribe depended. Nevertheless they allowed their males their hobbies and strange industries as a way to relieve their boredom while their females were out hunting and gathering. Despite their single-mindedness, they sometimes accepted some of their males' inventions that assisted their hunting, gathering, defence and offence. Bawaki was more modern in her attitudes and realized all such technologies could be useful. She saw in them ways to improve her people.

Just before dawn she stood a while at the northern edge of the Loddi Plains and observed the taunting mountains in the distance, their tops covered in thick mist. She had not yet experienced any dangers, although having heard several cries of wild beasts coming from the west.

The light morning breeze persistently blew from the north and those factors prevented her scent from getting to local predators. Except from the south where she had journeyed from and that path seemed to be relatively clear. It was now early morning when most of the plain's larger cat predators would be returning to their burrows to sleep during the hot daylight hours. She glanced in the southerly direction and viewed her clan's fief in the misty distance for the last time. Then she took a deep breath before descending the first gradient towards a small valley between two mountains.

She realised where two mountains met were usually dangerous places, for it sometimes offered shelter and water to its denizens. That area was covered by thornbush and she also knew that variety was poisonous. Therefore the chances of finding predators within that area were equally slim.

She removed her climbing rope and hung it over her shoulder. She ascended the other side, taking the more difficult route along the mountain ridge. She arrived at the summit in good time and rested from her climb while viewing the surrounding areas for a safer route. From her present standpoint she could view her clan's fief unto the misty Sadana Sea. To the left was the chasm's wall which appeared to hold the eastern part of the desert in place. Below, could have flowed a river in ancient times, but major upheavals in the past had separated those areas and it was not possible to take that route into the desert.

At its lowest end was the fief of the Zadi Clan. They were an unfriendly neighbour that hated trespassers. Therefore the only preferred route was the one from the north through the eastern pass and across the uninviting mountains.

Lumak could have observed many parallels between that area of the planet and the part of his home-world where he was born. On his world were waters in abundance, while here instead were deserts in widest expanse. Their chasms, although much smaller by comparison, held memories of dangers for him. Nevertheless the northern areas were quite similar to those on his own world, although this one much smaller in size and a thousand times more extreme and inhospitable by comparison. Where their small city of Marawi stood on the Sadana sea, his massive home city of Lud stood close to the Sea of Jessel, not too distant from the Ocean of Gibro. The area was like a miniature map of his own family's fief and almost identical in every detail, but for the extremely high mountains and associated deep trenches and gullies in the northern regions just before the desert. All those low lying levels would have been filled with water in ancient times.

On Tarran as the oceans dried and receded many crustaceans adapted well to the remaining waters deep within the deserts' sands.

Bawaki journeyed for another ten hours through the thorn-bush infested valleys and hills until she could see the high plateau in the distance. In another two hours she was at the plateau's sandy rim. There she stood safely on the highest point viewing the distant horizon. She could observe the smaller star amidst the few more distant constellations. The largest and most vicious of Tarran's binary slowly fell behind the western horizon, giving the planet a little time to recover and dissipate some of the day's accumulated heat. She had journeyed for more than half a day and keen on finding a suitable place to rest until morning. She realized that during the semi-dark hours many of the larger nocturnal predators left their burrows to hunt well away from any direct exposure from the harmful rays. During all this time she had faced the extreme heat while moving in and out of the shade. However she was well shielded from the direct rays and had timed her journey well.

Cat people had evolved their cultures to be active during the day. For that purpose their bodies were almost completely covered with special hair to resist harmful radiation. Only their eyes were at risks and those had an extra membrane and long thick eyelashes. Anyway, they knew better than to look directly at their main star and wore broad rimmed straw hats during the daylight hours. The less massive and more distant sister star was much younger and too far to have had any significant effect on their world.

Lumak thought of making contact with Bawaki but did not wish to scare her away. Nevertheless he had learnt their language and could communicate with hand and vocals while using an appropriate feline mask with his Shadite's Cloak.

She decided to spread her small leather tent, which was no more than six groundsheets sewn together at all edges to form a Constantina-like cube that expanded with poles in place. It included a small entrance at one of the corners with fasteners, through which the occupier could enter. Three thin tubular telescopic iron poles kept the uppermost surface away from the lower, with several netted vents for breathing. The males had learnt the use of such metals years ago.

Although such tents were quite tough, they offered little protection against any of the larger predators, so hunters were extremely light sleepers.

Bawaki found a large boulder to use as a seat and removed her other harnesses to release her burden, while keeping her weapons at arms length. She then exposed her rations and began to eat with a little of her precious water.

As the sun disappeared so did the heat and she began to shiver from the cooler air at that altitude. Although cat people used fire in their cities, which they ignited with large mirrors and lenses, hunters knew little of the principles involved and even less of the iron-flint-stone fire boxes.

'Bawaki!' Lumak cried, without fading into her world and Bawaki immediately turned around to see whether she had been followed by Siri or one of her other companions, but there was no one there.

'Bawaki! I am a friend...,' the voice again said. This time Lumak faded into the dark form while wearing a female feline mask. She snarled while quickly moving backwards, her bow already in hand, and began to retrieve an arrow. She had never heard or seen such a strange aberration in all her short existence. Cat people were incredibly fast and could complete almost any movement at lightning speed; for such were the ways of a supreme hunter.

'Don't be afraid. I am a friend,' Lumak, now a strange cat-woman, said in a mild voice. He had learnt their disposition and facial expressions. By now she had fitted an arrow and was ready to shoot, but held her aim.

'How do you know my name? Are you god or demon?' she inquired, while maintaining her distance, but closely scanning the stranger. Then he took something out of his cloak pocket and fired it at a small rock. The rock became a fire, but did not melt or flame.

'It's getting a little cold. This will keep us warm well into the night. Now we can talk,' he said, calmly.

'Thanks!' she replied, still shivering a little.

'I am a messenger from our lord, but I am not a god. I know your name because I have observed you. I also know of your interest in many things outside of your clan's knowledge and interests. How would you like to fulfil all your dreams?' he said, with candour.

'First, I must past my tests of bravery and survival.' She moved slowly towards the warmer rock for greater comfort, while holding her eyes on the stranger.

'That is the simplest of all tests and is only relevant to your clan. It is of little importance to the Grand Lord of our universe. To be truly great you must think effectively and strive for real and true greatness. Look at the distant stars for instance. Many are like your own sun, with worlds even similar to your own. They are inhabited by many creatures unknown to your world.

How would you like to visit any of those worlds in the future?' he said with sincerity.

'I would say it was an impossible feat for anyone except a god,' she replied, utterly astonished.

'I myself was from a star beyond all those you see and yet here I am talking to you, away from my own world and I am not even a god,' he said.

'If what you say is possible and I could also help my people in the process, then I would accept such an adventure, providing it was not too costly to my people and myself,' she replied, nervously.

'Spoken like a true princess, with a high regard for her own. Some systems like yours are extremely harsh and inhospitable to its inhabitants while others like mine are so kind and loving, that people like us are allowed to evolve and live upon them in peace and happiness, with only the minimum of effort. Yet, even those most beautiful and loving worlds that are taken for granted can change in the course of time into harsh parents, taking their fury upon their innocent children, but so also can the hash ones be turned into beautiful worlds with technological assistance,' he said.

'That is my world. Full of fury against her own, both young and old alike. You imply that my world may one day be changed into a better one. Is that really possible?' she replied with curiosity.

'Those problems may appear insurmountable, but in time even you can change that situation with the assistance of our Grand Lord. I give you my word as a hunter of greatness, that it can be done. My beautiful princess, Bawaki,' he said and she felt more at ease with the supposed female in the strange garment than she had felt with many of her own people.

'It will only cost you your commitment and nothing more, but you will be expected also to help others and respect life in its many habitats. They also have their ways of living and rights by virtue of their existence,' Lumak said, seriously.

'I must contemplate your words while I travel to the desert's floor,' she replied with commitment in her manner.

'In that case, I shall leave you this small memento and the insignia of my god-clan here on this stone. It will dispel any doubts you might hold about my existence. You can place the small box with its reflective face upwards in your nets when hunting for mulloks and throw it towards the ground when you are in danger,' he said and slowly faded into the air leaving her even more nervous than when he first appeared.

 Bawaki eagerly waved to the strange figure as she faded into the mist and began to make ready for the most dangerous challenges ahead.

Despite her considerable fears she was very courageous and walked towards the stone to collect the items. She soon moved her tent nearer the warm rock and closely examined the strange and apparently insignificant objects. When she had finished her examination, she put them in her small pouch for safe keeping.

CHAPTER 36

Unto the desert

At dawn, Bawaki fastened her belts and leather sleeves, then her holdall before traversing the high plateau. Then she began the slow downward incline into the orange desert. That part towards the east was not well-trodden, with many hills and crevasses. She was a gifted climber and tracker, and could detect smells for miles around in the now relatively slow breeze, so she persevered.

At her present rate of descent it would have taken her another six hours before entering the desert's rim. Then she would spread her tent and wait a few days until detecting signs of ascending mulloks. That was assuming the mulloks hadn't already laid their eggs and returned to the deepest areas of the desert's sand. If that was the case, she would have to travel elsewhere, much deeper into the hostile desert with a correspondingly smaller chance of survival in the extreme heat.

Nevertheless she knew what to observe so when she entered the sands carefully checked its contours and distant dunes for mulloks' markings. Those were small depressions in the sand that marked their points of entry and exit when they dived out and back into the sand while laying their eggs. They always leapt outwards and entered at two distinctly different points which left two opposite shapes that represented size and movement.

As she viewed the desert's floor she could find no such markings or signs of local sandstorms that could remove such markings in her local patch, so she decided to set up base in that area close to the hills. However unknowing to her, Lumak had a small hand to play in her fortunes.

She dug six long ditches with her bare paws and laid her small fishing nets within the ditches. Those she marked with vertical arrows pushed into the sand before filling them in. Then she placed Lumak's black box above the most central of the ditches with its reflective surface pointing upwards towards the sun and waited to see whether it worked.

Within another hour there was a distant rumble as of thunder. The rumble increased in magnitude to such an extent that it scared her into taking to the local hills. Safety was barely five hundred yards away, and she made it in seconds, leaving all her equipment behind.

While she watched she could observe swarms of mulloks boiling over the desert's floor to lay their eggs and dive back into the sandy and watery depths from whence they came. When the swarms had died away, she joyfully ran towards her base with a knife in hand to excavate her tent and other items. They had been completely covered by the sands brought up by several waves of mulloks. By now the nets were completely filled with struggling mulloks that had been captured while trying to return to their watery depths. There they struggled in her nets while beating themselves to death in the intense heat of the hot surface sands.

'Yawi! Yawi! Yawi!,' Bawaki cried, ecstatically in her catlike fashion; for never before had she observed so many mulloks in any one place. Even so, she was careful not to fall into deep crevasses created by their downward motion. Such crevasses were like quicksand and could slowly pull an unsuspecting hunter into the lowest depths until suffocated or drowned.

Using her knife she quickly removed their stinging tails, then their shells. After that task had been completed she drained them of all their juices to fill a large water bladder. Then spread their flesh out to dry.

After another hour she began to pack them into her large holdall and tightened her harness for her return journey. Then she tied her long climbing rope around her waist, hoping to take an easier and more northerly route with less climbing on her homeward journey. She did not intend to travel too northward and be cheated by the northern clans, who would doubtless have taken half her mulloks for passage through their territories.

Finally she collected the little black box and kissed it for luck before placing it back into her small front pouch.

Bawaki reflected on the strange visitor, her even stranger clothes and wand of great power. Power enough to heat a large rock without fire and realized the strange one must have been a servant of God. Either that or she was dreaming. But she had proof that she was not dreaming, so all those experiences must be real. In that case, who else could wield such incredible powers. Powers enough to command the mulloks to rise from the watery depths beneath the desert sands.

'Even so and with all those god powers, how can I help my people from their savage existence on such a hostile world. How can I, a mere princess, be exalted to the stars and be given equivalent powers to assist my world,' she thought for a while.

Then she realized any visit from a servant of God must be very important. After all the angel did call her by name, so she must have come all that way from the stars to see her on purpose. Which meant she was chosen for greatness, else why give her the special items for her protection.

Bawaki pondered those thoughts as she mounted the first small plateau out of the desert's sands. The sacks she carried were awkward and heavy, which meant her progress was slower than expected. She had to take extra care with each foothold as she climbed unto the main plateau. Then she would follow its mild contours for several miles towards the north west. At that point she would once more take to the hills.

'So father and his other males were correct all along, with their strange technological inventions. Even at the displeasure of my mother and the other females. I always thought our females reacted against change for no real reason other than the changes it brought. That was because they were scared about where those changes led, whether for better or worse. All such changes away from our well established norms needed much faith in the future and sometimes meant taking a leap in the dark in order to grow.

'Nevertheless, we had always gained by such technological advancement. Even the ability to write symbols on a map to explain the same routes to others. Now, that would definitely be a great gain if I could create a proper map of hunters trails, showing the many dangers on the way to the hunt and warn them in advance of places to avoid. Such a map could save the lives of our many brave and fearless hunters,' Bawaki thought as she considered those ideas.

CHAPTER 33

The route home

Although she had carefully plotted what appeared to be an easier route on her map, she had never followed that path before. There were areas on the original map that indicated places of danger. Nevertheless, she had little choice if she wanted an easier journey home with her more difficult load of mulloks.

The more well trodden route further north would have taken Bawaki into the northern territories with greater risks from bandits and others who would doubtless have stolen her expensive catch of mulloks. Having foregone all those risks on her own, she had decided not to freely give any amount of her catch to anyone, least of all bandits and greedy northerners.

As she climbed out of the plateau and unto the first thorn-bush vale she heard a distant roar and an old hungry cat appeared out of the dry desert pine bushes across her trail. Those miniature pines had long roots that penetrated the thick crusty sands for the odd moisture. Other desert plants would wrapped themselves around small rocks to collect the odd drops of water that accumulated on rock faces and sometimes penetrated the sands earlier in the day. They also absorbed the morning's dew with their large spongy leaves which made good shelter for predators.

While glancing at the shaggy beast, she cut the desert pine close to its roots and began sucking out its juices. All her precious water was gone so that stumpy plant was a godsend. What little mulloks' juice she had left was too salty and although nutritious would make her more thirsty.

'Oh! How I feel better for that!' she whispered to herself.

It was a large quadruped that growled and stamped its paws as a gesture of its territorial rights, with full intention of making Bawaki its first meal for many days. But despite intentions it could muster little strength and was just putting on an aggressive show with what little energy reserves it had left. Such cats were never seen outside of their dens during that time of day, so this one was desperate for a meal. At that time Bawaki was willing to pay a small price in mulloks for getting past the stubborn beast in order to make good time before nightfall. It would also lighten her weight a little. After observing the poor starving animal she didn't even bother to retrieve her bow, but walked directly towards it.

'You want food?' she inquired, sympathetically, of the shaggy beast, placing her paw into her mouth to signify eating in an attempt to bribe the giant beast into submission. Those cats were highly intelligent and would have known what she meant, although not having any precise language of their own. It growled again, this time accepting her advances and began showing submission by laying on its back and rolling in a playful mood. She couldn't help but sympathize with the animal, so she removed her sack of fresh mulloks and placed three large ones close to the cat while partly filling one of the mulloks' shells with mulloks' juice. Then she made her retreat as soon as it began to eat the first one.

She tried to maintain a respectable distance between herself and the cat in case it took a liking to her sack of mulloks, so she followed steadily ahead. She made as much progress as she could during the daylight hours. That was the time when most desert predators were asleep in their dens and burrows, and preserved their energies for nocturnal hunting. In those areas only the extremely hungry would venture out during the hot daylight hours.

She made slow progress through a long rocky ridge with the seemingly ever increasing weight of mulloks on her back. She continued that way until she became too exhausted to proceed any further and waited there for a while after sipping some mulloks' juice. She was too thirsty to wait.

The terrain soon worsened as she passed many dangerous precipices and crevasses on the way until she could see part of the Loddi Plains in the distance. Those plains bordered her clan's territories, but were a free hunting area and no-man's land. She hoped to cross into it just at the neck of the great chasm. By then, it would be dusk. Large predators would be out in number and roaming for food.

She knew she had little chance of survival while carrying her catch of mulloks. They had a strong and lingering smell that carried and her load would be detected for kilometres around once she had arrived at the lower plains. Luckily for her the air had become relatively still, but that might not be the case on the plains below.

The cats of the Loddi Plains were skilled at hunting in packs, ranging from six to several dozens. They could stealthily follow their innocent quarry for miles until the time was right for them to strike. Then they would pounce at once and tear that body into little pieces before their prey could have shouted a word for help. Those thoughts ran through Bawaki's mind while attempting to find a way out of her dilemma. Having weighed the situation, she thought she had little chance of survival with or without the mulloks during night time, so she decided to take her chances and persevered. At least the sack of mulloks and their shells added to her protection.

As she approached the plains, her problems were further compounded when she realised she was being followed. She didn't know by whom or what but could hear the occasional muffled growl coming from behind. Those occasional sounds tended to speed her progress towards the lower plains. When the distant growl had ceased, she rested for a while and glanced at her map to take a bearing, but many of the mountains were not where they should have been. She soon realised her position when she glanced towards the distance from a taller peak.

She had travelled more than ten miles towards the north and was not as close to the chasm's neck as she would have liked. She had arrived at the lower end of Cus-Veldi. That was one domain of the swarming horned vipers. They were small fang-less snakes with singular poisonous horns on their foreheads and sharp saw-like teeth. Those ferocious snakes with their piranha-like teeth were designed for tearing flesh in the quickest possible time.

A swarm of such snakes would hide beneath the sand and await their quarry. Each swarm could contain several hundred individuals and they were never seen until it was too late. They would quickly ascend out of the sand and dive towards their prey in the hope of sticking their sharp poisonous horns deep within their victim's flesh and those horns could penetrate deep into thick leather to release their neuro-toxins. Such poisons also made the kill uneatable by other types of predators. Luckily for her they hunted mainly during daylight hours and became dormant as it got cold.

There was another hour to go before the furious sun disappeared below the crimson horizon and another before she reached the Cus-Veldi. Then it would take half an hour to pass that area at quick pace. If she was fortunate perhaps she could just make it, or so she thought.

She travelled quickly and stealthily while looking for any snare pits, paw prints or movement in the soft sand but there were none. She tried to get as close to the chasm's neck as she could for more safety, but she was still too far away and the quickest route home was the one directly southward.

When she passed the land of the snakes she could observe a disturbance of dust in the distance. She wondered whether it was due to a small whirlwind which occurred frequently in those parts.

As the cloud of dust approached she soon realised they were caused by speeding feet. It was five large cats that moved towards her. They gained position so quickly she had little option but to take a stand where she stood with bow and arrow. Visibility was very low so it became quite difficult to hit any of those quickly moving targets. While they surrounded her position she fired and impaled the first one, but the closest was too fast for her and pulled her to the ground before she could shoot another arrow.

The others were soon on the scene to assist their companion in ripping off her clothes to gain access to the mulloks and her person. While they struggled, and she did put up a fight, Lumak's small black box fell from her pouch. As it hit the ground there was a mighty roar and then a blinding-flash of white light that lit the plains for miles around.

The cats screamed with fear and dashed away from their prey as fast as they could, leaving Bawaki superficially torn and with mild concussion. There she remained for a while, slightly dazed and temporarily blinded by the sudden flash of light. Soon the light dimmed as her pupils adjusted to ambient conditions.

'Now I know what the god-one meant and he was really from God after all,' she whispered to herself, with eternal gratitude, while shifting her load and redoing her harness to relieve the discomfort felt by their misplacement. Bawaki was lucky that she had not been bitten or severely wounded. She went to collect the little black box, but was surprised by what she could observe barely twenty metres away. There stood the large shaggy animal; the one she had given her mulloks to in the vale. She didn't know whether it was the bright light or the loud roar that sent her enemies away, but either way, the animal had helped to save her life and it could have her sack of mulloks and all her remaining rations as reward for that great service.

Slowly it walked towards her and began to lick her paw, trying to gain her affection. She stood in front of the large beast and stared into his eyes.

'So you are a grateful friend and not a foe? But you are supposed to be wild and vicious and not a pet. How did you know I would be in danger, or did you follow me for more of my mulloks? Anyway, you saved my life, so either way it doesn't matter,' she said to the kindly animal while pulling at its large ears, playfully and with loving gratitude.

She collected Lumak's black box and kissed it, then she hugged the shaggy cat and both began their long and fearless walk towards her clan's fief. Despite the many predators about at that time, she was sure none would take the risk to attack them; for she now had company and a little black box she could use to frighten them away. It took her until dawn to arrive at her clan's borders. When she converged with the main pass she was surprised to find several tents pitched to one side.

'Bawaki! Bawaki!' Siri cried, as she ran to greet her closest friend, but Siri slowed her progress when she observed a large cat following at Bawaki's rear.

'Do not be afraid of my friend Tokai. He will not harm you!' Bawaki yelled and her other companions soon followed. Bawaki undid her harness and removed the sack of mulloks, tent and other heavy items. Those she distributed among her friends to carry.

Siri and her companions had rightfully assumed that Bawaki would survive her trials to join them within three days from the day she left and had mounted their tents in the most appropriate place, patiently awaiting her return.

Bawaki told them of her journey and her meeting with God's messenger on the plateau. Then she showed them the box of many powers or god-box, as she called it, and the colourful insignia. They were utterly astonished by it all. To them the journey of endurance had not only made her the most worthy hunter in the land, but had transformed her into a god-child. Who else could have taken on the mountains and desert singlehandedly. To have won so many mulloks and the heart of one of the wildest of the desert's beasts.

It took them until noon before they arrived at Marawi City. She was greeted by many fearful onlookers as she proudly rode on the back of the large ferocious mountain beast as if it were a cart-cat. Her mother had since given up on the search and recalled the trackers by signalling mirror, so she was quite happy when her only daughter survived the ordeal of her tests.

When she entered the city gates, she was cheered by many, but they kept well away from her large pet.

She told her mother of her strange encounter and experiences and showed her the insignia and god-box of many powers as she called it, that Lumak gave her. The queen stared at her in utter astonishment.

'Never in all my life have I heard such a strange tail. You have been chosen for a great purpose, my daughter. God has saved your life and now you must become his servant in return. From now on, you will lead the hunt with our best hunters until you are called again for your Greater Purpose. That way our tribe will once again become the greatest among felines,' the queen said, joyfully.

Tokai, the desert cat, was made a royal hunter and given his own guard duties within the palace. From that moment on princess Bawaki had gained the reputation of being the greatest hunter in the land. Many would seek her company during the great hunts. Her reputation had travelled far and wide so that even the greedy northerners showed respect by not extracting bribe from her group while wandering through their territories.

Part 5
Back on Earth

BACK ON EARTH

'Darling! Darling! It's time to go,' Sarah shouted. Lumak realised he was dreaming of brave Bawaki, her cat people and the harsh world of Tarran. He knew she was Shadite material and her training would take her to Earth, so he looked forward to their future meeting. He also realized the next time they met she would most likely have been transformed through the Mind into a most beautiful female human form.

Since his move to the USA, Lumak felt a lot safer for Sarah and his friends left behind in Turkey. At least, the extreme religious elements in that country could not have followed him to his new country of residence, or so he thought.

Nevertheless he soon installed a most sensitive security system about the large manor, just in case.

CHAPTER 34

Shadite Plato pays a visit

Earth time ... 2041 CE

Place ... North Dakota, The United States of America.

Lumak was having a brake from his scientific program and decided to visit the stream near the large fishing pond to collect his thoughts. Sarah had christened that place Little River in her Turkish dialect and made it her favourite spot. Nevertheless Lumak called his preferred area close to the neck of the pond Beaver's Bank, since that area was inhabited by a family of friendly and inquisitive beavers. As he followed the winding footpath he felt a presence. He glanced behind to find the hooded figure of his Andromedan friend Plato following.

'Let me congratulate you on your recent achievements and bring you glad tidings from Gemmi and others including family and friends. The Grand Lord kept us informed of progress, so don't be too worried about them.'

'That's incredible news!' A surprised Lumak replied.

'Lord Vektron has sent me here to prepare the way for my people. Earth has been chosen to assist in the evacuation program and I would like to make a start.' Plato was joyful at their meeting and Lumak still couldn't believe his eyes. There they both stood in human form together and with little need for brain implants to translate their complex communications while showing similar human emotions.

'Plato, what a pleasant surprise! I thought you were on Caefon?'

'I like your human form. You now resembles my twin brother,' Plato remarked in jest.

'I suppose yours was the only logical choice for a functional template, but I think it's a great body all the same. Anyway, how are you occupied these days?'

'I am still assisting my people. However, the bulk of the work is now at an end.'

'It is indeed a great surprise and pleasure to see you here on Earth, my friend. From whence have you come?' Lumak inquired.

'I have just arrived from your home world, Kanaefon. I was there to arrange delivery of the Omegron Portal. It has been disassembled and is now being transported to Under-Caefon on a specially shielded craft. The other part is to be placed on a special ship for transportation to this system.'

'That's very good news. I was quite worried for your people in Andromeda. I suppose those ghastly Javols are yet several years away from your world?' Lumak said, but Plato shied away from that painful question and changed the subject.

'Gemmi has become a Grade 3 Shadite. She sends her love and expects to see you soon.'

'That's great news! I always knew she had those abilities. Please give her my love when next you meet,'

'I have been told of your recent marriage and must take this opportunity to congratulate and wish you well for the future. May both your lives be filled with happiness and good fortune. As customary, I brought you a small present. An ancient golden tiara set with diamonds and other jewels. I hope your wife likes it,' Plato said, handing Lumak the beautiful box, but with sad reflections of his own family since departed. It once belonged to Lucia, his brother Meron's wife over 3000 years ago.

They both saluted each other again by placing their fists on their left breast and Plato bowed to his senior. Then they embraced each other. Plato was in his Shadite's cloak and Lumak was afraid his present form would frighten Sarah. As an Andromedan human he also exhibited six fingers and two thumbs. Therefore both went for a stroll along the track towards the forest where they could talk without being observed or overheard.

'My real program here has only just begun. It will take me at least two more years before a single LPD can be produced. They will be required for any mass interstellar evacuation to a suitable planet within the vicinity of Earth.'

'And that journey will depend on the placement of the Omegron Portal', Plato replied.

'The inhabitants of this world will not accept your people in those quantities. They are xenophobic and will feel threatened by anyone more advanced than themselves. The situation may be further compounded when they realised the evacuees are from another world. They are xenophobic to the nth degree and will decimate your people if they knew of those facts. Further, this world is passing through a critical period in its history, with population growth as its main concern. Therefore I have a duty to the poorer countries like Africa; to assist their suffering before it's too late for them and their starving children.'

'I understand,'

'My friend, my task here is truly enormous so I will accept whatever help I can receive from you during this period. Nevertheless, anything to do with the evacuation of your world must be carefully planned and realised by a few responsible individuals. As a matter of fact, the bulk of your people will never set eyes on this world for the common-good,' Lumak said and Plato was saddened by that fact.

'Perhaps to another local world. The evacuation program will commence in about two years and I have no idea of Lord Vektron's long term plans on the matter. All I know and worry about, is that the first swarm of Javols will appear in our stellar system at about that time. The underground city of Lower Cantor is already full to capacity and there are more than ten million left on the surface. Those have to be fed and cared for during this time,' Plato said with concern in his voice.

'In that case, my friend, when you are not too busy elsewhere, you can be here assisting me. That should speed progress at this end and ensure that this path is clear and waiting. However, you must never use the cloak while my wife is about. She is not yet trained to accept our form and ways.'

'I see!'

'You must keep a set of clothes in the workshop and change whenever you arrive, until I can arrange a room for you at the house. Your hands will be accepted as a simple birth defect. This planet has many such cases due to chemical pollution and certain dangerous drugs taken by mothers during pregnancy. You can be thought of as one of my trouble shooting scientists. That occupation will explain your frequent absence.' Lumak added.

'That's fantastic!'

'I shall arrange some clothes for you and place them in a small case. The case will be hidden in one of the lockers in the workshop for which you will have a key. Visit me tomorrow so dressed and I shall introduce you properly to my wife. After that, I will let you have a room on a permanent basis,' Lumak said.

'That will suit me fine. You have made me a very happy person, knowing that I can do something positive to assist both programs,' Plato said and faded into the air.

Plato appeared again just before lunch and found the clothes Lumak had hidden for him in the locker.

He rang the door bell and Sarah answered.

'My name is Plato and I have come to see Doctor Longhurst,' he said, pretending.

'Darling, I would like you to meet Doctor Plato. He is now a member of our science team. He is one of the best in Micro Robotics and will be one of my senior troubleshooters when the project commences. Let me also introduce you to Harry Lennox,' Lumak said as he shouted Lennox's name and he was soon through the sitting room door.

Later that day he called Lennox into his study for another one of their private discussions.

'If at all possible, I would like you to head a separate team of scientists. We are to develop an anti-fertility device. Hopefully, the parent bacteria will not be required until the human population exceeds twelve billion. Then it should only be used when a firm decision has been made by those in authority. Any such decision can only be taken by those in power, but you are to keep our intentions in greatest secrecy for now. All computer models predict the extinction of humanity and most life on this planet within a short time if the human population is allowed to grow beyond that point,' Lumak said.

'Wow! That disastrous, eh! Do I have a little time to consider your appointment? I shall have to mention my new position to President Arnold. If it's ok with him I shall accept. Can I mention the terminal bio bug to him?' Lennox replied, with fear and trepidation in his manner.

'He is one of us and already knows. I keep very little from him these days. Explain exactly what I have told you. I find the extinction of any form of life to be intolerable. It is better stopping people from having children for a few decades than the alternative. Once this Terminal bacteria is placed within Earth's atmosphere it will multiply and prevent all types of human procreation. However, during that time a few families throughout the world will be randomly selected for procreation, by ensuring they receive a constant supply of the antidote. This device must show no symptoms and the infected should live out their normal life-span. That process will continue until the human population falls well below one billion throughout the planet,' Lumak said.

'I can't believe we are so far gone as a species, but I'll do whatever I can to help our world and its many species.'

'In that case, the sooner you tackle that matter, the better. We have lots of interesting work to do together, and it's all quite urgent, Pal. You are now playing in a different league with no where to go but upwards.'

The large logo of Solarian International comprised the disc of the planet Earth with two silvery wings on either side and that logo was displayed on all their documents and buildings.

Construction work was still continuing on the micro robotic development plant and several prefabricated structures added to that area for accommodation, recreation and training. Lennox had accepted the new position as Lumak's deputy in his bio division and his special group used a local building for their Bio-engineering programs.

The President didn't mind losing Lennox. After all, he had only recently joined the group and his interest lay more with the type of work Lumak was developing. Anyway, he had the brilliant mathematician and scientist, Professor John Laroche, to take up from where Lennox had left.

The LPD development was carried out at the most distant base within a security bunker. That place was being renovated and contained more prefabricated buildings for accommodation, recreation and training.

Although Sarah enjoyed the country life best, she was not a typical housewife and was soon bored with the same daily routines. Lumak realising the situation soon got Joseph, the manager, and his wife to assist in the manor, while their eldest son became the new manager of the ranch.

Lumak also needed someone to handle the conservationists side of the organization, so he decided to train Sarah and her father Ben for that purpose. He soon placed them on a correspondence course and aided their learning with small doses of microids and special memory drugs.

Instead of the temple at Sarah's family home, Lumak now had to contend with an area near the pond for his contemplations. That was until a new temple was built at the rear of the house to a similar design as the one near their country home in Turkey. For that great miracle of miracles several architects were sent to turkey to take photos and measurements and locate craftsmen and materials. Once constructed it was one of the most beautiful temples in the States.

He built that one specially for Sarah and her father Ben.

CHAPTER 35

Lord Vektron visits Lumak

Earth time.... 2041CE.... late.summer

Lumak was presently training many of his Turkish students in the new processes of micro-robotics. He had decided to develop most of the special equipment used in their production in house. Since the technology did not yet exist on Earth, he had some of the more intricate devices constructed by a few special companies in the field of Nano-technology. Although new to them, they were quite capable of completing those designs with his technical assistance. It also gave them several new directions to follow. As always he tended to take over those companies once they realized they had much more to gain by his new concepts and incredible designs. There was also a need for anti-gravitation devices during the mixture's suspension.

Since he was unable to build a laboratory in space, he had to utilize the Mind for some special prototypes. Nevertheless most of those particular units would eventually come with his LPD project, so he also had to begin that project on schedule. His main problem at that time were in finding suitable personnel willing to work away from home for long periods. Although most of his original Turkish students had been imported for that purpose he was still short on the ground. He soon had a large agency involved. Rewards and salaries offered were irresistible.

Lumak was completing some urgent paperwork in his study when he sensed a presence, to be followed by a greenish glow and then Lord Vektron, the Ploran, appeared. The black sphere moved about the room for a while before stopping in mid air in front of Lumak.

'Sut, you have achieved much since your short stay on this world, including a most beautiful and loving wife. May I complement you on such progress and congratulate you on your

recent marriage?'

'Thank you, my gracious lord!' A surprised Lumak replied.

*'As customary, I brought you a small trinket for your bride. It consists of rear stones unknown to this world and some powerful built-in technologies.'*Lord Vektron grew arms and handed the crimson box to Lumak.

'I thank you sincerely for your gift and compliments, my lord,' Lumak replied, humbly.

'However, my main reason for this visit concerns another important matter. It is to do with Plato's people. We have decided to use this system for the evacuation. For reasons I am unable to explain at this moment and that you have probably deduced, Earth is not suitable for accepting that many people. I have therefore decided to utilise Mars as their first port of call before transfer to another local system. That system will be discovered at the appropriate time. Before then, however, your LPD's will be ready, but will not be required if certain other plans have been successful, and there is a high probability of success.

'Nevertheless, you are to continue with the idea of giving any direct assistance should anything go wrong by way of delays in their evacuation program. Your other projects here are also important for solving the problems of this world in preparation for the Javols arrival in this galaxy, so please carry on as usual.

'Most importantly, you will be expected to give accommodation to twelve very important Andromedans when they arrive here in about two years. Therefore you are to make the necessary preparations. They will be extremely fragile from their experiences, so you must be gentle with them for our Lord's sake.

'Plato will continue his program on Caefon, including reassembling and testing the Omegron Portal before it is initiated. After that procedure has been completed, one of those units will be installed on Mars.

'Within six months from that time the evacuation should be completed and they will finally be safely away from those terrible Javols. It's regrettable that a complete galaxy was lost in the process, but there was no other way.

'As time passes more will be revealed to you.. We must secure Osmaron and that in itself is an enormous task, with so many

civilizations to consider and bring together for the common-good.

'Finally, my son, there is Triangulum to consider before the final battle is fought.'

'My lord, the house will be ready in a few months and my projects within two years. By that time I shall have a very competent team of scientists to assist the evacuation program. I can't visualise any major problems during the intervening period.'

'I always have great confidence in you, my son, and so also does our Grand Lord. You should however get your wife within our organization as soon as possible. As you know, humans are very fragile and she will be protected from certain dangers, including accidental death and ageing. However, the ring and bracelet will protect her to a certain extent if frequently worn.. There are some things one cannot hurry and some people are more sensitive than others in such matters.

'I must leave you now, but I shall be back before the evacuation commences,' Lord Vektron's sphere slowly faded into the air. Sarah sensed something was amiss and was soon knocking on the door of his study.

'Darling, is everything all right? I just had the strangest sensation of a presence. I wonder if this place is haunted?'

'That woman is acquiring a super sense. She will make a good Shadite, if I could only tell her the truth?' Lumak thought.

'Yes, Darling! Everything is all right! Must be to do with the special drugs that you've been taking for your studies? They do extend the senses, you know. Anyway, I have a small present for you!' He shouted.

She soon entered his study filled with curiosity. He opened the box to remove a most beautiful necklace. It was composed of strange greenish beads that had been grown from some type of stone and a pendant with an even larger greenish gem that was kept in a platinum ring. While she held it they could see it change from an emerald green to turquoise. Sarah wondered what strange powers made it behave in that manner. She also wandered whether it had similar powers to the ring he got her in Turkey. That one saved her life.

'My love, it's my duty to place it around your neck,' Lumak said and she handed it back to him.

The moment Lumak placed the item about her neck it changed into a deep purple and glowed for a while, as if synchronizing with its wearer.

'It's out of this world, Darling,' she said and kissed him passionately. Yet she was not concerned about the strange nature of her jewellery.

'If only you knew how close you were to the truth,' he thought.

'You must always wear it for me!' he said.

'Yes, my darling. I will!' she replied aloud.

Sarah and her father Ben (Bengizara Khan) had finally come to the end of their training and were presently filled with every type of knowledge of planet Earth regarding its endangered species and their habitats. Lumak's special drugs and microids had extended their minds to such an extent that they had no problems in absorbing almost any amount of information. They were equivalent to very exceptional doctors within relevant fields. However Lumak wanted them to take brain implants the moment they became available on Earth. That part of his list of complex projects, like the Terminal Virus, came under the control of Professor Harry Lennox, presently his second in command.

CHAPTER 36

A little snag

While doing some important research via the Internet, the phone rang and Sarah got up to answer.

'It's Lennox, Darling!' she yelled and Lumak took the call in his office.

'I have been speaking with John recently and he reckons it's time you gave a comprehensive press interview. The main newspapers and other important periodicals keep pressing the President and others, including myself for more information regarding you and the new projects. They are quite aware of the new Space Drive and Micro Robots. There could have been a leak from the White House since our last president's meeting. Although the placed is frequently swept for bugs, it's difficult to check every nook and cranny. Some areas of that building could be bugged,' Lennox said.

'Well, they could have guessed most of it or read it in magazines. My presence here is no secret. Anyway, does that make things difficult for us?' Lumak replied.

'No! Not really! It just means you will have to give an interview on one of the main TV networks. Don't worry, it won't be a lecture on any of our important new projects. The TV Station will be well chosen, so that the program is viewed by as many people as possible. However, you should be careful about what you say. I have arranged a briefing session with John for Thursday, if it's ok with you. If the press and others are satisfied with that interview it will stop them from nosing around or coming back for more.'

'This should not be a great problem at this time if I fit it into my daily schedule,' Lumak said.

'I think those people are quite persistent and always come back for more. In future we might have to create our own publicity agency to handle those persistent reporters and organizations. Then we can pass on relevant information as and when they become available by holding the occasional press interviews and conferences.' Lennox said.

'I agree,' Lumak replied.

'That way we can give them what we want them to have, with a lot more control. Anyway, I think we need to hold this interview as soon as possible.'

'Yea. That suits me fine. I am still collecting information and ordering equipment for the new laboratories. I also have to assist in the building program, otherwise my hands are free. If anything, this is the ideal time for such an interview, before the more serious work commences,' Lumak replied.

'In that case, I shall make the necessary arrangements and contact you later to verify dates,' he said and hung up.

Several days later Lennox called and told Lumak the interview had been arranged on a particular Sunday at 7 p.m. It was to be held at one of the main Washington DC studios at peak viewing time. Lumak realized it was going to be a show instead of a serious scientific interview. Nevertheless, being Shadite, he was always prepared for almost any eventuality.

Joey Donaldson, normally known publicly as Joe, had spent many of his best years with AOM Broadcasting. He always enjoyed the pain-giving process of brightly illuminating his accused subjects under the magnifier of public scrutiny with brightest studio lights. During that hour he would attempt to expose them to their barest bones. He was used to lengthy interviews on many universal topics and was knowledgeable in many varied technical subjects. With such experience he could navigate around scientific jargon and quickly get to the facts of the matter. With a brilliant and inquiring mind he had attained a Grade A degree in science at MIT, but because of financial reasons did not continue his career in that field. Nevertheless he still read all the necessary scientific journals and kept abreast of all new advances in those fields.

He had spent many years reporting for the press and a few scientific journals. Thus far his job had taken him to many places which had included topics from tropical hurricanes to the most devastating earthquakes and volcanoes. As a result had written numerous articles on pollution from nuclear power stations and disposal of used nuclear fuel rods. He was always impartial and gave good and bad reasons on both sides, but chose his questions to emphasize worst case scenarios.

All that was before he became freelance, which to him was the worst choice he had ever made. He found that choice very tough going particularly after his divorce. He was not the easiest person to employ or utilize and with a young daughter, found the job of being his own boss a very difficult one. During the course of his work, his potential as an interviewer was recognized by one of AOM's executives, who immediately offered him a contract. Soon after he gave up all his freelance commitments for the job he most loved. That job happened to be sitting in one of the main TV studios while exposing his opponents to the anger and fury of his audience and the public at large.

In all his time in television and elsewhere not once had he found such a unique individual as Lumak. From what little he had learnt, the man was a supposed technological genius with cures for cancer and a range of incredible inventions hitherto known only to a few members of humanity.

'Even when educated in England how could anyone from that backwater part of the planet, namely the remote hills in Turkey, come up with such unique ideas. And he was unknown by the best scientists and universities in the western world. He must be a very clever magician and therefore must be a fraud. Now he is over here in the USA and had even convinced our President, of all people, so he must be bloody good,' he thought.

Having a very busy schedule, Joe soon called his daughter. She recently graduated and was out of university.

'Jane, I might have a job for you. Get your travelling clothes laundered and documents in order. You are going to Turkey to interview some people for me.'

'But dad, I am supposed to be going to Miami on holidays next week with friends.' She was disappointed.

'Why not have a holiday out there as well. Will ten grand do? This is very important for me. It's to do with Professor Jeffery Longhurst. You know, the English scientist from Turkey.'

'You don't mean the cancer guy?' She replied, now quite enthusiastic.

'Yes! The same. I am doing an interview with him next Sunday and require some independent info of his life, religious beliefs and attitudes in general. I know it's at short notice, but I would like you to interview some of his family and closest friends. Any real background info will require a bit of digging and we don't have much time for that, so that aspect can be ignored for now.'

'In that case, I accept. But I am going to have some very pissed-off friends in Miami,' she replied.

'What would you say if I offered them front row seats in the studio, plus a slap-up dinner afterwards.'

'I think that might just swing it, but only if you promise,' she replied, realizing her father's irresponsible ability to change his mind at short notice.

'I promise. Now go and get ready. I expect you to call me from Ankara within twenty-four hours.' He hung up.

An enthusiastic Jane was soon on her way to Turkey. Although she had acquired a preferential list of topics from her father, time pressing, she decided to choose Lumak's three main friends. Jean-Claude, Jeremy and Jeremy's wife, Karen. Anyway, Lumak's father-in-law, Ben, was not available and she did not wish to risk the journey to the remote hills where Lumak began his experiments.

Joe had offered Lumak (Doctor Jeffery Longhurst) a large sum of money for his interview plus a follow up article, but Lumak declined any remuneration in serving the public. However once Lumak had given permission for the interview Joe decided to make it a big affair. The studio was revamped with much advertising on stream globally.

In a short time his daughter, Jane, had covered much ground and interviewed all relevant friends and colleagues, but everywhere she went the stories were the same; the man Lumak was caring, responsible and a genius, with knowledge of virtually every topic imaginable. She had checked hospital records and acquired several reports on worst-case terminal patients. They had all been miraculously cured within a week of taking the special serum. And that was not all; most of the patients had become much younger as a result of the special medication.

From the information she collected, Lumak had definitely found a cure for cancer, had invented a space drive of immense power and speed, and had found a way of manufacturing robots the size of a human cell. Professor Jean-Claude Chaimowich had also given her notes and a video disc of all the recent lectures, which she viewed constantly in utter amazement. Jane soon realized that many things did not add up. If it was all true, Lumak was not only a genius, but a super genius with the ability to create virtually anything from raw concepts.

Once she had acquired all the relevant information, she dispatched it to her father by special courier and decided to see the sights and view some ancient buildings.

'Dad, I am calling from Ankara. You should have received my package by now.'

'Yes, I got it when I entered the office this morning, but I hadn't time to go through it.'

'Well, I had a lengthy interview with Professor Jean-Claude Chaimowich, who was one of doctor Longhurst's closest friends when he lived here. He is now a director of all anti serum operations in Turkey. Anyway, his story like all the others, make the doctor a very clever and strange individual. Further, everywhere I go they call him The Lord or The Saviour or The Saint. I suppose it's because he had saved so many lives in that country.'

'Really?'

'Yes! The man has no enemies whatsoever, except for some jealous Moslem extremist wanting a share of his popularity. From what little I've gathered he is like the Messiah himself. One more important thing; many of the people he cured had become at least ten years younger. The anti serum has the effect of reducing the aging process. It boosts the immune system and extends the lifespan of the average cell, so they will live much longer as a result.'

'That's incredible!'

'One of the doctors I met reckoned that if the anti serum was made available to all and taken on a yearly basis after the age of thirty, no one need ever age. Can you imagine that dad. Being able to live for bloody ever without even the slightest chance of getting cancer! Personally, I think he is really the true messiah. He will change the whole of this world in a short period of time, so you must go easy on him.' She was quite emotional.

'Wow! They really have you convinced. Do you think he is going to form a new religious sect or some such organization over here?'

'Dad, I think he is the true sect and the real religion. He doesn't want anyone to follow a specific religion and does not like to be honoured or praised. When he arrived in our country, the first place he visited was the Washington National Cathedral, which is non-denominational. Whenever he visits a place he will enter the first religious building for prayer and meditation and seldom uses the term God. Instead he uses the term The Greater Purpose, which to him embodies the process of evolution and continuity throughout the Cosmos.'

'Wow! How intriguing!'

'I will not be able to visit England to check his family records, time not permitting. Anyway, I have collected a lot of other background info which should be more then enough for the interview and a follow up article,' she continued.

'In that case, I've wired ten grand to your account so enjoy a little holiday on my behalf. I hope I can expect you back here in two days to assist. You can help me with some of the background work. You seem to know a lot about the man which is not all written down and I need a little dialogue to build the scenery,' he said and hung up.

Lumak knew that sooner or later his complete past would be scrutinized, but also knew he had acquired the true identity of the real0 Doctor Jeffery Longhurst. That doctor was a Doctor in Physics who was educated at Cambridge University, England. He had gone to Africa to do some research in one of its desert regions on climatic change. Since his work took him to many distant areas through the desert he was always at risk. As with many people in his field, he was never one for taking along assistants on simple alignments and instrument checks.

One day he didn't return at the expected time. Neither had anyone of his group received communication from him for assistance. Many of his colleagues soon mounted a search and found his Landrover, but sadly there was no Jeffery. Although skilled trackers had followed his foot prints to an area of jagged and cracked rocks, it was an area infested by several large predators and he was eventually given up for dead.

In fact, the real Jeffery Longhurst had climbed that rock to get a clearer view of the area and fell within one of its larger cracks. He was presently a bleached skeleton in that rough rocky area within the desert. Although slightly wounded from the fall, he had died from thirst and exhaustion several weeks later without anyone hearing his fearful cries for assistance.

Therefore, if anyone queried his disappearance, Lumak could always say he had been lucky to have escaped the desert and had lost his memory for a while from sunstroke or such like. Lumak was always clever at engineering situations to back his story. His urgent mission was too important for Earth and the galaxy, therefore all such clandestine steps were necessary while on Earth if he was to function freely within the public domain.

Lumak was given all relevant information about the doctors past with the money he had received while at Sarah's family home in the Turkish hills. He had since absorbed all the information on the real Jeffery Longhurst within his brain implants, so to all intents and purpose had become that person.

Being always so thorough, Lumak realized he would have no problems with the doctor's distant relatives. They lived in Scotland and had only visited his supposed parents once when he was a boy of nine. In any event, they would most likely have backed his story, while any closer scrutiny with friends would have led up a blind alley. Therefore he was quite safe from all such scrutiny from the press and elsewhere. Further, his more recent life was an open book, so he had nothing to hide from anyone other than his past alien identity, which was too incredible for anyone on Earth to believe.

Although Sarah realized his strange powers, she always considered him the true profit and remained his most loyal wife. In any event they had been through much together and her loyalty could not be swayed by anyone.

CHAPTER 37

A youthful miracle

Madeline McCririck, known to all her family as Ma, was now in her mid nineties and disabled. She was an Iris immigrant who had arrived in the USA at the middle of the previous century. She married an American farmer but were not successful and lost their property to an unscrupulous and uncaring bank when their loan was called. Having a large family to feed their only alternative was in managing the large ranch for Lennox's uncle.

He knew the family for sometime and had on occasion given her husband George the occasional job. When his manager left the managing job was offered to George. He soon became General Manager on a more permanent basis with the house thrown in.

George McCririck was an experienced farmer and excellent at his job of managing the large ranch. While in his hands the ranch had become very productive. Sadly, George died from bronchial pneumonia and his eldest son Joseph continued in his father's footsteps.

Joseph was never as well trained, energetic or enthusiastic as his father. In the ensuing years the ranch had become uncompetitive. After the death of Lennox's uncle they gave up on the land and most of the McCriricks took jobs in the local town. That was until Lumak took over the ranch and made them a better deal.

Although having aged gracefully at 95, Madeline had mild cardiovascular problems, plus a few other internal organ deficiencies. For those ailments she had to take her daily prescription, which included several tablets and capsules. Presently her only pleasure was sitting on the veranda in her rocking chair while observing the scenery and passers-by.

While passing her house one day Lumak glanced in her direction and nodded his head with respect. Taking all her will power she eased her clumsy body with a walking cane out of the rocking chair to wave to him. Lumak, observing her difficulties immediately left what he was doing and walked towards the frail and crinkled figure to assist.

'Doctor Longhurst. I would like to thank you and Madam Sarah sincerely for all your kindness and assistance to my family,' she greeted, in a half Irish accent. She held on firmly to her cane but was shaking wildly. Lumak soon realized it was taking her all her efforts to remain standing.

'I am very pleased to meet you, Mad!' He said, and placed his arm out to shake her hand, but instead she lost her balance, so he had to assist her back into her chair.

'I'm sorry, Doctor. But my poor frail body sometimes find it difficult to take my weight.'

'Would you like to walk again without the use of that cane?' he inquired.

'Of course, Doctor! In my condition who wouldn't?' she replied, thinking his suggestions to be most humorous and not believing for a moment in such a possibility.

'What would you say if I told you, I have the technology to transform you into a most beautiful young woman again. You know, not everyone would like the idea. I think we humans have been cheated by providence for giving us so little years. Why, even some turtles can sometimes live in excess of 200 years, you know.' Suddenly she realized he was stack serious and not kidding her.

'You are really serious. Aren't you?' she said, astonished and gazing into his eyes.

'Yes! You should know me by now? I am always serious when it concerns life and death issues regarding family and friends.'

'I would relish the idea and be forever in your debt, if such a thing was possible,' she said, enthusiastically.

'Be careful what you wish for and don't hurry that decision before giving serious thought to both your current situation and the new you. You will be the first person in the whole world to have undergone such a procedure and your family might think it strange having a grand parent that looked even younger than her great, great, grand children. Not to mention all the publicity and television interviews you will receive. However, it will also make you and your family quite rich, even beyond your wildest dreams.'

'Wow! There's a lot to consider! But how can anyone wish to miss out on all that beauty and glamour of youth. Not to mention, good health and happiness. You know, Doctor, I have slaved all my life to bring up my family, with little help from anyone. So why should anyone begrudge this poor old lady a little indulgence. Not to mention some remunerations in her old age.'Lumak smiled at her carefree attitude.

'Well, you think seriously about what I've said and talk it over with your family. Then if you decide to go ahead with the conversion, maybe we could meet at my house to discuss and plan the procedure,' Lumak said and left.

That very same day Madeline brought the senior members of her family together to discuss those matters.

'Kids, Ma is getting young again and I want no problems from any one of you!' she said, in her usually hoarse Irish voice.

'What do you mean, Ma,' her youngest son, Philip, inquired. Phillip was now in his early sixties and had several grand children of his own.

'I had a recent visit from our Doctor Longhurst. He tells me he now has the technology to make me young again, so I've decided to take his offer. If I decide to go along with his treatments, I shall become a woman of about thirty years and remain so for a very long time to come. Since I will be the first person to undergo the procedure, it will make our family rich beyond our wildest dreams. Think of all the television interviews and journeys to Europe and elsewhere,' she said with a twinkle in her eyes.

'Are you sure about all this? I have read about the doctor's work in Europe and elsewhere in curing cancer, but this youth drug or what ever it's called is untested. Anything can go wrong, you know,' her most concerned eldest son, Joseph, interjected.

'I am going to die anyway in a couple of years or so. My heart is aching even more and my kidneys, bladder and other organs are beginning to fail. I don't know much about you, but I want to live as long as I can,' she replied.

'But Ma, we are Catholics and all this must be against God's will,' her eldest daughter in law, Ann, interjected.

'Since God is all powerful and all knowing, everything that happens must be God's will and purpose anyway, otherwise it would not happen. Would it? I have given this matter very serious consideration and have made up my mind, to go along with the conversion. So I want no more negatives from anyone and I would like you all to sign an agreement document for the good doctor. He will want the whole family over to his place soon to discuss everything relating to the procedure, so I want no more speculative words on this topic until we have more information.'

Madeline sent one of her grandsons to deliver the message to Lumak, and he patiently read the note.

'Doctor Longhurst, I've decided to accept your offer, so please arrange a time for an interview with my family. As you said before, they are against the idea, but that's expected,' Lumak read.

'My dear, I think we have another patient to cure,' he shouted to Sarah and she came running out of the kitchen.

'What do you mean, Darling?' she inquired.

'Old Mrs. McCririck would like to become young again, so I have decided to fulfill her wish. She is to become our second special patient. It will only require a simple injection of the modified serum. Although the anti cancer serum reduces age by about ten years, it is not optimized for age reduction and longevity. The new product Jeremy has put together with my assistance will fulfill all those requirements. For that great work I am sure Jeremy will receive his first Nobel prize.'

'It's like Marion's situation all over again. Are you sure it will work without any hitches,' Sarah inquired. Suddenly it had brought back all those memories of Marion's cure from cancer. All such experiments on people always worried her.

'Yes, my dear. I am sure. When they give the go ahead, I would like you to administer the serum,' he replied, in a most positive manner. She knew her husband well, with his uncanny powers and realized her patient would soon be whatever he said she would be.

It was not long before the postman delivered a large sack of letters. Many had been sent from Turkey, but several were from Europe and elsewhere. Lumak carefully selected several of the European letters from the pile and opened the first, to be astounded.

'Darling, I have received a letter regarding my Nobel Prize on the anti cancer serum,' he yelled and Sarah came running out of the kitchen again. This time she embraced and kissed him.

'We are to visit Europe after the interview to receive the accolade. Then if you don't mind, we can spend a little time in England on our way back.' Sarah could not contain her excitement.

The McCririck family visited the house on Tuesday and were sat comfortable in the main sitting room. Lumak had prepared a video on his anti cancer and longevity serums. It was about after effects on worst case cancer sufferers and the aged. They watched the video for an hour, then the lights were turned on and they were given refreshments. Then Lumak began to speak.

'I know many of you have your doubts about the conversion process, but it is not an operation with the usual high risks. All that is required is a blood sample from the recipient. The blood is then processed to create the serum with the new genetic changes and accelerators. The worst that can happen is that the recipient does not forego the full age reduction. If that was the case, we would simply administer a second dose. The weakness or strength of the dosage can be altered for best effect, depending on age, sex and weight of the individual.

'What you should seriously consider is the social impact and changes to your present way of life after the change. However, you should never worry about your home here with us on the estate, providing there is always someone to take care of business in your absence. If for any reason you decide to leave us in the future, you will always be free to follow that destiny,' Lumak said.

They listened patiently and carefully to Lumak's words and accepted all his advice and arguments, until all their questions were answered. It was now just a matter of acquiring a small amount of blood from Madeline.

Soon Lumak had a small room in the manor prepared for his special patient. That way she could be isolated from the outside world with its many unknown variables. He also realized that after Madeline's conversion, with the exception of her children, no one would recognize her. Therefore he made a list of her main characteristics and attributes for comparison before and after the procedure. Those were genetic and dental records, finger prints, retina scans, birth marks, tattoos and such like. Finally she was given a bracelet with a unique combination lock. The bracelet was to be fitted by her eldest son who was the only one with the key combination. Anyway, there were things about her family history only she and some older family members knew about.

Madeline was made ready and the serum administered. Within minutes she was fast asleep. Her temperature rose to the limits while Sarah kept a constant check on her metabolism. When she woke the first time she was very thirsty and was administered a nutritious drink. After that she fell asleep and her body became wet with sweat as the serum made up for those many years of decay and wear and tear.

After the first day little change could be observed. That would come with an abrupt reduction in temperature, when the serum went into its final stages of the process.

The following day a small change could be observed as her skin cells and muscles began to repair themselves to the new format. Bones, ligaments and neurons would be the last to change, and those were triggered when certain chemicals rose to reasonable levels in her system.

After the second day her temperature had dropped and she decided to get out of bed. During all this time her eldest son and his wife would make frequent trips to the manor to observe Madeline's condition. They were pleased by the caring attention shown by Sarah, who was always at her beck and call.

The real changes took place on the third day. In the morning she was about fifty and gradually changed to about thirty by 5 p.m. There was still many crinkle lines, that would disappear in time. However, their reduction could be further accelerated by the application of special creams and massaging. Bones would take a bit longer to change. A new set of teeth could be regrown with local injections to be given in her gums. The whole process was nothing less than a miracle.

Finally, Lumak gave her a thorough medical and found she was in peak health, with no further need for medication.

'There is going to be a little problem the next time you visit your doctor, so you might have to postpone that visit for a fortnight or so, until after my television interview. At that time I shall brief him about your changes. Anyway, you are now in peak health as would be expected with any young healthy thirty year old woman. And how do you feel?' Lumak said, little believing the young figure of the woman that now stood before him was really the one that struggled out of her rocking-chair a few days ago.

'I feel fantastic! Doctor, you have given me my youth back and I don't know what to say. It's a bloody miracle!'

Having spent several minutes gazing at her new self in the large mirror, she could not contain her emotions of gratitude any longer. She went up to Lumak, then hugged and kissed him on his lips. Sarah was amazed by her impulsive actions, but realized she would most likely have done the same in Madeline's position.

Lumak glanced at Sarah and shook his head not quite knowing what to say and Sarah smiled in return.

'Doctor, I'm sorry if I embarrassed you in front of Sarah, but I couldn't contain myself. I now have so much excitement and vigour. It's like I am bursting with energy.'

'In that case, I think you might be able to do me a little favour in return. How would you and your family like the idea of being television celebrities?'

'I don't know. I've never been on television before. But I'll do anything for you.'

'Don't worry, you will not be required to answer awkward questions. Just show your face as the first converted person in the world, now at a ripe old age of ninety-five. I will treat you and your family to a delicious meal afterwards. Transport and all other costs will be taken care of, so please make a list of clothes and other items that you and your family require for the interview,' Lumak said and she agreed.

CHAPTER 38

Lumak's 1st interview

Lumak had chartered a small passenger aeroplane from a local airport for the interview. He didn't like travelling by car or helicopter all the way to Washington DC. He had others to consider in his travel plans. The destination airport was not far from the television studio so he could conveniently take along the McCririck family to ensure everyone arrived on time.

On arrival they took a large limousine to the studio. It had been pre-booked for the day by his office. Lumak was wearing his strange white cloak with crimson cape. His golden sandals with cris-cross straps matched the two golden shoulder rings that held the cape.

About his neck was a large starlike medallion which hung on a golden chain. That medallion was given to him by King Olav on one of his previous missions.

This time the many large pleats of his white cloak had shrunk to more resemble an ancient dress. Perhaps more like the type used by the wizards of old. The white cloak was of a micro-robotic design of very high technology. Therefore it could change its shape and colour by simple visual adjustments through Lumak's brain implants. His left shoulder boldly displayed the winged insignia of the Shadites, his priestly clan.

Sarah was in a light blue suit with large winged diamond broach on her left lapel. Around her neck hung the special jewellery Lord Vektron had given Lumak. This time it was in radiant blue to match her outfit. She realized the strange necklace always changed to blend with whatever she wore. It also changed subtly to reflect her moods.

As they approached the building Lumak was surprised by the large crowd awaiting his arrival. Several approached him for autographs for which he patiently obliged.

As he entered the lobby of the studio there were many senators and scientists, all waiting patiently to observe the strange saintly figure. Lennox was known by many so he took Lumak away from his admirers. Then introduced him to all concerned, including Joey Donaldson, his daughter Jane and senators.

The McCririck family and Sarah followed at the rear and were also introduced. Finally Lumak was taken to the make-up department for the usual make-over before his television appearance. Not that he needed any of it. Sarah and the McCririck family were guided to a specially reserved area in the front row of the audience.

The large studio was exorbitantly furnished with an array of technological effects and the audience keen and cheerful. The band played an introductory theme and Joey stood up to introduce his important guests. Joey Donaldson never spared any costs by way of getting the best out of his interviews and audience.

'And now, ladies and gentlemen, I would like to introduce the most powerful brain on the planet today... Please give a big hand to Professor Jeffery Longhurst. Professor of bioengineering and a range of other equally important fields of science,' Joey announced cheerfully. Lumak walked on stage and everyone stood up to chair. The McCririck family was the first to stand and applaud and the last to sit.

'You may call me Jeff and I trust you won't mind me calling you, Joe,' Lumak said and gave his usual broad grin.

'I would like that very much. Now please seat over here, next to Professor Kane Powell. He is also an eminent professor in the field of Bio-engineering. His presence here is to give a balanced view during our discussions.' Lumak introduced himself to Powell who showed little interest and they sat down.

'Jeff, I think your anti cancer serum is an incredible cure, but it has a side effect. It reduces the aging process by about ten years on average. Why is that?'

'Why? Don't you think it's a useful side-effect to have?

'Yes! If it really works!' Joey replied.

'Cancer can sometimes be a persistent problem and even after a complete system cure, can rear its ugly head time and time again. Genetics has an important part to play in such cases. However, if the body is returned to an age before the onset of such reoccurrence, there is a much better chance of a permanent cure and the patient will not have to forego the discomfort of regular checks. This can further be assisted by diet and a moderate change in lifestyle. So in answer to your question, this is an essential part of the serum, necessary for thoroughness,' Lumak replied.

'But surely, if a patient continues to take the serum even after they are cured, they could live forever?' Powell interjected.

'The anti serum is not optimized for that purpose. During the healing process the patient is bed ridden and will undergo discomfort due to a high rise in body temperature. Furthermore, the dosage is fixed for a given weight and type. However, with the optimized longevity serum such discomfort and temperature rise can be minimized. Only the very old need have those discomforts and the dosage can be precisely adjusted for a particular age reduction. So in answer to your question; there are better methods available for longevity,' Lumak replied.

'You are telling us you have already created such a serum? An Eternal Life Drug?' Joey commented, ecstatically.

'I am sure, Joe, if you are very kind to me during this interview, you may have a sample free of cost,' Lumak replied and Joe became even more enthusiastic. The audience saw the humour and began to cheer.

'If that is the case, don't you think commercialization of such an incredible youth restoring serum could have a profound affect on human population growth?' Powell enquired.

'Before its introduction into the public domain, every negative aspect will be considered and population control will be top of our list. What I have at this time is the experimental prototype.'

'And does this prototype work, Jeff?' Joey inquired.

'Yes! It does!' was Lumak's reply.

'I can't believe such nonsense for a second! You must think us all to be the most gullible fools and morons!' interrupted Powell. Who by now had as much as he could take from Lumak's most positive manner, even to the point of arrogance.

Lumak displayed a most carefree attitude at the onset of such an incredible discovery. The man, Lumak, overflowed with confidence and seemed able to do even god's work for him. Powell was of the old school and didn't believe a word of what Lumak said. After all, he Powell had spent the best part of his life searching for all relevant basic genetic links unsuccessfully. Lumak made it sound all too easy. By now Powell was fuming and getting ready to bust his arteries.

'Madeline, would you please stand!' Lumak shouted and a young woman in the front row of the audience stood up.

'Friends, in answer to Powell's queries, the person you now observe standing was a ninety-five year old great, great, great, grand parent a fortnight ago. As you may observe, she is now a young woman in her early thirties. Sitting next to her is her son and step daughter, both in their late sixties. Although she is still a great, great, great, grand parent, she is now as young as her great, great grand children. Without even taking another dose of the drug she will easily live for another 100 years, barring accidents, of course.' The crowd was stunned by that revelation. Madeline lifted her skirt a little and spun herself around so that the audience could get a better look. They remained silent while observing the beautiful figure with little signs of aging.

'Don't worry, we have genetic, dental records and other information to identify her as the person in question, including her children's testimony,' Lumak added.

'Please Madeline, come and join us on stage,' Joey pleaded. She was soon escorted towards that area. Before sitting on the long couch she turned her attention to professor Powell and gave him some of her own words on the subject.

'From what you just said to the doctor, you can't know a lot about anything, and you call yourself a professor of science. Think of all the documented cases that doctor Longhurst have cured in Turkey and elsewhere. Don't you ever read your own medical journals and magazines? Never you cast such aspersions on my doctor again or you'll have to deal with me. You people are just jealous that he is a genius while you and your type are all useless failures,' Madeline said, looking directly into the eyes of Powell.

It all became too much for Powell. He unclipped his microphone in utter rage and disgust and threw it towards the central table. It fell into Joey's drink and created a splash over his question papers, which he nervously wiped with a tissue. Then the professor walked out, fuming with rage and leaving the studio audience stunned by his unpredictable behaviour. It was as if Lumak had staged the whole sequence of events to discredit him and his profession. Nevertheless everything Lumak had said and done was factual.

'What was all that about?' a disturbed Joey commented.

'I am afraid most people like him are like children competing on skate-boards. Well, I am not a child and I am yet to fine an honest equal with which to cross swords,' Lumak replied, also annoyed by the so-called professor. But Joey turned his attention to Madeline instead.

'You have quite a tongue on you, Woman!' Joey commented in jest, but Madeline was still seething with rage.

'He deserved what he got and I'll do it again, if I thought it would do some good and convince all those unbelievers,' Madeline replied.

Suddenly Joey changed the topic to the more personal aspects of Lumak's life.

'I have heard from a reliable source, that our President and his senators admire you. You have only recently arrived in our country, so why is that?'

'I suppose it's because I also admire the president, his loyal and hardworking senators and officials in their tasks of creating a better country for all its citizens,' Lumak replied.

'Ok, so I led myself into that vague answer,' Joey apologized, smiling. He soon realized that Lumak was not a soft touch and was clever enough to manipulate the audience and others to follow his own plans. That strange control occurred even without their knowledge.

'So, you are not a hoaxer or a brilliant magician?' Joey added.

CANCER CURES AND LONGEVITY

'Well, all I have to say in answer to that question, is; the tree shall bear its fruits or as some might say; the taste of the pudding is in the eating. One can only show real scientific discovery by results in the field and not by pure theory alone. Therefore, if I am a fraud you will all find out soon enough. However, very soon you will realize that all my serums do indeed work and the anti cancer serum currently cures thousands of poor sufferers on a daily basis, globally,' Lumak replied.

'Yes, I must admit in all honesty your cancer cures do work, and it appears, so also does your life-prolonging serum,' Joey said.

'At present the anti serum is licensed for use as an anti cancer device. Before the variant or longevity serum can be used certain assurances must be given. Only certain people past their pensionable age will be allowed its use with certain assurances. Furthermore, a choice can be made between longevity and procreation. In other words, those wishing to live forever should give up their rights to have children by a simple operation. Nevertheless it will be available to all in due course. By being careful, such methods can have the least impact on population growth.'

'I suppose enough said on the topic of cancer cures and longevity. Perhaps the audience will like to ask some of their own questions,' Joey said and turned his attention to a young well dressed gentleman in the second row.

'You seem to have a clear picture of most things. How do you think the universe began and what is our purpose here?'

'Wow. that's a tall order. Would you like to take that question or should I take another?' Joey asked Lumak.

THE UNIVERSE AND COSMOS

'It's a straight forward enough question. I shall attempt to answer the first part first. Contrary to what most people may think about our universe, it is a living, breathing entity that is but a small part of a system of many planes of universes in several dimensions. Some call these planes multiverses. Think of a universe as you would a tree, with branches of galaxies at different stages of development. Imagine each galaxy like a fruit that contains a seed that will eventually grow a new child universe and this process may continue to eternity. By such methods a universe is capable of creating as many universes as there are galaxies.'

'And how do galaxies create these seeds,' Joey inquired, innocently.

'In time almost every galaxy will develop a cycler at its nucleus. This cycler is just another name for a ginormous black hole. It will contain an event horizon with a temporal gradient approaching zero time. At this level of Space-time there are dimensional changes leading to the required dimensional transformations. The Cycler is the seed that will eventually puncture a hole in the fabric of space-time to begin the expansion process in what we may consider to be the other side of that singularity not in our space-time. Because of certain indeterminate factors within the Sea of Chaos and of All Possibilities, that puncture is always within a new and different space-time from all others, so the chance of two universes occupying the same space-time is highly improbable. Therefore, what we observe as a big bang, is just the puncturing from the other side, in the parent universe. Think of a tree with many branches of fruit, where each fruit contains a fertile seed. A universe is very similar.

'Furthermore, there are numerous facets to our universe. Most of them cannot be seen or detected by our limited senses or crude technologies at this time in our evolution. Also, many can only be realized while in combination with others. As a matter of fact, the forces, fields and diverse forms of energies so far detected and utilized are but an insignificant fraction of the whole. As we become advanced as a species, more will be revealed and their effects utilized. But first, we must find the gems and joins to fill the gaps in our knowledge,' he said.

'So the Big Bang does exist,' interjected Joey.

'It exists only in the sense that it is the only part of the process that we can observe. On the other side, the parent universe will contain numerous galaxies and may be virtually unaffected by the process. Therefore, there are planes of galaxies and planes of universes, ad infinitum. Nevertheless, each universe is unique and those within a given plane will pass on certain characteristics of similarity to their children, in much the same way as an apple or pear tree may pass on certain characteristics to their siblings through DNA.

'One way of coming to terms with this concept, is to think of yourself as a small cell exploring the inside of a tree. If you were such a tiny object, everything within your vicinity would be massive by comparison and behave differently from what you would expect. First of all, the world you observe would depend on the vicinity in which you explored. Surely, a cell in a leaf would have a different view to a cell in a branch or a root perhaps. In a not too dissimilar manner, our view of the universe is limited, not only by our senses and our brain's interpretation of what it considers to be reality, but by what we observe in our vicinity. Therefore, our view of the universe from the inside can never approach that of the external observer, who is able to view the complete tree in many dimensions. To the single cell, the system is magnified on a gigantic scale.'

'If what you say is factual. How does such a complex organism form out of a simple explosion, like a Big Bang,' Madeline asked, innocently and the audience cheered, thinking she might get one over on Lumak.

'Universes are formed from a state of All Possibilities driven by Chaos, so the initial seed will take whatever it required from the absolute randomness of the Quantum World to create the required template. The action of Chaos will destroy all those possibilities that are not strong enough to resist certain changes, thus allowing only elements that are part of the template. That template is a kind of reflection in multiple dimensions that cause certain lines of invariance, distortions or cracks within The Sea of Chaos and of All Possibilities. In other words, the probability of the sibling universe being similar to its parent is the most likely outcome.

Once that happens, a type of orderly decay sets in and a disturbance forms in the Sea of Chaos. That disturbance will grow as many more cracks and branches of cracks develop, to perpetuate the new form. That new form of order creates a vast amount of random energy which we observe as explosive heat, and hence the big bang. Nevertheless, only specific cracks will develop or else the process will go no further and be absorbed by the Sea of Chaos. So universes exists only because certain changes within the Sea of Chaos can lead to further changes add infinitum. During this process parallel internal universes leading to time-lines and other multi-dimensional structures will be created. However, if the template is flawed or any of those changes are incorrect, the process will begin to decay back into the Sea of Chaos from whence it came.

'For instance, atoms the size of oranges will not naturally exist within our universe and the amount and balance of particles, fields and forces will be of a similar format to the original parent universe, which has a proven survival matrix within its space-time continuum. Hence, some form of coding will exist at the quantum level. It is not too unlike our genetic coding. Universes can also experience and select the best future from parallel internal universes for optimum survival. Life can be caused to exist if it enhanced their survival scenario, and it does,' Lumak replied.

'In that case, how old is our universe?' Joey inquired.

'That's a difficult one to answer. I shall use another analogy. If you observed a small forest, how could you tell its age? Well, in most cases you would conjecture that its age would be older than its oldest tree. However, in the case where it could self-perpetuate by dropping new seeds, such a forest could be almost any age. We know our universe will lay seeds, but the seeds it lay are never in the same space-time, so that leaves the forest analogy out of our speculation. Nevertheless, like most life-forms, universes are constantly evolving and finding better ways to survive. For instance, our universe has several mechanisms for maintaining itself.

'Primarily, there are many types of Dark Matter and Energy most of which can condense into normally vectored matter to alter its expansion rate. Therefore, using this method a universe can oscillate between two extremes. It will expand to a maximum level then contract to a smaller size and expand again to that level, ad infinitum. During this process there is an interchange with dark matter and normally vectored electromagnetic type matter to form new galaxies and universes. Here again, it's like a tree changing its leaves and fruit-bearing to handle the different seasons. However, it is unlikely that any universe will contract or expand all the way. So in answer to your question, our universe could be several hundred billion years old with a 32 billion year cycle. In each phase, like leaves, new galaxies are formed and the old galaxies with their new universes are cast off and may become powerful quasars at its outer extremities.'

'How does it know when to expand and contract?' Madeline asked.

'That aspect is controlled by the density of Dark Matter and Energy, with the added effects of turbulence to speed the process of change when it occurs.'

'Now in answer to the second question posed by the audience. Why are we here?' Joey ask.

WHY ARE WE HERE

'That one is an arrogant question, and may suggest that we are an important life-form that requires special treatment. Whether we like it or not, we are simply another evolving life-form, so that same question could be asked of a snail or indeed, any other. About one-hundred million years ago we would have been considered equivalent to any of those so-called lower life-forms, and in a hundred-million years from now any of the so called lower life-forms on this world may become the dominant species asking this very same question.

'Therefore, each and every life-form is unique and important to the Greater Purpose when viewed over a long timescale.

'Life is just a higher state of electromagnetic type matter and exists throughout our universe and elsewhere, where conditions are favourable. Like water changing its natural state to ice, liquid or steam, depending on environmental conditions like temperature, pressure and such like. Electromagnetic type Life is also necessary to create a certain type of order within our universe. That unique order is necessary for its future survival.'

'How does this life begin on a suitable world?' Madeline asked.

'You know, every constituent part of our universe is for a purpose. For instance, there are many types of stars, from the small ones like our sun to giants, millions of times more massive. Small stars like our sun are meant to nurture life while the larger ones create the heavier elements and seeds of life in the process. Such massive stars will frequently blow off large volumes of their atmospheres. By so doing, large complex nebulae are formed which will enrich space.

'In the process, many will form large molecules, including nucleic acids which form the basic building blocks of all carbon based life. During their travels, many of those molecules will land on worlds like Earth by several methods to begin the process of life. Hence, the creation of life is not by accident. It is a universal process. You should believe me when I say that our universe is teaming with life, in much the same way as our wildest jungles here on Earth. However, initial conditions must be right for the process to take root and flourish.

'Therefore, in answer to your question, all life has purpose and may lay the seeds of more life throughout the Cosmos. Here, I use the term Cosmos to include all universes, all spaces, all dimensions and all times. As a matter of fact, the probability of life in any suitable world is about 3 billion to 1. Life becomes a certainty within 3 billion years from the cooling of suitable planets.

'However, life is not just matter. Each of us contains a unique identity which makes us different from all others. Our identities cannot be destroyed. This simply means we are constantly recycled. Even if clones were made identical to us, they would all have different identities because of different memories and experiences,' Lumak replied.

'One more question,' Joey shouted, while turning his attention to the audience..

'What other projects are you currently developing and how will they change our lives,' another person in the audience asked and Joe decided to pose a similar question.

'Yes, on the topic of space exploration, we have been told by a distinguished professor of mathematics, that you are currently developing a space drive and some form of Nano-technology with incredible possibilities for the future. Can you expand, Professor, on these new technologies?' Joey said.

LINEAR PROGRESSIVE DRIVE (LPD)

'While utilizing energy from the fusion of hydrogen, it is possible to modify certain symmetries, with certain resultant changes.

'Thus, at the sub-atomic level inertia may be separated and channelled in such a manner as to cause motion in a singular direction. That simply means that all negative reactions to motion can be removed and turned around to assist in forward motion. By using certain fields all matter within the vicinity of such devices may be aligned for that purpose. For instance, when we accelerate an object that acceleration may be caused by any given force from a single point, yet that force may propagate its effect throughout the complete solid mass. In like manner the reverse action may be initiated and focussed to a single point. Then that point of extreme force may be focussed or neutralised. Further, any mass must be overcome before its speed will increase, due to momentum. However, if we remove momentum the object becomes massless and may attain incredible speeds almost instantaneously.

'Because of the method used and object can be made to travel within its own inertial frame of reference, thereby taking itself outside of our universe at high velocities. By so doing, such a device may travel many times faster than the speed of light. Also, because it utilizes its own frame of reference, the aging process and time differences predicted by Einstein is nullified. In other words, if a visitor left Earth today for the nearest stellar system, when he returned in a week's time his family and friends would only be one week older and not several decades as would be expected from Einstein's Theory of Relativity.

'It works on a similar principle to an electronic diode, that can change a.c. current into d.c. current or alternating directions of current flow into a singular direction of current flow. Such devices are very efficient in channelling and converting energy into that type of inertia for a given mass. We intend to hold the first demonstration with a working model in about two years. Then humanity will be able to visit the nearest stars and by so doing expand our knowledge of the universe and the Cosmos in general.

'Wow! That is incredible! Man, I wish I was on that first flight to the stars?' Joey replied, amazed by the possibilities.

'Of course, Joe, anyone can come along. Since such a ship will have virtually no inertia and simulated gravity, everyone will be able to travel in luxury and comfort as we do on Earth. You should also realize that our planet is a giant spaceship.'

'How long before we can use these advanced technologies on Earth?' Joey inquired..

'After they have been demonstrated worldwide and production begins through our organization, they can be franchised globally. This is better for all. However, all our products will be supplied through accredited and vetted USA agents and kept away from military usage as long as possible. Those agents will be chosen at the appropriate time,' Lumak replied.

CHAPTER 39

Lumak's 2nd interview

FREEDOM

Several persistent hands went up in the audience.

'Yes, You! The third from the end!' Joey called out.

'My question is, "do you believe in the concept of universal freedom for the individual?" he asked, but Joey was baffled by that question and turned his focus on Lumak.

'Joe, it's a straightforward enough question and I shall answer, if you don't mind. No one in this universe can truly be free. We depend on others for our very survival. For instance, if there was no oxygen left we would all die a relatively quick and painful death. Oxygen is generated by certain types of algae in the seas and oceans and by trees on land. So if anyone thinks they can be free to do as they please without giving due consideration to others, that person must be either a fool or completely insane.

'Personally, I only know of responsibilities. What most of us consider to be freedom is always gained at the expense of others. While trying to be politically correct, let me be blunt in this matter. Are chickens free, sheep free, cattle free, pigs free? Is our planet free for its other life-forms to evolve naturally. I can go on and on to describe your freedom to you.

'You have imprisoned virtually all life on this world in order that you be free. Who has given you the rights for such freedom over other innocent life, to do with as you please? They also have rights to this world by virtue of their existence. What type of freedom is this, with everything else a prisoner of your making.

'A species is truly free when it is free by the bounds it sets and not those set by others for any reason,' Lumak replied.

'But they would be prayed upon if released into the wild?' the man shouted.

'And who is to blame for that? They have survived this far even without the help of man. Survival is an intricate mechanism.

Many creatures soon evolve ways and methods to avoid predation. However, survival for many life-forms become difficult when they become semi-domesticated and are bred by man for his own selfish purpose. Anyway, we are also part of a complex food chain.' The audience were startled by that response and suddenly became conscious of their savagery towards the so-called lower life-forms.

Joey didn't like to continue with that sensitive topic, so he abruptly changed the subject.

MICROIDS AND NANO-TECHNOLOGY

'There is also your work in micro-robotics that you have displayed so vividly in your demonstrations abroad. Is there a special project in that field?' Joey inquired.

'As you know, micro-robotics is a branch of Nano-technology. With this new technology we can build robots of virtually any size. Such flexible machines can perform virtually any tasks about twenty times faster than the fastest human. They can function within virtually any hostile environment and perform intricate operations on the human body, make precise connections within the brain, connect nerves and even repair individual cells. There are numerous applications in all fields, from the sciences, to the more basic operations like building a house. They may also be used for automatically changing wallpaper patterns or in altering the shape and size of a piece of furniture by a simple command. The first demonstration model will be ready in approximately two years from now,' Lumak replied.

A BELIEF IN GOD

'One more question, anyone?' Joey shouted and another put their hand up.

'Do you believe in God?' another one shouted.

'Do you want to answer this one?' a more sombre Joey asked

Lumak.

'This is another straightforward question. The answer to that question is an unequivocal yes. However, you use the term god, when our universe may contain numerous gods. If we took a trip through our universe today, I wonder how many gods we would find.

'First of all, what is a god? Let me expand on this topic to put a clearer picture in your mind, then we may compare like with like. I am0 afraid that my god may not be anything like yours. In the past almost every civilization believed in some god or another. It can be shown that our concepts of gods have been embellished over several millennia and handed down to us in different packages over the years by religious leaders.

'However, while considering any type of god, I shall do away with such concepts of tradition and religion. These concepts relate to the individual. Who is to say his or her belief is truer than the next man or woman's. Therefore, do all-powerful gods really exist and do they affect our lives, the galaxy and universe? Here again, I must give an unequivocal yes. Everyone of us affects our world and our world must surely affect our Solar System and so on ad infinitum. Therefore, everything in existence is connected and must affect all others, even like a single drop will affect the complete ocean. It will take numerous drops to form an ocean and even less its numerous waves, but an ocean cannot exist without each individual drop.

'Gods of all shapes and sizes exists throughout the Cosmos. For if any of us had the technology to move the Earth and live forever, wouldn't that person be considered a god by others. So gods are just very advanced entities with tremendous intelligence and power. Nevertheless many lower life-forms on this world may consider us gods, because we can sometimes do miracles with our brand of technologies. Therefore the term god is quite relative and depends to a great extend on technological advancement.

'I suppose the god that most of us subconsciously believe in, must comprise the three unique forms that are embodied in:

'(a) The Cosmos - contains All and is bounded by All

Possibilities within the swirling Sea of Chaos.

'(b) The She - contains the nature of all things. She is also called Mother Nature and embodies all forms of evolution. Since every facet of our universe is constantly evolving she must permeate all things and transcend all dimensions. However, she is more like a natural mother and is not technological.

'(c) The Greater Purpose - embodies a progressive change in a positive direction to improve cosmic existence and includes all forms of technology. There is also a negative side or Lesser Purpose. However, all life is of The Greater Purpose.

'Since the natural bi-product of evolution is intelligence and since technology is from such intelligence, technology must be accepted by The Greater Purpose and The She or else it wouldn't exist. However, since free will is involved, we must always ensure our technologies are for the long-term benefit of all life.
'So in answer to your original question, I believe in the true God of the Cosmos which is embodied by all that it contains.

SPIRITUAL GODS?

'Is there a spiritual god that takes care of us?
For what purpose would any super-intelligent creature desire to waste any of their precious time to assist us in such a manner above all others. What makes us so special when we are just another basic and uncaring predator species. Why... when last did any of us try to assist any of the so-called lower life-forms or our planet, other than for the purpose of hindering, killing and eating them? We must all give freely before we may receive in like manner.
'Take it from me when I say that the Cosmos is based on specific rules of physics. Wanting something to happen doesn't necessarily make it happen. That is the reason why we can't bring back the dead or move mountains using our minds in the real world. However, we may use technology and move a mountain

with a large bulldozer.

'In our universe many invisible forces exists. Forces like, gravitation, electro-magnetism, electrostatic and others. As a matter of fact our universe abounds with numerous invisible forces. So it doesn't take a great stretch of the imagination to imagine evolution taking place in such realms or at higher dimensions. Even within parallel universes that might interpose with ours from time to time. So even what you may consider to be ghosts may exist, but usually not in the way that you think.

'Although what you may consider to be spiritual gods do exist, they are required to follow certain laws of the Cosmos. So even those supreme beings and deities may rely on others for their survival.

HEAVEN AND HELL

'Here again the most advanced technologies throughout the Cosmos is quite capable of creating such a Virtual World wherein everything can be made possible, even a Heaven or a Hell. Further, one's Identity or Soul may be channelled to such places after the end of their corporeal existence.

'Since all living things contains Identities, all such Identities may be channelled after death to such places. So in that sense, I do believe in Heavens, Hells, and other Virtual Worlds and Universes. Here again, this process will follow rules, whether natural or technological.

THE EXISTENCE OF REAL MAGIC

'Although virtually anything is possible within the Cosmos, which contains many planes of universes. Every universe is unique. For instance, in any given universe only certain types of matter and its associated fields and forces may be distilled out of the Sea of Chaos and of All Possibilities. Therefore only that part of the Quantum World is visible to us through the Laws of Physics.

'This is because a universe is like a tree that will follow certain rules of survival that was handed down by its Parent Universe. A pear tree is not the same as an apple tree. This process is analogous to our DNA, which is a type of template or plan that our bodies will follow for our general longevity and survival. However, if the plan is corrupted in anyway serious problems may arise. A similar situation may occur with all universes. That way The She's time is not wasted in creating too many dud universes by the process of trial and error.

'There are many universes occupying many planes of universes. Most of those universes follow different rules to ours. For even the force of gravity in one may be different to another. In some of those universes even what we consider to be magical effects may exist. However, since magic works contrary to evolution I am certain that any naturally evolving creature would not have developed such powers outside of the natural order.

'This is simply because, if it was possible to do anything by thought, then most would simply die when we had bad thoughts about them. We could quickly destroy ourselves the first time we had a dislike for some part of our body, even as a child. If not by ourselves, by our peers. If only looks could kill. Further, we would be prey to every psychic lion, tiger or other predators, who would doubtless have developed such powers to subdue their prey, so this notion of existence is impractical and will not exist. Therefore all such powers due to our good or evil thoughts directly controlling matter could not naturally exist in evolution. Nevertheless, that doesn't mean a sense of well-being is not good for mind and body. Also, prayer has a type of spiritual power that can sometimes transcend matter to assist our evolution. But all such powers work at the subconscious level.

'Therefore some types of extrasensory perception does exist and is manifested by all life during the process of evolution. This is another important power of The She that enhances progress and the survival of all her children. In other words, we are inter-dimensional beings and therefore a lot more than the sum of our parts.

'Now, let me take a final question from the audience,' Joey said.

Several hands went up, but he took the one furthest at the rear.

'If an alien came to our world, how do you think he would explain us to his people on his return home?' an Englishman asked.
'Another difficult one, I am afraid,' Joey said to Lumak.
'No. I will answer.'

ALIEN VISITS

In answer to your question, I will not mince words or tell you exactly what you would like to hear.
'I suppose, at this late time, any aliens visiting earth could be for the purpose of collecting souvenirs of a once lovely world that was inhabited by numerous life-forms. So they might want to take away a souvenir as reminder of that once living world with its many dead, overgrown and ruined cities.
'As for commenting on this world when he returned. As a life-form that only cares about proliferating its own kind at the exclusion of all others. You should have realized by now that everything on this world is geared for that purpose, ie the human family, even when it will inevitably lead to the extinction of all life. At this time our planet can hardly sustain a mere 750 million humans and yet current population is almost 10 billion and rising.
'Most of the planet's surface is now covered with buildings and roads, dissecting and removing natural habitats, not to mention the destruction of the once fertile forests. Why this urge to have a family for its own sake, without giving a single thought to the future of our world and its diverse species.
'I suppose it's a natural response most humans have to life, given that not many are clever enough to see beyond their nasal extremities. In other words, if all fails have more kids and pray that everything works out the way we want.
'Nevertheless, all is not lost. We can always genetically improve humanity and give him a larger brain. Only then will he be able to visualize the more delicate issues and plan constructively for the future. However, only a few can be chosen

to take the species forward after the destructive turbulence of our immediate future.' Suddenly his audience became quite nervous while reflecting on his last few words. But everyone realized it was not in the nature of viral mankind to change.

Someone once said:

"To deny our own impulses is to deny the very thing that make us human". And in so doing, without having learnt the basic rules of self-control or the necessary emotional controls, Earth's humans can only define their world by misery and suffering. Such a species would feel misplaced in any world closely resembling Heaven.

A truly intelligent species will have long-term goals and you have none,' Lumak said.

'Wow, Man! You seem to be quite pissed off with us all!' Joey exclaimed.

'I have little choice other than being mad when I observe the damage done to our beautiful world and its eco-systems in the name of financial benefits, commercialization, GDP's and such like.'

Without giving too much away, Lumak had answered most of their probing questions. He realized that most of his projects were way beyond the abilities of even the most brilliant scientists of the time and had little to fear from those areas. He had given the press much to consider and hopefully all that information would keep them occupied and well away from him and his projects in the immediate future. That was until his working demonstrations. Nevertheless he had decided to create a team of his own publicity experts to keep them up to date on his progress.

The interview terminated shortly afterwards and the audience cheered. Yet many could not absorb the strange concepts put forward by Lumak. He was no doubt a brilliant mind, with many facets to his knowledge.

Joey Donaldson had given up trying to expose Lumak on television. Soon after Professor Powell left he realised how biassed and stubborn some people were to change. They were scared that such change would make them obsolescent or diminutive. Anyway, in that short time he had grown to respect

Lumak and his vibrant attitude in general.

CHAPTER 40

Trouble at the Manor

Since their move to the Manor in North Dakota, Sarah's father Ben was made responsible for all security. He had given the external building contract to a large city company but there were constant delays during construction. Thus far no one had arrived to instal the perimeter fencing and towers.

The more advanced monitoring and CCTV systems were to be installed by another company specializing in the field of electronic surveillance. During that time security was lacking at the manor so unbeknown to its residents criminals decided to take advantage of the situation.

One day many trucks arrived and workmen began to add the security fences and the four high towers at each corner at the perimeter.

Then three men entered the house to install several pieces of the electronic equipment. Thinking the work was presently underway, Lumak and Sarah ignored them and carried on their normal duties.

Although Sarah sensed danger, so far everything had occurred normally. The men appeared systematic and knowledgeable in installing the equipment, so she remained unconcerned.

At an appropriate time they decided to seize the opportunity.

'Come now! Let's go and see your husband,' one of the guys ordered while pointing his gun at Sarah's head. The other knocked on Lumak's door and entered his study. The third acted as lookout just outside the main door.

'Can I be of assistance?' Lumak inquired, innocently, but the second gunman removed his pistol and pointed it towards Lumak.

Using his brain implants Lumak immediately sealed the room. In an instant everything in that room was transferred into the Greater Mind. It was like a different universe of Virtual Reality where he could alter every aspect of matter, mind and body at will.

'Are you sure you wish to continue with this ridiculous plan?' Lumak inquired.

'What plan?' the man interjected.

'The one to kill me and my wife.'

'Yes! And I have a message from a professor. He told me you would know who it was. Anyway, he reckons you should hear these words before you hit the floor. He says to relay his complements and wishes you a safe trip to hell and 'no more will any young upstart like you ever insult him on TV again,' he read the last words from a piece of paper. Then he fired point blank at Lumak. As if in slow motion Lumak simply stretched forward and caught the bullets in mid air. The man emptied the clip, but as the bullets touched Lumak's garment they simply fell to the floor still smoking. He could have vectorized and allow the bullets to pass through his body but there were too many breakables in the room.

'Incidentally, I think you should know that among other things, I am indestructible. So please put your gun away,' Lumak said. Then Lumak focussed a thought.

'Yes Sir, I must put my gun away. I must give myself to the police and tell them of the plan to kill you and your family and I must not harm anyone,' he said as if in a trance.

'Now I command you to go and arrest your other friends,' Lumak said and he left. Lumak had recorded every bit of data from the man's mind and now knew the people that were involved in planning his demise.

Sarah was still in danger. When her captor saw his colleague leaving Lumak's room he assumed he had completed his share of the task. But to his dismay his colleague lifted his gun against him.

'What's this? Another bloody traitor!' he shouted and fired at his colleague killing him. Then he fired a round towards Sarah's head but the bullet simply dissolved on impact as strange greenish fields enveloped her body. The other gunman hearing the shots soon entered. It was then that he saw his senior lying close to the door.

'So you were the bloody stooge all this time!' he shouted and both men began firing at each other until both lay wounded and dying on the floor. A sensible Sarah went towards them and took away their weapons which she placed on the near table.

'Darling! Are you ok!' Sarah yelled. Lumak was soon out of the door to embrace and comfort his shaken wife.

'I really thought I was a gonna....but... but... the necklace came alive to protect me.'

'That was a close shave. Thank goodness we had our wits about us and recognized the dangers in time. Always wear your necklace. It will protect you in times of great danger. But the ring is also there as backup.'

'I thought they were part of the Islamists extremists.'

'No Love! They are a different lot this time! Now, my dear, please call the police and Lennox. I have arranged a transcript from one of the assailants. They can get rid of this mess and arrest the perpetrators forthwith. I have more important work to complete and I'm afraid its urgent,' he said and went back to his study unconcerned. It was soon found that professor Powell was in league with one Senator Murray. The senator was involved with a few major petroleum dealers who considered Lumak a major threat to their industries. Once the secret service was on their tail they were soon arrested. Then the whole matter was cleared up in secret. After that close shave the Manor's security was improved to a level equivalent to the type used at Forth Nox.

CHAPTER 41

Family matters

After the interview, Lumak and the McCririck family were in great demand. Lumak realized he had to focus on his demanding projects. Therefore he arranged his plans in such a way that Madeline and family would take most of the publicity pressure and heat. He placed Sarah in charge of all their escapades so she arranged interviews and transport for the family globally. Sarah, Lennox and his girlfriend, Joan, would sometimes accompany and prepare them well for each interview. Later, their publicity agency took over the tasks of all such activities. After many such interviews, Madeline became quite rich and popular. Despite her youthful appearance she had 95 years of human experience under her sleeves. Not to mention her bubbly personality that everyone admired and loved.

Despite everything, her family had grown to accept the idea of a youthful bubbly grandparent, with a tendency to make up for lost time by enjoying life at its fullest whenever she could.

Just out of curiosity, one day she visited the small ranch the bank had taken away from her family decades before. The place was in utter disrepair. As she leant against the broken fence to view its wild expanse all the memories of that sad episode of her life came flooding back.

'If only you were now with us, George, to see how your children had grown. I know, my husband, we had some awful luck, but finally we have come through, thanks to a great and most brilliant man called Jeffery Longhurst, and look at me how young I've become. So don't you worry anymore, my love,' she said to the field, while turning around like a little girl to show her colourful dress. As she did tears fell from her eyes.

Soon after she bought the small holding and assigned it to her eldest son Joseph.

Nevertheless Lumak soon made them an offer they couldn't

refuse. One day he called them into his living room and made them comfortable for what he had to say.

'People, I have decided to give you all a partnership in my ranch, excluding the manor and four hundred acres below Little River. The partnership will be 33 percent of all profits incurred. It is too much land for me to handle and your family are very good at farming, so it's only fair that you share in the profits. Think about my proposition and don't worry about money and equipment. I can get whatever you need at short notice. We can always review the partnership details on a yearly basis, if you wish,' Lumak said, while focussing on Madeline.

'No Sir, after all that you have done for my family, no way am I going to take another free dime from you! So we have decided to take up your offer and pay you for a 33 percent share in the business on offer,' Madeline said. Lumak immediately went forward to shake her hand and seal the agreement, but instead she hugged and kissed him. This time the kiss was on his right cheek and not on his lips as before.

CHAPTER 42

Sarah's negative reflections

After his arrival in the USA, Lumak had gained much popularity. Since his last television interview he had found many new friends in every strata of society. Even so, he also had his enemies, due to jealousy, economics or fear. Many realized a storm was coming that would shake the planet to its very foundations. During that time their well established livelihoods and wealth would be sacrificed. To many Lumak seemed to dislike their blind competitive capitalistic efforts and sacrifices for monetary gain. He was more on the side of the planet and its other life-forms. Those attitudes placed him outside of their ambitions.

Under Sarah's control, Lumak's anti-cancer serum was presently in use globally. Rewards from that businesses and other investments were truly enormous.

With the help of Lumak, Sarah and her father Ben had educated themselves well in matters of ecology and other relevant subjects. They were fully qualified in those areas, and literate in most of the main European languages. Finally they were ready to take on many of the planet's ecological problems. They hadn't been given brain implants, but with the special microids and drugs Lumak administered, they were equivalent to brilliant doctors in relevant fields.

Lumak realizing the serious tasks and heavy workload ahead, with the many projects of his own, soon placed all business controls under Sarah. She was always good at handling financial matters and was presently in control of billions of dollars. Sarah soon decided to create their own banking organization for giving help to the poorest countries. It soon expanded worldwide. She had applied to the US and other governments for tax concessions for their many charities and had been awarded substantial benefits. All those benefits she would use to assist poor students in getting a good education and improving global health by supplying free medicine to those at risk.

The main global organization she called Solarian Banking, under Lumak's advise.

One day she glanced at her image in the large hall mirror and became scared out of her wits. That day Lumak was away on business.

'Oh my God! What's happening to me?'

She thought of something nice and her mirror image changed to her pleasant self, but more beautiful and radiant than ever before. That better image of herself she could not let go and would have done anything to remain that way. She soon found that by thinking of good or bad, her mirror image would reflect those feelings. Sometimes she would reflect the most evil witch with dark and sharp features. That image always scared her into changing her thoughts.

'The Neckless or Broach must be changing my looks for a reason. It's guiding me to do what's right.'

It was as if she was being guided along a particular course in helping humanity. It also enhanced her psychic abilities.

Sarah was always sincere in thoughts and deeds and committed to saving the planet from the callous hands of humankind. Once she realized the dire straights the planet was in, she became furious, and when Sarah was furious the fallout was extensive. She began to place many adds in news papers and magazines to make the global public aware of the distress felt in many parts of the planet. She contacted numerous charities and relevant organizations to further stress her points. Many of those were coerced and offered substantial financial benefits.

Since Sarah's main organizations were presently the most wealthiest on the planet, she never had problems with funding. She would generously assist those charitable causes that followed closely her aspirations. Sarah and her father Ben were subsequently made honourable members of many such organizations.

For once in her brief existence, Sarah began to consider the attitudes and attributes of humanity and found the scales wanting. She soon realized the innate biases of selfish humanity against all things not of their own. When there was famine in Ethiopia mankind would send rations in truckloads to save his own, but when the species were different they couldn't have cared less. It was as if they disliked all other life in the universe and would sometimes go out of their way to accelerate their demise. Thank goodness there were a few good human souls about that really cared, but those were significantly less than 10 percent of the global population. The problem was how to increase the number of such caring people and assist them in their tireless efforts and campaigns.

'A pretentious self-indulgent species with such self-importance, that would even pray to his gods to save him in some paradise he calls heaven, after having committed so many crimes and atrocities against God's own creatures on Earth. And mostly in the name of having fun. If there was a place like heaven, I am sure mankind would decimate it as much as he had done to Earth. No god in his right mind would ever allow such a species into any of his beautiful realms. If there was such a god, of all species, hypocritical mankind would be the very last on his list. God is a god of all things and all life, not just of mankind.

'We humans must be the most arrogant of creatures to think the universe was only made for us. We enter areas like the Amazon rain forests and decide to clear it without giving any consideration for its original occupants. Like a bull in a China shop, we disturb their habitats and dwellings, remove essential sources of food and other supplies and willfully decimate their livelihood without giving due considerations, or even a thought to their future survival.

'Despite our over-population of this world, we still procreate like pigs and have children without knowing why we need them, relying only on our hormones and emotions to guide us along that blind alley to eventual extinction. How backward, primitive and instinctive can this so-called intelligent species be? How could anyone trust such a species like mankind to even take their dogs for a walk!' she thought, vehemently.

Sarah reasoned it was time every species were given some form of legal representation by proxy. Once a human lawyer was given the task to defend them, he would put himself in the place of an individual within the said species. With all the knowledge gained about other species over the years, one could be in a position to fully represent them in a court of law. After all, if someone decided to take our lands and property away from us illegally, we could take them to court and resolve the matter that way.

'Although human courts are only for humans, I can see no reason why others couldn't have legal representation by proxy. I shall seriously consider this matter after my return from the field. I am sure a legal president has been set in the past by someone in this regard.

'You know, when anyone enters this material universe they have little choice in the matter. They rely on others to give them a start in life, in order to get established. That basic right applies to all life-forms, prey and predator alike. We cannot ignore the innocent and assume there will always be enough resources for them to utilize. As a senior and more intelligent life-form, it is our responsibility to take care and protect those beneath us in the so-called food chain, as if we were their parents.

'Anyway, isn't it a fact that all life is equivalent to each other within the Cosmos. We humans were little more than slugs 100 million years ago and even the lowliest slugs today might evolve to supremacy in a few million years. It so happens in evolution, that every poor dog will have his day sooner or later, providing he doesn't become extinct in the process. And that's assuming the poor slugs and dogs are given a fair chance to evolve naturally on their own.

'If things go the way they are at present, it will be necessary to isolate humanity from all other planetary life.

'Humans could be placed in large sealed environmental domes with their own atmospheres, thus completely sealing off their populations from the planet. Such a progressive step would allow the Earth, our loving Mother Gaia, to breathe again, instead of being stifled under the trampling feet of self-indulgent humanity.

'That way they could be limited to specific areas of the planet and not devastate its important fertile areas as they have done in

Amazonia and other critically important parts of our planet,' she muttered, annoyingly, while typing one of her essays for the Scientific American.

In the year 2042, the human population was over 10 billion and rising uncontrollably to a level of mass extinction. Any such extinction would affect all life globally, but mostly mankind. So no wonder Sarah was at the end of her tether with regards to humanity. She realized that short of culling the human population with some deadly microbe, a quick and humane solution would have to be found immediately for planetary survival.

Nevertheless, she wanted a few children of her own and didn't wish to be too pretentious or hypocritical in placing too much blame on parents with a strong desire to have their own. However since becoming active in BioLive she had taken a stand against all frivolous adventures without forethought and would only bear children if their main purpose was to assist the universe, and be thoroughly trained in that manner.

Having given her ideas further considerations, she soon realized it would be more economical to isolate all endangered species from the effects of mankind. It was then that she came up with the unique idea of building massive dome environments with their own self-contained rain forests. All controlled by master computers.

'Darling, can I discuss an important matter with you?' she said and Lumak left his pile of paperwork and followed her into the lounge.

'What is it, Love?' he asked, patiently.

'I have been giving serious considerations to the present problems faced globally, including the decimation of many species by mankind, and have come to a single conclusion. If we cannot separate man from the other life-forms we have to separate them from man. We shall build massive dome environments throughout the planet, where original habitats can be re-created in their entirety. Here, I am thinking of structures many miles in diameter and miles high into the air. They must be thoroughly isolated from clever poachers who might attempt entering by air. The problem is, how to build such massive structures. Perhaps instead of domes, just very tall spherical walled perimeters is all that's needed, with enough security,' she said and Lumak remained silent for a while, regurgitating his thoughts on the topic.

'That's not going to be a problem. With my new Microid Robots such structures could be constructed in weeks, given a good source of raw materials,' Lumak replied.

'You mean to say, you can really do that with your robots?' Sarah exclaimed, innocently.

'Yes! The moment they begin to role off the production lines. But I am afraid it will take another year or so. There is also the problem of getting the large areas of land from the authorities. But since money is not an issue, I can do my part if you and your father are willing to travel and purchase the land.'

'My father and myself can visit all countries involved and offer them certain incentives for their cooperation. What if we decided to employ their people on several of such projects? In return we could buy large swathes of land for such construction. Further, many of those countries either haven't the payed manpower or desire to implement the necessary security measures to stem poaching and such like. In any event, we have a major task ahead of us.'

Lumak realized most of the present weather problems centred on South America, which was one of the main lungs of the planet. The Amazonian rain forests served the planet with most of its oxygen. With current and past deforestation, the amount of carbon dioxide created by their crude farming methods and practices had been larger than even the main industrial countries. All this was due mainly to their logging and slash and burn activities.

Out of all those South American countries, Venezuela was the poorest. In the year 2042 its population was just over 63 million and starving. That country had borrowed billions from international banks in previous years and had overstretched their economy in an attempt to repay those loans. During the previous years most of her natural resources had been used and abused to such an extent, that hardly anything was left to feed her still growing populations. Venezuela was presently within an economy of crisis.

Lumak realized the situation and decided to get them out of their current dilemma, so he explained the situation to Sarah and Ben. Ben was now Sarah's second in command.

'I know there are many countries in Africa awaiting our assistance, but I think we should make Venezuela our first project. Here is a report I recently compiled on that country. Study it well and learn as much as you can about its economies and political structure,' Lumak said and handed them their files.

'Darling, you almost read my mind. Dad, you know what we have to do,' Sarah said.

'My team is ready, just point the way,' Ben replied.

The shrewd negotiator Ben was to visit the bankers involved and take over several such loans from them at a modest fee. He would explain to them that the poorer countries were presently on the verge of bankruptcy and that his offer was a better choice than the alternative. Then he was to visit Venezuela and make their government an offer they couldn't refuse.

If that process of reclamation worked with one, it would work with more, so Sarah was optimistic of her new method to save endangered species.

CHAPTER 43

Sarah in South America

She continued her speculations and realized amongst other things the weather pattern was slowly changing for the worse. Those erratic variations placed extra pressures on the planet's numerous eco-systems. The global temperature had increased by almost 3 degrees and sea levels risen by over 3 feet, way above predicted values. At present rates the maximum temperature rise could eventually be over 7 degrees. If all the ice in Greenland and the southern polar region melted, water levels would rise by over 65 metres. However this was a worst case scenario. All coastal cities were slowly being submerged while many innocent creatures were being displaced on a global basis.

Once the weather pattern had regressed, the distribution of flora and fauna would change throughout the planet. Therefore, controlled environmental domes could play a significant role in saving all those threatened species. Further, all tropical regions of the planet could soon become uninhabitable by most animals, including humans.

There were presently two possible scenarios, namely the Deep Freeze and the Pressure Cooker. If the Gulf Stream suddenly stopped, the Deep Freeze scenario could be triggered, leading to another prolonged ice age. The ice would begin to build in the northern and southern latitudes, leading to more extreme changes in flora and fauna. If on the other hand, the Pressure Cooker scenario took effect, in the extreme the oceans could rise by over 80 metres (about 250 feet) with other undesirable changes. Either way the planet was stuck in crisis.

She wanted to assist but the only way she could accomplish her aims was to gain experience. That meant being in the field and facing those problems like everyone else. Her father Ben was a good negotiator and the correct one to get in touch with the governments involved for acquiring lands necessary for their large scale projects. Nevertheless she was saving the planet's endangered species from the callous hands of man and that must count for something, even among the most unconcerned politicians.

Sarah soon acquired a kit for her jungle travels and practised many worst case scenarios until she knew almost every square foot of planet Earth. When Lumak was convinced she was ready to handle her own missions independently, he gave her one of his special insignias. Those insignias could be used as monitors and trigger Lumak's new security system when pressed anywhere on the planet. Since Lumak's own insignia and computer systems were linked directly to his brain implants he could always observe her progress and communicate in an emergency.

One morning while having breakfast the phone rang and Sarah got up to answer.

'Is this BioLive as advertised?' the person inquired.

'Yes! The same! How can I help you?' she replied.

'We have a serious problem in the South American rain forests, with many important species of flora and fauna going down the plughole. The situation has become so critical we will take whatever help we can get. At present we have several conservation groups dispersed far and wide throughout the planet and find ourselves overstretched. However, every one of our projects have equal importance, so we cannot move operatives as we would like. Can your organization help?' he said while Sarah listened patiently.

'Where did you see our add,' Sarah inquired.

'It was in the New York Times.

'I see!'

'I am very sorry, but let me introduce myself. I am Doctor Harris Munroe of the Save-Our-World conservation charity.'

'Well, you are speaking to Sarah Longhurst. I am in charge of the organization, BioLive. I am certain we can assist you once we know of your problems,' she replied in a most positive manner.

'You don't mean... the wife of our eminent Professor Jeffery Longhurst?' he inquired.

'Yes, the same. However, we have only recently started this project and lack the necessary organizational skills to tackle matters of life and death. I was hoping to get some experience in the field before getting actively involved within the organization.'

'Mam, we have people all over the world including three separate teams in South America alone. Why don't you tag along with one of my best teams,' he replied.

'Do you have a team in Venezuela?'

'Yes! My wife and her team are in that country on their way to Columbia. They are currently assessing deforestation in the Barinas district and a few other local states. You may join them if you wish. We have all the necessary papers for dealing with government officials over there.'

'That's fantastic! But I will need a few days to prepare.'

'That's no problem. I shall arrange for them to meet you at Bolivar International. I shall fax them the minute you are ready.'

'Ok! Email me the details. I shall be ready for the trip in one week,' Sarah replied.

'It's on its way, Mam, and thanks for your kind assistance,' he said and hung up.

'That was the head of Save-Our-World. They need our assistance in South America and I've decided to make it my first mission. This is the only way I can assess their needs and damage done to those areas. Now we know for sure where we are going. Dad can visit the politicians and make the necessary arrangements and agreements,' Sarah said. Ben was also at the table having breakfast while listening to his daughters words. He was a military man and took everything in his stride in an unconcerned manner.

'I bet it's Venezuela!' Ben remarked to Lumak and he nodded positively.

They knew once Sarah had made her mind she would not detract by the smallest fraction, so they began preparing for her trip. As always, the Shadite Lumak thoroughly prepared and briefed her and Ben for worst case scenarios. He decided to give them all the necessary vaccines and repellants as needed during their trips.

Nevertheless, Sarah was now a heightened spirit. She had developed a super sense and intuition that could sniff a dangerous situation days ahead. Despite those powers she tended to follow dangers in order to gain more experience in the field.

Sarah and her group of six uniformed assistants arrived in Caracas a week later and was met at the airport by Doctor Munroe's wife. She was currently in charge of all their efforts in that continent.

'I am Catherine Munroe, but you may call me Cathy. I am very pleased to meet you, Doctor Sarah Longhurst,' she said and they shook hands.

'The pleasure is all mine, Cathy. Let's hope we can get some real work done while I am here. I have booked many rooms in the Hilton hotel, so I trust you and your team will remain with us there for a while. We have much to discuss, before our travels to the areas concerned,' Sarah said. They glanced at her in utter astonishment. After all they were just a poor charitable organization that could not afford luxuries like expensive hotels.

'This is not the Hilton Caracas Residencias? Are you sure, Mam. This is about the most expensive hotel in the city. Yes, I am sure!' Sarah replied, unconcerned.

Soon several limousines appeared on the scene and took them and their baggage away. On arrival, they were welcomed by the manager and his senior staff, who had informed the press to gain further publicity. Sarah always liked such initiatives from her staff.

The moment they entered the foyer they were bombarded by many reporters. Then the manager went forward to shake her hand and introduce his more senior staff. Sarah didn't know that she was also famous in that part of the world. However, she soon realized most of it was because of her husband's past assistance to those so-called poorer countries. Nevertheless Sarah saw her present country as another beautiful spot on the planet, but with much potential for improvement.

'My name is Carlos Martinez. I am your current manager, Mam. I hope your stay here with us will be a most pleasant one,' he said in good English, and everyone suddenly realized that she was the owner of the hotel. Sarah had simply bought the whole group of hotels of that name throughout the planet to make her visits to those places more comfortable.

'Carlos, I am very impressed, but I am here on business, so will require a special team of jungle trackers in a few days. Can you arrange that for me.'

'Yes Mam. I have some good contacts,' he replied.

CHAPTER 44

BioLive supreme

While in the hotel the phone rang, and Sarah took the call.

'My dear, it's me, Jeff. Is everything ok over there?' he inquired.

'Yes, Darling. I had a good reception and like the people. I feel I can do some great things over here. The only problem is the extreme heat. It must be close to 45 in the shade,' she replied.

'Your adds have been very successful. Our office received correspondence from most of the largest organizations. Many require funding and will go to almost any lengths for financial assistance.'

'Let them know that I will be holding a conference in Caracas over the next two weeks. Everything will be free, even their flights, so if anyone wants funding they will have to be present at that conference. I am not pussy-footing around anymore, with everyone's half baked efforts and ideas on conservation. Now I mean serious business,' she said. Lumak was surprised by her determination and change of attitude.

'Ok, my dear. Be careful, and I love you!' Lumak replied and hung up the receiver. Lumak used his large publicity organization to forward all the necessary brochures, invitations and tickets to those organizations.

Soon the representatives of many of the largest conservation bodies and charities were on their way to the city of Caracas in Venezuela. They were keen to know what was going on, but wouldn't miss the possibility of a large cheque in the process.

Later that week she called a meeting of all those concerned. The conference was held in the main dining room of the hotel which was filled with delegates from all over the world including numerous reporters. Sarah tapped the microphone and shouted at the top of her voice, silencing everyone.

'People, quiet please! I want to say a few important words.

There are many organizations with high aims and ambitions, but the sum of all their hard endeavours is just a token effort when faced with the enormous task of solving our planet's problems. Those problems increase exponentially on a yearly basis. So I have decided, in the interest of Mother Earth, to become responsible for all such organizations planet wide.

'You will still continue as before, but with a lot more power and funding through my BioLive organizations. Think of it for a moment. What gains have your charities accomplished in previous years. You are flogging a dead horse and you know it. Having assessed the situation globally and observed many worst case scenarios, I am afraid this is the only way forward for optimum effect.

'I know many of you will not agree to my methods at such short notice, but we have the finances that you require so if you really desire in your hearts to save our world for its future life-forms, this is the only way forward.

'From henceforth, we shall tackle the governments involved and acquire large swathes of land on which we shall build massive dome habitats. These habitats will contain all our endangered species, thus completely isolating them from deforestation, poachers and adverse weather conditions. They will each contain the strictest security. Many of the poor farmers can be retrained into animal welfare and security,' Sarah said, in no uncertain terms and they were amazed by her ideas.

'But Sarah, such domes will cost enormous amounts and they will not be large enough for many of the wandering species, like monkeys. They will also take many years to construct and the situation is now quite critical,' Cathy shouted from the front.

'Would domes three miles in diameter be large enough for you, Cathy. We have plans to build seven such domes within the amazon basin. They will cover an area of over 100 million hectares, with large sealed access tunnels between them for easy migration. With our current levels of technologies virtually any size can be constructed and be modelled to fit within hills and mountains. However it doesn't mean we cannot assist those requiring our immediate assistance when necessary.

'Cathy, your organization will soon be given a plan of such

structures. The head of your organization will also be made a director within BioLive, so you guys have nothing to lose, but everything to gain under our guardianship. And that freedom goes to all of those who would like to become part of the greater whole. In future we shall offer the usual immediate assistance to those endangered species, but also assess their environment for suitable siting of such domes,' Sarah said, and Cathy was numbed by the power of the woman that stood before her. It was like Sarah had changed into a different person.

'But Mam, even with all your resources, such structures will take years to construct. In that time many species will surely face extinction,' a reporter shouted from the rear.

'All our domes will be built by the most advance robots. The robots I speak of will be mass-produced in one of my husband's factories. Such Microid designs are intelligent and can work about twenty times faster than the fastest human. They do not require tea breaks, sleep or indeed any rest until the job is done. Given a continuous supply of raw materials, each dome can be constructed within a few weeks,' she replied.

'There is also the acquisition of large areas of land. How will you convince the relevant authorities of your good intentions,' another delegate shouted.

'My father, Doctor Bengizara Khan, is currently making a deal for such an area of land from the Venezuelan authorities, and he seldom fails. He will simply make them an offer they can't refuse,' she said, and they realized they were going places and quickly with her at the wheel.

'One more thing, people. Once you are members of BioLive you may stay in our most prestigious hotels free of cost and that freedom extends to all your main representatives, and I own all such hotels globally. That also includes one of the largest banks on the planet. This unimportant information is just in case you are not aware of the powers involved. We now have the finances to make a change, so why don't we all work together to save our world from certain disaster,' she said. They clapped and cheered as she left the stage.

From that moment on they could sense a wind of change

blowing through the corridors of their organizations and that wind of progress was for the better.

CHAPTER 45

No refusals

'Mister President, the representatives from the World Bank are expected here on Tuesday. They will remain for a week. Therefore we should organize a suitable team to show them around,' Emanuel said, while standing at attention in front of his president and bowing his head with respect.

'Isn't that Gomez's department? Anyway, where is he today?' an absentminded Carlos asked, innocently.

'Killed a week ago, Sir. During a border dispute,' Juan replied.

'Yea. I remember now. How could I have forgotten? He was a good man that will always be missed.' Then Carlos shook his head as if to dissociate himself from the painful thoughts of yet another crisis. After many years of such situations and crises he had grown a hard emotional crust to cope. It had also numbed him from the pressures of state and other more important matters like pollution and deforestation.

'As always, these people will try to squeeze the last drop of blood out of a stone and that stone happens to be us. They know everything about our situation here, but every time they come dressed in their smart suits telling us how to run our country. You know, every time they change the rules and add new stipulations. How can we ever repay our debts if we are to prevent exploration for gold and restrict logging to only the few areas of replanting. Our oil is almost gone, so how are we supposed to exist. Yet, if we are to supply electricity to our people we need hydro power, and they are also against our current plans to create the dam.

'Anyway, Emanuel, see what you can do to make our guests comfortable during their stay,' Carlos said with annoyance. Emanuel suddenly realized he had been promoted to Gomez's position.

Carlos Caesar Alonso Bolivar was a distant relative of the great leader Simon Bolivar, who had taken their country from Spanish hands in 1821. That was now over two centuries ago and Carlos, although a Caesar in both words and deeds could not take his country away from the hands of international bankers or stem the flow of foreign debt repayments. Not ever, with inflation levels in excess of 200 percent and rising. The days of cheap oil was over while his country's many oil fields and wells were empty.

Ben arrived in his private jet in Caracas on schedule and was flanked by many of his special security. Although he hated such flights he had taken special medication to overcome his fear of heights and air sickness. His plane was an incredible sight to watch, with the large insignia of their organization emblazoned on both sides. It glittered a bright silver and stood out like a jewel in the bright sunlight.

Emanuel soon came forward to shake his hand.

'My name is Emanuel Gonzalez. I represent the President,' he said in broken English with a strong Spanish accent.

'I am very pleased to meet you, Emanuel. My name is Bengizara Khan, but please call me Ben.' Ben was holding a beautiful ivory walking cane with embossed golden figurines throughout its length. What appeared to be a dragon's head formed the ornate handle. Ben replied in perfect Spanish and Emanuel was taken back by the power of the man and his calm attitude. Not to mention his own personal jet and security people. They were uniformly dressed Chinese and Japanese. All wearing dark suits and sunshades like ninja warriors. He immediately got on his mobile to his president.

'Mister President, it is not a team this time. Just a single individual and he want's to see you immediately!'

'Do you think he is after our guts?' Carlos inquired.

'I don't know, Sir. But I wouldn't keep him and his team waiting if I were you!' Emanuel replied silently while whispering those words.

'I have an appointment due in five minutes with one of my ministers. I suppose that one can wait. Get him over here right now. One way or another we are going to have it out with them. I've had enough of those bankers!' Carlos shouted and hung up.

'Sir, the President will see you now. That is unless you would like to visit your hotel first to freshen up.'

'No, Emanuel. That is not necessary. My jet is also a hotel with all the necessary facilities,' Ben replied and Emanuel was even more uncomfortable with the tall and powerful man standing next to him.

They took the president's limousine and were at the government's building within the hour.

'Carlos, my name is Bengizara Khan and I have come to make you a proposition.' The president scanned the powerful figure that stood before him and was amazed by his calmness.

Ben was wearing a most expensive and beautiful cream suit with an insignia pinned to his lapel. His hair was jet black with a bluish tint and his skin slightly tanned, almost like the president's. All that masculine beauty and perfection had come from their special diet and the use of other more advanced devices and drugs.

'Please come into my private study, Sir,' he said.

'Carlos, I have taken over your loans from the relevant banks and placed them within our own banks. So all your critical problems are now over, but not quite. We still would like you to repay about 25 percent of your current repayments, but you can do that with your coffee and other exports. This will give your country some time to breathe. However, in return we would like a few favours,' Ben said. Carlos was waiting for the crunch; for never before had anyone done his country any big favours.

'Carlos, my friend, we are global ecologists. Although we would like all your people to be well fed and happy, we are also concerned for the state of our world. Many poor species are becoming extinct, and when they are all gone we will be next, so we have to find ways to stop the rot. I have chosen your country because it is currently one of the poorest in this part of the world.'

'Well, what ever we can do to stop the rot,' Carlos replied, sarcastically. Thinking Ben's intention was to stop the building of his dam.

'I have no intentions of stopping any of your current projects. However, we would like to build large dome environments that will contain their own rain forests for the benefit of all misplaced species. That is until most of the natural forests in those areas are regrown. They will contain all endangered species which will be isolated from the hands of mankind. Such structures will be an attraction to tourists and bring you in much foreign currency. But the domes I speak of will be truly enormous. I am talking of structures several miles in diameter and miles high into the clouds. But, my friend, when the words of our intentions leave this room, I am sure every state will want their own. Their presence will employ many of your countrymen, either as security or assistants. Along with these domes will be large recreation and play parks for all those visitors. So you see my friend, wherever we build our domes will also be a most beautiful Disney World type park,' Ben said.

'This is truly an incredible plan, Senior!'

'And my friend, you don't have to pay a penny. All you have to do is mention the master plan to your other ministers. Anyway, I don't want anymore loan repayments from you for another five years, and when the time is right I shall pass the word around on the stock market and in a short time your country will become very rich again. Believe me when I say we have the means to virtually swing anything, so what do you say?' Ben said, with a broad grin in a quiet voice.

'I say yes, Ben. I say Yes!,' a happy Carlos iterated in Spanish.

'All we have to do now is find the area of the first sight. It will have to be about 100 million hectares of the worst lands. Your farmers will be well compensated for their losses,' Ben replied.

'Emanuel! Emanuel!,' Carlos shouted. 'Come here and get us both a drink.' Emanuel soon entered to take their orders. He had never seen his president so happy before.

'Ben, I thought you had come to virtually take our country away from us, but you have given us hope and a lot more besides. Who are you people really?' Carlos said.

'You have heard of the eminent Doctor Jeffery Longhurst and his organizations for saving our planet and its people? Well, I am his father-in-law and we form the organization.' Carlos couldn't believe that such a selfless organization could ever exist in the world of humanity.

Soon word of Disney Parks and environmental domes were on the grape vine. But that was not all. His ministers were told that they had been given a reprieve of five years for loan repayments. They cheered Carlos for swinging those negotiation their way. Carlos had soon become a most popular president and once again free to guide his poor country along his intended path. Which was to build his country and put an end to their poverty. He also realized the construction of large environmental domes would give the many endangered species a reprieve and that process would also calm world opinion against the devastation and pollution in his country. Not to mention employment for many.

Soon he made it difficult for the most unscrupulous logging companies to exist and they moved elsewhere.

Several areas of deforested lands were found in most of the states. As a matter of fact, most of the decimated lands were unsuitable for farming. They caused flooding and massive landslides during the rainy seasons, resulting in numerous deaths and other losses, so Sarah had many choices in her very first selections.

Carlos had assigned an army of soldiers to accompany Ben on his travels through the rough areas of his country. There were always border disputes. Those areas proliferated local bandits that would seize any rich person for ransom.

After Ben had completed his surveys and made his choices, he was pleased with the outcome of that mission and dismissed the local soldiers on loan from the army. He had allocated a week for his present project, which was completed in three days. Having a little time to spare with his personal guards, Ben decided to visit Sarah and her company to experience more of the country and its people.

CHAPTER 46

Jungle trek

'Mam, these are our guides,' Pedro said. Sarah scanned the figures of poor scruffy bushmen stood in line with all their pitiful shapes and sizes. There they remained still and at attention as if parading for their most esteemed president while awaiting scrutiny by their most boisterous Sergeant Major. Those poor bedraggled souls patiently remained that way for her inspection, while dressed in their best rags and Sarah could not believe her eyes.

She was dressed in military fatigues to take on the jungle with everything it would throw at her and her group of explorers. The only object that made her different to the others was her broad rimmed straw hat. That one included a veil that could be brought over her head and face to shield that part of her body from the blood sucking insects. She soon walked up to the first in line.

'His name is Emanuel, Mam. He is good with snakes and reptiles. He can sniff an Anaconda or Crocodile from over a hundred metres away. He is in charge of the trackers,' Raul said, and shifted his focus to the other as Emanuel bowed his head.

'It's nice to meet you, Emanuel,' she said in perfect Spanish and he bowed his head again. Since her hotel manager was also Emanuel, she realized it was probably a common name.

'Carlos is called the bird man. There is little he doesn't know about our exotic species.

'Cristos is an excellent tracker, but so is his friend Josepe. They work better together as a team,' he said. Sarah was impressed and bowed gently.

'Are all these guys fed?' Sarah asked in English, making sure they were strong enough to face the hazards of the jungle trek.

'Yes, Mam. They can also live on jungle food if they have to,' he replied. To Sarah that meant they were capable of eating live insects and animals for survival and she swallowed hard.

'Raul, here is some money, take them along to a good restaurant in the local village and treat them for me. Mind you, no alcohol. I want my guys fully sober. Also, get them each a holdall, some new outfits and rations. Include four new machetes for each of our guides and trackers. I want them to feel good with themselves on this trip. That also applies to you. Five thousand bucks should cover those requirements and use whatever is left over to buy some anti-malaria and anti-snake medicine. We might require some medicine for the sick in the village. I am also a nurse, so get a few syringes as well,' she said and Raul took them away.

Later that day Sarah's father Ben arrived with his six security guards. As always those Chinese and Japanese warriors were unarmed and serious. However those guys were trained in the martial arts and didn't need weapons at close range. To Ben they were his chosen Scimitars that were treated more like sons and daughters. They were most loyal and would follow him to hell if need be.

'Hi, Dad!' Sarah greeted and they shook hands like professionals.

'Sarah, we've got what we wanted. All 23 states are interested, but so far only four have given consent. I think the others will come across after they see our first miracle. But I had to offer them Disney-like Parks close to those areas to attract tourism. Anyway, our domes can be designed with entrances and passages for visitors and we can train some of the locals to show them the sites,' he said.

'That's fantastic news, Dad. Is there a local one?' she inquired.

'Since this is the most polluted and deforested state, we have a choice of three in this area alone,' he replied and she was intrigued.

'Wow! That's fantastic!'

Then he briefed her and showed her the location of the chosen areas on the map. Four states had given permission to build. They were currently in one of the states and close to a large area of deforestation.

Raul was responsible for the whole group. He soon got his local map out of his jacket pocket and placed it on the small retractable

table used for camping.

Pedro was responsible for their protection and carried a powerful snipers rifle and a handgun in a side holster. He was very keen on the safety of his group and carried a long scar on the right side of his face.

The weather had suddenly changed and it was pouring.

'Mam, this is the route to the village. It's about forty kilometres away. Although the village has a militia, there are bandits about. Mam, that area so close to the border is very dangerous. Most of it is infested with bandits and guerillas. I don't think you should visit that place.'

'You are too worried for our safety?'

'Yes Mam, I am! Most of them move across the border from Columbia. The army can only patrol these areas once every three months. They rely on the local militia for law enforcement, but they are not very reliable.'

'Don't worry, Raul, I am sure we can travel another forty kilometres without serious danger. We are virtually unarmed and do not pose a threat to anyone. But just in case, I shall tell everyone to be alert and aware of possible dangers. Anyway, Pedro is always on alert,' she said and called the team leaders together.

The rain stopped. This time they left their land rovers behind and decided to mount the mules, horse and donkeys for the rest of the journey through the denser jungle. That area of land was just before the village and contained about ten kilometres of track, so the trackers were required and led the group on four donkeys.

Having cleared the most direct route through the jungle eight hours later, they found themselves on a well trodden path. They were soon over a bridge that covered a small stream. As they viewed the area towards the village it appeared burnt and bare as far as the eye could see. All that area had been destroyed by slash-and-burn methods in the past. From their hilly viewpoint they could observe six large routes that led away from the village in different directions. Well trodden routes were always to be avoided due to hidden bandits and guerillas.

'The border village lay just ahead. We must be very careful from now,' Pedro insisted, taking his small gun to hand.

'This is definitely the place,' Sarah said while checking her hand-held DPS for accurate coordinates. Then dismounting her mule. The others did likewise as she called her group together.

'We are here people. This is the place where we shall build our first animal refuge. We have full permission from the authorities, even to build a local airport. They were intrigued by her authority in such matters.

As if by magic about fifty armed militia suddenly became visible on the banks on either side of their route. They were in the middle with guns pointing in their direction.

'Pedro, hold down your weapon and try not to pose a threat,' Sarah advised and he did as said.

'Mam, I should talk with them,' Raul said in local Spanish and moved forward towards the one that appeared to be their leader.

'Tell him we represent the government and are doing a survey in this area. We want to remove all the pollution and reestablish normality in this part of the rain forest. Mention, we brought medicine for those in the village and give him this authorization document,' Sarah said, and handed Raul the piece of paper.

After much negotiation, the militia's leader accepted his explanation and decided to guide them into the village. Sarah and Ben went to visit the local chief and took him a present. It was a beautiful grey stallion that Raul had used on their journey. Apparently the chief was the father of the militia's leader, who always scrutinized newcomers.

They had many problems in the past with the government due to their involvement with drug criminals across the border. Since recent reprisals by government soldiers, they were more careful within their jurisdiction, with no intentions of repeating the same mistakes.

Soon after Sarah visited their local health centre and made herself available for treating their local ailments. When she was finished there, she visited several of their dwellings to help the very sick and infirmed. Then she gave them medicine.

Very soon everyone in that village considered her a saint and she gained respect by all. Even the militia's leader, Pueblo, considered her his personal responsibility after she had saved his youngest daughter from a serious bout of malaria.

CHAPTER 47

Capture and rescue

They had left their large tents behind with the Jeeps but carried three smaller ones on their supply donkeys and mules. Anyway, they wrongly anticipated the availability of living quarters in the village. The small village had no hotels or guest houses and they could find no suitable accommodation anywhere so they compromised by camping in a local field. They chose a suitable area close to the village to set up camp. It was during the rainy season and the mud and insects were everywhere. Not to mention the swarms of pestiferous flies.

They soon mounted three tents in that area and decided to place the women in one, the men in the second and the freelance trackers in the third. Since there were more than enough sleeping bags to go around, and with little personal belongings to carry, they had no problems with roughing it for a while. The conservationist teams were experienced in such exploratory treks and usually carried bare essentials for their immediate needs.

The guerillas in that area had contacts everywhere and were well briefed about the visitors arrival. They were in desperate need of funds and saw the visitor's arrival as a godsend. Even so, there were about twenty people in Cathy's group and far too many to capture and feed, so they set their eyes on the women's tent. In the dead of night and while they were fast asleep, their captors restrained them in their sleeping bags and dumped them on mules.

Five kilometres later they stopped under a large tamarind tree to remove them from the sleeping bags to make them prepare for the long journey ahead. Then all the women mouths were securely taped. When they finished relieving themselves, their hands were taped behind their backs. Luckily for them Sarah had managed to press her hidden insignia during their capture, as Lumak had previously advised.

Ben heard a buzzing sound, then a voice in his head and wondered if he was dreaming.

'What! Who!' he panicked frantically.

'Its me, Jeff. This is a telepathic communication. I think we have a serious problem. Sarah, Cathy and two of their female assistants have been captured by Columbian guerillas. I now have their precise location. We are to arrange immediate rescue. The less people know of our plans the better. We must attempt this rescue ourselves.' Lumak repeated the message twice. Ben immediately jumped out of the sleeping bag. Everyone was fast asleep so Ben sneaked out. Lumak didn't want anyone else to know in case their rescue was compromised.

'Dad, try to speak to me telepathically, without using your voice, while keeping your mouth closed,' Lumak stressed and Ben was surprised that it was possible to receive information in that way through his mind. During his training he had inhaled several types of microids, but didn't realize they were permanent additions to his mind, and could function without brain implants. Those microids could operate through the small but powerful insignia he wore. He tried as Lumak had suggested, but was still furious that the girls had been captured and couldn't restrain himself.

'From what I overheard they must have a base camp locally. Perhaps within a twenty-mile radius of the village. If we are to build in this area they must be removed from the equation or else we shall have continuous problems with drugs and such like. Sarah and her friends will be quite safe for now, not having received information from them regarding a ransom. They must be still on route to a rendezvous point where their boss will make their next decision for them.

'This is a very delicate situation and we do not know who to trust in the village. I am sure some of the villagers and militia are in with them for a share of the ransom, so we have to thread carefully,' Ben replied.

'What do you suggest?' Lumak asked.

'We find the location of their main camp, rescue the girls and call the military to rain bombs on the place when they least expect. That way we can flush the nest of vipers and get rid of the nuisance for good,' Ben said. Lumak wondered at his father-in-law's take-no-prisoners strategy, but never agreed with taking life for any reason. However he realized more lives could be at stake in the long run because of their unwelcomed activities.

'I suppose you are the military mind, so it's in your hands. Do what you think is necessary for the greater good and make sure my wife is safe. Even so, do not be too hard on them,' Lumak said and disconnected.

Ben soon called the group including scimitars and trackers together, and explained the situation to them. They had taken along a small communicating station that could handle several transceivers, so he split his men into three groups of four, including himself, giving each one a transceiver and left Raul to take and relay messages. Then they would track the rebels toward the location given by Lumak until daylight.

They were to shadow them until they arrived at their main base. Then create a diversion and when they were not looking, rescue the women. It was a simple enough strategy but one fraught with many dangers.

While they progressed stealthily they constantly kept in contact. It was not long before they came upon an old campfire underneath a tamarind tree. It was still warm and Ben's tracker soon found their tracks, including those of the donkeys and mules. By now it was daylight. All three rescue groups merged and were moving through a narrow pass between mountains across a small stony river.

The place was polluted with oil spills everywhere. Ben concluded they were close to a large oil refinery. The area of dead forest and swamp was visible for miles and stank to high heavens. The guerillas had chosen well for an area avoided by the locals.

'This is a bad place, Senior. It will kill all animals that enter including us,' warned one of the trackers.

'Yea, let's hope it gives us an edge. It can't be the same all the way.' Ben replied, undeterred. The petroleum fumes were everywhere. Many dead birds and small animals could be observed everywhere. They placed their handkerchiefs and rags over their faces but it didn't hinder the stench.

Ben always carried a walking cane, although appearing innocent enough, was a most deadly weapon. Over the months it had become another part of his body. With it, he gave outsiders the impression of an innocent and well respected mature gentlemen. That cane however was really a small rifle with a hidden barrel. The barrel was secured by a hinged thimble-like end for walking. There was also a hidden latch underneath the handle. Once the latch was released, the spring-loaded trigger mechanism slid down as the front barrel lifted. The handle contained several magazines of bullets that could be automatically loaded with a simple twist of the handle. That was not all, the barrel was in two parts and contained a long bayonet that was spring loaded when not released.

Ben was once a captain in the Turkish army and knew all the tricks and methods of his quarry. Even so, he had others to consider in his dangerous plans.

The large abandoned oil refinery hadn't been used for years and was well hidden on the side of the river between two mountains. From their high standpoint they could observe many prefab buildings in rows. In the centre was a large two storey complex. All around were large cylindrical containers linked with pipes.

Once again he split his main group and sent them in three different directions towards the central complex. That was in case one of the groups were captured. The refinery complex seemed the most likely place. Even so, their progress could be halted or changed at any time by radio. The main idea was to partly encircle the refinery and acquire a good working knowledge of its layout, weaknesses and strengths, including the position of the captives.

Carefully, Ben and his group progressed stealthily between the prefab huts until arriving at the larger building. Once close, he could here male Spanish voices and knew it was the men. Anyway, their tracks, including those of their mules had led directly to that building. Also, one of the men had a distinct limp which gave the group away.

Ben carefully climbed one of the pipes to get a better look. While there he checked the area for lookouts, but there were none. From that standpoint he could observe the four women on the concrete floor with mouths, hands and feet securely taped. Five men sat around a table cracking profane jokes while playing cards and drinking potato rum. They were unconcerned and appeared to be waiting for their main group to arrive. Their captors had considered their operations too well done to expect any opposition that quickly. It was assumed they had collaborators in the village and were sure they would contact them by radio if the mission was compromised.

Once his quarry had been located, Ben signalled his fighters and they carefully followed to the location from three directions. Since there were no doors on that building, they simply held their positions until the time was right. To mislead the guerillas, Ben followed from a different direction and took them by surprise.

With cane in hand he walked directly towards the five men and fired point blank at the two closest to him. Suddenly his other fighters sprang from their hideout and subdued the others. Since the men were quite drunk their reflexes were slow so it was not a difficult effort on the part of his men. They were soon subdued with tape and dumped into a local shed. In the process, Ben had killed two of the men. Sand and dust was used to cover their blood and tracks.

'Are you ladies ok,' Ben greeted, while removing the tape from their faces.

'Please get us out of this mess. Every part of my body aches and the concrete floor and local insects didn't help. How did you find us so quickly?' Sarah asked, while dragging herself upright and shaking her limbs to relieve the numbness.

'I think your husband must keep tabs on us from afar,' Ben replied and Sarah nodded her head to agree.

'Thank God he had it all planned from the start or we would be in a lot more serious trouble. Those guys had no intentions of talking with us until their boss was present,' she replied and he shrugged off the painful thoughts of worst case scenarios.

'You didn't have to kill them? Did you, Dad?' Sarah queried.

Not fully agreeing with her father's callous and uncompromising actions.

'I had no choice! Having assessed the situation it was purely a military decision if I was to save you guys without bloodshed. And sadly, the most important choice was made.' Although she would have liked to resolve the situation in a more peaceful and less violent manner the damage was already done.

'Listen, everyone! We have to leave this area immediately and cover our tracks in the process. So we must travel once around the complex and take a route along the river towards the east. From what little I learnt from the men, the others will be here in about three hours, so that gives us enough time to clear the area before the bombs start falling.'

'What Bombs?' Sarah asked.

'The government also wants these guys and we have to remove them from this area before we begin building our dome. If not, this place could become a nightmare for everyone! I am now chief of security and must look at the broader picture!'

Sarah swallowed hard and continued to follow the larger group. Then Ben made a call at presidential level.

'I shall stay behind with three of my men and one of the trackers to warn the air-force the minute the guerillas arrive,' he said and Sarah realized her father meant serious business.

Ben didn't like the idea of taking his captives back to the village. Neither did he wish to take any more lives, which would have been the case if left where they were, so at the appropriate time his men freed their hands and feet. Then he spoke to them in English while using one of his men to translate.

'Listen carefully, Morons. Very soon this place will be bombed to a cinder by the air force, so if you guys have any brains and want to live, you must travel west along the river. That way, you will avoid their ground troops and dogs. And don't you guys ever show your miserable faces in this area again!' Those men would have given anything to exit their present situation.

'Si! Si!,' they pleaded and were already out of the building. Ben knew they would never be back within that area again, and neither would they have time to warn their fellow collaborators. Anyway, Lumak's colossal robots some 100 feet tall were to guard all such structures. They had weapons that could freeze any unwanted trespassers.

Ben had passed on the location of the refinery by radio to the military authorities. They had been after that particular group of guerillas for years and at last had the opportunity to remove them from the map. There was a local hill from which Ben and his men could observe the arrival of the guerillas. By that time the air force bombers were already in the area and ready to strike.

The Sand-Viper was about the fastest European combat aircraft fighter in existence. It could bomb from high altitude, take off vertically and land in the worst terrain while awaiting the arrival of an enemy and they seldom missed their targets. The moment the guerillas entered the building, Ben relayed the information of their position and in seconds the place became a virtual inferno.

Being an old oil refinery didn't help as most of the dead forests and swamps in the area were soon ablaze. There were many massive explosions that could clearly be seen ten miles away in the village to the east. Soon after the planes streaked overhead and everyone knew the government had blasted the local rebels to hell. Yet, no one knew of the kidnapping or of their visitor's involvement in that rescue mission. Ben had planned the campaign to have as little impact possible on the local community and their plans in that area. Yet, they had removed one of the worst guerilla outfits and in the process cleared most of the polluted region by fire.

Soon the women were well rested and could only joke about the experience suffered in the field of duty. They realized Ben and his daughter Sarah were not ones to be trifled with.

To the locals, the army and air force were always to blame for their misfortunes. This time the responsibility of the forest fires were laid squarely at the doors of the air force. Luckily it was rainy season.

Soon Sarah placed a large map of her projects for the area on a village wall, with the intention of bringing lots of work and wealth to the area and all their fears dissipated.

Sarah and the others remained there for a further week, surveying and analysing the area for the new construction. They also acquired a list of local species from those who knew the area before its destruction. She made a pact with the chief of that village to build a small hospital, if they would assist in guarding her future ventures in that area and he agreed.

Sarah had become very fond of her hired trackers, with whom she constantly joked. After all, even though freelance, they had assisted in her rescue at their own peril. She remembered them as the most shabbily dressed when she first visited the camp. Now, they looked like respectable trackers in their military fatigues. There was also an air of responsibility and dignity in their strides. Strange what a little money and kindness will do, or so she thought. While playing a mean game of football, they would frequently communicate tales of their dangerous encounters and escapades in the South American jungles with the most vicious of creatures. She sometimes wondered how any of them could have survived such ordeals. However of all their tales, she was quite sure the one told about her rescue would be the truest. That one would be told the most frequently of all their dangerous adventures and escapades.

One day she called them into the main tent and spoke to them in local Spanish.

'Guys, I realize you like to work independently, but how would you like to work for me in future. I can get you some powerful repeating rifles, including your own Land-rovers and you can earn big money for your efforts. So what do you say?'

'We say a big yes, Mam!' they said together, now dressed in their military fatigues and saluting like real hardened soldiers.

'Ok then. I shall arrange all the necessary paperwork. Go now and get something to eat and have a drink on me to celebrate our victory!' she said, and they were the happiest trackers ever.

Now all they had to do was find good sources of raw materials for producing the relevant plastics and other materials that would soon be required in the bullet resistant glass for the construction of the domes. By so doing they intended to supply the whole of South America from that country.

Since Venezuela was still rich in certain resources it did not take them long to locate the information from their Department of Industry. Those projects were placed in the hands of a company soon to be bought by Sarah's organization and production soon went on line in that country within a year. Nevertheless, at the beginning of all such new ventures there was always unavoidable delays. That was until Lumak's efficient and super intelligent microid robots became on line.

CHAPTER 48

Consolidation

After Sarah's visit to South America she had a clearer picture of the devastation caused by oil spills from oil refineries, their inadequate means of transportation and cleanup. But of all the savage and irresponsible scourges done to the planet's lands, deforestation caused by slash and burn were the worst. Second was the illegal and unscheduled logging within areas of the Amazon rain forests which led to climate change. Governments had been given meagre incentives in the past to stop such callous operations, but they were poor countries and the temptation was always to take advantage now and pay later.

The numerous environmentalists had used many tactics in the past to stem such activities, but to no avail. The effects of such neglect was now apparent and prevalent everywhere. Many countries in that area had begun to realized the bigger picture, and were willing to shut the door even after the poor horse had bolted and died of neglect in the process.

Sarah's friend, Cathy, and her husband soon became permanent members of BioLive. They simply transferred their organization, lock stock and barrel over to BioLive. Nevertheless they still had their own campaigns and fund raisers. They were now co-directors of BioLive and enjoyed their new financial freedom with more resources and assistants in the field.

During the intervening years many of the large conservation groups joined with BioLive, until it became the largest of such charities on the planet. Occasionally Sarah and her father Ben would visit areas at risk and make her usual assessments before the teams were sent in to make more permanent changes. They focussed mainly on Africa which was still a country in turmoil, with many wars and misplaced people. Further, as the Sahara desert expanded southward so did many become misplaced, homeless and destitute.

Within a single year several massive domes had been built in chosen areas of South America. Those were even larger than the ones in Venezuela. They soon became another wonder of the world. Hundreds of Egyptian pyramids could be fitted within each one and they contained their own internal weather systems, all controlled by large intelligent computers. Even on a clear day one could observe wisps of clouds at several levels of the massive structures from tens of miles away.

Their frames were of special non-rusting reinforced steel alloy and with the aid of repairing robots they could remain that way for a thousand years. Those first few were used as an example to the rest of the world and attracted tourists from every country on the globe.

Soon every country in South America and Africa wanted their own, so robots were constantly on the move.

Giant digging machines scoured the many left over forests' areas for suitable clumps of trees. Those were subsequently transplanted lock stock and barrel within the great domes to make environments more homely for their many active species. That way, even the oldest trees could survive. The ecologists would maintain a mix of fauna and flora known only to that area of forest. By so doing each dome would only reflect the life in their part of the Amazon rain forests.

Soon, Lumak's powerful robots were on show throughout the planet. They were truly fascinating to watch and made people feel insignificant and unwanted. Although very human-like in appearance, they were extremely intelligent, could speak all the main languages and perform any task about 20 times faster than any human. Such tasks could be completed in virtually any environment.

Being of microid design meant they were unaffected by climatic conditions and the environment. As a matter of fact, they made the ideal astronaut, and were able to exist in space without the need for oxygen. Being virtually a solid mass of liquid metal, they could withstand any amount of pressure or vacuum and transform to most shapes.

Like supreme magicians, they would perform clever tricks that could mislead the human eye. One of their more common ones was with a pack of cards. They would get someone to select a card from the pack then throw the pack into the air and while the cards fell the robot would quickly scan the cards and select one from the pack so quickly that no human could observe the action. That card was usually the previously chosen one and they were formidable players at poker.

Once people were aware of their capabilities many organization were against the use of such robots, but they couldn't stop the flow of progress. Large organizations and governments saw their use in many sensitive and dangerous jobs, including operations like organ transplants.

They could surgically operate on an individual and complete the task in minutes as opposed to hours, causing less trauma and suffering in patients. Not to mention the reduction in blood loss during the procedure due to incredible accuracy and a more thorough charting of the human body.

Such robots were not allowed for military use and could never be used to take human life. Lumak had many fail-safe features built into their design, including a dormant virus for self-destruct, which made them completely safe.

Lumak had began to test his LPD prototypes and could now harness such drives to a spacecraft for their first trip to Mars. However as yet not even the new president of the USA, namely Gerald Fraser, knew of their successes with that project. Nevertheless unlike the microid robots, that one was considered a Class 5 project that was outside the public domain until demonstrated to the president and his chiefs. That particular prototype had the capabilities of taking a crew to Mars in weeks instead of years. It would soon be used in a special project to clear debris and meteor from Spaceway. That motorway of the Solar System was to be a standard highway from Earth to Mars. It followed a computerised corridor between their orbits.

There was also the Plasma Gun. That weapon used a micro fusion reactor that accelerated hydrogen atoms within an intense magnetic field. When a part of the magnetic field was altered and released, a beam of plasma incased in a strong magnetic field over 100 million degrees centigrade would be ejected from a special nozzle. Such a device could easily have created a large crater on the moon when fired from great distances in space. Although Lumak began developing several such weapons for space, none were meant for Earth. Once those prototypes had been tested they were mothballed until required to fight the invading Javols.

Plato would frequently visit from Andromeda to assist Lumak with his many projects. That way Lumak's projects advanced faster than scheduled. Although the Javols were on their way to harvest his people on planet Caefon in Andromeda for food, they were still several months away. Yet, their relentless progress worried him. Even so, at that time none of his people on the surface world knew of the Javols or of their future arrival to destroy them all.

Most of that galaxy was now dead of all intelligent life and only a few civilizations remained towards the galactic rim. All those few remnants would soon follow the faith of the Ancients, to ultimate extinction.

Within 200 years the Javols would begin to arrive in our galaxy. Then all significant life would follow the same faith as the Andromedans, to ultimate extinction or slavery. They would be used merely as food rations for a rapacious predator that cared nothing for primal evolving life. To them all such biological organisms were inferior and could not sustain themselves away from planetary systems and their closed environments.

Despite the slow and undeterred progress of the Javols, many of the most powerful minds in the universe knew of the dangers and were taking a stand against them.

Lumak and Plato were Shadites and on Earth for a purpose. They had the powers to create the necessary weaponry to repel the Javols, but the Javols destruction would come with the Son of Destiny. He had the powers to transpose stellar objects like our sun. The new Patriarchs would be the all powerful Titans. They would be relentless in their fight against their foe until they were safely contained to posterity.

NEXT IN THE SERIES

Chronicles of Galaxy Osmaron
Escape from Andromeda

Epilogue

Earth-time... 2042 CE (Lumak arrives on Earth in 2041 CE).

After the appearance of the Nano-bot Javols in Galaxy Andromeda - due to a failed experiment - most of the primal life in that galaxy had been made extinct. The Javols saw all such naturally occurring organisms as their natural food and did not hesitate in removing all those civilizations they considered a threat.

The seven Gohran Grand Lords of our plane of seven universes soon put a plan in operation for the survival of all primal life. However only one could directly intervene and locate suitable intelligent worlds for assistance. Those worlds would be converted to a higher technological level and given the necessary abilities to fight the Javols.

Grand Lord Gerra, whose responsibility it is to safeguard our part of the universe, put forward his plan for ridding the universe of the Javols once and for all time. Using his Shadites, who are his special priests, many suitable life-forms are being recruited and new worlds probed and accepted within the Greater Purpose for their mutual survival.

The Shadite Lumak discovers a Class 1 civilization in a hitherto uncharted part of Osmaron (our Milky Way Galaxy) and despatches interstellar probes to investigate. Lumak, previously a sexless Semonite worker (a giant bee-like creature), is subsequently transformed into a human and transposed to the world they call Pleron. That previously unknown world is called Earth by its human inhabitants.

Lumak under the guise of one Doctor Jeffery Longhurst is to advance Earth's technologies to Class 5, from its present, Class 1. This classification represents advancement on a scale to the power of 10. By this method Class 5 may be taken to be about 100,000 years more advanced than Class 1, our present levels. A Class 1 civilization would have discovered, understood and developed nuclear devices.

During Lumak's visit to Earth he lands in the hills of Turkey and meets the shepherdess Sarah and her father Bengizara Khan (Ben). Sarah later becomes his wife.

Lumak soon finds a general cure for cancer, introduces Micro-Robotics, Stellar Drives and a Longevity Serum.

Yet, with Global Warming many problems become insolvable without a drastic reduction in human population.

A most drastic solution is found to solve all their problems. Knowledge of that particular solution must be kept well away from the greater public.

However, the almost indestructible Javols are presently on their way to Osmaron (our Milky Way galaxy) and will arrive on Earth within 200 years.

www.ingramcontent.com/pod-product-compliance
Lightning Source LLC
Chambersburg PA
CBHW020254120726
47904CB00001B/197